Drawn from the Life

Drawn from the Life

A Memoir

ROBERT MEDLEY

ff

faber and faber

LONDON·BOSTON

First published in 1983
by Faber and Faber Limited
3 Queen Square London WC1N 3AU
Typeset by Wyvern Typesetting Limited Bristol
Printed in Great Britain by
The Thetford Press Limited
Thetford Norfolk

British Library Cataloguing in Publication Data

Medley, Robert
Drawn from the life
1. Medley, Robert
2. Painters-England-Biography
I. Title
759.2 ND497.M/
ISBN 0-571-13043-7

Library of Congress Data has been applied for

Contents

Illustrations

PLATES

between pages 128 and 129

LINE

Man is a history-making creature who can neither repeat his past nor leave it behind; at every moment he adds to and thereby modifies everything that has previously happened to him. Hence the difficulty of finding a single image which can stand as an adequate symbol for man's kind of existence.

W. H. AUDEN

from 'D. H. Lawrence' in *The Dyer's Hand*

Preface

There has long been a need for an authoritatively researched survey of the extraordinary resurgence of poetic drama during the decade before the outbreak of the last war, written from a theatrical rather than a literary point of view, and emphasizing something of the part played in it by those whose imagination and enterprise as producers, actors, musicians and designers enabled the dramatic works of T. S. Eliot, W. H. Auden and Christopher Isherwood, Louis MacNeice and others to be brought to life before living audiences. In the meantime I thought I might make a contribution towards such an undertaking. A whole epoch of my life was dedicated to the Group Theatre, to a collaboration with Rupert Doone and those others most closely involved with its activities. As a committed participant I am not best placed to make a critical assessment: I thought, rather, that I might draw a picture. It has not been my purpose, then, to write a history, but to concentrate on that part of the events with which I was most intimately concerned. However, I soon discovered that the private and the public were so inextricably interwoven that what follows is as much an autobiography as a memoir; and also that as the first light throws long shadows I would do best to begin at the beginning. What was unique about the Group Theatre was its insistence on recognizing the artistic integrity of all those who contributed—whether as performers, writers, composers or designers: it was as a painter that I played my part, and my life as a painter naturally became a part of my account.

I am inured to the pangs of giving solitary birth to a picture but, when faced with a block of ruled foolscap on which words must be written, it did not take me long to realize that I would need a midwife if a readable and coherent book was to be the outcome of my labour. I needed somebody not of my own generation, but younger; somebody outside the events I wanted to describe and the relationships I wanted to trace, but sufficiently knowledgeable and sympathetic to be able to work with me on the basis of a shared understanding of them. At this point I turned to Mel Gooding, whom I knew as the son-in-law of my close friends Ceri and Frances Richards, a writer whom I felt would bring to the task a sympathetic apprehension of the complex experience of artists of an older generation, and a privileged insight derived from his close relationship with Ceri and Frances.

In the making of this book he has been much more than an editor; there is no part of it in which he has not played a creative, and critically collaborative, role. For all that, I must claim any errors, omissions and infelicities as entirely my own.

R. M.
December 1982

Acknowledgements

For permission to reprint copyright material the author and publishers gratefully acknowledge the following: the Estate of W. H. Auden for writings by W. H. Auden; the Editor of the *Observer* for reviews by Ivor Brown; Mrs T. S. Eliot for the use of two letters from her husband to Rupert Doone; the Estate of Duncan Grant for a letter from Duncan Grant to Rupert Doone; the Editor of the *Listener* for a review by Desmond McCarthy; the Estate of Louis MacNeice for two lines from 'The Coming of War' from *Plant and Fountain*; Mr John Piper for an extract from 'Designing for Benjamin Britten' from David Herbert (ed.), *The Operas of Benjamin Britten*, London, Hamish Hamilton, 1979; the Society of Authors on behalf of the Strachey Trust for a letter from Lytton Strachey to Rupert Doone, © The Strachey Trust, 1983; Michael B. Yeats, Anne Yeats and A. P. Watt Ltd for an extract from a letter from W. B. Yeats to Rupert Doone.

The letter from Serge Diaghilev to George Lifar from which an extract appears on page 93 was published in full in Lifar's book *Diaghilev—His Life, His Work, His Legend*, London, Putnam & Co., 1940, p. 474. The author and publishers regret that they have been unable to trace the copyright owners.

Acknowledgements

Prelude: August 1914

Summer holidays were divided between Walberswick in Suffolk where my grandmother lived, and the Mercers' farm in Westerdale, a remote village on the edge of the Yorkshire moors, where the River Esk, which trips down to Whitby, sixteen miles away, is no more than a beck. Except for a smallholding reached by cart track, ours was the last farm at the head of the valley. It was remote and wild enough to give us children an incomparable feeling of liberty and adventure. It was blessedly far from London and we had the whole place to ourselves.

It was a considerable upheaval to get us all there. Four children between the ages of 3 and 11 and 'Old Nurse Eldin', who went everywhere with us, had to be organized, and because we had to bring our own linen we were accompanied by a vast amount of luggage: four or five trunks (one of them with a rounded top to prevent anyone putting another on top of it); two tin hip baths (one with a very awkward high back to it) and a confused bundle of fishing rods, creels, walking sticks, mackintosh sheets, overcoats, and two picnic baskets with food for the journey. After what seemed weeks of preparation, the excitement began with the appearance of a Great Northern Railway private bus outside the front door of 42 Campden Hill Square. (In previous years this bus had sometimes been horse-drawn.)

The arrival in Kings Cross Station yard of our vehicle, the roof piled high with luggage, attracted the immediate attention of porters. Many directions having been given and many assurances made that it really was the right train and that this was certainly our reserved compartment, my brother Christopher and I were allowed to dash off to the bookstall, and *Comic Cuts* and *Tiger Tim*, ordinarily pounced on as vulgar trash, but permitted on long journeys for the sake of peace and quiet, were purchased.

On the way to York, where we had to change on to the Scarborough line, we were fed calves-foot jelly, which I didn't like but which was supposed to nourish and soothe over-excited stomachs. At Goathland, the junction of the branch line from Scarborough to Middlesbrough, we changed again, to the train which was to take us over the watershed and as far as Castleton in the Esk valley. Here there was always an hour or more to wait for the connection, which gave us time for a picnic in a nearby field. This picnic, although it brought us the first smell of moorland air, was also an occasion for anxiety. Separated from the railway line, what would happen if the train should suddenly appear and leave without us?

At Castleton, Mr Mercer with the pony trap and George the elder son or Frank the farmhand with the cart-horse and hay waggon for the luggage, would be waiting to take us to Westerdale, another three miles up the valley. I was determined on this particular occasion to complete the last lap in the hay waggon and refused to join Mother, Nurse and the two younger members of the family, whom I regarded as infants and thus not to be associated with; nor would I walk with Father: Christopher was older and could, but I wouldn't. It had been expected that I would walk, but in the end I gained my point and, contemplating the great swaying rump of the cart-horse between the shafts, I was allowed to hold the reins while the friendly beast took its own time to negotiate a road it knew far better than I. Nothing is slower than a walking horse, so I arrived half an hour after everyone else. Then there was cocoa and 'fat rascals' for supper and Mrs Mercer making us all feel at home once more.

At bedtime the final ceremony of arrival had to be undergone: the ritual dosing, after any long journey, with a powerful laxative, a vile-tasting powder stirred into a tooth mug of water. Mother believed that the nastier it tasted, the better the medicine. As castor oil was threatened if this didn't work the following morning, it usually had its effect.

The metalled road from the village came to an end at the Mercers' farm which faced up the valley and on to the moors. Beyond was the haunt of black-faced sheep, curlew and peewits; a country of purple heather, brown with peat and scented with tufts of reed grass and harebells. Opposite the house and separated from it by a cart track was a cattle pond with ducks on it, and a front garden, not for flowers but for vegetables. At one corner of this, scarcely concealed by a gooseberry bush, was a double-seated outside earth closet. The farmhouse itself, solidly built of stone and with a slate roof, had the simplicity of a child's drawing—a front door in the middle, with a carefully pumiced doorstep, a window on either side of it, and above, symmetrically placed, three more windows. By the back door was a hand pump which drew all the water that was needed, and beneath this was a stone basin. The farmyard was a simple quadrangle formed by the back of the house, the stables, the cowsheds, a great barn and hayloft, and a dairy with slate shelves and generous glazed earthenware bowls of milk from which cream was skimmed for making butter in the wooden churn. On the far side of the barn, at one remove from the house, were haystacks, pigsties, and a chicken run. Most of the hens enjoyed the freedom to peck around wherever they fancied, and laid their clutches in the most unexpected places. (The results of an after-breakfast egg hunt were always gratefully received by the management.)

In those days, when there were horses and harnesses in the stables, and wooden carts and waggons in the sheds instead of tractors and trailers, the economics of an upland dairy farm—there were also, of course, sheep on the moors—depended upon its being more or less self-supporting throughout the year. There was therefore something of everything, and we learnt, without being aware of it, many basic facts of life and death. (We were always sent out and away when a pig was stuck for they squealed most fearfully and could be heard even in the distance; not that this put us off enjoying the 'faggots' and 'chitterlings' that soon appeared on our plates.)

The Mercers were extraordinarily kind, and with their sons, George and Jack, who were already working with their father on the farm, to show us how, we soon learnt to be sensible and could be trusted to help. So there was always something to do, even on a rainy day.

The summer of 1914 was exceptionally hot and fine but in spite of the golden weather I had for some weeks been vaguely aware that Father and Mother were preoccupied, overshadowed by something I could not be told about. I don't know quite how it happened that without a particular reason I should be alone on that fateful afternoon, gazing absent-mindedly at the now colourless hills shimmering in an oppressive heat. With nothing better to do, I had been stamping around on the corrugated-tin roof of the earth closet in the front garden, purely and childishly for the sake of making a noise. Bored by this meaningless occupation I was now sitting warming my arse on the hot metal, when Mrs Mercer, in her kitchen apron, appeared suddenly at the front door and I heard an unforgettable cry. Three times she called, her voice echoing up the valley: 'War's been declared! War's been declared! War's been declared!' Then, banging the door behind her, she vanished as abruptly as she had appeared.

The real significance for me of this momentous announcement was the immediate awareness that I now lived in a world of adult events, the meaning of which could no longer be entirely withheld from me. I was no longer wrapped within the self-absorbed cocoon of infancy. I was a person.

I have always thought of that moment as an emergence: the beginning of an accountable life; something more than a number of unrelated remembered incidents. The image remains of that frozen moment of time: the apparition of Mrs Mercer shouting to her menfolk in the fields beyond—and me, an unseen witness sitting on the lavatory roof.

1 Starting Points

Nobody's life is entirely his own.

This book is an autobiography containing an element of confession, a memorial to chance and circumstance, and a remembrance of some of the people who have played a part, great and small, in the making of a life. Foremost in memory is Rupert Doone with whom I lived for forty years, and I will begin at our respective beginnings; but first I remark that, though our meeting may have been simply a matter of chance, as our love and friendship developed I learnt of occasional portents strange enough to give momentary credence to the possibility of a fate predetermined and inevitable. Rupert and I had little in common by way of family background and upbringing, and the paths by which we arrived together could hardly have been more different, yet from the moment of our meeting the compact by which we subsequently lived and worked together seemed irrevocably sealed.

Born Reginald Ernest Woodfield on 14 August 1903, the younger of two sons, Rupert Doone was brought up in Redditch, Worcestershire, where his father was a skilled worker in a needle factory. His father was humorous and bright natured, belonging by inclination to the country rather than to the town. His mother, intuitively understanding and sensitive, came from a background of respectable Victorian yeomanry. Reggie was a pretty little boy with fair curly hair which, in the Edwardian fashion, on grand occasions, his mother dressed in Little Lord Fauntleroy ringlets. It would be a mistake, however, to suppose that he was made a spoilt darling, for there was far too much common sense and liberal Nonconformism in the family to allow that to happen. (His uncle, angered by the jingoistic hysteria, had torn down the Union Jack on Mafeking night.) As a schoolboy he was a notable scrum half with quick reactions and a turn for speed. He received a fair formal education at the local grammar school but this came to an abrupt end when at the age of 15 he ran away from home, with no money in his pocket, intending to get to London and become a dancer. In the event he got no further than Birmingham where his uncle, Edward Morris, and his aunt Flo were building up a small engineering firm into a considerable business. Wisely, his parents allowed him to leave home, and a job as an apprentice draughtsman at Austin's motor works in Birmingham was found for him. This sensible but uncongenial occupation lasted for about a year until, making a further bid for freedom, he arrived penniless in London. Mr and Mrs Woodfield were helped to reconcile themselves to this wilful behaviour by the fact that he went first to the house of an uncle who lived near Olympia and managed the cake department of Cadby Hall for J. Lyons & Co. This last tenuous contact with family security did not last long and for a while he was virtually homeless, usually hungry and often cold. He turned to modelling for painters in order to pay for lessons at Madame Astafieva's School of Ballet in the King's Road, Chelsea. Alicia Markova and Anton Dolin, both of whom became firm friends, were studying with her at this time. With his first professional engagement he took the name of Rupert Doone—this was rather more romantic, and memorable, than Reginald Woodfield—and so he remained.

The Woodfield family had lacked nothing in the way of security and affection: the reasons for his running away and becoming Rupert Doone must be explained in other ways. In his own words: 'I simply felt that I did not belong to where I had been born.' It may not be unusual for an artistic and exceptional boy, particularly one who early recognizes his homosexuality, to feel this way, nor would it be surprising for him to wish to escape from provincial life into the theatre. But Rupert was determined to become a *dancer*, and there was in him some kind of daemon or extra driving force, for though it is now quite acceptable for a boy to want to become a ballet dancer, in 1919 this was an extraordinary ambition for a working-class boy in the Midlands. In retrospect I think perhaps his predisposition to performance would have been encouraged in a family which liked dressing up in fancy costumes; and Rupert remembered with unaffected pleasure enjoying the limelight at entertainments at home and at school. He never spoke of an actual visit to the theatre, except for the annual pantomime, and much more likely to have been an influence upon his unerring choice of career was his early addiction to the silent screen. The cinema cost only twopence, and Rupert spent endless hours watching his favourite stars—Mary Pickford, Lilian Gish, Charlie Chaplin and the early Mack Sennett comics—all performers balletic and gestural in approach, whose films would be accompanied by the musical improvisations of a local pianist. It was a caprice of Rupert's that his uniqueness, his strangeness in ordinary surroundings, was due to his mother's family being, however remotely, related to the Shakespeares.

Of Rupert's subsequent early career I know very little. After an enjoyable and professionally satisfying engagement in Basil Dean's production of James Elroy Flecker's play *Hassan* he went to Paris to find work for himself. At the age of 20 he was a close friend of Jean Cocteau and collaborated with him in the production of his dance-drama *Romeo and Juliet* at the Théâtre Cigalle. Through Cocteau he was introduced to Serge Diaghilev but he turned down an opportunity to dance in the *corps de ballet* of the Ballets Russes, his vanity foolishly demanding more than that. Before this he had been on an extended tour of provincial France with that famous figure of the *belle époque*, Cléo de Mérode. This experience with the tight-fisted, ageing ex-mistress of kings taught him how to hand a lady out of a railway carriage, hold her dog, and present her with a floral tribute. It also gave him a permanent distaste for touring and hotels. About this time, too, Rupert danced in New York with the Swedish Ballet, in which he appeared on stilts in Darius Milhaud's *La Création du monde*, designed by Fernand Léger, but after a typical contretemps about costumes he left precipitously for Europe, once more penniless but now at least with a decent overcoat. He worked thereafter mostly in variety and revue, understudying Léonide Massine in C. B. Cochran's *Keep on Dancing* among other things. At the time of our meeting in the late autumn of 1925 he was fresh from the success he had made in arranging the dances and appearing in Nigel Playfair's production of *The Duenna*. By this time he showed no trace of his provincial background. His exceptional beauty suggested Ariel; his temperament was mercurial, by turns impish, serious, fiery, gentle and insecure.

Born under different stars, worlds apart, there was yet one thing in our early upbringing that we had in common. We were both born into that generation that grew up in the afterglow of the great Victorian liberal tradition of free-thinking Nonconformity in which strong ethical discipline was tempered by a principled tolerance. In my father's vocabulary the poles of behaviour were designated 'tolerable' and 'intolerable'—terms which deliberately avoid self-righteous moral censure. Rupert enjoyed a childhood similarly marked by tolerance and forbearance. There the similarity ended.

I was born on 19 December 1905, into the professional and cultivated middle classes, the second child of a family of four sons and two daughters. I was christened Charles Robert Owen in the Allen Street Congregational Chapel off the High Street, Kensington, a formality acknowledged by my agnostic father in deference to his family's Nonconformist convictions. Mother, who had little say in the matter, would have preferred an Anglican introduction to the community.

Father, Charles Douglas Medley, tall and rightly considered handsome, was a distinguished member of the legal profession. He had a first-class mind and as a classical scholar of 16 at the Leys School, Cambridge, he already had the necessary qualifications to enter the university. However, my grandfather, a Baptist minister, was unable to afford the expense. He was therefore put to the law in a well-known solicitor's office, chosen by his maternal uncle, the Right Honourable Augustine Birrell, QC, MP, under whose aegis he soon rose to become the recognized authority on authors' copyright. His intellectual attainments and consuming passion for literature and scholarship were therefore to find expression in acting for, and enjoying the friendship of, practically all the great writers of his day. George Moore and Harley Granville-Barker were among his very closest friends, and he acted for William Somerset Maugham, George Bernard Shaw, Noël Coward and many others. In spite of a developed sensibility and a capacity for acute literary judgement, he had, as he one day confessed to me, no creative gifts of his own. He was, however, a man of considerable imaginative vision. In the 1920s he acted as a legal adviser to the first Lord Leverhulme, and he endeavoured to persuade that irascible tycoon to endow the old Grosvenor House (a great Regency mansion then standing in its own grounds in Park Lane) as a foundation for the arts. In this endeavour he was unsuccessful, but the ideas that had been forming in his mind were to come to fruition during the thirties when he formulated the terms of the foundation of the Barber Institute of Fine Arts in Birmingham. He insisted that there should be a professorship of music and a concert hall as well as a professorship of fine art and an art gallery. He remained Chairman of the Trustees of the Barber Institute until he was in his late eighties—he died at 93—when he was succeeded by my elder brother Christopher.

Father also held the chairmanship of the Guardian Assurance Company for many years. This made him of some eminence in the City, and it might have been expected that he would have accepted some of the advantages that go with such a position, but he refused even the chauffeur-driven car put at his disposal, preferring to be beholden to no one. His day's work done, he would make his own way home by bus or on foot, and then after the formalities of return had been observed he would as often as not seek shelter behind a book. Proud and egotistical, he was a man who did not like to be touched or to display feelings openly. Too much was hidden from us children; we never saw an open embrace or overheard a confidence between him and our mother. His apparent inability to respond with spontaneous warmth I later came to understand as a sign of human frailty: when I was a child, however, it added to my sense of him as being remote and apart. Any aspect of life which he regarded as 'human folly'—and all of us were touched by it—he treated, lawyer-like, with ironic contempt. It was not until I was past 50 that he finally disclosed an unsuspected aspect of his real feelings. Some time after Mother's death we were talking of the past when he confessed that, if we had been afraid of him, at the same time he had been afraid of us: 'You were all', he said, 'so infernally charming.' How characteristic that it should have been our capacity to draw out (and expose) his feelings for us that should have made him fearful and increased his reserve!

Father was kind but formidable: he was not an easy man to deal with, but he looked after us with real concern for our individual ways, and his affection for us, if not undisguised, was genuine. As children we had the free run of his library which, as far as standard collections of English literature go, was very complete. He was a reader, not a bibliophile. Once a year it was our duty to invade the library for its annual spring cleaning—the gilt edges were dusted and the rough cut banged together. The dust was then allowed to resettle. In this practical way we learnt the elements of classification—that Cardinal Newman's *Apologia*, for example, did not belong on the same shelf as the letters of Byron or *Roxana*.

For all his love of the country—he would take us out for long walks over the moors, and taught us to fish with a wet fly in the limestone streams of North Yorkshire—Father was essentially a Londoner and belonged to the culture of cities. Mother, though also born and bred in London, longed for the country—to make a garden and keep bees and goats. This sounds like a Kate Greenaway idyll, but anyone who has actually kept goats and bees will know otherwise. She would also have liked to keep a village shop, but unlike the goats and bees this did not materialize.

Mother, Anne (Nancy) Gwendoline, née Owen, was married at the age of 22; my father was ten years her senior. As her maiden name indicates, on her father's side she was Welsh. At the time of the marriage the prosperous Owens lived in a large house in Holland Villas Road and were part of a cultural and artistic circle that included G. F. Watts (then regarded as an universal genius), the Maughams and the Ionideses, and was centred on Holland Park and Campden Hill. The family interests were artistic and musical rather than literary. My mother was slightly built, attractive and talented; she could have graduated from the serious art student she had been to become a good artist. That possibility was closed by her early marriage and the responsibilities of a family. She had a good eye and a natural facility for drawing about which she was over-modest: I still have a charcoal drawing she did at Walberswick when I was a child that stands up in its own way to a Harpigny or a Jongkind.

As my Grandfather Owen lost most of his money soon after I was born, the vivid memories I have of the Holland Villas house must be imaginary. But the house that they built for themselves at Walberswick, and to which they retired in 1909, with its white walls and pargetted exterior in the domestic style of Voysey, is still vivid to me. It was perfectly in keeping with the taste that characterized the late-Victorian liberal circle in which my mother was brought up. It was a taste that tended towards the Liberty style, William Morris and dress reform. (She hated tight corsets.) Father's education had been sternly moral and political, high minded and public spirited: seeing in Nancy Owen a child of nature, simple and transparently direct, it is easy to see why he should have fallen in love with her. Nor is it surprising that she, naturally trusting but not uncritical, should consent to marry the handsome and intellectual young lawyer who was such an ardent suitor. As opposites they were complementary: he tended to resolve experience by rationalizing it, being critically minded and verbal; she was more directly emotional, intuitive and creative. They did not always see eye to eye and at the end she had come to understand him better than he did her.

As children we were loved and encouraged but rarely praised. How much this stinting of approbation was a deliberate policy to ensure that we were treated equally and without favouritism, I do not know. There are many things we can never know about our parents, and the degree of premeditation in their treatment of us is one of them. When speaking of the things hidden from me as a child I should remind the reader that this was an age when the father in a middle-class or professional household would rarely set foot in the kitchen or nursery.

For twelve years, from 1914 to 1926, it was necessary for my parents to practise extreme economy in order to make proper provision for our education, and though this circumspection may have become habitual it does not entirely explain why, when there was no further need of it, they never really let themselves go and pushed the boat out. Except for the occasional dinner party for two to four guests I do not recall any occasion when they entertained on any scale. How much better it would have been to see our parents enjoying themselves to the full! That they couldn't seems to have been largely an outcome of my father's difficulty in showing or sharing emotion, which may be understood in the light of the High-Victorian orthodoxy that self-indulgence was wicked. I remember once trying to persuade my father to buy a very fine sketch by Delacroix, *The Stoning of Stephen*: it was a small picture and very moderately priced. He greatly admired it, and could easily have afforded it; but he refused it on the grounds that it was far too fine a thing for him to have, and so it went to the Barber Institute instead. Although I have tried to overcome this family tendency to carefulness, I nevertheless detect traces of it in my own behaviour. I dislike buying new clothes and I am often inhibited by the idea that if I should fancy a jacket or some such thing that I do not actually *need*, it would be self-indulgent to buy it. I once refused to accept an expensive pair of crocodile shoes on the same grounds as Father refused the Delacroix—they were far too fine for me to have.

Father never wasted his time, but he frequently failed to make the most of his money. Like him I would rather spend time on my friends than money; it happens that I often end up spending both. Having written the foregoing I will let it stand, but I slightly regret it, for it seems to suggest that I hold my father responsible for faults that are my own. But there are far too many ungovernable factors in our shaping; like Tristram Shandy I believe that random circumstance plays all too great a part.

I like to think of myself as a normally rational being but nevertheless I find it difficult to account for the coincidence attached to the moment of my decision to become an artist. That moment is precisely placed: I was 15, and in the West London Hospital recovering from a broken arm. Mother had brought me a copy of the illustrated Royal Academy Catalogue for 1921 to look at, and I became fascinated by a reproduction of a Glyn Philpot picture of four nude Michelangelesque youths apparently clambering over the rocks of a misty mountain. As I looked at it I knew that I must become a painter: I cannot say why. Some time after I had met Rupert Doone—four years later—I discovered that it was he who had posed for Philpot's painting.

We tend perhaps in retrospect to give unwarranted significance to such coincidences (and this was not the only one of its kind). Whatever the case, it was an extraordinary sign connecting in such a way the most important elements in my future life.

2 Lost in the School Woods

For a fairly bright and intelligent boy I contrived to make a pretty thorough mess of my school education, and caused a fair share of worry, not only to my parents, but also to myself. Before going to Gresham's School, Holt, I had hated my preparatory school and had got into trouble there; and applied to join the Navy as an officer cadet but failed the written papers after passing the interview. I arrived at Gresham's as a late entrant, more by accident than design, in the spring of 1919 a few weeks after term had begun. A year and half later, I was very nearly killed in a street accident and was absent for six months. Then, on the eve of my seventeenth birthday in December 1922, I left Gresham's for good and became an art student.

Reviewing this stark outline of my education, it would be easy to conclude that my parents might well have been spared the expense of boarding me out. Upper-class convention, however, determined that sons should be sent away from home, preferably at about 8 or 9 years of age. This was supposed to toughen up the tender little sprig, and removal into a community of his peers was seen as the first step up the ladder of life. The object of the prep-school curriculum was to prepare him for entry into a chosen public school, whose requirements were likely to have changed very little since Queen Victoria's Jubilee or the Relief of Mafeking.

Neither in range nor in method could the instruction at Langton, the preparatory school to which I was sent, be regarded as imaginative. The natural sciences were non-existent and 'art' an extra. I could say that I hated the place, but it would be truthful to admit that I would have hated anywhere. I really did not enjoy the years of puberty at all: I made no success of them and it was a period of disillusion and disappointment with myself. There seemed to be no starting point from which to begin to assert myself, and much though I revered my elder brother Christopher, who had been there for some time before me, I felt hampered by being Medley Minor and was pleased when he left. I thought that now I could make it on my own. In spite of an inward conviction that I was more intelligent than most, I failed to justify this opinion of myself and never came out in class as well as I thought I deserved. Nobody seemed impressed or interested in my uniqueness. I lost interest in the school and, having no idea why I was there, knew only that I had to be.

This is not to say that I was a wretchedly lonely or neurotic child—I was perfectly normal and healthy. The wind-swept downs, the butterflies (for which Purbeck is famous and which I slaughtered in bottles of cyanide), the sea, and diving off the rocks at Dancing Ledge: I enjoyed all these. I kept grass snakes in my school desk and made fun of the headmaster's wife's great Edwardian hats, whose wide brims covered with monstrous artificial roses seemed even then out of date in a world of soldiers, tanks, battleships, land-girls and rationing. I also loved the coarse wartime oatmeal buns or 'wads' which bulked out the diet, because they tasted like the pig's-bran mash at Westerdale. But I lacked the competitive team spirit. It was not loneliness, but rather the desire to be left alone which was the trouble; and there wasn't any privacy to be had. What I needed was some kind of creative activity or guidance and there was no one to open the door. It was quite the wrong kind of school to have been sent to, a fact which my mother recognized, for after I had failed—thank goodness—to get into the Navy, she insisted I be sent to Gresham's, a new and modern school.

This desire to be left alone, which I was experiencing for the first time, was to recur at regular intervals throughout my life, and I now know it to be largely the product of self-doubt. I wasn't a day-dreamer, building fantasies of endurance and success, but a wool-gatherer, whose mind was filled by clouds of swirling, formless plucks of cotton wool, nameless and numinous concepts awaiting birth, adjectives seeking nouns, nouns without verbs, and free-floating verbs with neither subject nor predicate. I was constantly in that state in which a metaphysical suspension of activity is, paradoxically, called a vacant mind. Needless to say the news reached my parents in the form of unacceptable school reports that 'Robert could do better, lacks concentration, etc., etc.' but it seemed to me among my clouds that I was busy about something important—though I could not say what.

The periodic failures of self-confidence that accompanied this irresistible tendency to wool-gathering produced, in time, an internal attitude of self-criticism that I have had to keep under very strict control. It is not the function of the artist's intellect to question the products of his inspiration but rather to provide the ordering conceptual frame within which his imagination and sensibility can play. (I have ruined too many pictures by premature self-criticism.)

But to return to Father, and to Mother (whose support in what might be called my 'cause', was crucial), whom we left contemplating a succession of dismal school reports. The conclusions they arrived at were revealed one Sunday morning during the Christmas holidays, about six weeks after the Armistice had been signed in 1918, when Father asked me to go for a walk with him in Kensington Gardens. Father had a distaste for intimate confrontation, and conversation did not exactly flow; indeed it was not until we turned into the park by the Bayswater Road entrance that silence was broken. Pointing across the road to the Coburg Court Hotel Father informed me that Marie Corelli and her dogs had apartments there. A pause. Was the dreaded subject not going to be mentioned after all? I vigorously held on to the picture of white Pomeranians. We had hardly proceeded a hundred yards more when an opening shot was fired from an unexpected angle—I had anticipated a broadside. 'This is your last year at Langton and you are getting on: would it not be wise for you to consider what you intend to do in life?' Wildly groping for an answer to a question that I had never anticipated, and feeling myself put on the spot, suddenly and to my surprise I found myself declaring that I would like to join the Navy. Father was even more surprised than I was. Dumbfounded, he lost the initiative. The image of myself as a cadet, one of the glamorous elect dressed in a reefer with white flashes and brass buttons on the lapels, must have given me confidence in this spontaneous avowal of naval ambition. My voice gained conviction even as my father demurred. I became obdurate; he capitulated. I have always been surprised that I was allowed to brazen it through so easily, for it must have been apparent that the idea was an ill-judged resolution compounded of panic and bravado. I was made perfectly aware that neither parent particularly liked the idea of the Navy, but it was a relief to have something settled, and I enjoyed an illusion of security, for it never occurred to me that I might fail. My future settled, I continued my usual holiday pursuits.

Bicycles! How important it was to possess one! I had wanted a Hercules but an uncle had given me something less expensive from Gamages. The significance of this instrument of escape and self-expression lay in the liberty of movement it provided. Exploring as far afield as Acton and the Tower of London, riding down so many streets and alleys to warehouses and City churches (to some of these we had been taken on Sunday mornings by Father, whose religious interests were architectural rather than devotional), I acquired a sense of time and place, history and art. In those days it was possible to leave a bike quite safely leaning against the railings inside the portico of the National Gallery overlooking Trafalgar Square and I frequently went there on my own. The interior was impressively solemn; the pictures in their gold frames hung against dark, heavily embossed 'Lincrusta' walls and the polished museum parquet floors smelt deliciously—a Proustian aroma—of genuine turpentine and beeswax. Mother wisely left me to find my own level of appreciation, but unobtrusively encouraged me. I also took to buying old books for a penny or so in Kensington Church Street or from the stalls in the Farringdon Road.

Optimistically expecting the Naval Board of Examiners to turn me down, my mother, who had a clearer idea than anybody of what I needed, had insisted that my name be put down for Gresham's. (My Father would have preferred a classical rather than a modern education for me.) Her choice was providential, for I was to make many friends at Gresham's, whereas from Langton I cannot recall the name of a single one.

An important part of the process of education—and we all believe that we have to some degree educated ourselves—is the making of friends. For a small school in a remote part of North Norfolk, Gresham's seems at the time to have had more than its fair share of exceptionally bright boys. As the boys had no choice in having been sent there, it is worth asking why between 1920 and 1928 there should have been not only Wystan Auden and Benjamin Britten at the school but also, to name only those among my exact contemporaries, John Hayward, Erskine Childers (who was to become President of the Republic of Ireland) and John Moorman.

There is a tendency to forget that the Edwardian age was not really a frivolous one at all, but a critical and experimental time. Gresham's and Bedales (both founded in 1905) were the two best-known 'new' public schools to have survived from this period after the end of the Great War. Those progressive and predominantly middle-class parents whose social, moral and ethical ideals owed much to John Ruskin and William Morris had very little choice but to send their offspring to one or the other. Those who feared that educating adolescent boys and girls together was a bit risky, and that a background of Arts and Crafts Guild and Fabian Socialism might not provide a proper academic discipline, sent their boys to the far less radical Gresham's. The seminal homogeneity of our cultural backgrounds—for no parent sent his children to either school out of tradition, and certainly not for snobbish reasons—accounts for the extraordinary frequency with which links and connections of one kind or another could be traced between so many of the pupils at either school.

William Nicholson, the painter, sent both Ben and his younger brother Christopher—my contemporary—to Gresham's, whilst Muirhead Bone sent his son, Stephen, whom I was to meet at the Slade, to Bedales. Marriage often confirmed the links between those who went to either of the schools: John Moorman married Mary Trevelyan, a cousin of Julian, who was at Bedales; and Winifred Roberts, a cousin of Mervyn Roberts, my closest friend at Gresham's, was to marry Ben Nicholson. All this made for complicated interconnections, and it indicates fairly the affinities that existed between those families who chose one or other of the schools during a remarkable period.

When in 1975–6 I was asked to write a memoir of Wystan at Gresham's and needed some help from our contemporaries, I thought of John Moorman, who was now Bishop of Ripon. John, who had befriended me in my first year, was the son of a distinguished professor of English at Leeds, and an early bond between us had been a shared interest in literature and history. We had not met for many years, but from the opening of the front door of the Bishop's House at Ripon it was as if our conversation had never been broken off. He recalled Wystan as an apparently lazy boy, pink and white, who never did any work, and talked incessantly about psychology. (John also recalled that I had lent him a copy of *The Chronicles of Jocelyn of Brakeland, Monk of St Edmondsbury*, a document of twelfth-century monastic life. This book, given to me by Father, had apparently affected him deeply and had been influential in forming his own interests as an ecclesiastical historian. It gave me great pleasure to learn of my having accidentally played a small part in his vocation.) It would have been a pity to sour the agreeable reunion at Ripon by reviving memories of the 'honour system' at Gresham's, but my experience of that vexation to the spirit—Howson's long-abandoned method of dealing with the sticky problems of adolescence—must be described if I am to convey adequately something of the ethos of that remarkable school at the time I met Wystan Auden there.

Within about two weeks of arrival every new boy was individually invited by the headmaster for a welcoming chat. For reasons that became obvious, when my invitation came, nobody warned me of quite what was in store. It was in the evening after prep, and when the lamps had been lit, that the headmaster, Mr Eccles, invited me to be seated in one of the ever-so-homely, chintz-covered easy chairs, and matron, who had shown me in, was sent to bring us both a cup of tea. After kind enquiries as to my comfort, he assured me that Gresham's was a friendly place where everybody trusted each other. The interview then took a more awesome, not to say sinister, turn. There was to be no smoking, swearing or drinking—he was sure I never did these things at home—and would I solemnly promise 'never to say or do anything indecent'? I felt as if I had been stabbed in the stomach. I was already tainted with guilt—for towards the end of my time at Langton there had been an outbreak of 'terrible vice', with its consequent terrible row. Had it been thought necessary to warn my new school that they were taking on a convicted criminal? Struggling against a tide of shame, I ardently promised. But worse was to come; compliance was required with the following demands: if I broke any of these promises, I should report myself to my housemaster; if I saw anyone else break them, I should endeavour to persuade him to report himself; and if he refused, I should report him myself! On my honour to abide by this code, I emerged from the interview.

This shocking and unethical procedure effectively ensured our moral behaviour. But as it was morally wrong the effect on the school was not entirely healthy, for it meant that the products of such a system—with its licence to spy upon one's peers—would all too often be innocent neurotics or consciously virtuous prigs.

In practice I did not find the system unduly oppressive, and the promises extracted with such foreboding over tea with Mr Eccles faded from the forefront of my mind. It was not until two years later that an innocent incident revived my consciousness of being 'on my honour'. Wystan and I had escaped from cricket and gone for a walk and a talk in the school woods. Late in the afternoon we emerged from the shadows to be challenged at once by an unpleasantly priggish prefect. This unprepossessing youth persisted with a number of mysteriously loaded questions: What had we been up to? Where had we been? Lost in the woods, were we?—He had a good mind to report us! Having nothing to own up to we stood our ground, and with a singular lack of grace the prefect withdrew. Wystan, who seemed relieved, observed tartly, 'It's quite clear—he was jealous!'

I failed to follow the implications of Wystan's remark—he had seemed to take this absurd threat more seriously than I. Indeed it was not until the Christmas holidays after I had left Gresham's and while I was staying with his family in Harborne that the idea of homosexual love was to be broached at all. We had talked late into the night and Wystan had read some new poems. In the morning Mrs Auden discovered on our bedroom floor a manuscript poem containing a description of me at the swimming pool, in which she discerned an erotic element. For myself, I had never thought about Wystan in that way, and I had totally suppressed any such feelings about anybody else; it took some time for me to understand what this episode must have meant to Wystan, who was for the first time seriously in love. In fact it was not until three years later, when I found myself in a similar predicament, that I came to a realization of it. By then Wystan was at Oxford and it was too late. To have been loved, and not to have been aware of it, still less to have returned it fully and physically, was unconsciously to have caused Wystan distress. Emotionally and intellectually more developed than me, he had felt more and known more, and I regretted the pain he had suffered.

Revisiting Gresham's in 1974, when writing about Wystan for Stephen Spender's tribute, to prepare a short memorial of the poet for the school magazine, I had the strange experience, not of sentimental nostalgia, but of being on the wrong side of the mirror: the boys whom I encountered on their way to various classrooms, to the swimming pool or the open-air theatre, or seated at the next table to mine in the library, might, in their school uniform, have been ourselves. Politely ignoring the existence of the elderly stranger in their midst, they never spoke. I read old copies of the *Gresham* and studied the relevant school lists. Yes, there I was, and progressing far too slowly up the school! And then in 1921 a gap—my name was omitted and then reappeared in the Michaelmas term list in brackets and at the bottom of the class. Thus recorded is a prolonged absence from school caused by an accident which set me on the course I was to follow, finally making me a painter.

The accident was the result of a thoughtless misjudgement. Trying to pass a heavy vehicle in the Chiswick High Road, I caught the front wheel of my bicycle in a tramline, skidded and fell flat on my face in front of it. The vehicle in question was a heavy Foden steam wagon with solid tyres—a member of the steamroller family. The result was a crushed left arm broken in five places, and a hand which God miraculously spared from amputation. The whole affair was so grave that I was never reproached for the carelessness that caused it. But it could also be thought of as a Freudian accident, a mistake-on-purpose; inwardly worried about my persistent lack of progress, I had perhaps secretly longed to be exempted from the society of my equals. The accident and its consequences marked the decisive break between the schoolboy and the student and caused the transition to be engineered by my Uncle Cecil and Aunt Christine Pilkington.

While I was in the West London Hospital, in Hammersmith, I had seen Glyn Philpot's picture of the naked youths struggling through a mist towards a mountain summit and it had mysteriously seemed to symbolize my own condition. While in hospital I also read Vasari's *Lives of the Artists*, and G. M. Trevelyan's *Garibaldi and the Making of Italy*. As soon as it became possible to move me I was sent, heavily encased in plaster, to convalesce under the care of Aunt Christine and Uncle Cecil in Lancashire. The reason for this fortunate removal was that during the war the Pilkingtons had added an orthopaedic wing for wounded soldiers to their hospital at the glass works in St Helens.

That part of my education that I do not owe to my parents I owe to

Christine and Cecil. As the accident had distanced me from Gresham's so also it distanced me from home—and psychologically at just the right moment. A remarkable dynasty, the Pilkingtons demanded of themselves a very high standard of intellect and character and it was a great experience to endeavour to live up to their ideals.

Even among the Pilkingtons Cecil was exceptional. A physicist and natural scientist of great distinction, he was restlessly energetic, experimental and creative: ideas had to be tested by practice. At work, his passionate concern was with the physical: earth, rocks, plants and animals. Music was his relaxation. His opposite and complementary—creating a calm at the centre of the hectic hyperactivity of his life—was Christine. She was an observer of human nature; detached yet involved. She was concerned with the imponderables: art, philosophy, and theology. She loved to discuss what she had been reading. Doomed to live in isolation in a splendidly ostentatious Victorian Gothic mansion on the outskirts of St Helens, too large for their needs and which neither she nor Cecil had wanted, but which had been forced upon them to maintain the prestige of the Pilkington patriarchy, she felt cut off from the intellectual company and cultural contacts she needed. She therefore spent much of the time in her sitting room and library, and in order to keep *au courant* she had a bookseller in Liverpool constantly sending her new books. The large drawing rooms were never really lived in, and in Aunt Christine's room stood the piano on which she studied the scores of recent music by Sibelius, or Scriabin, or Delius, which arrived along with the books by John Masefield, John Drinkwater and Dean Inge. Because she had come to neglect it after her marriage, Christine was very reticent about her musical accomplishment. I asked once why it was she could so rarely be coaxed to play and got the answer, 'Oh, my dear, I do so hate to disappoint myself.' Like her husband, she was a perfectionist. They were well matched and proud of each other.

When it came to the visual arts they were conservative in their tastes. Perhaps the strongly Nonconformist background from which they both came, with its strict control over emotional experience, predisposed the sensitive but analytic temperament that they shared to the abstract qualities of the Chinese ceramics and Japanese prints with which they liked to live. Knowing how devoted I was to

Christine, and how much I owed to her, Cecil, when she died, gave me a beautiful unglazed T'ang horse to remember her by. Bought from the Eumorfopoulos sale in 1929, it had stood imposingly for years in the new house that they had built for themselves in thirty-five acres of unspoilt land on Boars Hill, outside Oxford.

Though life at Briar's Hey could never be dull for any length of time—Cecil once converted the floor of the baronial hall into a pool with black mackintosh tanks filled with water, across which garden canes were laid at measured intervals in order to check angles of refraction for the making of Vita glass which cut out ultraviolet rays—they entertained very little. And with Cecil working long hours at St Helens or away in Canada or Belgium, where there were other glass works, Christine was often deprived of company. It was into this situation that I arrived shortly after Easter 1921. With Father to deliver me safely, I was assisted out of the large blue Daimler sent to fetch us from Edge Hill railway station, shamefaced to be arriving as an almost helpless parcel. My other visits had always been on festive occasions, when the drawing room was opened for Christmas parties. On this occasion I was helped from the red-sandstone Gothic porch down a medieval tiled passage which led to the hall and the wide pitch-pine staircase ascending to the gallery and the surrounding bedrooms. Immediately after supper I was put to bed. There was a close bond of understanding between the Medleys and the Briar's Hey Pilkingtons; but I was to be like the boy in the story, who mounted the stage to assist the magician in a disappearing act: it was not the same boy who returned to his unsuspecting parents.

The arrangements for my education, which meant keeping up with school work, were quickly settled. In such a large house there was, of course, a room known as the 'school room', and Father was to send from London a resident tutor who under Christine's and Cecil's supervision would take me in charge. What went wrong with this simple arrangement was that Father proved not to be a good judge of tutors. Only one, a Miss Grant from Rothiemurins, came up to the exacting Pilkington standards. The first, who only lasted a few weeks, was such a crashing bore that Christine and Cecil could not put up with him. The last, a young man just down from university, survived largely because he had the tact to remove himself as soon as dinner was over. It was always a great relief, while coffee was being served in Christine's library, to hear the crunch of bicycle wheels on the gravel drive outside as he made his way, presumably to the Rainhill Arms, for a well-earned pint. Unfortunately Miss Grant, a 'temporary' between tutors, and the only one with the breadth of culture and sharpness of wit to be welcomed, was with us for but a short time, and in spite of being pressed she could not stay.

As the time spent on remedial exercise at the works hospital diminished, so the hours in the school room increased and with it the boredom of lessons under teachers who could not teach. It was Christine who brought me out; there was never any question that what interested her would interest me. In the evenings when Cecil returned from the glass works, he relaxed, not like Father with silence and a book, but with apologies for having been away—no, we had *not* been bored—and jokes, and eventually Christine would have to insist that he calmed down. Their concern for each other was openly expressed. After dinner the conversation ranged widely and freely over many subjects, and while I was never left out it was up to me to interest them in what I had to contribute.

At Briar's Hey I became sure that I wanted to be an artist, but of what kind I was, as yet, uncertain. Allowed to paint the walls of a remote box-room, my head stuffed full of William Blake, Christina Rossetti, Michelangelo and Sir Edward Poynter, I failed with a *River of Life*. *Cortez—Silent, upon a peak in Darien* (a single figure seated over the door) was slightly more masterly, but hardly the definitive start to an artistic career. I did not miss friends of my own age (for there were none about) and when the Pilkington children, Mary and Arnold, returned from school, I shamefully resented it, for I was no longer the only pebble on the beach.

Returning to Gresham's in September, I was outwardly pleased enough to be back, but I realized that the school had little further to offer me. If I was to become an artist I must be responsible for my own development and, if a beginning was to be made, the sooner the better. In order to pursue the kind of life I had glimpsed at Briar's Hey, I embarked on a policy of non-co-operation at school. Using the pretext of a recently fractured arm I got excused (temporarily) from the obligation to play games, and for the same reason—how could I go hurling rifles about in the air?—from the weekly absurdities on the parade ground of the OTC. When this excuse wore thin, I continued to object on conscientious grounds—what was the League of Nations for?—only to find, however, that although it was listed in the prospectus as 'voluntary', unless parents objected the boys had no choice. Already unpopular with the sergeant-major, I was consigned to 'Signals', an untidy unit composed of the awkward and the intellectual who couldn't be bothered to distinguish a left leg puttee from a right. (Such a unit was to be admirably suited to Wystan's attitude to uniforms as well as to his conspiratorial sense of humour and one of our earliest moves together was to get him enrolled as a signaller.) This policy of passive resistance, by which I asserted my identity and gained as much independence from community obligations as possible, was well advanced by the spring of 1922.

Such was the state of affairs when Wystan sought me out in March 1922 during a visit of the sociological society to a boot factory in Norwich. He had contrived to sit beside me on the return bus journey, and this was the first moment that I was aware of his existence. He told me that he had wanted to speak to me for a long time: he was very determined and it was quickly arranged that we should go for a walk on the following Sunday. Cherishing views (which I thought very adult) about my superiority with respect to the rest of the school, I found it rather strange to be out with a small boy, two years younger than me, with a smooth, pink and white complexion, the fairest of fair hair, and a very confident manner. I have no idea what we talked about, for Wystan did most of the talking, except that we soon discovered that we had a good deal in common, including a detached attitude towards the school.

Awarded a scholarship after entering Gresham's in the autumn of 1920, Wystan had transferred to the top end of the school early in 1921. He surveyed the social microcosm in which we lived with clinical detachment and evident distaste, and he was very soon giving me the benefit of his insights into an exhausting variety of topics. The only area in which I did seem better informed was literature and poetry, which with two years' seniority was hardly surprising. Even so I very quickly lost that advantage—by the end of 1922 Wystan's first published poem (unsigned) had appeared under John Hayward's editorship in the school magazine, the *Grasshopper*, while my only contribution was postponed until the following issue, and appeared after I had left school.

Having got along so famously on the first occasion, other meetings immediately followed. During one of these the relationship inevitably took a more personal turn. We were trudging across the fields on the far side of the Sheringham Road, and after airing my views on Blake, Shelley and Prince Kropotkin (a recent discovery) I embarked on an attack on the Church (amongst other self-assertive acts had been a refusal of confirmation). Expecting a sympathetic response to my ardently expressed, logical but unoriginal views, I was taken aback to discover Wystan flushed, frowning and offended. Wystan, I thus discovered, was devout. I could neither retract nor apologize; I could only stop talking. There was silence. To break the tension that was threatening to spoil a new and unexpected friendship before it had hardly begun, I found myself offering to share an intimate secret. Confessing that I wrote poetry I asked if he wrote himself and was oddly surprised to find that he had never tried. I suggested that he might begin and that started things off. The look of the rough field and of the group of trees behind us, the exact spot at which I had unwittingly touched upon a sensitive nerve, and recovered the situation with a suggestion of such immense consequence, was so implanted in my memory that when I returned to Gresham's in 1974 I thought, given luck, to rediscover it. But a new housing development had blotted out the gap in the hedge, and any real hope of identifying one field amongst so many, a mile away and so many years after, was impossible.

During the summer I liked to spend as much time as possible at the swimming pool, often getting there before breakfast when we didn't have to wear bathing slips. One day Wystan, having watched me larking about with other boys and taking them for double dives off the top board, asked me to do the same with him. A double dive is done by taking your partner on the shoulders, or pick-a-back. I explained to Wystan his part in the simple pick-a-back version and warned him particularly to keep his head down. After some difficulty in getting him into position without being strangled by his uncoordinated embrace, we plunged to disaster: Wystan predictably came unstuck on the way down and emerged from the water with a badly bleeding nose.

What was to characterize the adult Auden was, in almost every aspect, already apparent in the schoolboy at Gresham's: the vulnerability, the unsentimental passion, the ethical resentment of injustice, and the physical clumsiness that was such a contrast to the intellectual agility. That none of us at Gresham's, including myself, realized that we had among us an outstanding human being and a great poet in the making is excusable since he never indulged in the vanity of sharpening his wits at other people's expense. Precocious in intellect, he was not precocious in the exhibition of his genius: unlike Shelley, perhaps, or Mozart, or indeed Benjamin Britten, who came to the school a few years later, and for whom special arrangements had to be made, Auden did not as a young schoolboy shine in a way that made his future distinction obvious.

It was during this term—having rejected the proposal that I should try for the 'colonial service' (I was plainly not clever enough for the 'diplomatic')—that I made clear my intention to become a painter. 'Art' and 'handicraft', taught next door to each other in a newly built timber and thatched hut in the school grounds, were recently introduced and somewhat anomalous subjects, included in the curriculum as an either/or choice for juniors only. Occupying an equally anomalous position was Miss Bristow ('the Bristine'), for she was the only woman on the staff. A former Slade student, the self-effacing Miss Bristow left much to be discovered, for while she made no claims for herself as an artist she belonged to that highly cultured and courageous generation of pre-1914 women undergraduates. Her closest friend was Frances Cornford, the poet. Mother came to Holt and met Miss Bristow, in whom she was to discover not only an ally in the immediate business but a sympathetic and lasting friend. Mother's visit was the not usual half-term affair; she had come to confirm her own conviction that I should be studying art instead of marking time, and the support that she received from the intuitive Miss Bristow was immediate and direct.

With Father's agreement, the final move in my leaving school was made, and Mother took me, with a portfolio of my work, to F. E. Jackson's studio off the Kensington High Street. Ernest Jackson, now remembered best as a draughtsman and teacher, was a friend of my mother's from earlier days when she still had time to attend to her own gifts. He was also a moving spirit behind a periodic publication called *Imprint*, promoting the interests of the graphic arts, typography and authorship, for which Father had once written an article on copyright. On the easel was an as yet unfinished painting, *Pietà*, executed in egg-tempera, which now hangs in St James, Piccadilly.

Standing about or against the walls were several portrait heads on small wooden panels and highly skilled drawings reminiscent of the Italian old masters of the cinquecento. It was the work not of a plagiarist, but of a sensitive and eclectic artist-craftsman. This visit was my first introduction to the paraphernalia of the studio of a practising artist.

Wearing pleated linen overalls that his wife stitched for him, Jackson looked as much like a Yorkshire farmer as an artist. At the Byam Shaw and Vicat Cole School of Art, and at the Royal Academy, he was the most influential teacher and the strongest personality.

My portfolio was left in the corner while he showed his recent work and turned over the pile of drawings in the press. I gazed at the little glass pots of powder colour, the quantities of clean brushes, hogshair and sable, the drawing boards and sticks of charcoal and crayon. Could I ever attain all this? What would result from the easy flow of discussion between Jackson and my mother, and the comments I was occasionally called upon to make? Eventually my own work was looked at. Feeling by now that it didn't look any good, I just had to make the best of it. How far this introduction into the mysteries of art schools was a formality I never enquired, but Jackson obviously had to see my work before I could be admitted to the Byam Shaw School of Art.

Wystan and I continued to meet after my departure from Gresham's at the end of the autumn term 1922. My parents, who were not easy to please, became fond of him, and he fitted well into a family of six, being an avid player of card games, and always a vital addition to the party. His visits were always looked forward to with pleasure. Father never complained of the disturbance of his library, nor Mother of the books left all over the drawing-room floor, and they even tolerated his habit of banging out fugues and popular hymn tunes on the piano before breakfast. To be expected to give serious attention to such music-making, or to a Beethoven symphony played on a gramophone when the rest of the family were locking each other out of the bathroom on the upstairs landing was occasionally tolerable, but life could not go on being lived at such a pitch. Although everybody felt a bit flat after Wystan had gone, there was also a sense of relief; for his visits were stimulating but exhausting.

In London we frequented Harold Monro's poetry bookshop in

Old Gloucester Street and went to the theatre and the opera—we saw Basil Dean's production of the Čapeks' *The Insect Play* and *RUR* (the early robot play), and Rutland Boughton's *The Immortal Hour*. During this period too Wystan wrote long letters and sent with them sheaves of poems. My opinions were called for, and, as his handwriting took so long to read, I took these manuscripts about with me in various coat pockets to study on buses and while walking over Primrose Hill and Hampstead Heath. In this way Wystan's juvenilia became eroded. I fear, moreover, that I did not always answer him promptly; years later I was reproached for this. Wystan kept copies of course and when he allowed a few to appear in Christopher Isherwood's *Lions and Shadows*, I recognized them as among those I had received years previously.

In the following August Wystan joined us for a week during the holidays at Appletreewick in Wharfedale. It was a very wet Yorkshire summer and much of the time had to be spent indoors waiting for clothes to dry. Wystan added greatly to the fun of the occasion, organizing cards and progressive word games, and we noted with amusement that he always liked to win, and usually did.

The limestone country around the house my parents leased was very much to Wystan's taste. On the moors were the workings of ancient lead mines, which had fascinated him from childhood, and in Troller's Gyll, where the beck runs underground, the entrances to caves and potholes. It was the sort of landscape that always held a special significance for him:

Dear, I know nothing of
Either, but when I try to imagine a faultless love
Or the life to come, what I hear is the murmur
Of underground streams, what I see is a limestone landscape.

In January 1923 I had embarked upon my career as an artist by undertaking what would nowadays be called a foundation course at the Byam Shaw School of Art in Campden Street, W8, and I could be found daily travelling in all weathers on the wooden seats of the open-top number 31 bus which then as now followed a singularly unglamorous route from Swiss Cottage via Westbourne Grove to Notting Hill Gate. The reluctant schoolboy had by now become the enthusiastic apprentice anxious to learn from fellow pupils and masters alike. As was to be expected in those days before there were diplomas and government grants, most of the students came from upper- and middle-class families who could afford to indulge their daughters' talents until they married, or were elderly amateurs pursuing a hobby. The Byam Shaw, however, was serious, high-minded, and a place of extraordinary innocence—we brought our own sandwiches and drank tea or lemonade. But by the end of the year it was apparent that Campden Hill was not the centre of the art world, which was surely either in Gower Street, at the Slade School, or South Kensington, at the Royal College of Art. I felt the need for a larger horizon. There were too many girls (however talented they might be) and too few boys. I wanted more competitive and challenging surroundings, and associates of my own sex. Moreover I became convinced as the year wore on that Jackson's powerful personality was too one-sided an influence and must be resisted; and in this I know I was right. I set my sights on reaching either the Slade or the Royal College. My need for a more demanding situation was recognized by Jackson who now regarded me as one of his most promising protégés, whom he would expect in the normal course of events to progress to the Royal Academy Schools where, as drawing master, he would continue to oversee my development. Because of their admiration for, and belief in, Jackson my parents would not disclose my real reasons for wishing to leave, and I was in no position to insist upon having my own way. In any case the RA was a senior establishment, and I could pass from 'private' to 'diploma' level without a break in continuity. So I went after all to Burlington House, where it was hoped I would settle down. But I did not do so, and within a very short time I was once more on the move. I discovered years later that part of my mother's objection to my going to the Slade was that she considered me too young and feared that I might become prematurely involved with a Bohemian girl student!

At the Byam Shaw I had made no new friends of any consequence and I was pleased enough to be leaving for *terra incognita* even if it was not quite of my own choosing. I was to start at the Royal Academy Schools in January. Meanwhile I was invited to Harborne to see the New Year in with the Audens.

I had not seen Wystan since the summer holidays in Yorkshire; and with the change in my own prospects there was a lot to talk about. Meeting Dr and Mrs Auden for the first time I was on my best behaviour. The family house felt comfortable and lived-in. Over the white table-cloth at dinner it was obvious that Wystan, in looks and build, much resembled his mother. Taller than her husband, and a powerful personality, she had a refined and remote dignity, a withdrawn circumspection. Her face had many fine lines, so fine that at first glance they would not be noticed. I felt I was being inspected, which was quite natural since I had probably been much talked about. I formed the impression that Dr Auden's was the more accessible personality.

After dinner we went to Wystan's room, into which an extra bed had been put for me, and at last we could talk freely, and Wystan could read to me the new poems he had written. I have never to this day been able to understand how I could have missed the import of Wystan's poem about the swimming pool at Gresham's, but it passed over my head as just another poem. How far Wystan himself, as we lay three feet apart in our separate beds, intended the reading of the poem to be a proposition I do not know. In any case it was extremely careless of him to leave it lying on the floor for his mother to find in the morning. Summoned by Dr Auden to his study, we had no difficulty in convincing him that our relationship had never been sexual; indeed it must have been obvious to an experienced psychologist that the idea had never entered my mind. Dr Auden explained gently that he himself as a young man had enjoyed a 'close friendship' but that such a thing was not desirable, nor had he gone 'that far'. Had we gone 'that far'? We gave him an assurance that our relationship had always been and would remain purely platonic and left the study, numbed by the implications of the discovery but thankful that it had not been worse. The poem was not returned to its author; before we left the study Dr Auden, with permission, burnt the poem, and Wystan never referred to it again.

All conspired to bury the incident as quickly as possible, and Mrs Auden, who had been absent from the drama in the study, never mentioned it, at least not in my presence. The outcome of the crisis was to precipitate exactly what Wystan's parents had feared most: an open acknowledgement to me of his homosexuality, and a revelation to me of the full dimensions of his feelings. That I did not and could not feel the same did not seem to matter. In the rush of holiday events that followed it was understood, without inquest, indeed without words, that we stood together.

A welcome relief from a clouded atmosphere came next day, Saturday, when Wystan and I were swept off to lunch and a matinée of *Aladdin and his Wonderful Lamp* at the the Birmingham Grand Theatre by a medical friend of Dr Auden. As we were shown to our seats in the front row of the stalls, this distinguished doctor's wife explained, *sotto voce*, that her husband preferred a close-up view of the chorus girls' legs. This unsurprising revelation of the hypocrisy of adults served to confirm our moral solidarity, and did not pass without ironic comment. It was our good fortune that *Aladdin* was not only the first pantomime we had ever seen, but was a full-blooded entertainment in the great classless Victorian music-hall tradition in its last fling before provincial watch committees broke its spirit, and the Odeons and Commodores took over. As the Widow Twankey and her pranksome Laundry Boy, the incomparable comedians Stanley and Lupino Lane, father and son, embellished every ripe and Rabelaisian opportunity with the most wonderful traditional clowning. It was extremely filthy and hilariously funny and the ancient anarchy of pantomime provided just the relief we needed.

I returned to London on Monday morning with Wystan's Christmas present, *The Collected Poems of Francis Thompson*, inscribed 'To Bobo—with love—from Wystan H. Auden', in his already characteristic spidery handwriting. I had been aware, at the moment of his giving it to me, that his choice reflected a sensitivity to my taste at the time of our earliest meetings—a taste I had already somewhat outgrown—rather than that he was himself developing in his own beginnings as a poet. At any rate it was in sharp contrast to *The Poems of Edward Eastaway* (Edward Thomas), published by Selwyn and Blount in 1917, which I received with a letter and a packet of poems from Wystan soon after. The book I still have: it is signed 'C.R.O. Medley' and underneath in pencil and very small, 'hdd—W.H.A.' Wystan remained at Gresham's, isolated by his acute self-knowledge, and vulnerable to the pressures of the honour system whose moral viciousness he so clearly diagnosed. In London meanwhile, preoccupied with newly found companions in the excitement of Hampstead and Bloomsbury, I became the friend who 'answered some of his marvellous letters, but kept none'.

3 Unfinished at the Slade

The dark months of January and February did little to persuade me that the Academy, under Sir Frank Dicksee, was a proper place to be, in spite of the free tuition and the considerable list of prizes that could be won. The list was, in itself, a social document of an age already passed away—there were prizes for such things as *A Half-Length Portrait of a Lady in Evening Dress, Wearing Elbow-Length Kid Gloves.* The long passage leading to the studios, into which no ray of daylight could ever penetrate, was hung with innumerable monochrome compositions on biblical themes by generations of former students, the best of which was *Moses and the Brazen Serpent* by Solomon J. Solomon. The semi-basement studios, sandwiched between the blank and towering back walls of Burlington House and Sir James Pennithorne's great building (now the Museum of Mankind), were, in the winter months, it seemed to me, gloomy dungeons. The Academicians who were supposed to take it in turns to instruct us rarely turned up and were, with the cherished exception of George Clausen, uninspiring hacks. We waited in vain for Augustus John to stoke the fires of inspiration, but he never showed up and was more easily to be found at the Café Royal. John's son Edwin, and Morland Lewis, who left to become Walter Sickert's studio apprentice, were the only kindred spirits to be found.

Though the Keeper, Sir Charles Sims, and Ernest Jackson did their best to provide a coherent approach, it was obvious I must make an escape. Even though it meant wounding Jackson's feelings, it had to be done. By April I was working at the Slade School, having been welcomed by Professor Tonks as a deserter from the enemy camp. The relief was enormous. To enter by the central doorway of the neo-classical building and to be faced with Augustus John's assured and Rubens-like version of *Moses and the Brazen Serpent* halfway up the double staircase that led to the Antique Room, where beginners started, was enough. There were prize works by Orpen, Albert Rutherston and other distinguished predecessors, and Stanley Spencer's *Visitation.* In the semi-basement was the men's huge life-drawing studio, which was overlooked by a balcony which led to Professor Tonks' room. The walls of the studio were encrusted with the historic palette-knife scrapings of past and present generations. It seemed to me then a great school of drawing and painting.

The world of the art student of that period was effectively split between the rival kingdoms of Tonks at the Slade and William Rothenstein at the Royal College. There was no love lost between them and any cross-fertilization between their respective students was virtually impossible. Both however were united in their dislike of everything connected with Roger Fry. The pre-war Post-Impressionists Exhibition might as well never have taken place. To Tonks the mere mention of Cézanne was treachery: Fry was mocked as one who went about crying 'Cézannah, Cézannah in the highest,' a quip which I have always imagined to have originated in Ebury Street where Tonks, Philip Wilson Steer and Sickert dined with George Moore. As Roger, the 'Prophet', could easily have been cast as the Baptist in Nazimova's early film of Oscar Wilde's *Salome*, it was funny as well as being malicious. (Malicious wit was by no means confined to Bloomsbury.) Prophetic indeed he was, for it was he (supported by Samuel Courtauld) who was the driving force behind many important new acquisitions by the Tate Gallery; Van Gogh's *Chair*, and Seurat's great *Les Baigneurs* (both acquired in 1924) to name the two best known. Where would the National Collection have been without them?

The next two years were for me a period of great restlessness and personal uncertainty. I now know that I was seeking an identity at once personal, sexual and artistic. (The solution was of a kind that I could certainly not have predicted.) In spite of the dual hegemony of Tonks and Rothenstein over the official world of Art Studies it was possible to find outposts of unorthodoxy, and in due course, with others of like mind, I found my way to these. In addition to studying at the Slade I went to classes at the Central School (under William Roberts and Bernard Meninsky), to Walter Bayes at the Westminster

School of Art, and finally, with Eileen Agar, a fellow student at the Slade, I put my nose into Leon Underwood's studio where Henry Moore, Raymond Coxon and Vivian Pitchforth had found an alternative to the Royal College. For all this tireless activity the feelings of restless dissatisfaction remained. Why? Partly it was a matter of personal temperament—there was still something of the wool-gathering prep-schoolboy about the eager Slade student I had become—but in retrospect I see that there was more to it, and that my condition was typical of that generation of the early twenties, for whom pre-war values, and the sense of a permanence in things, had been shattered. At the Slade and the Royal College there were still young men whose development had been interrupted by conscription into the forces. For my generation the way in which the older cultural values were questioned was more personal than political. We were too close to the lost generation, whose loyalty to King and Country had led them into the valleys of death at Passchendaele and Ypres, to be impressed by the old ideals of State and Empire. Certainly, if we compare the records of many of those of our contemporaries, a clear distinction emerges: we were concerned with the quest for *personal* identity and *personal* loyalty, they with wider loyalties to community and cause. My younger brother Richard (who was two years younger than Benjamin Britten) went up to Cambridge from Gresham's with James Klugmann and Donald MacLean; among his closest friends at Cambridge were John Cornford and Julian Bell, both of whom were to die in Spain. In Auden's work with Isherwood in the thirties, and in his own poetry, the great theme of the Search is essentially a personal one—the hero sets out on a journey to find himself, as Auden himself had done.

There is no such thing as the State
And no one exists alone. . . .
We must love one another or die.

At the Slade in the Spring of 1924 I made a very good beginning, and at the end of the first term won a prize (or was it an 'Hon. Mention'?) for a life drawing—a modest success which established me amongst the promising. Doors began to open, and it was through Richard Carline that I was introduced to the artistic and social circles of Hampstead. Richard and Sidney Carline kept a remarkable open house for their friends in their mother's home in Downshire Hill, opposite their studios, where early works by her children, Dick, Sidney and Hilda, and by Stanley Spencer and Mark Gertler were hung with their father's anecdotal Victorian pictures on every available wall space. There were innumerable cabinets, bibelots, sit-down chairs and family bric-à-brac, and it had the cosiness of the seldom dusted. It was not the writers like S. S. Koteliansky, nor the talk about John Middleton Murry and Katherine Mansfield, that interested me, but meeting Stanley Spencer for tea on Sunday afternoons. The diminutive Spencer, looking slightly weather-worn and apple-cheeked, like a mischievous bright-eyed and ageless gardener's boy, read out loud from T. S. Eliot's *Poems 1920*. He gave repeat performances of 'The Hippopotamus' and 'Mr Eliot's Sunday Morning Service', particularly relishing 'Polyphiloprogenitive/The sapient sutlers of the Lord'. It was the first time I had come across Eliot and the lines have stuck in my memory ever since. Not yet the Cookham recluse, Spencer struck me as very sharp-witted and friendly. He had just begun the first large *Resurrection* and I was allowed to see it in its earliest stages. The huge canvas was stretched out on the wall of a room on the top floor of the Vale of Health public house in Hampstead, where Stanley worked and 'dossed down'. The composition, meticulously squared up and outlined in pencil, was begun at the top left-hand corner and, working with what were very small brushes for such a large picture (some of them water-colour brushes), he completed each area as he went along. I saw the top left completed and can only assume that, as when working on a fresco, he finished at the bottom right. After his marriage to Hilda Carline we lost touch and the last time I saw him was at a Slade dinner in the 1950s. Cheerfully inebriated, unwashed and not a little smelly, he recalled everything even down to an early picture that I had shown in Bond Street in 1932. I was touched to be so remembered. The exhibition at the Royal Academy in 1981 made me think that in any other country Stanley Spencer would have been treated with the honour and respect properly due to an artist greater and more original than many more celebrated European 'masters'—Max Beckmann for example. Instead he was reduced to churning out green landscapes for Arthur Tooth, and accused of pornography by a President of the Royal Academy who bored everybody at the Arts Club with his dirty jokes.

It was at a party in 1924 that I met Mark Gertler, who was at that time moving away from Garsington and his entanglement with Dora Carrington, about which I knew nothing. He had a studio in Willow Road and was working on his own fully developed style based on Chardin, Cézanne and Renoir: his outlook was far more accessible to a student than Stanley Spencer's imaginative and quirky view of things. He worked direct from nature, and his studio was full of his favourite objects: aspidistras, commonplace pieces of drapery bought from market stalls, Staffordshire china figures, a violin in its case (the Tate Gallery has a painting of this), and, in acknowledgement of Cézanne, a pedestal *compotier* with apples in it. His concern with the structural organization of 'what was in front of him'—the classical obsession of painters of easel pictures—influenced me for a long time. In emulation I bought a Staffordshire figure in a junk shop in Camden Town. When he committed suicide in 1939—he was not yet 50—Gertler was insufficiently recognized and rewarded, for the British show little understanding of their best painters.

As I began to discern the essential elements in the contemporary situation it was inevitable that I should come to realize that what I was seeking was not to be found at the Slade. That I should come so quickly to this conclusion had much to do with John Strachey (not to be confused with his cousin the politician) with whom I was to be deeply involved for the next eighteen formative months. He had been sent to the Slade not through any love of Bloomsbury or Professor Tonks, but because it was just round the corner from where he lived with his grandmother, Lady Strachey, at 51 Gordon Square. Since the death of his father, John had been the responsibility of his Aunt Philippa—'Pippa'—the anchor of that extraordinary clan. Tall and thin, and not unlike his Uncle Lytton in appearance, John had inherited his fair share of Strachey talent, wit and intelligence, but was wayward and rather irresponsible, and regarded the world as his oyster. He was known as 'Spotty John' on account of his complexion, which in no way diminished his success with the girls.

The exciting possibilities now opening up in Bloomsbury were considerably enhanced by the 1924 and 1925 seasons of Diaghilev's Ballets Russes at the Coliseum. Admission to the gallery cost 1/6 or 1/- for a seat, and 9d to stand. It was filled with art students experiencing for the first time living works by Picasso, Braque and André Derain, and the music of Les Six and Stravinsky. At home in Belsize Park I chose orange, black, lemon-yellow and white for the bedroom, which somehow fitted in with Bakst and Benois as well as Picasso. The effect of course was rather spoilt by the green lino already on the floor, and by having to share the room with my younger brother Richard.

It was Bloomsbury that was for a long time to shape my attitudes to art—indeed to life. My fall from grace at the Slade, however, was directly precipitated by my submission to a monthly Sketch Club Criticism of a still life based upon a sepia reproduction of a Derain I had found in a pocket-sized monograph in the 'Modern Masters' series produced by Editions Braun. This had been intended as a mild protest—a *Summer Composition* of a view over the back gardens of Belsize Park, influenced by Seurat and Gertler, it had been ignored by Tonks—but I did not expect the wrath of God to descend upon such a modest, and seriously intended, effort. Tonks never spoke to me again unless he had to: for example, when I bade him adieu in 1926 before going to Paris. I remember him however with affection, for he was a great figure in his way, and he stood up for English painting and for the dignity of his students at a time when their standing in the University was continuously in question. We made it up some years later when we met by chance at a performance at the Arts Theatre of George Moore's *The Passing of the Essenes*. He was delighted, now that he was retired, to meet a former student and the defection to Roger Fry and Bloomsbury was forgotten.

I would have eventually graduated into Bloomsbury through my cousin Francis Birrell, who at that time had just started a bookshop with David Garnett in Taviton Street, where I would sometimes meet up with my elder brother Christopher. My introduction, by John, into the domestic centre of the Strachey family at 51 Gordon Square was nevertheless fortunate, for the Stracheys, Stephens and Grants belonged together, and Francis, who belonged to the literary side of Bloomsbury, could not have introduced me into the artistic side of the company with such ease. Certainly an extraordinary galaxy lived and shared houses along the eastern side of Gordon Square, where before the war, at Number 46, Vanessa, Virginia and their brother Adrian had shared rooms. Here, after the war, lived Lady Strachey and her sons Oliver and James and their wives; Adrian Stephen and his wife Karin (Oliver's sister-in-law); Duncan Grant and Vanessa Bell until they moved to the studio in Fitzroy Street; Clive Bell (whose charming apartments had been decorated by Duncan and

Vanessa); Arthur Waley (in an apartment above James); and, in 1925, Maynard Keynes, now married to Lydia Lopokova, who had moved across from Fitzroy Square.

The Strachey family was extraordinarily close knit, even though they were so diverse a collection of individuals, and until Lady Strachey died the headquarters was at Number 51, where the delicate Lytton always had a room kept specially for him. When his sister Dorothy (the translator of André Gide, and, as Olivia, the author of *Olivie*) came with her husband Simon Bussy and their daughter Janie, somehow there was also room for them. (The Bussys lived in the South of France, at Roquebrune, and Simon had been a close friend of Matisse and Rouault since their days in Gustave Moreau's studio. He was himself a good artist who never made a great name.)

If it was John who brought me there, it was Pippa who remains the central figure in my memories of Gordon Square. Deceptively the plain-looking little spinster, the maiden aunt who looks after everybody and everything, Pippa belonged to that distinguished generation of great and cultured women that before the First World War had fought for its rights and gone to prison for it. She told me that it had been quite enjoyable—at least as she remembered it—because they had maintained their spirit: she recalled how, under the direction of Ethel Smyth, they had sung and blown tunes on combs wrapped in lavatory paper. As well as looking after her mother, running a large house, and being the selfless and devoted Strachey concerned about all the other Stracheys, she still found time to carry on with her own work, which was running the Women's League of Service. The League, a voluntary organization for women's rights, had its headquarters in Marsham Street near the Houses of Parliament so that, assisted by Ray Strachey and Marjory Fry (another of the 'greats' who worked in the same cause amongst the prisoners in Holloway), she could monitor legislation and lobby MPs.

From the vantage point of the front sitting room of 51 Gordon Square, with its well-worn furniture, and the unfashionable but important Burne-Jones that hung over the mantelpiece, incongruously flanked by the paintings of Simon Bussy, Bloomsbury did not appear at all as the critics have made it out to be. After supper, grouped around the grand piano which took up so much space, we sang, with the old lady loving to join in, snatches from her favourite

Gilbert and Sullivan operas, or played word games until Pippa saw her safely upstairs and to bed. One evening, by way of change, we introduced David John, Edwin's brother, whom we had met at the Café Royal, to play his party piece: a Bach fugue. Of course there were parties and talk—how they loved to talk! Discussion and gossip (the salt of civilized conversation) belonged together. *Everything* was talked about and they applied a common sense, seasoned by logical paradox (a mixture reminiscent of the eighteenth-century Enlightenment) not only to the moral inhibitions and prejudices of society, but also to the inspection of their own conduct. It was, therefore, not the mannerisms, the cliquishness and the arrogance that struck me, but the all-embracing seriousness. Everybody seemed engaged upon important and innovatory work. Duncan and Vanessa, painting away in Fitzroy Street, and Ray Strachey, after a day in Marsham Street making rugs after their designs, were always ready to talk—Ray could embroider, smoke and talk all at the same time. James, more remote, was translating Freud. The early and mid-twenties were the heydays of the circle: Lytton, after *Eminent Victorians* and *Queen Victoria* (1921), was famous; Virginia Woolf was writing *Mrs Dalloway*; Maynard Keynes was already a powerful influence upon thought and action. I took to Bloomsbury like a duck to water and soon caught the Strachey accent—the inflection that was characteristic of the Bloomsbury style.

In and out of 51 Gordon Square most days of the week, and familiar with the comings and goings of others, through taking on the formidable task of redecorating the entrance hall and five-flight staircase—in a complicated mixture of powder colours, whitening and size prescribed by Duncan and resembling 'French grey', and all of which I had to brew up over a gas ring in the dining room—it did not take long to be accepted as part of the surroundings. I was very soon shown Clive's Picassos, Gris and Derains. After Roger had set up house with Helen Anrep in Bernard Street, in 1925, I went to see his painting of *A Green Field* by Seurat, and I recall his resonant and beautiful voice trying to persuade me that 'every other blade of grass is red'. It was at the ample Victorian house in Dalmeny Avenue, where he had lived with his sister Marjory since 1919, that I went to my first large party of the inner circle of Bloomsbury and met Lytton, who had hitherto been a remote and special figure. Helping myself to food in the semi-basement dining room, I found that I had been followed by Lytton, who, noticing that the domestic helpers had retired, exclaimed, 'Thank goodness the Brownies have gone!' and planted a smacking kiss upon my lips. I was still under the illusion that I was entirely heterosexual, so this was not the fairy godmother's wicked entrance to awake the sleeping beauty, but I enjoyed being singled out and tickled by such a celebrated beard. When I told him I lived at home in Belsize Park he told me of the time when he had lived there and how one day, being late for an appointment, he had rushed out to find a taxi opposite the tube station. He had cried out in his high-pitched voice 'Are you free?' to which the driver had promptly replied 'Yes, but very expensive.'

This was all very intoxicating, and Wystan, isolated at Gresham's, faded from my mind. Written in the familiar hand, his long letters, often difficult to decipher, remained unanswered until they had almost disintegrated in my pockets. I read them in bits on the tops of buses or walking to Gower Street across Primrose Hill. The poems that came with them were also a problem because as they developed I became increasingly unable to say anything constructive about them. To have replied only that 'I like this one but not that one' would have been inadequate and shabby. It was the beginning of an awkward period between us.

During this period, not surprisingly, the literary side of things was not important to me, and it was ironic that it was not until the first months of 1925 when Lytton's play *The Son of Heaven* was given two performances at the Scala Theatre in aid of Pippa's League that I got to know Duncan and Vanessa at all well, and it was that occasion that marked the beginning of a working relationship that continued until 1934, after the launching of the Group Theatre.

The Son of Heaven was not at all a bad play but I could see why it had not been taken on by Max Reinhardt or Granville-Barker, in spite of their initial enthusiasm. The play concerned the affairs of the Empress Dowager and a Chinese Duke at the time of the Boxer Rebellion (1909). The setting was the interior of the Imperial Palace, Peking. It had been written in 1912 and the subject had lost its immediate appeal; but the fact that Lytton had written it and that the décor and costumes were by Duncan Grant was considered enough to guarantee sufficient response and to fill two houses. The designs were strikingly fresh and original, a characteristic chinoiserie fantasy.

Clear ochres and greys set off pinks, oranges and emerald greens. The costumes, some of them elaborately decorated, were hand painted by Duncan and Vanessa with a confident boldness that astonished me, but to which all their experience of the Omega Workshop days obviously contributed. Being two locally accredited art students, John Strachey and I were naturally enlisted as helpers—at least we knew what a brush looked like and as a boiler-of-size and a mixer-of-whitening my reliability had already been proved. We also appeared on stage—with my brother Christopher—as walk-on eunuchs, forbidden even to utter a castrated squeak. We had to shuffle and teeter around, our hands hidden in the inside sleeves of monkish robes, in the wake of the Chief Eunuch. Though the two principals, the Empress and the Duke, were played by named professionals, full use had been made of Cambridge connections to provide the rest of the cast as well as the producer, Alec Penrose (elder brother of Roland), who had recently made a success with the University Dramatic Society.

During rehearsals, Miss Gertrude Kingston, who had consented to play the Empress, behaved as well as might be expected, appearing to accept without too much demur the direction of a producer whom she considered an amateur. But secretly she had made her own plans. Duncan, going the rounds before the curtain went up on the first night to wish everybody good luck, discovered the great Ibsen actress dressed not in his costume but in what she declared to be the *real thing*, a heavily embroidered, hideous black-brocade Manchu robe—and nothing, not even respect for Duncan's overall colour scheme, nor his feelings as an artist, could persuade her to take it off. But worse was to come, for she had decided that the play would be greatly improved by adding to her part in it. She had seized the hour, and not only the eunuchs but the whole astonished cast trembled when she prolonged the climax of the second act by a full five minutes of drama of her own invention. Backstage it created a buzz of excited dismay. If Lytton had been there—he had gone abroad on holiday—she would surely never have risked it. For the second performance a compromise was effected: she would wear the right costume provided she was allowed to retain a shortened version of the interpolated cadenza.

The auspicious introduction to such friendly and distinguished mentors might have settled me down, but in fact it had entirely the opposite effect. The world opened up, and it was inevitable that I should plunge headlong into a year of great confusion, a period of disordered identity both artistic and sexual.

Art first, sex after seems the natural order in which to treat things here. The most important influences on the younger generation of artists were Roger Fry's *Vision and Design* and Clive Bell's *Civilisation*, and the concept of 'Significant Form'. These two books provided a secure base for new ideas as well as the essential ammunition for a rebellion against the out-of-date teaching rooted in the New English Art Club traditions of the Slade and the Royal College. Inevitably, the ideas they set in motion, by the ironic course of destiny, led to the overthrow of their authors. Art always outstrips theory. It was all very well for Roger to shake his head over the philosophical unsoundness of the concept of 'Significant Form': everybody knew what Clive meant. The anthropological galleries at the British Museum were stuffed with 'significant forms', they were open to us all, and we could draw on our own conclusions—Picasso's Negroid heads of 1907–8 were getting known. Roger, explaining that for the artist what is important about an egg is its oval shape or ovoid form, opening the door on to the enchanted fields of abstract thought, resisted the inevitable non-figurative, as well as the more disturbing surrealist, implications.

It must be observed that this failure of nerve characterized Bloomsbury art as well as its theory. There was never a Bloomsbury school of painting, and the work of Duncan and Vanessa lacked the vigour and drive necessary to create one. For all their talent and intelligence they remained essentially amateurs, in love with the hand-made and the decorative. By 1929 Roger was already regarded as a potential traitor to the cause of modernism. This was unfair: after all he had been the pioneering figure in its British career. In 1930, in company with Quentin Bell, Rupert Doone and Humphrey Slater, I attended one of the lectures in which he discussed the future of figurative art. Afterwards, if for some of us doubts remained they certainly did not for Humphrey, who was convinced that his treachery was complete. Some time later I recall Roger remarking of an exhibition of Henry Moore that 'The trouble with Moore is that he knows what a work of art is, and is trying to make one.' This dubious remark saddened me, for I had owed a great deal to Roger. This is to anticipate, and I must return now to that period of crisis in my life that did not begin to end until I had met Rupert Doone and was living with him in Paris in 1926.

Having for very good reasons rejected the school of drawing at the Slade, my attendance there became perfunctory. If I liked the model I would occasionally draw from life, but usually after signing the register, I would spend the time gossiping on the front doorstep, generally with Rex Whistler, Stephen Tennant and Oliver Messel—a very sophisticated and amusing trio. None had any reason to apply themselves, nor were they painters as I understood the term. Rex anyhow was Tonks's favourite: he could draw anything out of his head provided it was a pastiche of somebody else (usually eighteenth century). This is perhaps a little unfair, because he was endlessly inventive, and sensitive about the limitations upon which his success depended. Oliver, moving fast into the theatre—he made the gold mask designed by Braque for the Diaghilev ballet *Zéphire et Flore* at the Coliseum in 1925—might be perfecting for our benefit his impersonation of a spinster showing lantern slides of her travels in the Holy Land to members of the village Women's Institute. Stephen was delicately beautiful, as if he had strayed out of a novel by Ronald Firbank. They were enormous fun and belonged to the smart set (Duff Cooper, Glenconners, Sassoons) and they very much kept their own court. Tonks, who had the reputation of dining in Mayfair every night of the week, was a snob. There is nothing like being an artist for going up (or down) the social scale, and he was of the opinion that patrons should be well-born as well as rich. Under him this socialite element was a feature of the Slade, to which one might be invited as if to a select party, and made it quite distinct from the Royal College where scholarship students had to look seriously to the future and pass their diplomas.

John Strachey, Humphrey Slater and I were also identifiable as a trio: we considered ourselves to be the intellectual and Bohemian élite—the rebels. Humphrey was undoubtedly one of the most naturally talented and original students at the Slade. I never thought of him as an intellectual until in the early thirties he started playing chess and reading Lenin, which was a disaster, for he gave up painting and became the leader of an East End Communist cell. In earlier times he appeared rather scatterbrained, and was certainly conceited. He claimed to be descended from Sarah Siddons and liked to emphasize his likeness to Gainsborough's portrait in the National

Gallery by tying a narrow black velvet ribbon under the chin and round his well-formed neck. Regular-featured, with blue eyes and blond hair, he was a great success with the girls. Rather like the Three Musketeers, accompanied by lively and well-connected female students, we came together and performed not only at studio parties like the Carlines', but on formal occasions such as balls and dances given during the 'season' for débutantes where we were an accepted troupe. Our own connections were extensive, and with one thing and another, as opportunity provided, it was possible to get an entrée to a fair section of London life. It was perhaps all valuable experience, until one began to feel blasé, and complained of the 'wine cup' at Claridge's or the champagne at the Van den Burghs' in Kensington Palace Gate. It was so easy to get about town: transport ran late, there were always taxis to be found, or being young you could walk. Lyons Corner House was open all night and breakfast (delicious kippers) served from five or six o'clock in the morning. But I could not help feeling that this was not my proper milieu.

It was not the social round that was so wasteful a part of a misspent youth—it could aptly be described as ring-a-ring-o'-roses, it was so innocent—but the way in which John, Humphrey and I filled in the time away from the Slade. Humphrey, apparently unhampered by the control of a guardian, had the advantage of living and working on his own in a studio in Yeoman's Row. In the intervals between anathematizing Professor Tonks and all his doings, and getting drunk on beer and the importance of our own ideas in the pub at the end of the road, we painted in his studio some perfectly horrible pictures. However serious our intentions, we got into various scrapes, and kept late nights. It was all right for John and Humphrey, but the problems of concealing the red-eyed ravages of a putative Bohemianism from Father's silent disapproval at the breakfast table on the morning after could be countered only by actually doing something to restore order and discipline to both my art and my life.

The meticulous if rather rigid structures of William Roberts's drawing seemed a useful antidote. I joined therefore the evening life classes at the Central School in Southampton Row where he and Bernard Meninsky both taught. William Roberts, a compact little ball of a man, and rather plethoric, turned out to be a disappointing teacher. Meninsky, who is remembered with affection and gratitude by all those whom he taught, proved to be useful, for he was very much aware of what was going on in Paris. There is no doubt, however, that the seminal influence on students in the mid-twenties was that of Leon Underwood whose private school and studio was in Girdlers Road behind Olympia. I went there with Eileen Agar, who was also at the Slade, but too late in the day for it to be of much use to me. Shortly afterwards I was to leave for Paris with Rupert Doone. At Leon Underwood's were Blair Hughes-Stanton and Gertrude Hermes and, in the evenings, Henry Moore, Raymond Coxon, Edna Ginesi and Vivian Pitchforth. These last had all gone there for the same reasons—they had received no more understanding and sympathy from Rothenstein at the Royal College than I had from Professor Tonks at the Slade.

Underwood, whose reputation rests upon a small number of exceptional avant-garde sculptures made in the twenties, had started out as a painter. He was a sound and positive draughtsman, and having his own school (which was very well run) he had the advantage—as we saw it—of standing outside any educational establishment. He was extremely susceptible to any new ideas that were in the air, and this made him a natural ally for the young rebels who gathered in the School's studio, which adjoined his own smaller work room. Here he created an atmosphere of freedom in what was more a community than an academy.

Evening classes in themselves were not enough. Coming late in the day even a sympathetic master like Meninsky could not give more than supervision to part-time students. But they did however clear the mind and the earlier extravagances of Yeoman's Row were succeeded by a more consistent programme of work. During the summer of 1925 I shared a studio in the backyard of a house in Charlotte Street with John Strachey. Because it was lit by a skylight from above it was a real *studio* and I thought it splendid, but I quickly grew to hate it, and have never again worked in a room I could not see out of. Moreover it had the complications of being halfway between the Slade, where the attendant coryphées were still at work, and Bertorelli's and Poggioli's in Charlotte Street where it was possible to be well fed for 1/6, and get a carafe of Chianti for the same price. This inevitably lead to lunchtime parties that spread over into wasted afternoons in the studio, which became the scene of many a disorderly but innocent riot.

There was a crisis however that had been rumbling in the

background for some time, the causes of which it would take the analytic powers of Freud himself to disentangle. John and Humphrey were experienced and had easily established intimate relations with the girls, whilst I remained (not through lack of trying) a virgin, and I did not at all like being left behind. Whether the studio precipitated the crisis I do not know. Being there, with the only light coming from above, was like living at the bottom of a well. I felt enclosed, and began to feel ill. Every afternoon at the same hour I became dizzy and, seized by a tight constriction across the chest, I had to lie down on the floor until it passed and I was well enough to get up again. John, always starting pictures and never finishing them, was usually out, and did not know of the extent to which I was afflicted. In any case, I didn't want him to know. These attacks went on until I could stand it no longer, and one afternoon while lying on the floor, I decided that I must go home, confess and see a doctor. At that I fell into a deep sleep and when I awoke I knew that the crisis was over. A weight seemed to have been lifted, and I felt entirely light and free. I knew at that moment that the enchantment that John had held over me for so many months was dispelled and that I would never come back to the studio.

During this year of search and uncertainty on my part, Wystan, isolated at Gresham's, had come to terms with himself. I was still lost. However, when he visited me during the summer term it became possible to make some amends for the priggish rebuff of an earlier visit, when I had explained (how tiresomely!) that I was interested only in girls, and that on leaving school he would be too. Everything now came out in the open and we joked about the boys at Gresham's whom we had found attractive, and about those victims of the 'honour system' who had gone to the bad since leaving. He was also typically secretive and self-dramatizing, for instance announcing one morning that he was off to Piccadilly Circus to meet a poet, a most interesting and dangerous character, who was in love with the page-boy outside the Trocadero. He also told me of his intention to play Caliban in the school production of *The Tempest* for the enjoyment of being able to express his dislike of 'the Masters'.

By the autumn subsequent to the crisis I was established in a room of my own, the impoverished drawing room in a modest Victorian terrace house in Winchester Road, behind Swiss Cottage and a stone's throw from home. The rent was 12/6 a week. The smaller back room was let separately to John Strachey at Pippa's request, for in Gordon Square he was still a problem. There had never been any question of a break-up between John and me, but this time we had separate keys, and I had the advantage of the choice of room. Cleaned up and repainted in white distemper, this room with its Victorian marble mantelpiece and the mirror fixed over it was recognizably the prototype of all those rooms I have since liked to make. There was very little furniture, and with two large windows overlooking the street there was plenty of light. There was a gas ring in the grate and it would have been easy to live there had it not been understood that I should continue to sleep at home. The only large piece of furniture I brought with me was a narrow day bed—a mattress supported on a black ebonized wooden frame about twelve inches off the floor for which my parents had no further use. Except for sitting or lying flat it was pretty uncomfortable but with a cushion or two it suggested possibilities.

One of the first pictures I painted there was a portrait of Wystan who had come up to London for a week in September before going up to Oxford. I was pleased with this painting and we both thought it a likeness. Wystan, who with new-found independence was enjoying the part of grand seigneur, insisted, to my annoyance because it had been meant as a gift, on paying for it. Justly reproached for allowing Wystan's seminal early writings to fall to pieces in my pockets, I would much like to know what he did with my portrait—for I never saw it again.

Concurrent with this lost masterpiece, which should be at least on the racks, if not on the walls of the National Portrait Gallery, I painted a picture of the opening trio in *Cimarosiana*, a ballet I had seen during the Diaghilev season, with costumes by José Maria Sert, performed by two male soloists and a ballerina. This was very strange, because I had not yet met Rupert Doone, and it was four years later in 1929 that Rupert was to make his début at Covent Garden, during Diaghilev's last season, in this very trio.

The white-painted room in Winchester Road was the scene of a final attempt at heterosexual seduction. Although the girl and I had come from much the same background—Campden Hill and Bloomsbury—I had got to know her well only over the previous year. Claire had very beautiful dark brown eyes, and she was calm and sympathetic. Of all the girls that we knew at the Slade she was the only one I wanted to be with. It would be difficult to say after all this passage of time how far the attraction was sexual, but there was a genuine affection between us. I prepared the scene and invited her to dinner. She must have known the reasons for the invitation and came therefore to sound out how things really stood. I knew that it would be difficult to persuade her to become my mistress, but as we could speak quite frankly to each other I thought that the barrier of her Roman Catholic faith could be overcome. Gently and not without humour she wisely turned me down. I had been on the point of actually proposing that we get married—and had drawn back from that as dishonourable—when her refusal came as a relief. We parted friends and have remained so ever since.

Human nature is, however, without duplicity, double. I had been thinking, would it not be a practical step to get seduced? It did not seem to matter much by whom. Had I not after all once made a pass at Humphrey, pretending it was a joke? And why had I waited outside the stage door at the Coliseum, not to see the ballerinas but the male dancers? It was no good being adrift forever, and the compass pointed in the direction of Stephen Tomlin, the promising sculptor who was making a bust of Lytton Strachey and was Bloomsbury's latest artistic and intellectual discovery. Stephen, bisexual and several years older than me, had been markedly friendly whenever we met and an existing attraction seemed to make him the perfect initiator. Not surprisingly, perhaps, nothing worked out as it had been planned. It was not Stephen but his heterosexual brother Garrow who, after dinner one evening in Lambs Conduit Street, was the first person ever to seduce me.

After this, things happened very quickly. Wystan felt sufficiently established to ask me down for the weekend in Oxford. He was obviously enjoying life and conveyed the impression that he now had greater liberty than myself who was still living at home. As usual we talked until past midnight, and it took a very long time to get round to the conclusion—foregone on my part, as I knew I was no longer morally in a position to refuse. Neither of us was an experienced lover and did not know how to make the best of the occasion, and there was something typically clinical and Wystan-like in his remarking as the sheets were pulled back that 'everybody's resistance' was 'at its lowest by three o'clock in the morning'. I enjoyed the experience, and was very pleased that it had happened, though I had to admit to myself that it had been symbolic rather than passionate. I returned to London in a certain glow of satisfaction, and the thought that next time it would be better, for I assumed that with Wystan it certainly would, and that a heterosexual affair could be left in the course of nature to present itself when it would.

Within a week, however, all anchorages were swept away. One evening in November 1925, at the corner of Howland Street and Fitzroy Street, I ran into John Armstrong carrying a bottle of wine wrapped in coloured flimsy paper and on his way to a birthday party for Wells Coates who lived just across the road, next door to Duncan and Vanessa's studio. The objection that I didn't know Wells Coates was overruled. There would be plenty of people I knew, including Elsa Lanchester. So we crossed the road, and going in I was introduced to Wells (an engineer and journalist, not yet an architect) and his girl-friend (a dancer with ambitions to be a musical comedy star). I was then passed to John Banting who had been painting her portrait. Armed with a drink it was now possible to take note of the small groups standing about talking and drinking, and I realized that most of the company was new to me. They seemed more directly interested in avant-garde theatre than painting, and there were several references to Rupert Doone, who was expected to arrive late. I had no idea who he was, but gathered that he was an up-and-coming young dancer and choreographer and that the party would not be regarded as complete until he arrived. It was a relief therefore when Elsa entered, for her vitality and eccentric beauty were guaranteed to liven up any party that was rather slow in getting started. The same age as 'the Three Musketeers', she had been a frequent toast of that exuberant crew. She was also much sought after by hostesses of the upper-middle-class Bohemia who patronized the Cave of Harmony, a private night club and cabaret, open several nights a week, in a basement in Charlotte Street, where she and Harold Scott entertained with wittily salted revivals of Victorian street ballads. Elsa had a long skinny figure like a starving street arab and an auriole of flaming orange curls surrounding a mask of fine but irregular features, sparkling and prominent green eyes, a little *retroussé* nose and pouting red lips: she was alternately a Pre-Raphaelite waif, a Bacchante, and an angel.

One or two couples took the floor. I was a good dancer and I decided to show off with Elsa in a tango. I had obviously gone too far in my apache role for, holding me at arm's length, she suddenly announced in her clear voice, 'The trouble with you, Robert, is that you don't know what sex you are!' As everybody had been looking on, the only reply to this deadly shaft was to take off all my clothes and demonstrate the facts. This unpremeditated exhibition was greeted with a round of applause. It was evidently what was needed to get the party going and I was not allowed to get dressed again. Insisting however that a fig leaf would make the costume more classical, John Banting improvised one out of a small-sized gramophone record and a length of ribbon. Some time later, through the jostling crowd of dancers, I espied an impeccably dressed, fair-haired young man with slanting eyes, standing in the doorway with his head slightly tilted to one side, surveying the scene with the enigmatic and self-conscious air of one who, at last, has arrived. He had immediate 'presence'; his looks, slightly feminine, were strikingly unusual. Had I seen him instead of the anonymous little figures that had disappeared into the night from the stage door of the Coliseum, I might have recognized the Eros or Ariel that I had expected. Like Elsa, Rupert was not one to be overlooked in a crowd.

I felt I ought to put some clothes back on, but the figure came across and asked for a dance. Rather clumsily we danced; by change and change about a strange introduction was effected. I said I would feel far more comfortable if I got dressed and if he would wait for a few moments I would be back. By the time the party was over, and overcoats being sought for, we had arranged to meet again. One meeting led to another, usually in tea shops or restaurants in Charlotte Street, but sometimes discreetly at the theatrical lodgings in Guilford Street, where he was staying. His worldly possessions at the time consisted of a trunk and a heavy suitcase which contained all the books that an unsettled existence allowed for. Amongst these were Edward Gordon Craig's *On the Art of the Theatre*, several copies of Craig's *The Mask*, Havelock Ellis's *The Dance of Life*, selections from the poems of Swinburne, Cocteau's *Cock and Harlequin* inscribed by the author, and an omnibus Shakespeare. There was also a negligently kept book of press cuttings and a few photographs, mostly unmounted. By Christmas we were inseparable. Unexpectedly, and very much to my relief, my parents failed to spot the nature of our relationship and Rupert spent Christmas Day with us *en famille*.

As far as Rupert's friends were concerned there were no problems, but for me, there was Wystan to think about. I hated the thought that once again I seemed fated to wound him. I was quite prepared to risk anybody else's disapproval but not Wystan's. I wrote and told him what had happened and asked him to come to London to meet Rupert. The meeting took place in Winchester Road and Wystan arrived first. Nervously over a glass of sherry I prepared the ground. Would he understand that it was more than an infatuation with a pretty young dancer? Rupert was two years older than me, but looked younger; appearances could be deceptive. Wystan appeared to take it all quite easily, amused perhaps by his having been right after all about my homosexuality, and certainly curious. Rupert's arrival some minutes later removed any fears that the meeting might prove an immediate disaster. Equally curious about each other, neither showed the self-assertiveness that might have been expected. As it turned out, the awkward interim period of sizing up, of mutual probing and of establishing their separate identities, was cut short by the discovery that they both laughed at the same kind of jokes. We finished the bottle of sherry, and spurning public transport took a taxi to Bertorelli's, where with Rupert's aid I could afford a convivial luncheon. Leaving behind us two empty carafes of *rouge* we swept out just in time for Wystan to catch his train. Rupert was delighted with Wystan and declared the meeting an unexpected success. But for a time I wondered what Wystan, as his train rushed past Slough, Reading and Pangbourne on its way to Oxford, had finally made of it.

Before parting we had vowed to meet again before long, but in spite of those protestations it was a year before the opportunity presented itself, for Rupert and I were to be in Paris from May until the end of the year. And so began the relationship, as remarkable for its ups as for its downs, that during the thirties was to make the Group Theatre a theatrical and social force to be reckoned with.

4 Paris 1926

It is not easy to describe just how extraordinary a person Rupert Doone seemed to me at the time of our first meeting. The pure chance of our encounter at Wells Coates's party could not have happened at a more crucial moment for me. Everything seemed in the balance, and I needed help in almost every part of my life. Not that I clearly recognized my needs; I could not myself critically untangle the vague indeterminacies of desire, the uncertainties of purpose, and the muddled expectations that made up my personality. In truth, Elsa had been right, and that was only part of it. Rupert's great gift was his ability to help people to find themselves, and I felt during the first months of our life together that I was being taken to pieces and put together again. His reactions, often overriding the logical, were swift and intuitive. He seemed born with a natural understanding of painting, music and poetry, and his visual sense was particularly strong. He thought in terms of images and forms, but he looked beyond them to motivations and rhythms. I was never able to talk to Wystan about painting because he did not understand how a painter worked. Rupert did understand. And because dancing is physical and visual, I was able to reciprocate. I could see what he was about, and I could talk to Rupert about his work in a way that had been impossible with Wystan. Apparently self-assured—there was no trace of the provincial background from which he came—Rupert nevertheless had the air of a foundling, and needed the security that I could give him, a security that had hitherto been denied to him by a tempestuous and unsettled career of self-education. Over the next few months our understanding and our commitment to each other grew in spite of circumstantial difficulties.

Paris 1926

In the early spring of 1926, during an idyllic weekend in an isolated cottage in the country near Horsham, we laid plans to escape together to Paris. Rupert was better known there than in London, and there might be better opportunities to work: quite apart from his relationship with Cocteau, he had numerous connections there. For my part what could be better, after the Slade, than a period in the capital of modern art? We asked Duncan Grant, a friend of Rupert's since 1924, to write a note to my parents supporting the idea, and to this was added a similar letter from Roger Fry.

Rupert left shortly afterwards for Paris to await the outcome of our plot. The letters from Duncan and Roger were no doubt reassuring, and I had no difficulty in persuading my parents that it was a good idea. They knew of course that I would probably be joining Rupert but they had no overt reason for disapproval. On 6 May, the eve of the General Strike, a month after Rupert's departure, I set out for Paris, taking the last train to leave Victoria for Newhaven–Dieppe.

The doors slammed and slowly we drew out of the already darkened station. The great adventure had begun. There was a trunk full of clothes and painting materials in the luggage van, and in my pockets a letter of introduction from Roger Fry to Jean Marchand, enough money for the journey, and a letter to Thomas Cook and Son, allowing me to draw three pounds a week (five pounds in case of emergency). The excitement of liberty and anticipation ran high, but in the early hours of the following morning, as the train neared Paris, I got cold feet. The future that only a few hours before had seemed so desirable had suddenly and unaccountably become a step into the dark that once taken could never be drawn back from. In the grey dawn, as the train shuttled across the points of the many tracks converging upon the Gare St Lazare, and wound its way past the tall pale ochreous tenement blocks in which windows were already opened and curtains drawn, I was consumed by agonizing doubts. Should I be bound to anyone but myself? Was not the world my oyster? Should I not, even if it meant breaking my vows to Rupert, by an *acte gratuit* cancel the past and embark alone upon a new life? In the terminus, beneath the blackened glass roof, the steam hissed from the vacuum brakes and we came to a halt. Grey faced and demoralized I felt no joy in the arrival, only a paralysing indecision. To resolve it I sought refuge nearby in a seedy second-class hotel—perhaps to sleep, but above all to savour a sensation of being absolutely and completely alone. It was well past midday before I had the courage to descend the stairs, pay the bill, and order a taxi to the Hotel St Germain des Prés, rue Bonaparte, where Rupert had been kept waiting for many hours. Emotionally drained, like a guilty sleep-walker in a trance, I knocked on the door of what was to be our room for the ensuing months, fearing the worst. But at the sight of Rupert standing in the open doorway, the blackness was suddenly lifted as if it had never been. I was safe and where I had wanted to be. How could I have wanted to run away? After hours of anxious waiting, and on the point of telephoning London to find out what on earth had happened to me, in the immediate relief of the moment Rupert postponed the inquest into my unaccountable behaviour—how could I have acted so cruelly?—until the emotional crisis had subsided.

Perhaps an emotional scene was the necessary prelude to the real beginning. Certainly it was for me, now, that the first and most formative period of my development as an artist began. For Rupert, already more developed than me, the next few months were also to prove vital, for they led to his becoming the partner of Vera Trefilova, one of the three greatest ballerinas of Imperial Russia, and an engagement at the Scala in Berlin. But meanwhile I had to be played into Rupert's scene, for Paris was his terrain. To celebrate my arrival, that first evening, Rupert had assembled a welcome party of friends, and having restored our somewhat battered nerves with double brandies at the Deux Magots, we walked past St Sulpice and the Luxembourg Gardens to the Café Sélect in Montparnasse.

Since the days of le Bateau Lavoir the Bohemian centre had shifted from Montmartre to Montparnasse and the unprecedented invasion of international and polyglot artists of all kinds that swarmed in post-war Paris had adopted the studios and the cafés and the cheap hotels of the 6e and 14e *arrondissements* as their stamping ground. Into this melting pot of talent, in which Parisians played little part, I was about to be introduced. An arena in which only the exceptional could make their mark, it was also a playground where the feckless could fritter away their ambitions until they were forgotten or destroyed. It was typical of Rupert's style that he had chosen to live away from the hubbub, in the historically exclusive and more stable area of St Germain.

The most crowded of the cafés were the Café du Dôme, with its ranks of tables on the pavement, and on the opposite corner across the boulevard the Rotonde, which before the Revolution had been frequented by Lenin—or so it was said. For some reason the Rotonde was falling from favour, and the Coupole did not exist except as a workman's bar, or *zinc*, to which nobody went unless they were broke. But the café frequented by our circle was new, small, and aptly called the Sélect. The décor was nondescript art deco. The first to see us and to be seen as we entered was Mary Butts—easily recognized by the tangled mass of flaming gold-orange hair that refused to remain tidy. She had a clear pale complexion, small, bright green eyes, zany red lips, broadly rouged in a carefully chosen colour, and an infectious giggle. Her bangles slipped down to her elbow as she waved a welcome with a cigarette held in a long ivory holder. Sitting next to her was Mary Reynolds, a quiet, intelligent American lady, then living with Marcel Duchamp. Cedric Morris and Lett Haines swept in on their way to a party and arrangements were made for us to meet the following day. A number of people joined the table, including Alan Ross MacDougall (Dougie), who had been the devoted secretary and amanuensis of Isadora Duncan. At the age of 17 and on his first visit to London, Dougie, a stocky little Scot from Glasgow, had been arrested and flung into prison for taking part in a suffragette rally in Westminster in 1916. Infuriated by Sassenach injustice, he immediately fled to New York and became an American citizen. Living on his wits as an independent journalist, an entertainer and a maliciously witty gossip, he nevertheless led a life of endearing integrity. He did what he wanted on no money at all, and never complained, except of the mercenary demands made by the French *matelots* whom he couldn't resist. He had one best suit, which he wore at the Ritz when going to see Janet Flanner, and otherwise he lived in a trunk which contained every medical and culinary safeguard against the misfortunes of travel. He was the kindest of men both in giving and receiving.

Among those who frequented the Sélect there were Jacques Stettiner, Jean Aron and Raoul Leven (all friends of Cocteau); Nina Hamnett (who was sometimes on her 'grand tack' and off with the Princesse Violette Murat, the Countess A, or to tea with Cécile Sorel and Coco Chanel); Kisling, who had made drawings of Rupert; Foujita, the successful Japanese artist, and, rather to one side, Ossip

Zadkine, the sculptor, who preferred St Germain. In the Russian contingent at the Sélect—Paris was full of exiles and refugees—were Marie Wassilief, a lively little bundle of a woman, an avant-garde painter who had been stranded in Paris during the war and had run a soup kitchen for starving compatriots and was now making portrait puppets in leather; and Serge Maslenikoff, a refugee, sad, lovable and funny—he designed sequin embroideries for the best 'houses', but he had never learned how to make money and was usually broke. Also there came, with the reputation for being an independent and touchy recluse, Djuna Barnes: a shy unicorn, she was beautifully groomed, with a touch of the masculine in her attire, and she affected a walking stick. If in Paris it was Mary Butts, warmly attached to Rupert, who was our closest friend, it was Djuna who lasted over the years.

The following morning no city, it seemed, could be more beautiful than Paris. The trees in the Luxembourg Gardens, in the Tuileries, and along the boulevards were freshly green and sparkled in the clear spring sunshine. The light washed the eyeballs clean and it was a city for painters to live and work in. Everywhere down the rue Bonaparte and the rue de Seine there were art shops and dealers showing their own artists. The narrow streets, whose tall houses, the colour of calcined bones, blocked the view of the quai Voltaire, suddenly opened up on to the Seine and the vast Palais du Louvre on the opposite bank of the river, where the poplars on the embankments lightly fluttered in the morning sun. Whereas London is a mercantile city, built around a busy tidal river, Paris is a great land-locked capital, designed for public life, the marching of armies and splendour. From the avenue de la Grande Armée, the Arc de Triomphe and the Champs-Elysées, the great perspective focuses on the fountains and statues of the Tuileries, the Carousel and the Louvre.

Before leaving London Roger Fry and Duncan had discussed how I might best spend the time. Both had urged the value of making copies. Familiar with the National Gallery in London, whose scale suggests the country mansion, I found the imperial grandeur of the Louvre overwhelming. Stuffed with the loot of centuries, from the time of François I to Napoleon, to which had been added the more recent purchases of the Third Republic, the endless galleries had the appearance of gigantic auctioneers' salesrooms, the pictures, in the various style of earlier centuries, covering the walls, four or five deep and frame to frame from floor to ceiling. Many were in need of cleaning. What plenitude for the serious glutton of works of art! What discoveries to be made! The most staggering of all was the Salle Démon, which was filled by virtually all the great French nineteenth-century masterpieces. Here, hung from the cornice by great iron brackets, was Géricault's *Raft of the Medusa*, Courbet's *Funeral at Ornans*, and the great *Atélier*; in the centre of one wall Delacroix's *Crusaders Entering Jerusalem*, *The Massacre at Scio*, *Women of Algiers*—and among the Ingres, and the Millets, Daumier's *Harlequin and Pierrot*, Courbet's *Stags at Bay* and the refined works of Chasseriau. More pictures than I had dreamt of. It was not going to be easy to choose what I wanted to copy—and I was not going to be on my own, for there were plenty of students of all nationalities working away, as well as the professional copyists, an extinct breed now, but for whose works there was then still a market.

Meanwhile there were the grander dealers in and around the rue St Honoré, where the recent and more important Picassos, Braques, Matisses and Bonnards could regularly be seen. In London there was only a handful of dealers in modern art: here there were hundreds. Artists were socially important, not oddities. However ephemeral the gossip in the cafés might be, it always returned to what artists were doing. Art was regarded as important, and controversy between artists, writers and philosophers was news.

Vivid first impressions were accompanied by a new feeling of well-being and liberty; there were no parents to worry about, and under French law nobody had the right to interfere with our relationship. It was not on that first evening at the Sélect but several days later that Lett, whose humour was mischievous and sophisticated, suggested that now I had arrived I had better go in at the deep end. He arranged with Cedric and Mary Butts for a night out on the town before life became serious. The evening started off in the *apache* quarter on the far side of the Bastille where in the rue de Lappe there were a number of homosexual bars. We avoided the dressed-up haunts to which tourists were taken for expensive 'slumming' and went instead to a rather large café where there was music. To my surprise—for I had naïvely thought that only the young and preferably beautiful could be homosexual—tough, middle-aged navvies were affectionately dancing together and seeming to ignore the younger set, among whom were several *tapettes* made up with eye-shadow and rouge. I was asked several times for a dance with a formality reminiscent of the débutante balls in Mayfair and, more out of politeness than desire, I finally accepted a young man. My conversational French at 'la plume de ma tante' level was no match for my partner's working-class argot and though I did my best to keep in step with his jigging dance I was not entirely successful. After drinks we left in a taxi for a more fashionable night-club near the Opéra called the Jardin de ma Soeur, the name of which spoke for itself, although the company was mixed. The décor of red damask was discreetly lit by shaded ormolu candelabra, and a muted orchestra was playing the latest numbers. Among those who occasionally got up to dance in a rather verveless upper-class way were two retired British Guards Officers, plainly recognizable by the trim of their moustaches and the Savile Row cut of their tweed suits. But it was obviously a 'dud' evening at the Jardin, so we quickly left for the Boeuf sur le Toit where Mary, a regular smoker of opium at this time, was disappointed not to find Cocteau. Weiner and Doucet, the cult classical pianists, were improvising jazz duets, and here we ended the evening, and my first experience of Paris by night.

After a week of initiation into the joys of open life in cafés, the talk amongst painters and writers, and the delicious food and wine in newly discovered restaurants, serious work began abruptly. Not later than eight thirty every morning Rupert was on his way to work with Madame Trefilova in her studio in the rue Pergolese, off the avenue de la Grande Armée, and I had set off to the Académie Moderne in the rue Notre Dame des Champs in Montparnasse. We did not meet again until the evening and then usually for aperitifs or coffee at the Sélect.

My own daily programme of work began to take shape. I had intended that my time should be shared between the Académie Moderne and copying at the Louvre, but work at the Académie proved unrewarding. Except for a little French girl who painted some anemones in a blue bowl, the rest of the students were all American ladies, hell-bent on producing imaginary 'modern art' in the flat, semi-abstract style of Louis Ozenfant. Léger, whom I really wanted to meet, never turned up and Jean Marchand, the principal teacher, failed to interest me. After a 'criticism' during which Ozenfant had reduced the American ladies to tears by praising the blue bowl of anemones at their expense, I decided to leave. Thereafter I spent most of my time at the Louvre or at Colarossis or the Grande Chaumière, where there was always a model but no tuition.

The problem of choosing which of the discoveries at the Louvre to copy had been delayed by a (perhaps fortunate) obstruction put in my way. I was told that Watteau's *Gilles* was not available as somebody else would be occupying the space. This was a lie, for during the two months that I was working at the Louvre nobody at all showed up to work from the Watteau, which was hung in a room full of Louis-Quinze period pictures and away from the main galleries. In the course of my early wanderings I had chanced upon it as if by accident and this had made it in some way my own personal picture, unaccountably special to me. It is a full-length portrait of the artist's friend, Gilles, as a clown, dressed in the traditional white costume and a round hat that crowns his head like a halo. He confronts us full face, and looking slightly down towards us, for he is standing on the summit of a hillock that slopes away to a hidden horizon, the vanishing-point being below our line of vision. The simple upright figure, who stands so close to us that his feet almost touch the bottom edge of the picture, is seen therefore against a great expanse of a clear yet partly clouded sky, the sky of a late July afternoon. Behind him, and with their backs turned towards us and him, recline his fellow players, of whom, as the ground falls away, we can see only the heads and shoulders. On one side two men and a woman, dressed perhaps for the parts they are playing in the *commedia dell'arte* performance, look into the distance and pay no attention to Gilles. On the other side are the head and shoulders of a donkey wreathed in a garland of flowers, and a black-clothed, rather bucolic-looking fellow with a ruff round his neck, who looks not at Gilles, but at us—his expression is quizzical and mocking. The last picture that Watteau painted before he died, the image of *Gilles* stands for the predicament of the artist himself who, isolated and alone, gazes out at us, impassive and mute, as we act out the comedy of our own lives, on our side of the proscenium picture frame. A great masterpiece? Yes! The conventional imagery, the artificial subject-matter and the elegance of the handling might count against it, but as an icon of the human condition I found it deeply moving, and still do. Except for what I had seen in the Wallace Collection, amongst the ormolu and crystal, the Boulle furniture and the Lancrets, I knew practically nothing about Watteau except that he had died of consumption at the early age of 37 after an unhappy life. As yet I responded, consciously, only to the outward appeal of fashionable images of the *commedia dell'arte*—images that Picasso, Braque, Derain and Juan Gris were currently making use of in their pictures, images that recurred in the ballets of Serge Diaghilev. Pierrots, Harlequins—to whom must also be added sailors dressed in their white uniforms—like strange and magical beings no longer entirely earthbound, belong to a timeless tradition, and exert a lasting appeal.

Presenting as it does the portrait of a performer in a great classic role of pantomime I was also able to see *Gilles* as a celebration of Rupert's chosen vocation in a world of which I was now part. It was not until 1960, when I was writing a piece for the BBC about the Dulwich Gallery's *La Fête Champêtre*, that I finally came to understand that in this last picture Watteau had summed up and expressed, in the most elegant and poetic terms, a view of life that was profoundly Stoical. This meaning had been hidden from the youth who first saw it, but it has for me now all the force of a religious icon, and I have used the frontal composition in several variations in recent pictures.

It was fortunate perhaps that I was prevented from making an immature copy of so haunting an image, for by making a botch of it my early experience might have been blunted, and my memory less prepared to hold it in suspension until realization of its real meaning, many years later. After several days of indecision I made a second choice, of Poussin's *Les Bergers d'Arcadie* which shows three shepherds and a shepherdess who in their wanderings have come across an ancient tomb and are engaged in deciphering its inscription. The idyllic and moody serenity of the picture strongly appealed to me, but my choice was determined by more than my emotional response. I thought it would be good for me to submit to a strict classical discipline and through this perhaps discover what Roger Fry meant when he spoke warmly of Poussin as a master, and a major influence on Cézanne. I got so absorbed in copying Poussin as accurately as possible, however, that I forgot about Cézanne.

After so many delays and uncertainties in making a beginning, I started to work in a rush of over-enthusiasm. Having spoiled one canvas I started over again, this time squaring the picture up from a photograph and eventually ruling lines all over it. I thus began to discover a geometry I had never been told about. Every detail in the picture seemed to have its exact place. And not only that: the geometry was also tied up with textural relationships—the counterpoint of the undisturbed and the complexly worked areas of the surface. A rigorous discipline provided the structure of the thought and the feeling in the piece. The literary or illustrational was suspect in those days of 'significant form' and abstraction, but I succumbed to the ambiguous magic of the picture, its elegiac sentiment. The strength of feeling—the poetic element—in the painting derives in large part from the origins of its design and the monumental impersonality of the image which makes it so permanent and powerful. These were also the qualities of Eliot's poetry, which both Rupert and I were incessantly reading at the time. I did not bother with the inscription 'Et in Arcadia Ego' which I took as a simple epitaph: 'I [presumably a shepherd] was also in Arcadia.' In fact, as I learned later, the inscription embodies a thought in grimly direct conflict with the Virgilian serenity of the picture: 'I—Death—am also in Arcadia.'

I loved working in the Louvre, having to concentrate on a particular masterpiece while surrounded by so many others. Without consciously thinking about terms of reference, I developed a sense of comparative worth and standards of quality. It also ensured, when taken in conjunction with the immediate stimulus of the Ecole de Paris, examples of which were in all the art dealers' windows along the route of my daily journey to life-drawing sessions in the ateliers of Montparnasse, that my attitude to painting was no longer English but French.

The first months in Paris set the routine of work which we followed till the end of the year. For me it brought the beginning of an individual life in art, and for Rupert the full development of his technique as a classical dancer—a development which was entirely his own affair. Rupert was heading for maturity, while I was emerging from the student stage. This gave him the dominant role in our relationship, as I had more to learn from him than he from me. I was saved from falling into the trap of a plausible plagiarism of the contemporary styles that surrounded us—of putting on other people's clothing—as much by Rupert's irrational and intuitive gift of seeing below the surface, of distinguishing the genuine from the fake, as by the disciplined routine we had decided I should follow. As far as my work was concerned his reactions became—and were to remain—the yardstick against which I could measure my own development. Rupert's sensitivity to visible and physical signs enabled him to pinpoint, often and accurately, the hidden weaknesses of character that interfere with creativity and the successful and uninhibited production of work. I came to know during this time that Rupert was not at all easy to live with. The intuitions that gave him his insight into art also revealed to him, to an uncomfortable degree, the unconscious motivations within our day-to-day relationship. As a dancer who used his body as the instrument of artistic expression Rupert lived close to the nerve, and the self-will, aggression and violence beneath the surface, without which he could never have achieved what he did, would sometimes burst out in uncontrollable and unpremeditated storms. There was always a cause, but it was sometimes hard to discern. To put it simply, he was disconcertingly quick to anger if he felt in any way menaced. For a long time I was afraid of these possessive outbursts until I came to realize that they were for Rupert a temperamental necessity and that my part was to absorb the shock-waves that issued from the inner turmoil.

In August we moved to a cheaper hotel just round the corner in the rue Jacob. It proved a great success as it was more a lodging house than a hotel for short-stay visitors. The sanitation was primitive but we were allowed to move the furniture and enough room was made so that I could work. Both of us worked hard, but in spite of going less and less to the Sélect, where in company the little white saucers accumulated far too quickly, there remained enough social life to keep us going. Owing to a favourable rate of exchange, friends and acquaintances were always popping over for weekends in Paris and sooner or later were bound to appear at the Deux Magots, particularly as 'Bloomsbury', when in Paris, always centred on the Hôtel de Londres, at the bottom of the rue Bonaparte near the Seine.

The year of T. S. Eliot's 'The Hollow Men' and of our discovery of Marcel Proust and Ronald Firbank, 1926, was also the year of *Gentlemen Prefer Blondes*. We had just bought a copy when one afternoon Lytton Strachey, looking like a tall and thin grey secretary-bird wearing a panama hat, came wandering past the terrace of the Deux Magots and, casing the joint, found us. No, he didn't think Anita Loos was 'quite his cup of tea', but we persuaded him back to our hotel bedroom where the three of us lay on the bed while we read aloud, with much laughter, the adventures of Dorothy and Lorelei. With Lytton I went to the Galerie Georges Petit for an important exhibition of paintings by Matisse, who met us there by arrangement. I didn't have much to say to the master for he addressed himself principally to Lytton. Lytton, who had no confidence in his judgement of paintings—as Rupert discovered the following day when he failed to persuade him to buy a Douanier Rousseau very cheaply—appeared rather nervous. Matisse, dressed very correctly and looking like an eminent doctor-professor, gave us an energetic tour round the pictures, and then obviously feeling that he had done his duty by the great literary figure and his Bloomsbury supporters, apologized for having to rush to another appointment and signed an illustrated catalogue for Lytton, who with typical kindness promptly pressed it on me. Shortly after his return to London we received a characteristic letter:

Dear Rupert,
Your kind and amiable letter delighted me. It is wonderful to think that I am still thought of at the two Magots—a spot which has now become in my mind a romantic—an almost fantastic memory. Is it still possible that you and Robert still flit to and fro, and that coffee, vermouth sec, or Rossi (I daresay at this very moment) flows down your throats?

I wish I could look in on you once again but here I am, inextricably involved in damp grass, downs, blackbirds, etc., etc., and here I shall remain, it seems to me, until my hair turns white and my teeth drop out and I am finally scythed down by Old Time, among the rest of the vegetation. . . . I believe the Russian Ballet is in London now, but I have not been to it. A kind of paralysis has seized me, after my Parisian gaieties and I can do nothing but read antique books. Occasionally, I entertain speculations about the Purpose of Life; but they remain speculations. Perhaps the whole truth is contained in 'Gentlemen Prefer Blondes'. But this does not apply to Robert to whom I send my love—please also pull both his ears for me, and any other part of him you may fancy. . . .

my love,
Lytton

Duncan Grant came over to Paris on a short visit, and he and I made quick little water-colour sketches in the Louvre—a practice much to be recommended. More regular interludes however were provided by Sunday dinners with Mary Butts or afternoon teas with Mary Reynolds—the tea was from Jacksons, Piccadilly, and the cakes from the Reine Blanche, the famous pâtissier in St Germain who had supplied Marcel Proust. In a corner of Mary R's sitting room was an easy chair, permanently reserved for Marcel Duchamp, by the arm of which was a little table with a chessboard and various pieces in play set upon it. Introduced to Marcel, we were given to understand that he was a chess champion. We met several times and he carefully preserved this enigmatic persona: elegant and reserved, dressed in a Savile Row suit, he acted the part of an English gentleman.

In 1966, when Richard Hamilton was at work on his famous replica of the large glass, *The Bride Stripped Bare by Her Bachelors, Even*, in preparation for the Duchamp exhibition at the Tate, I recalled these meetings for the benefit of the Newcastle University art students, thinking that they would be amused by behaviour so typical of the 'modern master' who was now all the rage, only to find that they were shocked by my youthful ignorance of his work. Laboriously I had to explain that there was no reason why I should have known anything about Marcel, because he hadn't produced any visible work since the great 'Armory' Exhibition of 1916 in New York which was no longer art news in the Paris of 1926. Their shock might have been more profound had I been able to cap the story with Djuna Barnes's remark (made when we met in New York after the exhibition at the Tate Gallery—where many of the works on view were replicas of the originals): 'Marcel! We all know about Marcel—he never did a day's work in his life. He always lived off rich women!'

On Sunday afternoons, at Mary Butts's apartment (beyond the boulevard Montparnasse towards the Champs de Mars), it was possible to sink back into a familiar English laziness. Her brilliant instability was offset by a strongly maternal instinct, and after tea we would frequently stay on for a vast dinner of roast beef, for Mary liked to reassert the Englishness of the fifteenth-century Norfolk forbears with whom she identified as strongly as with the ancestor who had been the generous patron of William Blake. Surprisingly for a classical scholar, Mary was obsessed by magic. Separated after the war from John Rodker, by whom she had a daughter who was now at an expensive private school near Paris, Mary, against all level-headed advice, had followed Alistair Crowley to Cefalu accompanied by her lover Cecil Maitland. This escapade, which is more fully described in Nina Hamnett's uninhibited account of the period, *Laughing Torso*, ended disastrously, with Cecil's health badly undermined, and Mary disillusioned and embittered by Crowley's part in the affair. Nina had warned Mary against the visit to Cefalu. Now in calmer waters, her association with Jean Cocteau had naturally done little to break a drug habit which, unknown to most of us, had escalated from opium—which she shared with Cocteau—to heroin. One day in the late autumn, when Rupert was entirely tied up by rehearsals for the Berlin engagement with Trefilova, news came that Mary was in the agonizing throes of an essential disintoxication and needed help. It was unfortunate that Rupert couldn't go because he was always marvellous with people in trouble, and it fell to me to look after her. Arriving there the following morning I found not only Mary prostrate on one bed, but also the great hulk of Walter S, a handsome American gigolo, in a similar condition in the other bed. Every day and all day for the best part of a week, innocent and unprofessional, I became the male nurse. The job involved hypodermics, pills, placebos and drugs, in what I hoped were diminishing doses, though I couldn't be sure of this because the only other person allowed in was the very untrustworthy-looking doctor of uncertain nationality who visited us once a day. This glimpse of the lower depths satisfactorily removed for ever any fascination that hallucinatory drugs might have had for me. The only incident that brought a breath of normality to an otherwise nightmare week was the unexpected appearance of Roger Fry and Helen Anrep, glowing with energy and enthusiasm, who had called to take Mary out to luncheon. With my back firmly placed against the bedroom door I explained that Mary had a bad attack of the flu and a raging temperature.

Amongst the other intimations of maturity was the totally unexpected and delightfully reassuring Proustian discovery that I was not the only black sheep in the family. Rupert and I were to call on Francis Birrell at his hotel before being taken out to a nearby restaurant for lunch. 'Monsieur Birrell' had not come down yet—would we go up? We duly ascended, to discover Francis dozing happily in bed with a cheerful little Russian whom we had never met before. Naked and hairy, they looked like a couple of small black bears. This discovery altered the tone of the party, as Dorothy, in *Gentlemen Prefer Blondes* would say, 'quite a lot', and we went to the theatre where Boris, the little bear, was working with Charles Dullin and saw a piece suitably entitled *La Comédie des Bonheurs.* From that day there was a bond of secrecy between us, for Francis was afraid of his father Augustine's disapproval. I have often wondered how far he was right, for Augustine was the most humorous and humane of men—but for his generation the memory of Oscar Wilde still cast a long deep shadow.

Around café tables and in the company of dancers I had listened to endless and detailed talk about the ballet, and having watched various classes at Madame Astafieva's in London and at Madame Egorova's in Paris I knew the difference between a *chassé* and a *pas de bourrée*. I lived at the edge of the world of ballet, but I had not yet seen Rupert dance in performance. (In fact it was not until the Dolin–Nemchinova season at the Coliseum in 1927 that I actually saw Rupert on stage.) However, his final rehearsal with Trefilova before they left for Berlin, of the *Grande Adage* from *The Sleeping Princess*, was the first occasion on which I saw Rupert at work, fully stretched, as an artist. This took place on the bare floor of Trefilova's studio to music played on the piano by an accompanist. Both dancers were in practice clothes, she in a black leotard with her hair tied back into a small rose-coloured scarf, and Rupert in black tights and white vest, with a tightly rolled handkerchief round his forehead to prevent the sweat from running into his eyes. To be invited was a singular honour indeed, for great ballerinas do not like to be seen at work in the privacy of the studio where the sweat and struggle to create their art may be all too visible to the outside eye. Aware that I was thus uniquely privileged I sat quietly on a wooden bench, and watched as they worked through, and took to pieces again and again, a famous *tour de force*. It is a piece that demands from the male dancer a lyricism that will create a setting proper to the central performance. Watching them work I became aware that the abstract structure of the dance, and the phrasing of the movements, with the subtlest nuances of meaning, were crucially important; their technical virtuosity was but the means to the realization of the form, and not an end in itself. And this abstract structure, discovered through the virtuosity of such dancing, is itself nothing without the poetic expression that was the special gift of the great ballerinas of the Russian Imperial School. Such understanding can be handed on only from one dancer to another: there is no other way. It was for this that Rupert had specifically gone to Vera Trefilova, and it was characteristic of his single-mindedness and humility that he should go where he could learn. The experience of being an observer to such a process, of being in an entirely different relationship to the dancers from that of an audience, distanced by footlights and proscenium, and having none of the visual elements of theatrical performance to create the grandeur, was an unforgettable experience, and I felt I had never before seen such dancing, or understood at all what dancing meant for the dancers. I saw, too, how Rupert's approach to his art was essentially creative and studio-based, and that his understanding of my work grew directly from his own experience as an artist. From that moment—which itself signalled Rupert's trust in me (and incidentally indicated Trefilova's great confidence in him)—I recognized that our life's concerns were parallel, and that a pact had been sealed.

The following day, carrying Trefilova's hand luggage on the platform at the Gare du Nord, I felt like an untrained stableboy in charge of a precious and vulnerable racehorse, terrified that she might trip or collide with a porter's trolley, and injure her legs. As their train pulled out on the start of its journey to Berlin, I reflected that my life was acquiring light and shade, and taking on a more solid and graspable form. In becoming a person I was becoming an artist.

5 London 1927

We returned to London in time for my twenty-first birthday on 19 December, and Rupert was invited to stay over Christmas. Father and Mother gave me an HMV Portable (a classic model) and on it I could play the famous recording of Schubert's 'Trout' Quintet with Cortot, Thibaud and Casals that Aunt Christine had bought for me. My grandfather sent a note congratulating me on 'having achieved the easiest rung on the ladder of life' and enclosed the card of admission to the Royal Academy Schools in 1791 of my great-great-grandfather, Samuel Medley, signed by William Opie.

A lot of trouble was taken getting everything ready. Aunts and cousins of various ages, Bloomsbury friends, Pippa of course, John Strachey and Humphrey Slater and the girls from the Slade and Campden Hill were all invited, and after the Persian and Turkey rugs in the drawing room had been rolled back we all danced on the parquet to the not very loud strains of a rather limited number of 'hits', mostly borrowed for the occasion and played on the gramophone with a 'loud' needle. It was all very jolly, but nobody had sent the handsome cheque that Rupert and I thought we would need if we were to escape to a place of our own.

Neither of us had anticipated, however, so serious a deterioration of the friendly spirit in which our then-unsuspected relationship had been received during the celebrations of the previous Christmas. The liberties that my two brothers now allowed themselves in the expression of their hostility, and the innuendo that coloured their response to Rupert's feminine traits and lack of conventional schooling indicated that even if there hadn't so far been a great deal of unkind talk behind our backs there soon would be. Rupert decided to cut short his visit and take a room of his own in Charlotte Street. His tactful withdrawal meant that conventional civilities remained just about intact.

So began the pattern that was to regulate our lives from that point on, with both sides recognizing that it was possible to avoid the disruption of affectionate family ties as long as neither side saw too much of the other. For the next forty years I would make sure that Rupert and my brothers met only when there would be no opportunity for conflict, or even comment. To my parents I would be forever grateful, for whatever may have been their feelings on the matter, or their view of my future, they did not oppose my decision to set up house with Rupert. It was not possible, of course, to discuss the true nature of our relationship: I had with my family no common language—no vocabulary of sexuality such as Wystan and Dr Auden shared—and anyway in the circumstances of the time I would have had to deny any suggestion that we actually went to bed together. I was now of age and I was determined to be responsible for myself. My father made me an allowance of five pounds a week on the understanding that I should try to start earning something of my own as soon as practicable, and that Rupert would pay his share. On this basis, in February we set about finding a studio. This proved more difficult than we anticipated, and after several weeks of disappointment we settled for a top floor in a terrace off Shepherd's Bush. The neighbourhood was rather depressing but it had the advantages of a cheap street market under the arches of the Metropolitan Line on its way to Hammersmith, and a number of junk shops where it was possible to buy some fine pieces of Victorian mahogany furniture for very little money. As a studio for painting I had a pleasant little room overlooking a garden at the back of the house. The living room at the front, though we made it look attractive, was rather crowded because Rupert, for the sake of appearances, insisted on two 'divans'. As one of these was a double bed the appearances were less than convincing.

Soon after we had settled in, Mother and Father came to a grand dinner, which included everything from soup through to nuts, and which started with sherry and ended with port. The vegetables had to be served from saucepans as we had no dishes, but the occasion was one of memorable warmth.

A week or two later, when Wystan came up from Oxford, we

introduced him to Francis Birrell, which was such a success that on his subsequent visits to London Shepherd's Bush was shunned in favour of Elm Park Road, Chelsea, where Francis lived with his father, Augustine. For a brief and unrecorded period Wystan toured with Francis the literary establishments of Bloomsbury. Passed over in the unfashionable Far West we were piqued at his cavalier use of the connections we had given him to life at the centre, for we did feel very isolated out in Shepherd's Bush. The only painters in the neighbourhood were Raymond Coxon and his wife Edna Ginesi, and it was not until 1930 that I got to know them at all well, after an exhibition at the Goupil Gallery to which we all contributed, along with H. S. Williamson who was later to be the Principal of Chelsea College of Art. This was to lead to my joining the staff at the Chelsea Polytechnic School of Art and thereby becoming financially independent in 1932, the year in which, coincidentally, the Group Theatre was also officially founded. This, however, is to anticipate matters: there were to be a great many changes before then.

Our sojourn in the 'Bush' lasted only for six or seven months. But before we moved to Titchfield Terrace in Regent's Park Road an exciting prospect was opened up only to be all too quickly closed again. A letter arrived from Rudolf von Laban and Kurt Jooss inviting Rupert to meet them in The Hague to discuss the possibility of his engagement to teach the elements of classical ballet to the company of the Ballets Jooss, newly established in Essen. They thought that this would widen the vocabulary of their 'expressionist' dancers. Rupert, who had been introduced to von Laban in Berlin by his friend, the critic Edward Dent, would have been an excellent choice, for he was almost alone here at that time in being interested in the mid-European and German school of dance. He went to The Hague with two conditions in mind—that the money should be right, and that he should not be limited purely to teaching but free to participate in other aspects of the company's work, and to create new works of his own. It was his insistence upon the latter that proved to be the breaking point. There was no precedent for the employment of a British choreographer abroad and moreover Rupert was an unknown quantity. Jooss was the brilliant choreographer of a recently formed company that bore his name, and Rupert asked more than he would grant. Neither of them bore any ill feelings and when *The Green Table* came to London in 1933 they met as friends. Rupert recognized immediately that Kurt had already succeeded in doing the new kind of work that he envisaged for the Group Theatre.

With the disappointment came the consolation that our establishment in London was not going to be broken up by Rupert's going to Essen. He returned instead to Margaret Craske's studio, making the daily journey to Leicester Square, and I went on painting in the backroom, and for almost two years neither of us seemed to be getting anywhere. As a young painter, still struggling to find my way, I could not expect anything else, and I had the advantage of being able to work on my own. For Rupert it was a different matter, and in the absence of advantageous and interesting engagements he was thrown back on himself. This was no bad thing. Living together as we now were he was for the first time freed from the immediate pressures of having to accept work. He was always difficult to place on account of his temperament and ambitions, and the problem of finding opportunities was intensified by the professional status in the strict hierarchy of the ballet dancer's world that he had acquired by dancing as Trefilova's partner. There were plenty of good dancers around, and a growing interest in the ballet. Karsavina and Lopokova were married to Englishmen and living in London; and also from the Diaghilev company there were Ninette de Valois, Anton Dolin, and Alicia Markova (who had made her first appearance in 1926). However highly English dancers were esteemed abroad there was no centre at home around which they could focus and the only ballet company based here was Anna Pavlova's. There seemed only two ways out of this impasse: either to start a school or form a company. Ninette, Marie, and Anton Dolin were all trying one or the other. The existence of Margaret Craske's School in West Street was crucial for Rupert, who was not in a position to open a studio of his own and indeed not ready for it. First of all, with Margaret herself, who was in every way encouraging, he successfully arranged *Two Hungarian Dances* by Dvořák for Anton Dolin in the two-week Dolin–Nemchinova season at the Coliseum. With other dancers at the school who were prepared to work with him on new ideas purely for interest (though there was always a hope!) he created a solo dance, *Acrobat*, and a comic nigger-minstrel duet for which Duncan Grant designed the costumes. There was also an ambitious scheme for a ballet to music by Bach which Duncan would also design. In these projects, which came to little, Rupert was picking up the threads of a creative relationship with Duncan that anteceded my relationship with him. In a letter to Duncan written back in August 1925 Rupert had even touched upon the possibility of their collaboration in a permanent theatre: 'I have a lot to talk to you about when I see you next time, at least I think I shall. I am not however quite sure, it is about a small theatre with interesting plays, and simple scenery.' It was characteristic of Rupert that on a day when he had had two strenuous lessons from Massine (mentioned earlier in the letter) he should also be thinking about the possibilities of a creative theatrical venture. This was seven years before the Group Theatre was formed.

What Rupert was like at this time was well captured by Mary Skeaping in a recent conversation. Mary met Rupert in 1927, and worked with him first at Margaret Craske's studio. She was to become a great collaborator and friend in Group Theatre days and after.

> I had been working with Rupert at West Street; and he had been picking up all sorts of ideas. . . ideas so modern, so interesting, that I was keen to do them, because there was nothing to be had, that I was in touch with, that could give me such fresh ideas of movement. And he was full of ideas—they would come chasing out. I had to grasp these ideas and try to bring them to life. One had to keep a very observant eye because every time Rupert demonstrated his movements he did them differently: this was his search for something—a final form of what he wanted. So I had to keep watching . . . until I could snatch what I could demonstrate, which would enable him to decide of the many different things he was doing what he was really trying to express . . . I must say that this required a great deal of patience—but I could see the value of what he was trying to do, and many dancers couldn't. And you really *do* have to realize the importance of something when it's as new as this was. Rupert Doone's choreographic ideas were really very much in advance of his time, and I consider myself very fortunate in having had the opportunity of working with him. I was very impressed with Rupert's dancing, his technique. He had a very marvellous light quick jump, strong beats, strong turns and very beautiful footwork—it was the first time I had seen this

type of technique in an English male dancer for a very long time.

This was a time of trial and error in which we were both looking for a direction, for a breakthrough, and in which we rode as it were in tandem, with Rupert leading, and were not yet working in collaboration as we were later to do in the Group Theatre days. Life, however, was never dull.

In the spring of 1928, just after we had left Shepherd's Bush, a gracious letter arrived from Victor Dandré: Madame Pavlova was in need of a new partner for her next world tour and Rupert was invited to her house in Hampstead to discuss the matter. We carefully discussed the pros and cons and decided that the disadvantages plainly outweighed the financial benefit that would undoubtedly came from a contract. Pavlova had the reputation of eating her partners alive and no male partner since the days of Mikhail Mordkin had survived the ordeal with an enhanced reputation. We thought also of the horrors of touring, packaged into hotels, sleeping cars and ocean liners with a troupe of dancers confined to a repertoire of popular kitsch. But so complimentary an invitation could not be turned down out of hand, and Rupert duly presented himself at the appointed hour.

He was shown into a large reception room with a view of the staircase that descended from the private apartments on the upper floor of the mansion, and comfortably seated by the charming and devoted Monsieur Dandré. Surrounded by bibelots and silver-framed memorabilia he waited for half an hour. At last the goddess, in a purple robe with a short train, silently appeared and descended majestically for the interview. The conversation was enthralling, and unsullied by any reference to business. As she rose, offering her left hand for the ritual of departure, she mentioned that Monsieur Dandré would deal with all contractual arrangements. Rupert returned entranced but not beguiled, and the afternoon was spent in drafting courteous regrets at having to decline the offer. That evening an impeccable note was dispatched.

It was at this time that we became involved with the somewhat bizarre episode of Margaret Craske's sudden conversion to vegetarianism and Eastern transcendentalism. This was not, at the time, so odd an event as might be supposed, in view of the contemporary fashion for the spiritual enlightenment offered by Ouspensky and Gurdjieff (among others less respectable) to which several of our friends had already succumbed. (The celebration of the Maharishi and the success of transcendental meditation in the late sixties and early seventies came as nothing new to those who remembered the late twenties.) We were not entirely surprised at this development, as behind the disciplinarian mask of the highly trained ballerina who had chosen to devote her life to teaching there was the unconventional and creative temperament which made her such an outstanding teacher, and which responded so warmly to Rupert's own imaginative flair. We were, however, surprised by the completeness of her surrender when some months later she followed Shri Maya Baba, the master, to India. In London his temporary headquarters were in a private hotel in Bayswater and there one Sunday morning we were received by the Shri. In the large reception room everything was golden—the chrysanthemums that filled the vases, the apricot silk of the curtains, the master's saffron robes, and those of his Indian disciples grouped around him. We were introduced by Margaret, and Rupert, who was obviously further along the spiritual path than I, was an instant success. Clearly an earthbound creature, I was not equally favoured. Rupert soon discovered that Laurel and Hardy were the master's favourite occidental relaxation, and on several subsequent occasions we took the bearded sage to cinemas where their comedies were being shown. Maya appeared in mufti on these informal occasions, but his beard and manner marked him out as a more than ordinary personage, and turned going to the pictures into an event. The master did not mind that neither of us was inclined to join his following.

It was not so much for spiritual reasons as for reasons of health that Rupert decided that we must become vegetarians. The experience would not only be elevating, but Rupert, who was inclined to hypochondria anyway, hoped that the diet would dispose of his rheumatism, which if it got any worse might shorten his career as a dancer. Rupert never did anything by halves and we adopted a strict regime—even nut cutlets were regarded as an indulgence. Endless vegetables, however fresh, proved an unsatisfying diet, troublesome to prepare and very expensive. After two months of abstinence—I had also been argued into giving up smoking—we surrendered to the temptations of beefsteak and roast lamb, and with great relief I lit up again. I was pleased that the fad was over, but Rupert remained worried, and the signs of constitutional weakness stayed like a shadow at the back of his mind. It was a fear from which he was never to be entirely free.

Gillian Scaife and Rupert first met at the West Street studio in 1928, where her son Rollo Gamble, an alert and athletic youth of 17, had arrived to take lessons. The Scaifes were a theatrical family. Gillian's brother Christopher had formed a close relationship with Tyrone Guthrie when they were at Oxford together, and wrote plays. Gillian had expected that Rollo, the apple of her eye, would follow the family tradition and become an actor, and was a trifle disconcerted by his decision to become a ballet dancer. She perceived in Rupert a professionalism equal to her own, and was intrigued by his personality. She was especially pleased to find a dancer whose ideas extended beyond the conventional limitations that she had feared might circumscribe Rollo's development. As it happened, in spite of Rollo's physical aptitude for the dance, he became a producer and film director. Rupert for his part was delighted to find in Rollo an eager understanding and a receptiveness to the ideas he had been developing with Mary Skeaping. Thus by chance began the friendship with the Scaifes, a crucial link in the chain of events that led to the formation of the Group Theatre. It was also the first of a number of short-lived and productive nearly platonic relationships of Rupert's, almost invariably with heterosexual young artists seeking self-discovery, that I was to become familiar with over the years. Rupert had an extraordinary sensitivity to that special quality in a dancer or actor that others often failed to perceive. He had no doubt that I would be as interested as he was in the creative potential of those he took up. His instinct was so sure that invariably I was.

In the summer of that year, after leaving Oxford and before going to Berlin, Wystan came to stay with the Medley family at Colby Hall in Wensleydale. It was during this visit that he took care to explain why he was not going to Paris—it was overly fashionable and suited only to intellectual snobs. Wystan knew that I could not be expected to agree with such a preposterous view, and I took his remarks to be an oblique criticism of my relationship with Rupert—a ballet dancer with strong Parisian connections, and altogether the wrong sort of person. Instead of confronting Wystan—the family tendency to avoid 'unpleasantness' came into play—I let the matter drop. But I could not help wondering whether Wystan had or had not read a recent piece in *The Enemy* in which Wyndham Lewis had attacked, with characteristic violence, Parisian chic as exemplified by the smart set's craze for the Ballets Russes, and made fun of the English francophilia as exemplified by Bloomsbury and Roger Fry. Had we continued the discussion then Wystan might have discovered that Rupert and I both saw clearly the point of Lewis's polemic. Bloomsbury represented to us the older generation, and we were moving away in our own direction. Our friends, mostly artists and writers, or people of the theatre, had never in any case been confined to that one circle.

And Bloomsbury had nothing to do with my first opportunity to exhibit. This came about not through Duncan or Vanessa (enormously helpful as they had both been to me) but through R. O. Dunlop, whose sister Edith Young had been a friend of Rupert's since the days at Madame Astafieva's. Dunlop, who was a few years older than me, was just beginning to come into his own, painting very strong and lively pictures and portraits with a palette knife. He was also producing a periodical called *The Emotionists* with the assistance of Edward Ashcroft (Peggy's brother), a young poet whom we remembered as the brilliant and beautiful youth we had last seen in Paris at Michel Leiris's Galerie Pierre in the rue Bonaparte. The exhibition was at the Goupil Gallery in Lower Regent Street where Van Gogh had worked, and was one of those marvellous old-fashioned galleries hung with claret-coloured velvet (as Agnews still is) and with a very good natural light. Only one of the pictures stays in my mind, because it had some relevance to my future developments. It was an oil sketch on paper of a number of nude figures in movement, linear rather than modelled, and deriving from notes made in Margaret Craske's studio. It was the only picture I sold—I was tremendously proud of the red spot—but unfortunately I no longer remember to whom. (I would dearly like to know.)

Throughout the twenties it was extremely difficult for young modern artists to get a showing, though during the latter half of the decade there were signs of a relaxation. Apart from Oliver Brown at the Leicester Galleries there were no established dealers showing signs of a consistent interest until Duncan MacDonald at Reid and Lefevre and Ralph Brown at Tooth's came on the scene about 1930.

This limited the opportunities for young artists to open-exhibiting societies like the (already old-fashioned) New English Art Club, and to the London Group which superseded it, and which was controlled by Roger Fry. There were also several elective societies of which the Seven and Five was the most radical and influential. Later, in 1933, Unit One was founded by Paul Nash and, with Herbert Read as its publicist, contemporary British art began to take on a recognizable public form. That development was still to come, however, and in any case, although I was keenly aware of the stirrings of a new spirit, I was still very much preoccupied with my own problems as a painter and too young and unformed to be enlisted in the avant-garde of modernism.

The most interesting venture of its kind in 1928 was the opening of Dorothy Warren's Gallery on the second floor of an eighteenth-century house near Hanover Square. Henry Moore was given his first one-man show there—which created a great deal of interest and helped to secure his first public sculpture commission: high up on the fortress walls of the new Head Offices of the Underground Railway in Westminster. Unfortunately the gallery came to an end in the blaze of publicity, hysteria and scandal that greeted the exhibition of D. H. Lawrence's paintings, which followed almost immediately after Moore's seminal success. The attendance at this exhibition was so great that the floors were in danger of giving way, and the police came in and arrested the pictures for obscenity. This closed the gallery, but for posterity Lawrence got his own back on the Marylebone magistrate responsible, in the poem referring to Mr Mead as 'that old, old lily'. Regrettably the paintings were not very exciting and the pornography even less so. Lawrence was much in the air, for Rupert and I had just read a smuggled copy of *Lady Chatterley's Lover*. Meeting Vanessa one morning at the corner of Fitzroy Street we asked her what she thought of it. With a Mona Lisa smile she replied in her calm beautiful voice, 'Rather lovely descriptions of scenery don't you think?' As a matter of critical fact she was absolutely right.

Like all ambitious students still in search of themselves, with an awkward bundle of pictures tied together with newspaper and string, I had tried hawking my work around uninterested dealers in Bond Street. Once was enough. I was lucky to have the small mixed show at the Goupil, and later the backing of the London Group. Sales however could hardly have been worth more than thirty pounds a year, for pictures ranging from five to twelve pounds each. Something had to be done to make ends meet, and the obvious stopgap was teaching.

To disguise my age and inexperience I grew a beard; this was streaked with ginger and tickled my neck. It survived an abortive interview with the Headmaster of Wellington College after which it was removed. What I finally landed up with was two evenings a week at three shillings and sixpence an hour in a council school at the far end of the Commercial Road. Social conscience had prompted that this school should be partially open after normal hours as a play centre, in the hope of keeping 9- to 13-year-olds off the streets. It was in no way in the modern sense of the word a 'play centre'. There wasn't any equipment except a few games like table skittles, and some books, mostly torn, to look at and for reading aloud. 'Art' was apparently a new idea, and for this purpose the school hall and gymnasium, delicately smelling of dust, disinfectant, and pissy pants, was opened up. This, with two trestle tables and a blackboard easel or two, was the studio. This layout was to prove disastrous, for as soon as those playing organized parlour games or being read to got bored, they would erupt into the hall, and disorganized bands of little fiends took over. They raced from end to end of the great hall, climbed the walls, and stole the pencils and the coloured chalks. There was one small boy whose childlike concentration, however, remained impervious to the racket and who drew every kind of motor car, bus or lorry, out of his head and in the liveliest detail. And there was the goblin with a cast in one eye who confided that he had tried to kill his infant brother with a carving knife. I found it hard not to sympathize. The activities were supervised by a disillusioned young-old schoolmaster. Over cups of tea in a nearby café he explained that teaching was a racket run by Freemasons and that he couldn't afford to belong to a Lodge. I stuck it out for several months, but when this sad old-young man was replaced by an angular female who was always angry that I couldn't keep control of the pencils—I had taken to cutting them up into two-inch lengths—I decided that the experience was not likely to be of much use as a gateway to the higher fields of education upon which I had set my sights. In spite of a rise to five shillings an hour I retired.

About this time, and out of the blue, Mrs Lucy Wertheim, from Manchester, descended upon London and visited the studios of the relatively unknown, buying sufficient stock to open a gallery in New Burlington Street. The collection was formed round a nucleus of Christopher Wood's paintings, which after his suicide she had bought from his mother. I was an early beneficiary of her patronage, selling eight pictures to her for ninety-six pounds. None of these pictures was as important to me as the two paintings Roger Fry had bought earlier that year, but I was pleased and happy to receive for them the largest amount of money I had ever earned in a single transaction. In pocket, I was able to join Rupert at the Hôtel de la Grille in Paris where he was rehearsing with Bronislava Nijinska (for whom, after Massine, he had the greatest respect) in new ballets (Ravel's *Bolero* amongst them) for Madame Ida Rubinstein's extravagant season at the Paris Opéra.

Financed by her admirer Lord Moyne of the Guinness millions, Madame Rubinstein, an indomitable beauty and inspired patroness of the arts—though no great shakes as a dancer had surrounded herself with the greatest and most expensive artists—Stravinsky and Ravel for the music, Benois for the settings, and Nijinska for the dance—and of course a very large company and full orchestra. For the dancers it was a sought-after occasion and a great gathering of the clans in an off season. Everybody made fun of the absurdity of such *folie de grandeur* but nobody could afford to miss it. Diaghilev, like everybody else, was there, and in an hilarious letter to Serge Lifar he described the first night:

> My dear:
> Paris is an awful town, impossible to find five minutes for a couple of words even! Everyone seems to have collected here, it's the most awful muddle! Let me begin with Ida. The house was full, but there was a good deal of paper about, mostly her friends. Not one of us, though, were given seats, neither myself nor Boris, Nouvel, Sert or Picasso. . . . We only just, just managed to get in. *All our people were there*, Misia, Juliette, Beaumont, Polignac, Igor [Stravinsky] and other musicians, not to mention Mayakovsky, etc., etc. The whole thing was astonishingly provincial, boring and long-drawn-out, even the Ravel, which took fourteen minutes.

Amidst a great deal of witty and cruel ridicule, of dancers and sets alike, was a single positive observation that was to have far-reaching consequences of a directly personal kind: 'The best dancer turned out to be Rupert Doone, the little Englishman we both know.'

Six months later Rupert received an invitation to join the Ballets Russes of Serge Diaghilev as a soloist, for what turned out to be its last season, at Covent Garden in July 1929.

The great Nijinska was the most exacting *maîtresse de ballet*, and Rupert, who had to rehearse with the principals as well as with the company, would return in the evenings utterly exhausted and flop into bed. Frederick Ashton and William Chappell, under less strain in the *corps de ballet*, were able to view the operation with refreshing detachment, and Freddie enlivened us all with a cruelly accurate mime of La Rubinstein struggling to execute a proper *pas de bourrée* whilst endeavouring to make a long cross-legged, cross-stage exit.

It was during these rehearsals in the autumn of 1928 that Vanessa Bell had asked us, rather surprisingly, to keep an eye on Quentin, whom we had never met in London, and who had to come to Paris to study French and art. So one auspicious morning a tall and slender 17-year-old sprig of Bloomsbury presented himself at our hotel. This was the beginning of an enjoyable and lasting friendship. I can now appreciate Vanessa's concern, and have since learned that in spite of my 'slowness' she judged me sympathetic and reliable. She need not have worried because Quentin was well able to look after himself. The only looking-after I did was to introduce him to the Académie Ranson where after a day's work—he learning French at the Sorbonne and I painting at the Louvre—we would meet up for the evening drawing classes. Quentin was an immediate asset, relieving Rupert and me from endless talk about the ballet. Such talk was never exactly boring because I had learned to experience the dedication to the dance in my own terms, but one can always have enough of a good thing. With Rupert away by eight o'clock in the morning and often not back until late, Paris was a different experience from what it had been two years before. (The circle at the Sélect had dispersed.) I felt entirely familiar by now with the ways of the city and it had become my terrain as much as it had previously been Rupert's. To improve my French I read Racine, and Proust's *Sodome et Gomorrhe* which had just been published. The sound of Racine in my head spoke for itself, but when I later read Scott Moncrieff's translation I realized how much I had missed of Proust, in spite of an unexpected chance to enjoy briefly something of the *grand monde* his characters inhabited. I have forgotten from whose introduction I became on visiting terms with two distinguished Parisians, whose father had been a well-known surgeon and a friend of César Franck, and found myself partnering a teenage niece, who was about to come out into society, to those formal balls—white gloves were *de rigueur*—that etiquette demanded. An equally informative and not dissimilar social experience was provided by Harley Granville-Barker and Helen his wife, an heiress of the Huntingdon-Hartford family, who out of regard for my father invited me twice to dine and to go to the theatre. Not yet having read any of Edith Wharton's American novels, I found it difficult to slip into a style of living that descended directly from the wealthy New York high society at the turn of the century. Bidden to *Les Navigateurs* on the Quai des Augustins I looked forward to choosing from the menu of this famous gourmets' restaurant only to find that a dinner of *plain* roast chicken had been ordered in advance, as also had the white wine and Perrier water.

The Opéra season came to an end. There was no reason to return to London before Christmas Eve, and a week or two in hand gave Rupert the chance to surface for air after a gruelling experience that, apparently, had failed to provide the opportunities he had hoped for. There had been little opportunity for him to make an impression, but after two years in the wilderness the engagement had been necessary.

For my part, though I had returned to the Louvre, this time copying Chardin, I worked a great deal on my own in the Hôtel de la Grille, and sometimes at the Académie de la Grande Chaumière, painting from the nude. This latter exercised a hard discipline, because though dependent on a 'subject' I am a conceptual rather than a visual painter: the implications of which fact I had yet to learn. Surrounded daily as I was by the contemporary masterpieces of the Ecole de Paris, why did I continue to follow such a thorny academic path instead of plumping for one of the current styles, whether of Picasso, Braque, Matisse, Rouault or Derain, and exploit it? The answer is that to have done so would have been contrary to the moral and ethical traditions I had inherited from my parents, which forbade the idea that the achievement of anything worthwhile could be easy. My inhibition was further intensified by the fatal (for an artist) indecisiveness that derived from a predisposition, inherited from a classical liberal background, to the belief that there were always at least two sides to a question. Moreover, with so many styles to choose from—the art historians of the modern movement had not yet arrived to tidy up the terrain—the options were by no means clear. I have always associated the end of the cultural epoch that had begun with Les Fauves and cubism with the death of Diaghilev in 1929, neatly placed at the end of the decade. Interestingly, in 1931 Christian Zervos in *Les Cahiers d'Art* was to write a leading article on *Les problèmes de la jeune peinture—le retour au sujet, est-il probable?* The cubism of Picasso and Braque of the first decade of the century had disintegrated the object but not destroyed it, and young painters were advised by Zervos, in terms closely resembling the views of Roger Fry, to build upon the experience of Cézanne. 'Personne' he wrote about Cézanne, 'n' a posé aussi définitivement le problème qui nous préoccupe et sur lequel nulle autre oeuvre ne saurait nous fournir autant de clarté.' Had the article been published in 1928 these impeccable views would still have been as irrelevant to the daily practice of a 'jeune artiste' as Eddie Marsh's caution when he bought one of my pictures in 1931 that it was 'the duty of every young man to save'. I could be accused of being indecisive, but from experience I had already learned that however overwhelming a Picasso, a Braque or a Matisse might be, the facile use of another artist's currency was an unrewarding investment.

The real day-to-day problem that young painters emerging from adolescence during the late twenties had to cope with was that the Tradition, even if it was seen to culminate in Cézanne, seemed already far distant and vague in outline. A work of art now could be made out of almost anything: old matchboxes, the shapes of guitars, and collaged sheets from *Le Journal*. A pipe, a loaf of bread, a packet of tobacco and a wine bottle became a 'Holy Family'. The astonishing outburst of modernist creative vitality, temporarily held back during the war, also had a progressive political dimension. In reaction to the violence of the war arose ironically the aesthetics of the machine: the aeroplane provided a key image. The artist, like the airman-hero, allied to the new technology, would pilot the way to a new society. Through mass production, life-enhancing objects of beauty would be universally available. Over Léger's *Les Noces de la Tour Eiffel* the parachutist descended from the passing plane and Roger de la Fresnaye's tricolour was spread on the sky.

Having become a painter simply because I liked paintings, the political implications of all this passed over my head. Léger (who had expressed his views some years previously in articles I had not read) appealed to me because the commonplace denominators of everyday life were assembled on a flat and decorative plane with the mechanical frankness of industrial templates. The great exhibition in 1925 of *Les Arts Décoratifs* (art deco) in the Louvre also reflected an attitude to life and design which was basically optimistic and democratic, in spite of the fact that the really fine products, like those of the *haute couture* of Paris houses, were in their original form extremely expensive. It was this kind of chic that Wystan, in Berlin, reacted against.

It had taken some years since the end of the war before German art and artists were acceptable again in Paris. I may have been incurious, but I remember no young German painters in the *ateliers* until the last quarter of the decade. There was, of course, Max Ernst; and the writers Tristan Tzara and Claus Mann (Thomas's son) who had gravitated to France after the Communist and Dada revolutions in Germany had failed. There were lines of communication still open, in spite of Paris being full of White Russians, between Moscow and Paris via Berlin and via Diaghilev. Such connections entirely bypassed the German expressionist painters, which did not matter to me, for I was never to be fond of the erotic and social *Angst* of the likes of Schmidt-Rottluff and Kirchner. Such awareness as I had of the wider European horizons, however superficial, was gained through the theatre. Whatever may be said of Diaghilev in his last years, when he might have been accused of seeking novelty for its own sake, he brought to the attention of those who were prepared to look in those years, work by Jakouloff, Gabo, Pevsner and others in the modern movement. By way of the theatre also I encountered these and other constructivists like Alexandra Exter, Rodchenko and Popova, although not, of course, Malevich. Also missing from my experience at the time was the work of Mondrian, Van Doesburg and De Stijl; and I knew nothing of the Bauhaus. Such limitations were due as much to circumstance as to taste.

Although we were aware of the significance of contemporary events, we continued to be unconcerned with politics. Paris as the centre of international art was what mattered to us. In unfashionable Berlin at this time, meanwhile, Wystan took up progressive ideas of psychological liberation and, witnessing the violent politics of late Weimar, was becoming politically aware. For the time being our ways had parted; I had no word from him. For Rupert and me, however, the pattern of life in the early thirties was to be determined not so much by any economic or political set of events, as by the unforeseen death of the great impresario and the collapse of his ballet company.

6 Ending the Twenties

During the December of 1927 Duncan Grant was working on a large picture, *The Bathers*, for which he made a number of drawings from friends and models. It is not always easy to get two models who are not embarrassed to work together in the nude and who understand what a painter needs, and, knowing this, Rupert and I had posed for him on a number of occasions. These sessions were enormously enjoyable; we talked a great deal, exchanged drawings, and our relationship with Duncan was understandably deepened. Talking together Rupert and I came to a shared conclusion however about the way that Duncan's work was developing. We were concerned that his great talent for decorative invention—the quite un-English *esprit* that animated his best work—was being dulled by a misplaced seriousness. Under the influence of Roger Fry's rather puritan ideas of what serious painting should be, he was moving in the direction of a heavy, rather solemn, academic Post-Impressionism. In *The Bathers* (so consciously—indeed conscientiously—a Cézanne subject) Duncan seemed to be attempting to give expression to his native inclinations, and at the same time follow the stern dictates of the Fry aesthetic, which derived from a study of the line from Poussin through Chardin to Cézanne. We decided to try to persuade him to give greater play to his essential gifts—and we agreed that for this to happen he would need to make a radical break with the Bloomsbury world which had become, we felt, increasingly enclosed and self-regarding, and spend some time in Paris on his own. As Rupert had known Duncan since 1924 when they had met each other in Paris at the time when Rupert's affair with Cocteau was coming to an end, and as we were unstinting in our admiration and affection for him, we felt entitled to compose a letter suggesting such a course of action, and posted it under the studio door in Fitzroy Street. We knew we were treading on delicate ground but we felt a special responsibility and thought that someone had to do it. The strategy did not work—how could it have done so? Duncan was offended, and Vanessa annoyed.

Happily, after a short period of coolness our tactless interference was forgiven, but this slightly comic episode may serve to illustrate the truth of what I had thought but not spoken when Wystan had so unkindly implied that the Bloomsbury connection was all-important to Rupert and me. We were well aware of its limitations, but there were ties of affection and gratitude that it would have been silly, and dishonest, to deny. Our movement away from the spirit of Bloomsbury was given added impetus by the reappearance in our lives at this time of Edward and Fanny Wadsworth, neither of whom Rupert had seen since before he went to Paris in 1922. Both were fond of Rupert, and I was immediately accepted by them as a friend. Although he was no longer actively involved in the vendetta that Wyndham Lewis—'The Enemy'—was still conducting against Roger Fry, Edward nevertheless continued to regard Bloomsbury as the exemplification of provincial English ineffectuality and prettiness. His own house at Maresfield in Sussex contained works by Léger, and on the lawn outside stood a large wooden sculpture by Zadkine. Trained in Germany as an engineer before going to the Slade, where he had joined forces with Wyndham Lewis, Edward's views were rigorously modernist. The entire Italian Renaissance after the death of Giotto and Masaccio was written off as a disaster. Modern Art meant *construction* and *synthesis*. There was no room in his aesthetic for Post-Impressionistic approximation, any more than there was for the arty-crafty cosiness of Charleston's hand-painted furniture. A frequent utterance of Edward's was 'A painter does not paint what he sees but what he knows is.' This expresses a view of the creative process that endows the art object with an emotive or metaphysical significance, and which allows that the subject of a work might be entirely removed into a world of its own, either abstract or representational. One branch of this line of thought leads into the surreal world, and Edward was for a time influenced by Pierre Roy's small and meticulous *trompe-l'oeil* assemblages of psychologically evocative objects. Much though I appreciated the cogency of Wadsworth's clearly expressed and somewhat dogmatic ideas I could not adopt his concise style, nor could I find sympathy with a vocabulary of forms from which the human figure was entirely excluded.

Edward had a studio on Campden Hill, and from there, in a Rolls-Royce built, to his own design, like a boat, he used to drive down to Maresfield, where he and Fanny entertained at splendid weekend parties. To these would come a crowd of guests as diverse and interesting as those who attended Vanessa's and Duncan's parties in Fitzroy Street; it included Zadkine, Frederick Etchells, Yanko Varda and his beautiful mistress and model, known as 'Varda'—Yanko, a Greek of infinite wit and fun, made Byzantine-cubist mosaics out of broken mirrors, glass and crockery—Constant Lambert, McKnight Kauffer, and Marion Dorn.

One evening, during the Ida Rubinstein season in Paris, we were introduced by Zadkine to Valentine and Bonamy Dobrée. Now we were all back in London that brief acquaintance sprang into one of those friendships that are as stimulating as they are short-lived. Over those few months we saw much of them at their home in Well Walk, Hampstead, where they lived before moving to a charming Georgian villa near Diss on the border of Norfolk and Suffolk. Valentine Dobrée, who was the daughter of a British diplomat, had been born in Alexandria. Her choice of birthplace seemed appropriate: she was small and finely built, and the cast of her features with her jet black hair and lively dark brown eyes, gave her the enigmatic aura of a gypsy changeling who had strangely inherited all the assurance of a privileged and highly sophisticated culture. Although she was a gifted artist, she made no claims for her pictures, and her astringent and cosmopolitan intelligence perfectly complemented Bonamy's perceptive scholarship. With the Dobrées we talked about everything, but especially about poetry, drama and painting. The word *ambiance* was very much in the air. On Mount Athos, their friend Robert Byron was writing *The Birth of Western Painting*; his thinking on art was influential in the circle around the Dobrées, and when his book was published in 1930 I insisted upon it as a Christmas gift. Although the word *ambiance* as used had no exact definition, we all felt we knew what was meant by it. It was the attendant numinous cloud of meaning that was created by the power of the artist's associative imagination, and which might invest a modern work with the metaphysical presence that surrounded an ikon. The duty of the modern artist, therefore, deprived of Byzantine religious symbolism, was to create an image which had such *ambiance*—a quality that lay beyond the visual impression. To Rupert, for whom dancing was ceremony, in the performance of which the art of his dance often transcended the material he was called upon to perform, these ideas were highly sympathetic, and seemed to endorse his own experience.

It was at Well Walk that we first heard the name of Herbert Read, and the Dobrées were surprised that we had not yet come across a figure they regarded as quite obviously important. Both Valentine and Bonamy considered him the Great White Hope of English poetry, and they were at pains to tell us that he had been awarded the Military Cross for bravery during the war and, no doubt thinking of our pacifist Bloomsbury connections, added that he was *not in the least homosexual*. The associations by which they felt the need to refer to the war record of the poet and philosopher, and pay tactful deference to our relationship, which they understood perfectly well, may seem obscure now, but were, in fact, very much of the period, for the pacifism of the Quaker Roger Fry and the rationalist Bertrand Russell, and their Bloomsbury affiliations, had become inextricably confused with undertones of homosexuality. In spite of several attempts, a meeting with Herbert Read did not take place in Hampstead that year and it was not until the early thirties that we actually met, when I found myself introducing him as the principal speaker at one of those semi-political left-wing meetings in dim church halls that preceded the founding of the Artists' International Association. (Both Herbert Read and Bonamy gave lectures for the Group Theatre in 1933.) As the twenties moved towards their close Rupert and I were thus unconsciously laying the foundations for our work together during the next decade. I am aware of the danger of neatly packaging time, but the thirties were a very different kettle of fish from the twenties; and events were to make the transition for us definite and dramatic. The first months of 1929 found us in London, as *au courant* with things artistic and theatrical as might be expected of two young men, one a dancer and the other a painter, with a milieu as various, and friends as diverse and interesting, as fortune provided. Rupert went more often to the theatre than me with the benefit of 'comps' for matinées, but on Sundays we went together to see productions by the Stage Society at the Scala and the Royal Court of the seldom-performed plays of Jonson, Webster and the lesser Jacobean dramatists. At the New Cinema in Regent Street we saw Russian, German Expressionist and other experimental films (including Léger's essay in abstraction) for the first time. We read the poetry of D. H. Lawrence and of the Metaphysicals (newly in vogue), the novels of Dostoevsky, the psychology of Freud, and the reviews in the papers. I continued to paint and Rupert continued to wait, as it were, in the wings. And then one morning Diaghilev's long-awaited but unexpected summons to join the Ballets Russes miraculously arrived. Rupert was no longer the tiresome and demanding youth, the friend and protégé of Cocteau, who in 1922 had felt arrogant enough to turn down Diaghilev's invitation to join the *corps de ballet*: he had expected more than that. For the Covent Garden season that was to take place in July he was given two solo roles: in the opening *pas de trois* in *Cimarosiana*, and in the trio 'Ariadne and her Brothers' in *Aurora's Wedding*, which he danced with Vera Petrova and Nicholas Efimoff. For the rest he would dance in the *corps de ballet*, in order that he should learn the repertoire. Rupert approached the season with absolute dedication and professionalism. He knew that his moment had come: his stubborn refusal to settle for the second rate, to take any easy options, or to do less than he was capable of doing, had paid off. The season in London was the beginning; if he was aware of his limitations he was also confident in his ambitions—and these went beyond performance.

For the début at Covent Garden in *Cimarosiana* I sat in the circle and, very tensed up, awaited the arrival of the three dancers to take possession of the empty stage: they were Felia Doubrovska and Eleanora Marra, and Rupert, dancing beautifully. And then suddenly he slipped and dropped upon one knee. The recovery was so quick that the people sitting next to me seemed not to have noticed. During the second interval I met Rupert by the pass door from backstage into the auditorium. I felt that all might be over before it had hardly begun; he also was subdued, and only volunteered that the misfortune had to be seen in perspective. It was not until we had left the theatre that he told me what had happened. Coming offstage angry and disappointed with himself he had been confronted by Diaghilev himself, whom everybody had supposed to be ill and in bed at the Savoy Hotel. Cutting short the stammered apologies Diaghilev had simply said 'Vous ne dansez pas mal' and left the theatre. Leon Woizikovsky, who had overheard, came over and told Rupert that in all the years he had danced Diaghilev had never said as much to him. This small but significant sign of favour was not to escape the notice of a company prone to jealousy and intrigue, and there were dangers of the kind of divisive gossip about Diaghilev's intentions that Rupert was most anxious to avoid.

To mark the end of the season Pat Dolin gave a grand party in honour of Diaghilev, who, seated away from the crowd, looked like some sage and very grand lama. From his chair, with his large and magisterial head with its white streak running through greying hair, he received the homage of chosen friends. Introduced by Rupert I made my bow, glad that I was not called upon to talk: it was enough to have seen the man so much talked about. He looked very tired and his complexion was putty coloured, but everyone said he was better.

Leaving the company to finish the season with a fortnight's engagement at Vichy before dispersing for the annual vacation, Diaghilev went to Paris and from there on to Venice. Alone in London I packed the luggage for what was to be the most wonderful and privileged holiday, for Vanessa and Duncan had lent us their little house and studio in the South of France. Isolated amongst the vineyards of Colonel Teed's *manoir*, and about a mile from and above the little (as it was then) fishing village of Cassis, 'La Bergère' was in every respect perfect and private. For the celebration of what we conceived to be the dawn of a new life no more idyllic circumstances could be imagined. Burdened with enough luggage to last two months and an unruly sketching easel, I was met by Rupert who had arrived two days earlier direct from Vichy. With him was Alexandrine Troussevitch, Diaghilev's personal secretary, who was our first guest. I had heard about Alexandrine by way of Rupert's letters from Vichy, and she was to stay with us for four or five days before joining her mother and sister who lived in a small apartment in Nice. Nobody could become Diaghilev's secretary without being exceptional; but how to describe her? Alexandrine was small in stature and neatly built like a ballerina, and intensely Russian, by which I mean she was possessed of a special combination of intellect, intuition and mysticism: her nature expressed itself in devotion. Whether she had decided to look after Rupert of her own accord, or (as it now occurs to me) Diaghilev had suggested that she keep an eye on him, I do not know, but at Vichy she had made a point of advising

Rupert of the cross currents of personalities and powers within the company. At Vichy Rupert had been told by Serge Grigoriev that he was to be rehearsed for the male role (the poet) in *Les Sylphides*—a plum of promotion—and following Alexandrine's diplomatic advice a hint had been dropped that ultimately he would like to be tried out as a possible choreographer. For this it had been necessary to cultivate the confidence of Boris Kochno, not the easiest of men, who had Diaghilev's ear in these matters.

Alexandrine was entranced by the unpretentious style and artistry of Duncan's and Vanessa's cottage and studio at 'La Bergère', and there began a relationship that required no explanations and that was warm and hopeful. Elise, Vanessa's servant, came out every morning to look after us, and the sun shone. It was the first time in our lives that we were able to entertain in a fitting manner. Alexandrine left on 20 August and we happily looked forward to our next guests, who were to be Margaret Craske and Mabel Ryan.

And then on the very next morning there arrived from Alexandrine in Nice the fatal telegram: *Diaghilev is dead*. Stunned by the appalling news we took ourselves down to Cassis only to find that it was already over the front pages of every newspaper. Desperately in need of contact, we telephoned Lydia Sokolova and Woizikovsky at Le Lavandou and spent the following day with them. Backed by some dusty tamarisk and windblown pines we lay on a spit of hot sand, gazing towards the hazy silhouette of the Isle d'Hyères across a glazed and torpid sea.

Alexandrine's first letter dated 21 August:

> Mes Chers Amis,
>
> Yesterday on my arrival in Nice I found a telegram from Serge [Lifar] and Boris [Kochno] telling me of the sudden death of Diaghilev. He died at the Lido on the 19th of a poisoning produced by an abscess at the base of the diabetes. The abscess from which he had suffered in London was completely cured. The new one was entirely unexpected and developed into gangrene. I have as yet no further details—I have only the telegram, and also this morning I went to Monte Carlo to see Grigoriev who also had a telegram saying that they had buried Diaghilev in Venice. At the Lido were Serge and Boris. I believe that M. Koribout [Diaghilev's uncle] had time also to come. I do not know if [Walter] Nouvel is there. On

> Sunday they are all returning to Paris where M. Grigoriev also goes to discuss the questions of the ballet. It is too early to speak of them—there was no question of that this morning—but I think that everything will be done that the ballet exists.
>
> Those members of the ballet who are in this neighbourhood make a funeral mass on Tuesday (ninth day after the death is a great day for us) at the Orthodox Cathedral in Nice. They are: [Lubov] Tchernicheva, Obedennaia, Ladre, Lissanovitch who saw him in Monte Carlo and from Juan-les-Pins Tcherkas and I think [Alexandra] Danilova and Doubrovska. I think it would be good if Rupert were to send a telegram to Serge and Boris together they are at the Hôtel des Bains, Lido, or from Sunday next in Paris, Grand Hotel. Je vous embrasse mes chers amis. Mes amitiés à vos amis—
>
> Alexandrine
>
> —I am staying in Nice. I cannot afford to live in Paris although that is my great longing to be near Lifar.

In a second letter written some days later to Rupert ('cher petit Reggy'):

> . . . je reçois tout le temps les nouvelles des affaires. . . . We hear that as all the material (costumes and scenery etc.) of the Ballets Russes was Diaghilev's personal property a legal writ of trusteeship has had to be applied for to enable the ballet to use it! It is hoped that a satisfactory conclusion will be arrived at within a few days. All the contracts (Diaghilev's handsigned for the following year) are upheld. M. Grigoriev is returning in a few days' time—I shall have further details. In the case of a satisfactory settlement M. Nouvel will be the administrative director and Kochno artistic director. Your telegram to Serge and Boris is very good—I am going to Paris on the 15th September. Every day I have been running a small temperature but I hope that the remaining two weeks will put me right. . . .

In a postscript Alexandrine asks for news of our return to London, of Dolin, a film, and of what talk there is of Balanchine and of Fokine being out of joint—Balanchine had accepted engagements in the USA—and finally, 'Is Robert painting hard?' Because of Alexandrine's letters we were probably better informed than most; but

Diaghilev's death had caused immense confusion, and nobody really knew what to do, or what would happen.

At 'La Bergère' we did what we could to rescue the holiday from gloomy thoughts about the future. In Cassis there was a fair sprinkling of visiting international talent. Yanko Varda was staying with Wyndham Tryon, and there was Galanis, the Romanian-Greek illustrator of Djuna Barnes' *Almanack for Ladies*, and an adventurous element of local society. Roland Penrose, whom we scarcely knew except through my being in his brother's production of *The Son of Heaven*, had taken a villa some distance away and came down to the beach with his beautiful and temperamental first wife, Valentine, who was herself a remarkable poet. And so the days passed in a substitute social round. Faced with competition by so much international talent, which included a German painter called Von Paulen, my hard-worked landscapes, overwhelmed by the unaccustomed Mediterranean light, by the genius of Cézanne, and Duncan's *ambiance* which inhabited the studio, had little chance of success. I worked hard but was discouraged. Before leaving, several weeks earlier than we had anticipated, we had a great party at 'La Bergère'. Everybody, including Rupert, danced to the music of Wyndham Tryon's Spanish guitar, and the local music of mandolins and concertinas, until three o'clock in the morning, during which time I frequently had to run up the hillside to fetch another dozen of Colonel Teed's 'best'. However, it is not the memory of the party that survives so vividly as that of encountering one day in the heat of noon, as we returned from the beach, a distinguished figure in light grey summer suiting and wearing a great panama hat, accompanied by a young lady with a parasol. This was Alexander Benois, looking as if he had strayed out of a picture by Manet or an episode of Proust. Benois congratulated Rupert on his dancing and also conveyed how appreciative Diaghilev had been. There was no reason for doubting his sincerity but the well-meaning confidence served sharply as a reminder of what had been lost.

In late September we returned to the *gris clair* of northern light to assess what could be rescued from the ruin of Rupert's expectations. The pillar that had sustained ambition had fallen. What was to follow such a catastrophe? I had learned that Rupert was apt to rush to extremes but I was dumbfounded by the idea that he soon arrived at and proposed to me. Ballet was not the only form of theatre, so why not make a clean break? His hopes of working as a principal dancer for the greatest company in the world lay in ruins. No other company of comparable artistic and creative standards existed. But there were lessons to be learned from Diaghilev's vision—a theatre of all the arts—that were generally applicable. Why not open up the field in the straight theatre, and make other opportunities for himself?

To me this seemed to mean throwing everything away on a gamble in a field where he had no experience. And how on earth was he going to earn a living? Though it was mean to put money first I could not help but mention this practical objection, while at the same time I was conscious of enjoying the excitement of an upheaval. Rupert was always taking one with surprises, sometimes foolish, sometimes wise. There were also other and very personal factors involved, and these were discussed frankly between us. Rupert knew that in spite of the particular qualities that had earned him a place in an enclosed and hierarchical world, he would never become a star. Whatever his day-dreams might at one time have been of being a new Nijinsky, he knew he would always need to work in a company. Moreover he feared that his active life as a dancer might be shortened by rheumatism; and there was also the common belief that late starters finished early. Rupert had no intention of conventionally ending his days as a teacher or as a *maître de ballet* in a continental opera house.

There was also the question of temperament. It was acknowledged that he had originality and flair, but the reputation he had gained of being difficult to manage followed him around like a tin tied to a dog's tail. This aspect came out in his relations with Ninette de Valois who had been forming a company of eight or nine young dancers, from the school she had been running with Kathleen Dillon, in the hope of persuading Lilian Baylis to accept a ballet company as an integral part of the Old Vic establishment; in which endeavour she was to succeed. Both had respect for the other, but Ninette, beginning in a modest way—as Rupert was later to do with the Group Theatre—could neither afford to pay for a 'soloist' nor risk taking on an *enfant terrible*. For the future it looked as if Rupert would have to follow his instincts, come what may. His intuition told him what he must do, and I became accustomed to the idea; but it was not yet necessary to act immediately on what was, at this point, nothing more than an idea. After all the Ballets Russes still nominally existed. Meanwhile there was much to do. In November we moved to 6 Fitzroy Square—a move we had planned before going to the South of France. Alexandrine wrote to the new address and told us of Grigoriev's efforts to keep the company together pending the arrival of contracts for the annual engagement with the Opéra in Monte Carlo, which would carry things forward over the New Year and up to April. Wild rumours kept circulating that the ballet would be rescued by powerful millionaires. More coolly Alexandrine wrote: 'Les affaires des Ballets Russes se poursuivent. On est on train de signer les premiers contrats et Rupert a sans doute entendu que M. Goetz a été à Londres.' The contracts arrived, and then Grigoriev wrote asking Rupert to make enquiries about a Mr Van Loo, a Dutchman, who had offered to buy the Ballets Russes lock, stock and barrel. Grigoriev was plainly suspicious and the address in Shaftesbury Avenue looked dubious. When he called Rupert found a shabby and unoccupied room on the third floor of an office block. It was appalling to find the estate of the great Diaghilev fallen into the hands of rank speculators.

In February Rupert joined the rump of the company, much reduced by lacking a number of principal dancers, with mixed feelings and no great hopes. The spark had gone out of it. He hated Monte Carlo, and three months was a long time to be away in an unreal atmosphere of gambling and money. He was soon counting the weeks before it would be over. His letters described the events of that unhappy period, and gave a good indication of his state of mind. The salaries were low and the cost of living high. Shutting himself away from the endless gossip and the unfounded rumours about the future, he began writing a long story—*A Provincial Pianist*—about a young woman of difficult temperament who cannot find her place in the world.

Letter of 22 February 1930:

Dear Robert,

I received your letter telling me of what pleased you about my writing. I am a fellow full of doubts, always I am. Always asking if what I am doing is right or wrong—I am always dissatisfied with myself in the end after all the convictions I had the other day. There is no rehearsal only a performance tonight of *Quo Vadis*. The music influenced by Massenet is by Jean Nouget, a man I have

> met several times years ago—I had a letter of introduction from Mme. Astafieva when I first entered Paris. It is really quite a nasty Opera and what with M. Guinsberg's direction *c'est très bête*. In one scene we dance and pelt Nero with flowers, we hurry to change after he has left the royal box of the Arena to return as Christians mauled about by lions, we are supposed to be half eaten by them. Imagine how much we laughed over this affair. M. Guinsberg shrieked at Tatiana Chamié 'Don't laugh, it's *serious*' he cried.

Left without artistic direction—Kochno, Lifar and the other principals were in Paris—terrible things could and did happen, and of course there were no new ballets to rehearse, as would normally have been the case, in preparation for Diaghilev's great seasons in Paris and London. There were however, for Rupert, small social compensations:

> I had a very nice tea at the Bussys' at Roquebrune. André Gide was staying there; he was very reposeful and calm. There was a German Fräulein who had a complexion of shell pink and a dress of the exact colour. She spoke very little except in German. After tea André Gide's mail arrived. His letters are often from young girls of eighteen. I said, *like a film star's*, so Dorothy Bussy said *fans*. She told me a story about a man in the Casino who after gambling all his money away took aspirins; when hours later he awoke he found himself being drawn along inside a grand piano. Apparently it is the usual way they take out people who have committed suicide. They are always avoiding scandals.
>
> Turandot is given on the 25th, I think next Tuesday. Unfortunately the Russian princess who arranges the performances I am giving with Tatiana Chamié offered us Tuesday at 700 francs, but we were unable to take it because of *La Princesse Turandot*.

For *Turandot* Rupert took over one of the principal roles usually danced by Woizikovsky, who was not in Monte Carlo. It was the only occasion from which he got any satisfaction, and he sent me a copy of the programme. The alliance with Tatiana Chamié, one of Diaghilev's most trusted soloists, was enjoyable because it provided much needed extra cash without which it would have been difficult to save even enough money to pay the fare back to London. For their concerts they gave excerpts from *Les Sylphides*, and popular dances of the 'Columbine and Harlequin' sort which they fitted up for themselves, in various hotels and ballrooms in Nice and Menton. *Mentone*, as the English called it, was the less wealthy but more genteel winter resort: 'Coming in the tram I noticed that all the people except for the French were English ladies; Mrs Ledward said that Mentone is called the "Cats' Home"—it is full of the most odd sorts—ladies with high complexions.'

Rupert's letters from Monte Carlo tell their own story: full of sharp observation and gossip, they reflected also the frustration and boredom that afflicted him in what was a sort of limbo, in a town he hated and a company with which he had no future.

5 March:

> I have one of my restless periods when nothing pleases me; I am bored and irritable when I feel life holds nothing for me. It will pass I know. It is a period of feeling that I am not succeeding as I wish, that I am not gifted as I wish to be, that also I am not capable of learning. . . . I find that perhaps I am a little too—(I have tried to think of the word I wish for, but cannot)—perhaps after all it is to do with the fact that I am over-critical. I find it so difficult to accept authority, although I try so hard. How much I try you, but I know you are able to endure the way I am telling you this. I find it is perhaps not that I resist the authority of scholars but the thing I find difficult is my relationship with 'others'. I try to be patient and humble but emotionally I find it impossible at times. Things are so complexed inside me—do not take this for self-pity, it must not be so, though that is an element of it if I were to tell the truth. . . .

Looking from the window he sees the famous Lady McCarthy 'in sky-blue berri-basque to match her tailor-made costume', and the lady from Hertfordshire who started the conversation in the Casino gardens the day before by asking if he read the *Daily Express* and she had just lost five hundred pounds at the tables:

> 'By nature I am not a gambler,' she said, 'but inside there it takes one like that.' She told me of the fat German who took her by the arm, pushing her away from the tables—how like the period of *La Dame aux Camélias*. 'How dare you touch an English lady, you

> horrid man!' The director came. 'How can you permit such people in your casino?' she demanded. 'It is *lowering*—this man ought to be in a butcher's shop with a lemon in his mouth!'
>
> There, in the gardens, is the girl with the aimless look saying 'Yes, Mrs Rinnell.' 'I don't think we shall be alone down there,' says Mrs Rinnell. 'Oh no,' replies the girl, 'you see Captain Johnson and his party will be there.' 'I said,' says Mrs Rinnell with emphasis, 'I *don't* think we shall be alone.' 'Oh no,' replies the young maid. (She has a walking stick like her companion opposite, whose face is quite purple with blood pressure and the heat.) 'It is so *hot*,' she says, and changes her seat. . . .

The grandest occasion was the charity performance with Chamié in the Hôtel de Paris, Monte Carlo when the Grand Duke André came to watch a rehearsal accompanied by his wife, Kressinskay, the great ballerina and ex-mistress of the Tsar who was reputed to have left Russia 'with so many diamonds they would have covered a mattress':

> They have gambled all their money away sometime since, however he, the Grand Duke, still has a lord-in-waiting who copies him in style (in moustachios too). Less than six weeks I hope to be back in London. So far nothing has been arranged, and personally, taking all things into consideration, do not think anything of importance will come along. People have lost interest—the general theatrical world I mean.

And then came the firmer proposition: the possibility of a contract with Sir Thomas Beecham for an opera season at Covent Garden in May and June. Then a letter with less than a month to go:

> Everything has passed off as usual. Yesterday we rehearsed for an opera called *Satan* [by Raoul Ginsberg the director]. I am disgusted with it all. Everything has passed off as usual, that denotes my boredom. Nothing has been arranged, and it seems that nothing will be arranged by Grigoriev. My opinion stands good which I told you a month or so back, but from time to time we have been informed of different propositions that might have materialized. But alas it is said that Sir Thomas Beecham is seriously ill and—there is little chance before the autumn [by which time the penniless dancers would have dispersed]. The other affair concerning some collective, American persons, who were

> said to be raising money, have not yet replied but are expected to do so next week definitely. As I know that these certain persons are trying to get hold of the costumes, Grigoriev and his agents would seem to have a very good chance of securing the costumes and scenery. I intend to return directly to London. People say that Danilova has received an offer from Massine, who is interested in the Americans buying the costumes. Some people here are saying that Grigoriev does not wish to work with Massine. I am told that Troussevitch [Alexandrine had not answered a letter] is acting for Massine in Paris—but this is only hearsay. I shall break my journey and see her in Paris.

Without authoritative direction and split between Paris and an incomplete company, lacking many of its principal dancers, in Monte Carlo this sad and anticlimactic ending of a great company was inevitable. But the magical name of Diaghilev remained to be conjured with, and the achievement of the Ballets Russes could not be allowed merely to fade away. There was in London an abundance of talent and no shortage of support: Lydia Lopokova, Tamara Karsavina, Ninette de Valois and Marie Rambert, assisted by John Maynard Keynes, formed the short-lived Camargo Society; and at Sadler's Wells and the Mercury Theatre, Notting Hill, were to provide permanent centres for what were to become the first truly international British companies.

As for Rupert, though hindsight gives them the appearance of deliberation, his movements after the return from Monte Carlo were far from immediately decisive. There was in any case as yet no question of a choice between dance and the theatre; he continued to think of the possibilities of both. What he had learned from his past experience, and from working on his own ideas over the years between working with Trefilova and the engagement with Diaghilev could be put to use only in the right circumstances.

Life is made not so much by decisions as by events. During the summer of 1930 he partnered Phyllis Bedells, famous as the first English prima ballerina, who had made her debut with Adeline Genée at the Empire, Leicester Square, and the climax to a successful tour came with a concert performance at Norfolk House, organized by the Dowager Duchess for her favourite charity. Alerted through Gillian Scaife and Rollo that Amner Hall (always known as ABH) was preparing for a second season at the Festival Theatre in Cambridge, starting in October, for which Tyrone Guthrie was to be producer, Rupert arranged through Gillian that ABH should be invited to the performance, and persuaded to include Rupert in his Company.

The concert was given in the Great Drawing Room overlooking St James's Square. The setting was splendid; magnificent dark-red antique curtains in richly ruched architectural folds shut out the sunset glow of a late summer evening, and the room was lit by crystal chandeliers that hung from a deeply coffered Queen Anne ceiling. Closely packed rows of gilt reception chairs, fragile and uncomfortable, were provided for the audience. (I could not help but wonder if these were part of the occasional equipment normally carried by ducal establishments or whether they had been hired from Gunter's.) At the far end just enough space had been left clear for Prince George Charchavadze and his grand piano and for Rupert and Phyllis to dance among other things *La Dame Masquée* by the pianist himself (of which we have no record of choreographer) and a somewhat circumscribed version of Fokine's *pas de deux* from *Les Sylphides*. Nobody seated more than three or four rows away had any chance of seeing more than the head and shoulders of the performers bobbing about, or the top half of Phyllis when raised shoulder high. Seated somewhere in the middle, packed in with the dowagers and the city directors and their lady wives in white kid gloves, were Gillian and ABH, a jolly and impish little septuagenarian, who might just as well have been enjoying his cigar outside in the evening sunlight in St James's Square for all he could see. Standing at the back of the audience I saw what I could of this remarkable performance and after it was over recovered Gillian and ABH from the crush and took them into the white and gold drawing room (now in the Victoria and Albert Museum) which had been turned into a dressing room. A grumpy ABH, complaining that he had not seen a thing, was introduced to Rupert, and there, in a scene of stately farce, began Rupert's new career.

7 Beginning the Thirties

At the Festival Theatre Tony Guthrie and Gillian (who had a large part in the management) had assembled a youthful company around Robert Donat, Flora Robson and David Horne (a leading player and ABH's son). Amongst the lively company of forward-looking actors was Robert Eddison and a small contingent of student beginners. For Rupert, who was undertaking a theatrical operation comparable to the recutting of jigs for the component parts of a sophisticated machine, the set-up was ideal.

Though it had been understood that Rupert had not joined to make his name as an actor, Guthrie decided to throw him right in at the deep end and he was given an important supporting role as Cowper, the secretary of the eponymous hero in *Warren Hastings* by Lion Feuchtwanger, which opened the season in October. Dressed in a grey frock-coat, long waistcoat and knee-breeches, and wearing a close fitting pigtail wig, the best that can be said of this baptism by total immersion is that his sense of character and stage experience gave him the authority just about to carry it off. Though he spoke clearly he had the greatest difficulty in memorizing his lines, as I very well knew, having gone over them time and again as we sat together by the coal fire in his lodgings off the Newmarket Road before it was time to go to the theatre for the first night. Guthrie, faced with the responsibility of weekly rep, could not afford a 'slow study' to hold up rehearsals and thereafter confined Rupert to walk-on parts until the final production in December of *The Merry Wives of Windsor*, a jolly Christmas romp in which, corpulently padded, bearded and red faced, he exuberantly played Mine Host of the Garter. This was a typically mischievous piece of Guthrie casting, and it appealed to

Rupert's natural sense of comedy and bucolic fun to be made to hide his dancer's figure with pantomime padding, which was Tony's revenge on Rupert for his spectacular appearance in James Bridie's *Tobias and the Angel.* In that play a dancer—a slave—is required by the Caliph of a mythical Babylon to entertain his guests, Tobias and his angel guide. No appropriately short piece of music being ready to hand, Rupert went to see Edward Dent who suggested Boris Orde, the music master of King's College Chapel. Orde wrote a beautiful, sinuous piece for solo oboe lasting a mere two minutes. He also provided two undergraduates, Julian Trevelyan (the painter) and Edward Selwyn (who became a professional musician) to play their oboes gratis on alternate nights; an arrangement entirely agreeable to the management. Tony had no idea what he was letting himself in for, never having seen Rupert dance, and although Rupert had no intention of hogging the scene, he was incapable of playing down his role whenever he danced. The inevitable happened. The moment Rupert was on the stage he had total command of it, and at the end of his brief but spectacular moment he disappeared into the wings with an oriental leap *en arabesque* with such enthusiasm that he had to take several calls. Tony had not been at all pleased that the action of the play had been held up and subsequently, however prolonged the applause, all calls were refused. It became the thing for undergraduates to come to the theatre to see Rupert dance. The effect upon the company, who had hitherto regarded him as one of Gillian's oddities, was to establish Rupert as a personality and performer to be reckoned with and whose views upon the theatre might be worth listening to. There was nothing markedly original about these ideas, founded as they were upon Gordon Craig, Granville-Barker, Jacques Copeau, and his experience of Diaghilev's use of artists, painters and musicians. Indeed they were shared by Guthrie who was beginning to appreciate that Rupert had been shaped by a hard theatrical discipline. What was to be remarkable was the tenacity with which Rupert held to his concepts of a poetical theatre and the originality with which he was to carry them out.

Tony and Rupert were in every way contrasting characters. Tony was well over six foot tall, with a small head and hawklike features, and was a quick and organized worker whose directions in the theatre were always sharp and clear. Rupert was stocky with a large head and a misleadingly innocent expression, a slow worker, much given to apparently logical explanation, whose insight took longer to earn the confidence that Tony's decisive direction so easily inspired. As a result of the Festival Theatre seasons Tony became recognized as the leading young producer of his time, and rapidly established himself in the West End and at the Old Vic. He became famous, formed companies and built theatres both here and in America, while Rupert went on to plough a narrower furrow, but made his own distinctive and not insignificant contribution to the English theatre of the thirties. Before Cambridge it was Rupert who had the wider professional experience, for Guthrie until then had worked only in the provinces (notably with the Scottish National Players) and with amateurs. Both were idealists, and by the end of the season they had formed a good relationship founded upon a mutual and candid appreciation of each other's merits and limitations. For a short period in 1933 Tony became a co-director of the Group Theatre, and he was to give Rupert valuable assistance in the production of *The Dance of Death*.

What was to become the Group Theatre started in the autumn of 1930 with endless talk with the young student actors and actresses of the Cambridge Festival Company, who were eager to express their own ideas on what the theatre should really be about. Rupert, who had thought for so long about the possibilities of a new sort of theatre, became the creative force in the group, and out of their discussions there arose the determination to do something practical when they returned to London. An organization was clearly needed, and foremost in the hard work that went into its inception were Isobel Scaife, John Ormerod Greenwood, and John Allen, whose enthusiasm, idealism and willingness to throw themselves into the everyday mundane tasks behind the scenes were crucial to the carry-over of the group's ideas from Cambridge aspiration to London reality. A contributing factor to the sympathetic and creative atmosphere that prevailed at Cambridge was undoubtedly the imaginative conversion of the old Victorian music-hall out on the Newmarket Road that the Festival had once been into a flexible theatre to suit the requirements of modern and experimental methods of production. The conversion had been made by Terence Gray, a cousin of Ninette de Valois. He completely gutted the original stage and proscenium area, and replaced it with a modern flexible apron stage, and installed a permanent cyclorama which at that time was an innovation. He also installed a revolutionary lighting system designed by Harold Ridge, whose theory of stage lighting, later elaborated in his book on the subject, was to teach me so much about light and colour.

The design of the theatre, which included its inherited ample foyer of ambulatory bars and floor space (enough for a restaurant), was imaginative and innovative, and it was a tragedy when it was pulled down and replaced by the New Theatre, sponsored by Maynard Keynes, which though centrally placed instead of on the outskirts of town, was a conventional and dull building, too small for large companies and useless for the kind of experimental drama that a university should be interested in. I cannot help dreaming what Rupert and, for that matter, Wystan—for his plays were obliged to compromise with contemporary performance conditions—could have achieved had the bare spaces of the Round House in Camden Town been available. But perhaps our limitations did not allow us to see quite plainly.

I had no part in the seminal, purist, and no doubt immature discussions of the ardent disciples in Cambridge, for Rupert's career was still in a separate compartment, and while he was throwing himself with such commitment into a new creative adventure I was pursuing a rather more solitary career in London.

Shortly after our return from Cassis, and before Rupert's departure for the Ballets Russes' last season, we had moved to 6 Fitzroy Square, which turned out to be one of the happiest places we ever lived in, in spite of the fact that it was one of the most ridiculous. Carved out of the back half of the attic top floor, and reached by a narrow and ill-lit staircase (the grand stone staircase of the Adam house having come to an end on the second floor), it was composed of three small rooms and a cupboard of a kitchen lit by a skylight in the roof. There was a windowless bathroom and a WC next door, hidden beneath the stairs on the way up from the floor below. We had however a wide view over the rooftops towards the Tottenham Court Road and the dome of University College in Gower Street. The rather larger flat at the front, overlooking the square, was occupied by two prostitutes. Our peace was periodically disturbed by blood-curdling rows when their 'protector' came once a fortnight to collect the cash. Below us lived a *lady*, a parson's daughter, she declared, and most discreet, and from her rooms we never heard a squeak. This was surprising, as it turned out, for one night, returning without our front door key, we rang her bell, and she opened the door to us dressed in riding kit and carrying a whip.

This salubrious and well-placed property we rented monthly from a 'Mr Marsh' (Signor Marchi—an Italian Soho small-property tycoon). Some months later the girls next door left and their place was taken by two young students from the Slade, the first of whom was the painter Eleanor Bellingham-Smith, who later married Rodrigo Moynihan, and the second, Beth, was engaged to F. E. MacWilliam, who was at that time still at the Slade. These were more congenial neighbours.

I had a very small room to work in, but the light near the window was good. In those days we did not paint such huge pictures as later became the fashion, our work being intended for living rooms rather than museums or warehouse-like galleries. In Rupert's absence I worked hard, and as he said in a letter from Monte Carlo when he was struggling with his own difficulties, and trying to write, 'perhaps it is a good thing to be separated and to think things out'. Replying to his letters I gave some news of my work and our friends, particularly of Duncan Grant, with whom I became involved in an ill-fated commercial project. This was the outcome of a proposal by John Lewis of Oxford Street that an outlet for decorative works by Duncan and Vanessa and other artists from Bloomsbury might be set up. In the event nothing came of it. Just as Rupert left Duncan had sent him a characteristic note:

> My dear Rupert,
> This is to wish you goodbye and good luck. I was at Twickenham [his mother's house] until Saturday and came up this morning too late to wish you goodbye. I was sorry not to see you before you left. Your picture after all can wait till you get back. I have suggested to Robert that you should write a story or a book dealing with the true life of Monte Carlo. *No one* has yet done it properly. It is marvellous psychologically and the stage is so small. It ought to be like Racine in prose. However you will very likely not take this view.
>
> I hope you will dance divinely well and marry the Grand Duke or Duchess.
>
> Love Duncan

As his own letters showed, Rupert certainly had the material to write those stories but he never did. Instead after his return he kept us all laughing about them.

During these months, while Rupert was away, I was able to paint some modestly good pictures, and showed them in mixed exhibitions, which ultimately led to my first exhibition as an artist in my own right. One of the less successful efforts, I am reminded by one of Rupert's letters, was one of two bicyclists, a subject which then lay fallow thereafter for over twenty years until I made it particularly my own during the early fifties. It was a large and ambitious picture and to increase the *ambiance* I had merged the cyclists with running horses shown against a blue background. My failure was to have confused visual experience (the cyclists) with invention (the horses, not felt in the same way). I had made the mistake, so common amongst the ambitious young, that Wystan so neatly summed up in *The Dyer's Hand*, of producing not 'imaginative art but imaginary art'. More successful, I thought, was a smaller picture in which Blake's Tyger, 'burning bright', was seen in a Delacroix sort of way, a romantic effort incomprehensible to Bloomsbury. I liked this picture but one day, many years later, after Rupert had died, I found it at the back of the cupboard. Without a moment's hesitation I put a knife through it, for it was not as good as I had remembered it. This raises an awkward problem: is it the better to think that everything you do might be important (who is to judge?); or to destroy everything you think might not show you in the best light? (A word of advice to the young: do not put signed rejects into the dustbin—I did this once only to find that two years later they were on the pavement in front of a junk shop.)

At this time Eddie (Sir Edward) Marsh, invited me to lunch to see a portrait head of Rupert painted in 1922–3 in Paris by Nina Hamnett. He later bought two pictures of mine, and was, I suppose, my earliest patron, as indeed he had been to many others. His justly famous collection owed its origin to his admirable decision, taken as a young man, to devote the small annuity (two hundred pounds) that he received from the nation as a descendant of Percival, the assassinated prime minister, to the encouragement of young British painters.

Some time later, having received much encouragement over frequent luncheons (you had to be careful not to say 'lunch') and dinners at Raymond Buildings, Rupert and I decided to return the hospitality and invite Eddie to dinner in Fitzroy Square. The outcome was an embarrassing disaster. Because Rupert had caught a bad cold and the flat was filled with such heavy odours of camphorated oil and Vick rub, it was impossible to receive anybody, and we decided that I should entertain Eddie alone at the Eiffel Tower in Charlotte Street. A special treatment was obviously called for and I drew what I thought a more than ample ten pounds from the bank. Halfway through dinner I had lost my nerve, and was admonished for repeating myself, for I could concentrate on nothing but Eddie's choice of all the most expensive dishes—soup, sole meunière accompanied by a Chablis, followed by roast pheasant and an excellent claret, dessert and coffee. Sweating, I accepted the bill with trembling hand, and exhaled audibly with relief that the ultimate shame had been narrowly avoided. The palpable tension had somewhat marred the meal, but I was forgiven. Eddie Marsh was really the kindest and most sympathetic of men, but it was sometimes difficult for a young and struggling artist to keep up with a frequenter of great houses and friend of duchesses. He had the handsomest bushy eyebrows of anybody I have met, and liked to read aloud the translations of Horace's *Odes* that he was working on. Approval meant much to him for he was modest about his own achievements; and he genuinely loved the pictures he had bought.

Regarded as either the place which saw the culmination of an apprenticeship, or as where began a new chapter, Fitzroy Square has always held a special place in my memories, for it was there, in that tiny studio room, that I accumulated a sufficient amount of work for the exhibition at the London Artists' Association in Bond Street that put me on my own feet, and which led to the beginning of my career as teacher, and a long-desired financial independence, both events which coincided with the official start of the Group Theatre in 1932.

After Monte Carlo we had resumed the habit of going to Paris whenever possible. Usually this was for a break from the grey weather and to escape from British phlegm and philistinism. Now, more specifically, it was to see Alexandrine, who after Diaghilev's death and the ensuing débâcle had used her experience and understanding of artists to become a freelance *courier des tableaux* for various dealers, and particularly the Galerie Jeanne Boucher in the rue de la Boétie which at that time was showing Soutine, Pavel Tchelitchev, and Christian Bérard. Her interests were in the direction of the new figurative painting and drawing: it was a courageous but precarious living. With Alexandrine we visited a number of studios, and were introduced to Tchelitchev and Bérard, whom we had not met before. At a *vernissage* we encountered Serge Lifar looking amazingly dazzling. While Rupert and Lifar talked—they seemed genuinely pleased to meet again—I admired his spectacular *maquillage*, the gold bangles and the varnished crimson fingernails. In the evenings we frequently met up for dinner with Mikhail Larionov and Nathalia Gontcharova at the Petit St Benoît in the rue de L'Abbaye. They lived very simply, for though she had a longer active life as a painter than he, who had devoted himself to Diaghilev and the ballet, they were never well off, and they could have done with a fraction of the money that their pictures fetch now.

If I have since thought more often of Larionov than of Gontcharova, who is less clear in my memory, it is because he was so greatly lovable, like an affectionate Russian bear. The last work of his that I saw was *Le Renard* at Covent Garden, with its farmyard animals and acrobats, so inventive, fresh, and not in the least sentimentally 'folksy'. In the Ballets Russes he was like the child who strayed into the enchanted circus and forgot the world he had left behind. He stood apart from the intrigues of the ballet, and he was the trusted soother of temperaments. He and Gontcharova had no children of their own, but it was impossible not to love him as a father.

Thrown together by fate, Tchelitchev and Bérard were rivals and each intensely jealous of the other's growing success. Bérard was certainly more amusing, extrovert and friendly to meet, while by contrast Tchelitchev seemed coolly calculating, and introvert. Both had sharp claws. It was from talking with Tchelitchev, however, that I received one of the most valuable hints about painting I have ever had. He was using at that time a very limited palette of dark grey tones. (The early paintings are to my mind far better than the mystically rainbow-coloured later works.) Talking about the need for limitation he told me that he mixed up grey tones from dark to light and warm to cool on the palette, and then painted from these without squeezing out any more from the tubes of pure artist's colour from which they were made. I never went to his studio to see what he actually did, but it seemed a procedure worth trying, and when I returned to London I worked out something similar for myself. It sounds a very simple and obvious way of ensuring a total unity, but in practice there is more to it than that. By denying myself a little extra dab of this or that I became far more aware of what was happening on the palette. It led also to a refinement of distinction between *tone* and *colour*, and to the realization that there are as many off-whites or blacks as there are colours in the spectrum. Nobody becomes a colourist by reading a book—it is visual experience that counts and it can be of many kinds. For me the next important development was the result of using coloured light in the theatre.

It must have been some time in the autumn of 1930 that we were invited by Hooper-Rowe and Misha Black (later, as Sir Misha, Professor at the Royal College) to join a group of friends for a first reading of *Das Kapital*. The meetings took place in Hooper-Rowe's studio off Great Titchfield Street which was conveniently round the corner from Fitzroy Square. Neither Rupert nor I stayed the course: the Great Book was far too long! In spite of the mugs of brown ale, tea and cocoa, we dropped out, as far as I can remember, not long after a description of the making of a chair. We both responded to the poetic insight, but got bored with the argument. To continue our studies we bought a copy of the Communist Manifesto, which had the advantage of being short and dramatic, but those characteristic forgatherings served to immunize us against the orthodox Marxist dialectics which permeated the thirties.

Acting, music and clowning can be as easily adapted to polemical purposes as to simple entertainment and delight. This is not true, however, of painting, and socialist-realism follows conventions that are merely arbitrary and soon become routine and boring. Goya's *Fifth of May* and Picasso's *Guernica* transpose rather than depict the terrible events they commemorate: history is refracted through art. The guns are silent, the blood is paint. The effect is cathartic and it purges us of violence, enabling us to live with it—and not turn it against others.

In spite of its potential for propaganda, under Rupert's direction the Group Theatre put art first as a way of discovering truth, but it could not have existed at all without a degree of political and social awareness. For one thing it was impossible to ignore the tragic consequences of the slump—the poverty and unemployment. The Group Theatre inevitably took on something of the left-wing colouring of its time, but its aims were always to produce plays and performances that were intrinsically interesting, and well done. The directly political theatre came later and did good work at the Unity Theatre, but I doubt if it would have been so theatrically adventurous without having the example of the Group's work, and the productions of the German expressionists by Peter Godfrey at the Gate Theatre, to follow.

We made the sitting room in Fitzroy Square to suit our tastes as closely as we possibly could, but there was not much space to move around in. The only visual record that survives is a picture now in the municipal art gallery at Newport, Gwent. In this the composition centres around the treacherous Valor 'Perfection' oil stove—a just reflection of its importance. Over the mantelpiece we hung an early and entirely non-figurative picture that Humphrey Slater had lent us. It was a fairly large canvas and on an olive-green ground was placed a dot of light cobalt-violet, about the size of a penny, offset by a thin black rather hesitant and wavy line. We were pleased to have so revolutionary a painting in which we saw more than pure decoration—though Rupert had remarked a lady in Monte Carlo carrying a bag, an evening *pochette*, with just such a simple decoration. In spite of difficulties in getting galleries to show his work, Humphrey enjoyed the revolutionary role and was never observably troubled by self-doubt, and his conceit of himself was always undermined by his ability to laugh about it. It was not because my own work was more figurative that I felt his extreme position had been somewhat too easily come by; but his streak of exhibitionism—sometimes hard to disentangle from egotism—could be good fun.

Although opportunities for exhibition were gradually opening for painters of my generation it was nevertheless an awkward period. There existed a kind of invisible divide between those five or ten years older, who had taken an active part in the war, and those who had been just too young, and who had not yet formed an identifiable group. In my case there was another factor, in that I had gone to art school at an early age and left prematurely to go to Paris and live with Rupert. This had the effect of putting a certain distance between me and my exact contemporaries like William Coldstream and Claude Rogers who were leaving the Slade in 1929–30. Preoccupied as I had been with painting the human figure, and with traditional approaches, without a novelty of style to attract particular attention, it was not surprising that I should be somewhat isolated from those of my contemporaries and acquaintances who in 1933 formed Unit One to defend and champion modernism. At all events by that time I had been drawn into a commitment to the Group Theatre.

Things did not change immediately after Rupert's return to Cambridge. It made little difference to the pattern of our lives that after the daily practice *à la barre* at Margaret Craske's he was now working with actors rather than with dancers. My involvement certainly did not begin until some time in the winter of 1931–2 and at that time I was with Rupert's assistance preparing my first exhibition and getting pictures framed for it. During this time Rupert's career as a dancer and choreographer was by no means relegated to the past. There was an appearance at the Camargo Society as a principal dancer, followed by the opening of the Rambert Ballet at the Mercury Theatre for which he and Alicia Markova were engaged as guest artists, and, following a suggestion by Lydia Lopokova, Rupert was invited to arrange a ballet for the Camargo Society and the recently established Sadler's Wells Ballet—a challenge he could not resist. The music was Ravel's *Le Tombeau de Couperin*, and to give dramatic form to the succession of musical *divertissements* he imagined a party of aristocrats of the late seventeenth century—in the style of Louis XIV and Watteau—whose picnic in a sylvan glade is enlivened by the unexpected arrival of a troupe of strolling players and acrobats disguised as orientals from China. Duncan Grant designed the décor and costumes and provided a frontcloth depicting musical instruments strung like trophies across Couperin's tomb. The ballet, renamed *The Enchanted Grove*, was ambitiously conceived and stretched the available resources to the limit. The dancers found it difficult to follow the intentions of Rupert's unaccustomed inventions, and rehearsals were complicated by his idiosyncratic method of working. Though greeted by many as an important work of great originality—some thought it, along with Ninette de Valois's *Job*, the best thing since the great days of the Ballets Russes—it was never revived. I am not alone in thinking this a great pity.

It had been in the summer of 1931 that Rupert had first declared his primary commitment to the Cambridge group, and had begun to look around for ways to further its cause. It was a cause that few knew even existed, a venture that had hardly been given a name. Now, in the new year, 1932, between January and April, everything happened in a great rush: *The Enchanted Grove*, my exhibition in Bond Street, an invitation to join the staff at the Chelsea Polytechnic Art School, and the final preparations for the launching of eleven young performers on an unsuspecting public at the Everyman Theatre in Hampstead. This was the first performance of what was now called the Group Theatre. And as if all this was not more than enough, Rupert was engaged by Massine to restage the dances for Offenbach's *Helen of Troy*, which Max Reinhardt was transferring from the Adelphi Theatre to his Grosses Schauspielhaus in Berlin at the end of April. Rupert had to leave London immediately after the last rehearsal of *The Provok'd Wife* and the Group Theatre had to fend for itself on their first First Night. I became an inefficient 'front-of-house'.

Converted from a circus, the Schauspielhaus was the largest theatre in Europe. It was adapted for 'spectaculars'. Considering the size of the stage alone the operation could be compared to transferring from the Adelphi to Olympia. It turned out therefore that restaging meant re-inventing. In Berlin the production also had to satisfy exacting musical and operatic standards, and the part of Helen was taken by Jarmila Novotna the opera singer instead of Evelyn Laye the musical-comedy star, and A. P. Herbert's translation was buried within a revised text by two German adaptors. While paying as much attention as possible to Massine's original choreography Rupert seized with both hands this opportunity for his own creative purposes and made a great success of it. Instead of being regarded as Massine's understudy he found himself treated as a creative artist in his own right. The extent of the alterations can be guessed by Massine's reply to one of Rupert's very tactful letters:

16 April. 3 Albermarle Street

My Dear Rupert,
I received your letter of April 7th but could not answer you on account of rehearsals for the 'Miracle' [the reason for his not being able to go to Berlin himself]. I am glad to hear you are progressing with 'Helen'. What a pity the male dancers are so unsatisfactory. I cannot understand the necessity to dance an Overture. In which costumes? and on what occasion? I find it so good to begin 'Helen' with the Greek Chorus.

The original settings and costumes by Oliver Messel along with everything else had been completely redesigned by Ernst Schutte and Ladislaus Czette.

I was determined to get to Berlin even if it meant begging time off from the Chelsea School of Art which I had joined only a few weeks before. *Die schöne Helena* which I saw at the Schauspielhaus shared little in common with *Helen of Troy* but Offenbach's music, and even that did not sound the same when it was sung by Jarmila Novotna instead of Evelyn Laye, whose real gift was for musical comedy. Among the successful additions was a character dance for a 'slave' in the orgy scene, danced by Kyra, Nijinsky's daughter: she brought an unmistakable trace of her father on to the stage, in her looks—the eyes and cheek bones—in her bearing, and in her abandon in attack. I am sure it was not imagination. Arriving in Berlin several days after the opening night, I found Rupert established in a heavily furnished *pension* within walking distance of the theatre, and surrounded by a small circle of newly found sympathetic friends many of whom had been introduced by Edward Dent, and all determined to make my short visit a success. Later in the week we had tea with Stephen Spender who told us that Christopher Isherwood was not in Berlin at the moment, and so we did not meet Christopher until he came to London for the first performance of *The Dance of Death* at the Westminster Theatre in 1934.

While Rupert was occupied at the theatre I took the opportunity every morning to visit the galleries and museums. It was obligatory to look at the bust of Nefertiti, and the Hellenistic monuments from Pergamum. The most important discovery for me, however, was a picture at the Kaiser Frederick's Museum by Signorelli. This was entitled *The Education of Pan*, and was destroyed by fire shortly after the end of the war. I had always liked the Signorellis at the National Gallery, which were rather dark and solemn, being unrestored at that time, and this picture with its simple strong colour came as a surprise. The subject also was magical and enigmatic. Bang in the middle of the picture was a goat-legged Pan, his legs crossed, seated upon a rock. A crescent moon above his head was entangled like a halo in the girlish locks of auburn hair that fell to his shoulders, which were wrapped in a dark blue scarf embroidered with silver stars. This figure was closely hemmed in by three naked youths playing upon reed pipes, one on each side and the third stretched on the ground at his feet. The left-hand side of the picture was closed by a naked female figure also playing a single long reed pipe, and on the right an old shepherd, as if strayed in from a Nativity, was leaning upon his crook. The landscape behind the shepherd was wild and rocky, but behind the woman it had become a pastoral and cultivated land—where in the shade of rich trees two small figures meditated and there was a view to a distant and classical township. In the sky was a chariot drawn by careering horses. (I took the charioteer to be Apollo, but I have since been told that it was Horus.) The composition had the boldness and simplicity of an emblem and it stuck in my mind from the moment I saw it. Years later when we were living in Wimbledon there was an occasion when I was wandering around the house not knowing what to do. Rupert, in irritation, was driven to exclaim, 'For Christ's sake, if you don't know what to paint, copy something'—and at that moment the Berlin Signorelli came back into mind. It was a good choice since because the original masterpiece itself no longer existed I could treat it as I liked—I worked from an old monochrome photograph—without challenging direct comparisons. But what was the picture really about, what did it mean? If I was going to make my own version it had to be founded upon an idea, a concept and an image. I found that scholars, from Berenson onwards, had been puzzled by this mysterious image. The picture was plainly meant to be read, but how? Berenson, on the assumption that the long shadows that went from right to left indicated sunset, inferred a tragic element. But looked at from Pan's point of view, from inside the picture, it would be dawn. Anyhow, with Horus in the sky it was time's movement that mattered. Drawing the diagonals from the corners I discovered that Pan's genitals were at the exact centre of the rectangle. The placing was obviously symbolic. With their centre at Pan's penis, a number of irradiating circles could be drawn which referred obviously to the central group and probably beyond. Moreover, by inscribing a pentagon I found that the reeds of the musical instruments were related to each other by the pentangle. The pentagon also encloses the five-pointed star. These magical geometrical configurations, with their deliberate references to the symbols of the Neoplatonic universe, seemed then (many years before Frances Yates had so enlightened us to their significance) far more important than the direction of the shadows. On this occult

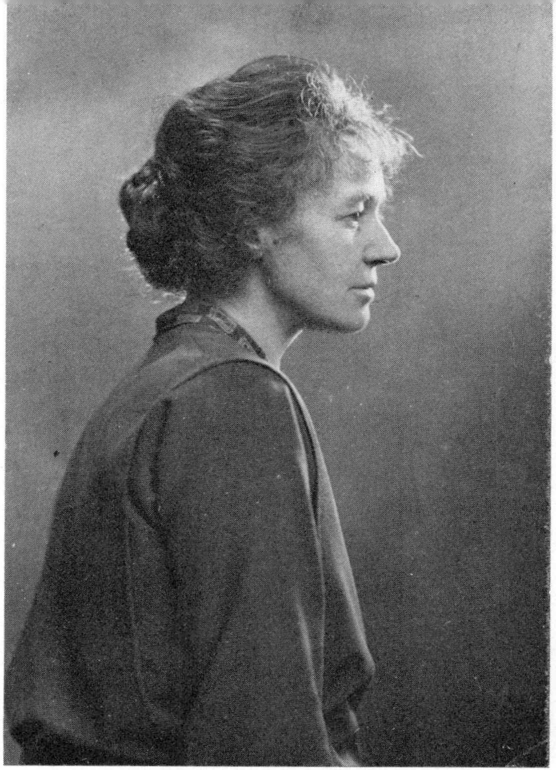

1 *The author's mother, c. 1914; photograph by G. C. Beresford*

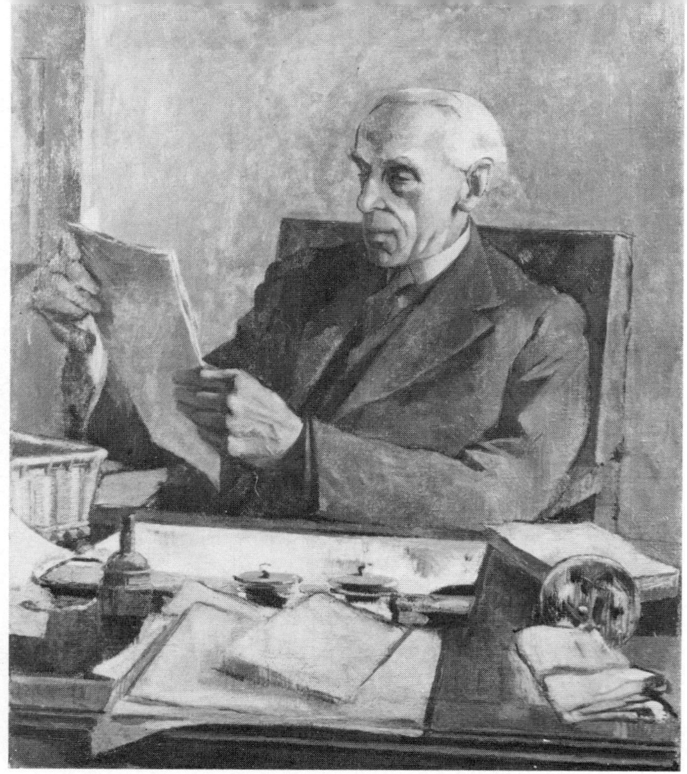

2 *The author's father, c. 1936; portrait by the author*

3 *Harvesting at Westerdale*

4 *Walberswick, c. 1912; drawing by the author's mother*

5 *Wystan Auden, 1926*

6 *The author, 1926*

7 *Rupert Doone, 1926*

8 *Rupert Doone, 1921; drawing by Edward Wadsworth*

9 *Drawing*, Standing Nude, *1926 (Arts Council Collection)*

10 *Rupert Doone, 1936; photograph by Ramsey & Muspratt*

11 *Christopher Isherwood, 1938*

12 *Rupert Doone dancing in* Chinese Dance, *1937*

13 *Rupert Doone dancing Death in* The Dance of Death, *1934*

14 Sweeney Agonistes, *1934*

15 The Dance of Death, *1934*

16 The Dog Beneath the Skin, *1936*

17 The author painting the front curtain at the Old Vic, 1938

18 *The author with Rupert Doone, Wharton Street, 1939*

19 *The author in Cairo, 1944*

20 *The author at Cyrenea, 1944*

21 Rupert Doone directing, 1951

22 The author and Ceri Richards at the Leicester Gallery, 1960

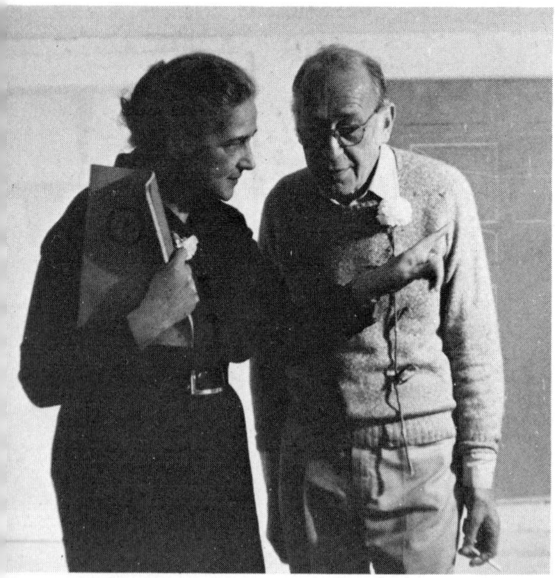

23 The author and Vera Russell at the Artists' Market, 1976 (courtesy of Jonathan Bayer)

24 Connie, 1969

geometry I reconstructed the picture, and using colour in support of it painted the wild background behind the shepherd red, and the contrasting pastoral landscape green. Horus and his chariot I eliminated. The result was one of my more successful pictures. (It was bought by Lord Bernstein and now hangs in the boardroom of Granada House.) What a disaster was the destruction of the original!

I returned from Berlin to resume the weekly life class for beginners that I had taken charge of. Rupert returned a week later. Before leaving he was cordially thanked by Reinhardt and invited back to Berlin. Why was it, Rupert reflected, that abroad he never had to fight for recognition? It was not that he was vain. Rather it was that he had a sense of his worth and felt with some justification that here in England he had to struggle continually to be understood. He had more than talent, indeed he may have had talents that in themselves were limited: what he possessed was that rarer creative quality, *vision.* The French have an appropriate phrase: *Il a du génie.* His experience in Berlin had fired him, and Rupert returned with creative energy to burn. By the end of another year Hitler had come to power, and Reinhardt's empire was in ruins. He fled to America and produced a film of *A Midsummer Night's Dream*, with Mickey Rooney as Puck, and choreography by Bronislava Nijinska. In London meanwhile Rupert had a new focus for his creative energy: the Group Theatre was at last underway.

8 Auden, Isherwood and the Group Theatre

One morning in the summer of 1932 after doing the usual shopping in Seymour Street open market I turned into the Home and Colonial Stores on Hampstead Road and found myself waiting behind a middle-aged man buying cracked eggs. I had never noticed anyone buying cracked eggs before, and the incident, though trivial, made a marked impression upon me. Neither *Das Kapital* or the *Statesman and Athenaeum* (read mainly for its art and literary news) had taught me much about political economy. *Economics* meant what you had in your pocket and what you could do with it. It had dawned on me that with prices falling as they were, living on a fixed income, however modest, meant we were a degree better off than we had been. I began to feel that perhaps this was unjust. We had moved from 6 Fitzroy Square, which however grand it looked from the outside was pretty horrid on the upper floors, to 46 Fitzroy Street, a few doors away. This was a middle-class Regency house, more domestic and better suited to conversion to flats. It was a sobering thought that it was as much to do with the slump as with the occasional sales of paintings to Eddie Marsh and Lucy Wertheim that we could afford the extra five shillings a week rent. Even so, living in Fitzroy Street things did not seem particularly grim.

Curtis Moffat had recently bought the whole of 4 Fitzroy Square and opened an ultra-smart avant-garde gallery for interior decoration and modern design: Bauhaus tubular-steel furniture and light fittings; textiles and carpets by McKnight Kauffer and Marion Dorn; fashionable jacaranda and black and white verneered-wood fittings;

Paul Nash and Edward Wadsworth paintings. There was clearly plenty of money about in some quarters. But the incident of the cracked eggs was a straw in the wind—and although we were preoccupied with our own affairs gradually it came about that the bleak and uncertain realities of the thirties crept up on us, entering our consciousness and then our conscience.

Meanwhile there was a lot happening around us: among those who had made Fitzrovia their centre of operations were Bill Coldstream and Claude Rogers from the Slade, Adrian Stokes, and Victor Pasmore, who was still working in his office at County Hall and going to evening classes at Central School. An important event for all of us was the establishment of Zwemmer's Gallery, attached to the bookshop in Litchfield Street, a step away down Charing Cross Road, run by the young Robert Wellington, the son of the painter Hubert Wellington who was Registrar at the Royal College. One of the first exhibitions there was of work by Coldstream, Pasmore and myself. Under Wellington's enthusiastic direction Zwemmer's became a focal point for young artists—'Objective Abstractions' in 1934 was a seminal exhibition and included important early work by Rodrigo Moynihan, Geoffrey Tibble, Ceri Richards and Ivon Hitchens among others. John Piper and John Armstrong were among others who exhibited there during this period. The gallery also provided a fertile ground for recruitment to the Group Theatre whose meeting rooms were just around the corner, and Bob Wellington became the Group's first business manager. His approach to this as to everything else was lively, perceptive and energetic, but not excessively businesslike.

It was inevitable, as the Group got under way, that our thoughts should turn to Wystan Auden as the writer most likely to provide new work of the kind it had been created to perform. We had just read *The Orators* and it was with some excitement that we wrote to him in the summer of 1932 at Helensburgh to ask if he would be interested in working with a small new company which had been together for a year, training in verse speaking, song and movement, and which was committed to the possibilities of a 'total theatre' particularly suited to poetic drama. We made no exaggerated claims but framed the proposal as provocatively as possible: of all contemporary poets, we declared (and this was true), he was our first choice. Wystan replied that he was indeed interested and that he would like to come and stay—he was leaving Helensburgh and had business in London. It could be a good opportunity to talk things over. Not long after he came to Fitzroy Street.

We were now, all of us, six years older than when we had last met together. I was no longer a student, Rupert was no longer primarily a dancer, and Wystan was well on the way to becoming the most famous young English poet since Byron. Although the circumstances were entirely different from those of our earlier meetings, for this time Wystan had come to discuss a collaboration, and one which might be very much in his interest, I felt, nevertheless, a certain anxiety. I was still afraid that the differences of temperament and background might prove difficult to overcome, and that seeing Rupert and me together might revive a latent jealousy in Wystan. Rupert had more at stake than Wystan: for him it was the next necessary and positive step towards the kind of contemporary poetic theatre he was aiming at; for Wystan it was simply an opportunity which if it looked propitious he might follow up. They both, of course, had the gift of creating the opportunities they needed for their own creative purposes. After dinner Rupert embarked on a lengthy description of his aims; what the Group Theatre was about, and so on. Rupert had the sometimes maddening tendency of the autodidact to verbosity, especially when he was nervous or feared misunderstanding. Wystan, who was verbally quick and sometimes impatient, interrupted these expatiations with the sudden, provocative pronouncement that 'Ballet was an art form fitted only for adolescents.' This defiant anathema, which I feared might precipitate trouble, was in fact an inspiration, for it broke the ice and enabled Rupert to come at once to the point: since the death of Diaghilev, ballet was doomed to become a middle-class diversion, and was no longer a viable form for contemporary use by artists with something new to say. Wystan quickly recognized that he was dealing with someone whose intuitions had led him to a view of the theatre that was close to his own. Sympathy having been established, we were able to move on to the main business of the evening: Wystan was asked to provide a suitable piece for an enthusiastic fledgeling company training together in a new way in movement, improvisation, singing and choric verse speaking. There would be public performances of some kind or other, of quite what had yet to be established. Rupert suggested the theme of Orpheus in the

Underworld for a spoken/sung chorus, with himself as Orpheus, for it was understood that he should play a principal role in a central dance/mime part. Wystan proposed the idea of a 'Dance of Death': he had recently discovered a medieval German poem on the subject, and the engravings of Dürer were also in his mind. Both suggestions had potential. Rupert could more clearly visualize the Orpheus, but he made no effort to influence Wystan in that direction. The outlook of the Group Theatre was clearly indicated: it would avoid the established repertoire of classics, concentrating instead on folk and medieval sources, and on experimental reworkings of classical drama. Wystan made many useful suggestions for suitable poems and ballads, and offered to adapt the Chester play of the Deluge (*Noye's Fludde*). Among the poems he suggested was Vachel Lindsay's *The Congo* with its rhythmic refrain 'Big Black Bucks in a Wine Barrel Room'.

To get an idea of the company in action, Wystan agreed to come to Sudbury, where the Group Theatre would be holding its first summer school in August. This was planned to follow a production at the Kenton Theatre, Henley-on-Thames, of *The Man Who Ate the Popomack*, a surrealist comedy by the poet W. J. Turner, that we misguidedly thought would attract an audience during Regatta Week. The school was held at 'The Limes', a local private school. There was a large lawn at the back for the movement classes, and singing and speech were supervised by Ethel Lewis, an excellent teacher recommended by Tyrone Guthrie. Wystan arrived with a half-open suitcase crammed with books and crumpled clothes. The following morning I went out to do some sketching and chanced upon an already exasperated Wystan, chain-smoking and seated on a hard chair, watching Rupert in shorts, a white handkerchief as *bandeau* sweat-rag tied round his head, beating a tambour while several young men and girls in bathing dress hurled themselves around and, now and then, as part of the exercises, fell down. It looked like a mixture of Delacroze and remedial exercises. Wystan had declined the invitation to join in. In the afternoon, to the accompaniment of folk songs and 'Big Black Bucks', he retired to work upstairs. After a school dinner of corned beef salad, apple tart and custard, the evening was spent rather like an open seminar. Wystan, whose level of boredom was very soon reached, held out for another day, and then took himself off. For genius, however, very little is allowed to go to waste: there are several moments in *The Dance of Death* when the images on the Sudbury lawn satirically reappear with startling fidelity:

> *How happy are we*
> *In our country colony*
> *We play games*
> *We call each other by our christian names*

About two months later Rupert received a script for *Orpheus*. It was a great disappointment, far too much a school piece, and without any of Wystan's spark. It was inferior to the piece of work that Rupert had expected, and feeling that he had been fobbed off, he promptly turned it down. Wystan wrote admitting that he hadn't liked it either; however, he was thinking more seriously about a 'Dance of Death'. We waited and waited. The typescript of *The Dance of Death* finally dropped into the letter box at Fitzroy Street sometime in the late summer of 1933. By midday Rupert, taken by surprise and rather baffled, handed it over to me to read. The script was as much in advance of what we had expected as the *Orpheus* had been behind it. On the second reading Rupert realized that this was what he had really been asking for, without knowing it. All our expectations had been fulfilled: the mime/dance part, a chorus, the unconventional structure—part medieval morality, part charade—all these features suited our purposes perfectly; and it dealt with an urgent contemporary situation in an original and unexpected way. What is more, nobody else would touch such tendentious political doggerel; we would, and we would make a success of it.

Since Wystan's visit in 1932 the Group Theatre had expanded. It now had rehearsal rooms of its own at 9 Great Newport Street, and it would be possible to draw on the number of players required to fill the stage at the Westminster Theatre, which was now open to us through the good offices of Gillian Scaife and Amner Hall, who had bought it after the success of Tyrone Guthrie's seasons in Cambridge. A composer had to be found to write the music, and Wystan came to London. He had recently met Michael Tippett and been impressed. He took Rupert off to meet Tippett and to listen to some of his music. Rupert came back with the opinion that Tippett was too grave a musician for the piece that Wystan had written. Wystan was not too pleased that his protégé was turned down in favour of Herbert Murrill, a composer with a lighter touch, who was then Musical Director at the BBC. We are unable to judge what Tippett might have done, but Murrill certainly produced music admirably suited to Wystan's text.

In scale and scope *The Dance of Death* was the largest production that the Group Theatre had yet undertaken. Halfway through rehearsals, Rupert, realizing that as the dancer 'Death' he was never offstage, and that he needed assistance, asked Tyrone Guthrie to co-produce. Wystan came to London for the final rehearsals at the Westminster Theatre, and was more than delighted to see his work actually on stage, and rehearsals in progress. It was essential that the momentum of the piece should be kept up, and he was enormously helpful in making suggestions, agreeing to cuts here and adding lines there. The speed with which Wystan, on the spot, could write just what was wanted on scraps of paper or the insides of cigarette packets, was extraordinary. The only major alteration was to the night club scene, which as first written was much too brief to make its point on stage. To build it up he wrote in a number of new lines on the spot, edited them overnight, and in the morning put the typed amendments into the actors' copies.

The Dance of Death was put on for two Sunday performances at the Westminster Theatre in February and March, 1934. It was preceded in a double bill by *The Deluge*, which with a few amendments suggested by Wystan was given in the original text. This was, in the opinion of many, one of Rupert's most inventive productions. To these performances of *The Dance of Death* and *The Deluge* came Bertolt Brecht, who was greatly impressed, and proposed to Rupert that he and WHA should become the English representatives of an international society of playwrights and producers which he was to call the Diderot Society. (The Society never became a reality.) For his part Christopher Isherwood mischievously brought Unity Mitford in the hope that she would yell and create a scene—which she didn't.

These performances were of vital interest to Wystan's friends and also to his enemies. They came to the theatre, having read the doggerel of the text, which Faber and Faber had already published, anticipating a poet's funeral. Few of them could have predicted the theatrical excitement. The performances were a resoundingly controversial success, and even the most sour-faced theatrical critics had to concede the arrival of something quite new and vital to the English stage, even while dismissing it as an adolescent romp.

The initiative was now with Wystan, Rupert and the Group Theatre, and the importance of what was to follow from Wystan's hand was evident to all of us. A breakthrough had been made—what next? Relations between Rupert and Wystan were now cordial and over the following year Rupert went down to the Downs School at Colwall on several occasions to help Wystan in the production of his school's end-of-term theatrical entertainments. I was not invited.

Wystan's next effort was *The Chase.* We received this in the autumn of 1934 and, once again, Rupert was disappointed. We began to plan a production, however, until Wystan wrote to say that he intended to make changes. Throughout December and into the new year he worked with Christopher Isherwood on a completely new version, and we received the result early in 1935 at the same time as we were negotiating a Group Theatre season at the Westminster Theatre. *Where is Francis?*—the revised version of *The Chase*, and the first outcome of the renewed collaboration of Auden and Isherwood—was a stunning development of the 'charade' style of *The Dance of Death* into a more than full evening's entertainment. Like *The Dance of Death*, and *The Ascent of F6*, which was to follow, it is based upon the archetypal themes of a Journey, a Quest and a Trial. *Where is Francis?* struck Rupert and me as an unimaginative title, and I rechristened it *The Dog Beneath the Skin*, which, if inaccurate, has proved memorable.

The season at the Westminster Theatre was launched in October 1935 with a double bill of Eliot's *Sweeney Agonistes* and *The Dance of Death*, both proven 'studio' successes. *The Dog*, the *pièce de résistance* of the season, was held back until after Christmas and was presented in the New Year on 10 January. It was far too long, but the censor with his blue pencil made a bad beginning to its abbreviation by mutilating several scenes, and a lot of unexpected troubles had yet to be faced. King George V died and this led to the cutting of the splendid Ostnia Palace scene (a blasphemous cod on the high requiem mass which the management would not countenance at such a time). Better a *Dog* without it than no *Dog* at all! During rehearsals it was reluctantly decided to cut the 'Destructive Desmond' act. With a character list of Shakespearian proportions the actors had to double or even triple their parts, but the excellent comedian, who also played

the GROUP THEATRE in

THE DELUGE

THE DANCE OF DEATH.

WESTMINSTER THEATRE,
FEBRUARY 25 & MARCH 4
1934.

Programme cover, Group Theatre, 1934

one of the journalists, simply could not make a success of Destructive Desmond. The principal problem however was the unresolved finale. This problem was structural—a matter of artistic irresolution—and could not be remedied by Wystan scribbling new lines on the back of an envelope. The staged version was theatrically successful in the event largely because of Rupert's choreographic skill in creating an effective stage picture. This was the first indication of a major limitation of the authors as dramatists: that they could not create dramatically effective endings to their plays. The last scene of *F6* was just saved by Benjamin Britten's beautiful lullaby for the mother; and in the last act of *On the Frontier* their misjudgements were to prove theatrically disastrous. In spite of the many tensions that built up during the production of *The Dog*, there was never a flare-up, simply because the necessity of putting the play on forced everyone to keep his nerve. The first night provoked strong reactions for and against. Audiences steadily built up and the run was extended for a further week. Though Gillian Scaife's and Amner Hall's confidence in Rupert and the Group Theatre had made the season possible we were nevertheless bound by a fortnightly rep contract and this was as far as the management of the Westminster Theatre was able to go.

For all its weaknesses as a play, *The Dog Beneath the Skin* focused attention on the importance of the Group Theatre. It also confirmed that the Auden–Isherwood collaboration had to be taken seriously. Like *The Dance of Death* it was conceived in a form eminently suited to Wystan's genius and also to the style of the Group Theatre. Its originality lay in a very individual and inventive combination of Berlin cabaret, musical comedy, pantomime and poetry, unprecedented in the English theatre.

The stir created by *The Dog* ensured that the next Auden–Isherwood play would be a *coup* for an adventurous management. It was Ashley Dukes who came forward, and under his management *The Ascent of F6* became the nearest to a popular success that the authors were to achieve. It opened on 26 February 1937 at the Mercury Theatre in Notting Hill, and after two months there, it transferred to Keynes's New Theatre, Cambridge, and subsequently to the Little Theatre in the West End where it ran for several weeks more. In 1939 we revived the production at the Old Vic, with Alec Guinness in the lead.

It has become their best-known play, but it is the one that I would least like to see revived. Their first endeavour to deal with three-dimensional or real characters, it is flawed by a fatal uncertainty as to what it is really about. Moreover, once again, the climax as written was dramatically weak, and bound to fail theatrically. Neither Christopher nor Wystan could think of a satisfactory solution to the problem, and consultations with E. M. Forster, the sage of Abinger, proved not surprisingly of little avail, serving only to muddy already disturbed waters. In performance it was only Britten's music, I thought, that redeemed the final scene.

W. B. Yeats wrote to Rupert praising the production, but criticizing the ending:

> . . . I thought your production of the Auden play almost flawless and the play itself in parts magnificent. My only complaint is of the final appearance of the Mother as demon. Why not let the white garments fall to show the Mother, or demon, as Britannia from the penny. That I think would be good theatre—a snow white Britannia. . .

Rupert's strength as a producer lay in his gift, developed in earlier years as a dancer, and carefully studied, for creating atmosphere without cluttering the stage with irrelevant detail. This gave the moral and poetic elements in the drama space to breathe. As designer I was acutely aware of the problems of presentation that were posed by *F6*. It was perfectly understood by Rupert that in the writing of a play the authors should not be inhibited by practical details. As producer it was his job to cope with such difficulties. Neither Wystan nor Christopher, however, seemed prepared to learn from those who as directors, designers and actors had the job of putting across on the stage what they had created on the page. They found it difficult, to say the least, to subordinate themselves to the imperatives of co-operative production. All this goes to show that they were reluctant to learn their job as dramatists the hard way, in the theatre. It was simply another activity in the promotion of their own careers, to which they were prepared to give only as much attention as they thought necessary. What sort of importance it had for them was demonstrated by the care they took in *On The Frontier*, their next play, to square the circle, and make a play in their convention which would also prove a commercial success. The near success of *F6* encouraged these ambitions. Notwithstanding all this, relations between Rupert and Wystan were always amicable during the period of rehearsals and differences of opinion and approach to matters of production were resolved in a spirit of give and take.

In the summer of 1937 John and Myfanwy Piper generously put their farmhouse near Henley-on-Thames at our disposal. It was planned to be a pleasurable get-together for the Group Theatre executive and its supporters, during which future plans could be discussed. We knew that Wystan and Christopher had not yet made a proper start on the new play, but we would need to know when it could be expected, for after *F6* the Group Theatre was closely associated in the public mind with Auden–Isherwood, and their new play would be an important event for us. It was naturally assumed that it would be put on by the Group.

Wystan and Christopher arrived in the late afternoon, accompanied by Beatrix Lehmann and Bertold Viertel, like two black crows, an uninvited professional backing. The authors had come to announce, without any previous warning, that the next play was destined for West End production. They were out for commercial success. In the absence of a legal contract, which nobody had considered necessary (quite apart from the fact that there was no money to pay for it) they expected that this betrayal of trust would be accepted as a *fait accompli*. As the matter was not open to negotiation they would speak only with Rupert; and this to everybody's acute discomfort was precisely what they did—in camera. The rest of the weekend party, who had arrived at Fawley Bottom in high spirits and with great expectations were left to get on with it in an atmosphere soured with disappointment and anxiety. The grisly scenario thus imposed came to a climax when Wystan teamed with an innocent and embarrassed Benjamin Britten to vamp hymns on the piano, and then to pick out with one finger, to Ben's brilliant two-handed accompaniment, an ironic 'Stormy Weather'.

For an entire day Rupert was locked up with Christopher and Wystan. None of the participants in this extraordinary meeting was ever fully to reveal what happened. But at last Rupert emerged with a communiqúe: *On the Frontier* would after all be produced by the Group Theatre. What feat of persuasion brought about this unexpected outcome was never disclosed. Some degree of good feeling was restored and social tensions were eased by the arrival of Nancy Cunard with her black boyfriend. Many years later, after

Rupert and Wystan had died, I became curious to know what had really taken place during that fateful meeting, and asked Christopher to tell me. 'It may surprise you but I simply cannot remember. Nature', he said, 'kindly removes unpleasant memories.' Essentially it had been a prolonged confrontation between Wystan and Rupert; Wystan's domineering attitude that theatrical artists were servants of the word was pitched against Rupert's unwavering assertion that he had equal rights as a creative artist.

On 18 January 1938, after they had completed *On the Frontier*, and plans for its production under the management of Maynard Keynes had been agreed, the Group Theatre gave a farewell party for Christopher and Wystan on the eve of their departure for China. Geoffrey Grigson, Rose Macaulay and John Hayward were among Wystan's friends from different worlds who were invited to what was planned as a very special occasion at Durham Wharf, Julian and Ursula Trevelyan's studios overlooking the Thames at Chiswick. There was plenty of space there, and the Trevelyans' only condition was that their bedroom should be off-limits. Rupert arranged a cabaret entertainment, the *pièce de résistance* of which was 'Tell me the Truth about Love', newly set by Benjamin Britten and sung by Hedli Anderson with Ben at the piano. The programme also included several well-known numbers from past productions.

Christopher and Wystan arrived suitably late for a star entry, accompanied, as if on a state visit, by Prime Minister E. M. Forster; Secretary of State Cyril Connolly; and supported by the drunken halberdiers Brian Howard and Edward Gathorne-Hardy. Predictably, these latter soon invaded the out-of-bounds bedroom and were discovered by Julian holding a private party on the bed. After a sharp exchange during which Howard loudly proclaimed that he would not have his best friend, Eddie, insulted by the worst painter in London, Bob Wellington was called in to attempt an eviction, and was immediately challenged to a fight in the small courtyard, in the centre of which was a newly planted magnolia. This ridiculous combat, which I witnessed less as a referee than as a kind of policeman on behalf of the management, lasted but a few moments, as Bob's spectacles were knocked off his nose, and Eddie was too drunk to press his advantage. The magnolia, for which I felt a special responsibility, stayed upright and is now a fine tree.

The following morning the celebrated authors, to the accompaniment of the clicking of numerous press cameras, departed for China. At Durham Wharf we were completing the washing up.

Arrangements for *On the Frontier* went ahead. Keynes would back the play for a preliminary run at the New Theatre, Cambridge, with the possibility of a transfer to the Globe Theatre in Shaftesbury Avenue. Christopher and Wystan arrived home just in time to see Beatrix Lehmann's splendid performance of Cocteau's *La Voix Humaine* which Rupert staged at the Westminster. *On the Frontier* was a Romeo and Juliet affair (drawing upon Christopher's ultimate failure to get Heinz out of Germany), with two opposing houses straddling the border separating (Fascist) Ostnia from (free) Westland: a theme providing many opportunities. It promised well and the most sinister and lively character was the Leader's foil, a homosexual delinquent and hit man called 'Babyface'. After the first flush of excitement, however, a cooler look showed that, once again, the last act was weak. Several private readings suggested that with very few alterations this could easily be put right, and Rupert wrote a carefully worded letter suggesting the changes we considered necessary. We waited for a longer time than we thought was required for a piece of simple surgery. When the final version arrived it was not the same play at all. 'Babyface' had been cut out altogether with the result that many scenes had had to be completely rewritten and none to any advantage. The play was deprived of its vitality.

On the first night of *On the Frontier* the curtain rose to a round of spontaneous applause as my double set of the Ostnia–Westland rooms was revealed. But it was not enough to sustain a play which, though it contained some beautiful verse, was plainly lacking in appeal—it would neither shock nor interest. Any personal satisfaction derived from the reception of my design did not survive the falling of the curtain to respectful applause and the realization that the play would not make the hoped-for transfer. It was given two performances on one Sunday at the Globe Theatre, and allowed to die a natural death. Long after, I asked Christopher why on earth they had taken out 'Babyface' and disregarded Rupert's recommendations. He confessed that he really did not know, but that it had been a 'terrible mistake'.

Rupert's reaction to the failure of *On the Frontier* was that the authors had dug their own grave: it was the disappointingly inevitable culmination of a long process. Essentially the fatal flaw in the Auden–Isherwood collaboration with the Group Theatre lay in the failure of the authors to take the theatre seriously enough. The ethos underpinning Rupert's conception of the Group Theatre was of creative co-operation between artists, performers and technicians—a co-operation based firmly upon an absolute respect for each other's contributions. I recognize that for Wystan and Christopher it was a matter of priorities—they had other fish to fry, and their feelings towards the theatre were deeply ambiguous, at times destructively so. As Christopher himself said (*à propos F6*): 'We were serious and yet not serious. . . . It was extremely aggressive towards a whole theatrical convention (i.e. traditional realist drama) and yet again, it was making use of that convention. . . .' (Quoted in Brian Finney, *Christopher Isherwood*, Faber, 1979.)

Throughout the collaboration it was left to Rupert, whose dedication and commitment to the Group Theatre were total, to deal with problems and emergencies, and the authors' consistent failure to create strong endings to their plays raised a great many difficulties. The authors were frequently away on other business: Christopher never even saw a production of *The Dog Beneath the Skin*, being in Portugal with his German boyfriend Heinz; and Wystan, away in Spain, left *The Ascent of F6* entirely to Christopher, only to complain when he saw the production!

On the personal level, Christopher, who had thoroughly enjoyed working with Rupert, Benjamin Britten and myself on *F6*, got on better with Rupert than Wystan did. The novelist in him appreciated and instinctively sympathized with the interaction in Rupert's character of personal ambition and artistic idealism. Wystan on the other hand could be impatient of Rupert's foibles, and easily irritated by his aggressiveness. This aspect of Rupert's behaviour could be traced back to the earliest years of his career, which had been marked at times by great hardships including physical privation, and to his protracted struggle for recognition. At times he could be, perhaps not unnaturally, defensive about himself and consequently insistent upon being treated as someone special. Wystan, who came from a secure and privileged professional background, and who had from the beginning been celebrated as a prodigy, found this irksome. The poet-pedagogue, unlike the novelist, was not concerned with the analysis of personalities, preferring to allot to different friends roles they were expected to play: Edward Upward was the novelist,

Stephen Spender the lyric poet, Medley the painter, and so on. By being with Rupert I was no longer acting the part he had assigned me, a fact which added at times to his irritation. Wystan's form of domination was to act the Super Nanny, looking after and organizing his friends indirectly. This habit of Wystan's conflicted with Rupert's more direct self-assertiveness: inevitably there was friction if they were thrown together for any length of time.

When all is said and done, however, it should be remembered that Auden's relationship with Doone and the Group Theatre was fruitful to an historic degree, and mostly enjoyable. We all got a great deal out of it, not least Wystan himself, whose contribution to the theatre was exciting if limited—and was, without doubt, shaped largely by the unique quality of the Group.

The prolonged association of the Group Theatre with Auden and Isherwood has paradoxically proved its triumph and misfortune, because it seems forgotten that it ever produced anything else. Its many other achievements have been largely ignored, subsumed as it were within the orbit of Auden's overriding reputation. But there was much more to the Group Theatre than Auden and Isherwood, and to that story I shall now turn.

9 The Group Theatre 1932–1939

The production of Vanbrugh's *The Provok'd Wife* at the Everyman Theatre in March 1932, though no more than a 'studio promise' and attended largely by an audience of friends who had in turn brought *their* friends, had been nevertheless a public occasion. It had meant giving ourselves a name and declaring our intention to found a permanent company—more than a Sunday club for unusual plays—which would bring together poets, painters, musicians, actors and audience. Also we had asked for money, a subscribed membership, to further that ambition. The name 'Group Theatre' had been chosen because it described the kind of theatre Rupert and the original troupe of eleven performers wished to bring about. It was not, as some people thought, a democratic left-wing affair in which everybody had a vote. There had been and would continue to be endless discussion and argument—that, after all, was how the Group had come into existence—but what finally counted were not the decisions of a committee but the imaginative purposes of Rupert Doone. Rupert was not interested in what has become known as 'director's theatre', or in the idea of an individually expressive 'interpretation' of a text in which the actors, designers, musicians and everybody else are deployed simply to a preconceived end: his vision was of a creative theatre, in which collaboration would lead to a new sort of expression unknown in the English theatre at that time. The first manifesto of January 1934 cleared the ground by stating what we were not, and what we thought we were:

> the GROUP THEATRE is not an ACADEMY,
> although it trains actors.

> It is not a PLAY-PRODUCING SOCIETY,
> although it produces plays.
>
> It is not a building.
>
> It is a permanent GROUP of actors, painters, singers, dancers, and members of the audience, who do everything, and do it together, and are thus creating a theatre representative of the spirit of to-day.
>
> It trains actors in the belief that by working together they will evolve a common technique with new means of expression.
>
> It produces plays from any age which are of importance to us to-day.
>
> It does not quarrel with the commercial theatre, but as the commercial theatre is not able to achieve these ends it sets out to find a new way.

There followed '7 POINTS about the GROUP THEATRE':

> the GROUP THEATRE is a co-operative.
> It is a community, not a building.
>
> the GROUP THEATRE is a troupe, not of actors only but of
>
> Actors
> Producers
> Writers
> Musicians
> Painters
> Technicians
> etc., etc., and
> AUDIENCE
>
> Because you are not moving or speaking, you are not therefore a passenger. If you are seeing and hearing you are co-operating.
>
> the GROUP THEATRE is a school for actors. If you cannot make your gestures as sensible as your

speech, if you cannot dance or sing, if you are afraid of making a fool of yourself in public, the GROUP THEATRE will take you in hand.

the GROUP THEATRE is neither archaeological nor avant-garde. It is prepared to adapt itself to any play, ancient or modern.

the GROUP THEATRE costs a guinea a year.

the GROUP THEATRE has premises at 9 Great Newport Street, W.C.2. (top floor).

By this time the Group had already gone a long way towards creating a distinctive identity. Behind the confident declarations of artistic policy, the published constitution and the list of over two hundred members lay two years of working, thinking and talking, during which we had been held together by shoe-string economies and the commitment of a small number of dedicated individuals.

W. J. Turner, who wrote regularly for the *Statesman and Athenaeum*, was the first poet-writer to join the Group. He had been enthused by the Everyman performance of *The Provok'd Wife* and immediately became a member-supporter. I do not recall whose idea it was that we should take the Kenton Theatre in Henley-upon-Thames, a charming red-brick Victorian survival in a street which ran down to the river and boat-houses, and present a play for Regatta Week; but this is what we did, and the play we chose was Turner's *The Man Who Ate the Popomack*. A witty, slightly surrealist comedy, the play is concerned with the unexpected dangers encountered by dilettantes in search of an identity. The play opens with a smart and fashionable private view in an art gallery, and ends with a dinner party given by a millionaire and connoisseur of mysterious origin, at which the rare fruit, the 'popomack', is bought on as a dessert by oriental attendants: on eating it all the guests turn blue. To advertise the performances in an appropriate way we put on an exhibition of paintings, shown on the stage, which was open to the public all day. We thought all this invention and fun would attract at least some of the flannelled 'undergrads' and their summer-frocked girl-friends (and a parent or two) who were not entirely bone-headed, but we played to empty houses, and all the Group got out of it was the experience. Gillian Scaife generously paid up the deficit on the theatre booking, and we had barely enough in the coffers to pay for board at 'The Limes' in Sudbury where in August we set up our first summer school, bloodied but unabashed. It was John Greenwood who had found 'The Limes', a local private school in Gainsborough's birthplace, where the enterprising headmistress was willing to provide board and lodging for the Group for a fortnight during the summer holidays. Behind the house, which was indistinguishable from other grey-brick houses in the street except for a highly polished brass doorplate, it was more promising than it looked from the front, for there was a large garden and a lawn for movement classes. Normally the school took in about fifteen boarders in addition to the day schoolgirls, so we could just about fit in, and there was a music room, with an upright piano, for Ethel Lewis to take lessons in music and speech. The food was institutional but sufficient, and the only discomfort was that the children's beds were rather small. The school was on the edge of town and the surrounding countryside and the River Stour were perfect for *plein-air* sketching, even though it looked too much like Constable to be true. Accepted as one of the group, I never attended the classes, but went on with my own work, leaving them at it while I hunted for subjects.

Sudbury proved such a success for the Group that a summer school, either at 'The Limes' or at A. S. Neill's 'Summerhill', became an annual event during which a 'show' suitable for performance at 'fêtes' in country-house gardens or village halls was put together. These summer seasons of study, rehearsal and performance away from London were crucial to the developing spirit of artistic comradeship that was a unique characteristic of the Group Theatre. The following year, 1933, we produced a programme of short pieces, songs and dances, and our tour of Suffolk villages was preceded by a presentation of the programme together with a production of *Lancelot of Denmark*, an early Renaissance secular play, at the Croydon Repertory Theatre. This had been arranged by Nevill Coghill who was on the Croydon board of directors, and whose connection with the Group was the result of his friendship with the Scaifes; he was also, coincidentally, a friend of Wystan, having been his tutor at Oxford. It was for this production that I made my first designs for the theatre, although I had been marginally involved in creating the *mise-en-scène* for a reading of *Peer Gynt* given one Sunday at the Westminster Theatre in February 1933. *Peer Gynt* was the first Sunday Group Theatre membership performance that we gave at the Westminster. It was early days as yet and the small audience scarcely filled the stalls, but it left a vivid impression on those who saw it. Using nothing but a bare stage and rostrum with a few chairs set well off centre towards the prompt corner, Rupert showed what he had been working towards with the actors, and what could be done with the simplest of means. By subtle changes of light, and a choreographic use of space, he created a setting in which the actors had to exploit all their resources of gesture and expression to define each dramatic situation, and detach each scene from the next, without the benefit of extraneous visual aids to create the illusion. The drama materialized in the acting and the movement to fill an empty space with imagined realities. The reading became more than a reading: it promised a way of playing, original but unassuming, complete in itself. It was Rupert at his best: it established the Group Theatre style, and showed that he could work on a broad canvas. It was entirely characteristic of Rupert's approach that recognizing the datedness of William Archer's translation he should immediately ask Randall Swingler to make a new version for future production. Such commissioning was of the essence of the Group.

After our disappointment with Wystan's *Orpheus*, his delay in producing anything else suitable was but one problem among many we faced at the beginning of 1933. First and foremost of these was the lack of rehearsal rooms and a proper permanent base for a membership paying a guinea a year. In March 1933 we at last found a home, on the top floor at 9 Great Newport Street. The rest of the building was severally occupied by sweated-labour jobbing tailors, but having climbed the steep, narrow and seemingly endless staircase you finally arrived in a large, empty and well-lit warehouse space, perfectly suitable for a rehearsal room and office. The rent was low, and the situation, just off the Charing Cross Road and close to Leicester Square underground station, was ideal. We scrubbed it and cleaned it, put a lock on the lavatory door on the half floor below, begged some furniture and borrowed a typewriter. Enthusiastic and prominent amongst the bucket-and-broom brigade was the Lady Constance Foljambe, a recent recruit who had just won twenty-five pounds on a twenty-five-to-one bet on a famous horse called

Kelsborough Jack, a sum she donated towards the expenses of our getting in. 'Connie' was to remain a devoted friend to Rupert and me for the rest of her life. 9 Great Newport Street was to be well known as the Group Theatre headquarters until war was declared six years later. Everything took place there—Rupert's classes (open to any member feeling the need for exercise: Sir William Coldstream remembers 'being a tree'), play readings, rehearsals, making costumes and building scenery. In the office, which soon became the wardrobe cluttered with wicker hampers, letters were written, and propaganda and programmes printed, often late into the night, on a small and ancient Platen press with a sans serif fount imaginatively bought on the initiative of John Greenwood. The Group Theatre Sign, selected from pages of calligraphy worked out between Rupert and myself, now appeared on all publicity: the sign derived from the male and female symbols, and was meant to represent our intentions to penetrate to the heart of things.

The Great Newport Street rooms were also the venue for the all important fortnightly committee meetings. These were more a meeting together of comrades than a formal convention representing the membership at large. In any case it was always after the last item on the agenda had been dealt with that the real business began. This was the formulating of new ideas and the discussion of future possibilities. Everybody contributed and as the character of these discussions derived largely from Rupert's personality and way of doing things they were usually long and discursive. Inevitably, personal problems and preoccupations came into the open: those at the heart of the enterprise came to know each other's strengths and foibles extremely well. Something very cohesive and vital was lost when the Group grew in importance—and size—and these ramshackle and intimate meetings had to give way to less time-consuming procedures. There was always the need to recruit new members and raise more money, particularly to cover the expenses of the Sunday productions at the Westminster Theatre as these became more sophisticated. Nobody got paid, neither the director and actors, nor the helpers who showed the audience to their seats and sold for twopence the programmes which John Greenwood, John Allen and myself had produced. The possibilities of the Group's rooms at Great Newport Street were fully exploited therefore for fund-raising parties, lectures, and for showing excerpts from projected productions or studio performances of new or hitherto unperformed works. The most important of these try-outs, early in 1934, was T. S. Eliot's *Sweeney Agonistes*.

Rupert had been thinking about *Sweeney* for some time. At the Group Theatre Rooms he produced it in the round and it proved such an interesting and remarkable success that it was revived in the following December and January and given a number of Sunday evening performances. A distinguished and élite audience climbed the precipitous and unsavoury stairs to see it at that time, amongst whom was W. B. Yeats (whom I was personally detailed to help up the stairs) and Virginia Woolf, brought by Eliot and a party of friends. Desmond McCarthy published a perceptive review, the longest yet written about the Group Theatre, in the *Listener* on 9 January 1935. This was the printed version of a talk he had given on Christmas Eve and it is worth quoting, for it expressed a considered and sensitive response to what we were trying to do:

> I had a rather out of the way experience as a playgoer the other night. I had received a notice from some players of whom I had not heard before. They called themselves 'The Group Theatre', and the circular announced that I should be able to see at No. 9 Great Newport Street the performance of an unfinished play by Mr. T. S. Eliot, which I happened to have read. It had interested me very much, partly for this reason—that it was written in a kind of verse which seemed to me more suitable for modern plays than blank verse. It was called 'Sweeney Agonistes'.
>
> I found myself in an L-shaped room on the third floor, round which seats had been arranged leaving an empty space in the middle, where stood a table with some drinks on it and some unoccupied chairs. It was in this space that the performance took place. We, the spectators, were in the position of Elizabethan swells; we were sitting on the stage itself. 'Sweeney Agonistes' is a slight piece of work, and a fragment at that—two brief scenes. But it makes its impression, and technically it is interesting. . . .
>
> 'Sweeney Agonistes' belongs to that part of Mr. Eliot's work inspired by his negative impulse to contemplate the sordid. The author had described it as a fragment of an Aristophanic melodrama, but the adjective does not seem to me right. It strikes me as being rather the fragment of a drama of retribution translated

> into the terms of squalid modern crime. It was thus that it was performed at 9 Great Newport Street. Mr. Eliot himself seems to have assented to this interpretation by quoting at the beginning a passage from a Greek play in which Orestes speaks of the Furies which are pursuing him: he says, 'You don't see them, you don't—but I see them: they are hunting me down. I must move on.' In this case the Furies of retribution are the policy, as well as the lashes of remorse, though it is the *feeling* of a haunted conscience that is most powerfully conveyed in this strange little piece. I must try to describe how the play was presented. That is the best means of conveying what this group of young men and women are up to: the kind of play they are on the look-out for, they describe as 'realistic fantasy'; they give their work for nothing; they are feeling their way towards a new contemporary form for the drama. As Mr. Doone, who is at the head of them, has written: 'the form we envisage for our plays is analogous to modern musical comedy, or the pre-medieval folk play, since in it realistic incidents are allied with fantasy—in our case the fantasy of the poet rousing emotion by means of conscious rhythm.' In performance, the realism became largely symbolic, and this effect was strengthened by all the characters save one in 'Sweeney Agonistes' wearing masks. . . . It certainly had a grisly impressiveness lifted above the matter-of-fact, partly by the symbolic suggestion of the masks, and partly by Mr. Doone's device of turning the audience itself into a kind of chorus (the actors were sitting among us).

These performances of *Sweeney Agonistes* were as important as *The Dance of Death* in drawing attention to the Group Theatre as a venture that had to be taken seriously: it was doing important things, and it was beginning to attract a lively and informed audience.

Just before Christmas Rupert wrote to John Johnson (Celia's brother, who was a new and enthusiastic recruit following the earlier performances of *Sweeney* at the Group's rooms, and who became editor of the *Group Theatre Paper*):

> I went down to see Wystan's school play, which I enjoyed very much indeed, and I think I learned things besides, from the children, especially in a short play that Wystan said they made up themselves. I must say that it bore an uncommon resemblance to a

'Folk Play', so one can take it that the 'master' guided them. It was about a cabbage, and a tree, and a king and his son, and a giant and a doctor and an attendant and a princess and father Xmas and a hare and and and. But very charmingly done. Apparently children are given to that sort of phantasy.

Were you at Sweeney last Sunday? Not that I expected you. . . . Yeats was there, and Bert Brecht, the writer of the German 'Beggar's Opera'. Who was very impressed, said it was the best thing he had seen for a long time and by far the best thing in London. He is going to send us a play of his, with music by Hindemith (the composer who has just been sacked by the Nazis) he was so impressed. Desmond McCarthy was there and is going to say something about us on the wireless next Monday (Xmas Eve) at 6.45 pm. So he says. I thought you would like to know. . . . Do you see we are going to give another two performances of Sweeney, owing to demand, in the New Year?

The promised play never arrived. (Given the conditions of exile which Brecht suffered at the time, this was not surprising.) We met Brecht again early in 1939 when, over coffee at the Embassy Theatre, we talked of the coming war and how best to survive it. Nobody was better qualified to give such advice than Brecht, one of the century's great survivors. Somewhat disingenuously he suggested the South Sea Islands. Needless to say he had already made his own plans.

In the October of 1934 Rupert had produced, at the Mercury Theatre, Notting Hill Gate, under the aegis of Ashley Dukes, W. J. Turner's version of Molière's *Amphitryon*, *Jupiter Translated*, with settings and costumes by Nadia Benois and music by Anthony Bernard. Shortly afterwards, Dukes had approached Rupert to join discussions with T. S. Eliot, W. B. Yeats, and Tyrone Guthrie about the possibilities of creating 'a home for poetic drama' at the Mercury. It would be initiated by a season of plays possibly including *Sweeney Agonistes*, *The Dance of Death* and something by Yeats. However much respect Eliot and Yeats had for each other, there were disagreements. Eliot told Rupert after one meeting that he felt like 'kicking Yeats downstairs', which at the Mercury were rather steep and narrow. Rupert saw quite a bit of Yeats during this period and was taken to hear Miss Ruddock read 'the poems' (an experience which led to his private determination that the 'sweet dancer' should never be allowed on the boards). There was also the occasion when, descending the stairs for luncheon at the Savile Club, Yeats stopped to gaze in the mirror and to Rupert's delight said, 'One must always adjust the Image.'

Rupert retired from the talks when it began to look as if he would be responsible for no fewer than five productions under Ashley's management. It was clear to him that this would compromise the Group's freedom of action and strike at the heart of its identity. What is more, he had but qualified sympathy with poetic drama of the Yeatsian kind, and he understood, quite rightly, that it was not in keeping with the spirit of the time or with the philosophy (however vaguely expressed) of the Group.

Nevertheless, Duke's proposition had been attractive and Rupert had taken it quite seriously. His decision to withdraw provoked heated argument at 9 Great Newport Street: was it not throwing away an opportunity for professional advance—a possibility of a breakthrough for the Group? Rupert was adamant: we would not put the Group Theatre at Ashley Dukes's disposal. It was better to wait—and in this he was right. On 20 March, Eliot wrote to Rupert:

> My dear Doone:
> I am so very sorry to get your letter of the 18th, and to know that after you have taken so much trouble and time over this business, you feel obliged to retire. Obviously it is impossible for any one man to produce five plays in the time at your disposal. I am afraid the whole thing has been badly muddled. Whether the issue would have been more successfully resolved had Yeats been able to be in London I do not know. And also, unless there was someone behind such a scheme with the time and influence to get adequate support for it, it could come to nothing. This end of it is obviously not yours and I don't consider it mine. I am sorriest on account of Auden, and I hope that you will be able to make arrangements with the Westminster Theatre to give him a show in the autumn. As for myself, I want to assure you that I found your criticisms very valuable, and but for the abortive undertaking I should not have had the benefit of them.

The latter part of this letter refers to *Murder in the Cathedral* (destined for Canterbury). Following the success of *Sweeney Agonistes* Eliot had sent Rupert a first version of the play, which to

Rupert's surprise was written entirely in prose. Rupert went to see Eliot and told him that by abandoning verse he was denying his essential genius; at this meeting they discussed scenes from the projected play in some detail. Rupert had hoped that the Group Theatre might mount the first production of what was clearly destined to be an important work. Correspondence about the production had begun in January 1935. The following letter from Eliot makes it clear how and why it was that Rupert and the Group did not produce *Murder in the Cathedral* first:

> 30 April 1935
>
> My dear Doone.
>
> Thank you very much for returning the newspaper cutting which may be useful to the Canterbury designer. I am extremely sorry you have had such a very bad time [Rupert had had flu] and Tonbridge will suit you. As for the play, please don't think that there is no chance of my ever letting you do it if you wanted to. It was only after Yeats' season having fallen through, I felt obliged to refer the matter again to the Canterbury people, and as they definitely felt their production would have a better chance if not preceded by another in London, I thought I should defer to their wishes. Do let me know when you are back in London, and let us have a talk.
>
> Yours ever TSE

Significant as a Group Theatre production might have been, I have always doubted that Rupert could have generated from *Murder in the Cathedral* the magical intensity with which he invested the fragmentary *Sweeney Agonistes*, which was in spirit and form so much closer to the style of the Group.

Rupert was not a born administrator and his conduct of negotiations was idiosyncratic, but he had the rarer gift of being able to see round corners, and seize opportunities that others might miss. Why not plan our own season for which we had already a small but organized audience? *Sweeney* and *The Dance of Death* were asking for a wider audience; Wystan and Christopher Isherwood were rewriting *The Chase*, which would provide the essential novelty if the season was to have any meaning; and the Group Theatre repertoire already included other possibilities such as *The Deluge*, and *Fulgens and Lucrece*, the first English secular comedy, which had been a success at the Everyman and also at the Maddermarket in Norwich where we had played at the invitation of Nugent Monck. Gillian Scaife supported the project and negotiations with Amner Hall (ABH) began. An over-ambitious list of plays was submitted for discussion which included the classics *Gammer Gurton's Needle*, *Arden of Faversham*, and the new version of *Peer Gynt* on which Randall Swingler was busy at work. Other ideas were discussed. Why not ask Michel Saint-Denis, whom we had known since the first season of his Compagnie des Quinze in 1933, to produce an English version of one of their plays? It would be a draw and express a certain solidarity, for it was with certain European theatres that the Group had more in common than anything here.

Rupert bore the brunt of the discussions with ABH, and a number of delicate compromises had to be negotiated, as was inevitable when an enterprise such as the Group was faced with a commercial management. Rupert, who at the outset had indicated that he personally wanted only to produce the Auden–Isherwood and Eliot plays, found himself co-director with ABH and Gillian of the entire season, principally responsible for its organization. ABH insisted moreover that the season should contain at least one production as a vehicle for the talents of Gillian: as far as he was concerned, *The Dance of Death* having gone over his head, Auden was likely to be a dead loss, and something lighter, more romantic, was needed. The second production of the season, therefore, was Rudolf Besier's *Lady Patricia*, which proved a disaster in every aspect in spite of the valiant efforts of John Wyse, who directed it. Such accommodations were necessary, however, to get what we needed: a repertory season in the theatre with which we were already associated.

The Group Theatre season opened on Tuesday, 1 October 1935, with the remarkable double bill of *Sweeney Agonistes* and *The Dance of Death*, which ensured an interestingly mixed full house of our own committed supporters and the inveterate first-nighters who could not afford to be left out of a new thing. There was also a full critical turn-out. The audience reception for *Sweeney* was mixed and somewhat muted. *The Dance of Death* created something of a stir and ended to enthusiastic applause. It is always difficult to judge from a first night what the critics are going to say. We expected a mixed bag of notices, but not the heavy-handed stupidity and condescending acrimony which we excited in much of the national press. Ivor Brown, whose critical versatility enabled him to write not one but three lots of knocking copy, in the *Observer*, the *Manchester Guardian* and the *Sketch*, went to town with something like a vengeance:

> It is, I know, very difficult to think of anything new, and it is always embarrassing to be trumpeted as the Last Word. None the less, the Group Theatre might surely have arrived with some less tattered baggage than a creed of masks instead of faces, of acrobatics instead of acting, and of the 'Liquidation' of a decadent bourgeoisie by the Up-and-Coming Saints in Scarlet. All these ideas have been knocking about in the Germanic and Muscovite theatre for years, and have been discredited because they are either dreary or nonsensical. . . . Mr Auden does not seem to be watching life at all. He is just taking the reach-me-down Aunt Sallies of undergraduate Communism and knocking together a charade which would stir the titters of a Left Wing smoking-concert.

Of *Sweeney* he could suggest only 'that this piece so performed is totally unintelligible unless you are in the movement'. He ended on an ironically positive note: 'The choruses and combined movements had been carefully rehearsed and were well done, and there were elements of good revue sketches. . . . Only it was the kind of thing that Mr Charlot and Mr Cochran do so much better. . . .' (*Observer*). *Sweeney* 'is the usual Left-Wing business, with people gibbering in masks in front of black curtains' (*Sketch*). 'Like other and more comprehensible things in life, this play stops after a while' (*Manchester Guardian*). For George W. Bishop in the *Telegraph*, *Sweeney* 'defied description and called for little attention. . . . It is dull and pretentious. . . quite pointless. . .the actors were in hideous masks by Robert Hedley [sic].' In the *Sunday Times*, Bishop (who, like Brown, had more than one outlet for his vituperation) wrote, 'I failed to make anything of "Sweeney Agonistes", which appeared to my philistine mind to be pretentious nonsense.' For the critic of the *Evening News*, *Sweeney* was 'a nearly meaningless nightmare' which he could personally 'outdo on half a pork pie without pickles'. *The Dance of Death* 'might almost have been written by Mr Noël Coward'. (Whether this was intended as a compliment or not was not clear from the context.)

The enormous coverage advertised us very well, however, and

though we never played to capacity the audience grew steadily and by the time the run came to an end we had received some reviews that were intelligent and appreciative. The critic of the *New English Weekly* put up a spirited defence:

> Nothing since the advent of Ibsen has so successfully exposed the wretched incompetence of our dramatic critics as these first productions of the Group Theatre. The best we get from our popular papers is the sort of 'criticism' that will damn a new play because Sarah Bernhardt could not have acted in it; and the vilest is the dogmatic obscurantism that abominates anything new simply because it is 'new and disquieting'. And again we have the type of sincere ignoramus, one of those downright fellows who in any sane community would have been much better and happier occupied in carting coal, but in England, writes dramatic criticism for the 'Morning Post', and dictates to thousands of theatre goers that they are to consider Mr T. S. Eliot's *Sweeney Agonistes* 'crude and sordid and pretentious' and that it is 'an attempt to prove that Life is Death'. . . . All I can say is that no one who professes . . . an intelligent interest in theatre can afford to miss the present productions. . . . Here is theatre springing from the rhythms and idioms of your own life . . . with its slang and jazz heightened into poetry. . . .

Among others who stood out against the common rot were Harold Hobson in the *Christian Science Monitor*, and the critic of *The Times*, both of whom emphasized the significance of the formal and stylistic elements and the vitality and ingenuity of the production. Most surprisingly, from the heartland of philistinism, *Punch* contributed a lengthy, lively and generally sympathetic piece to the public discussion. Rereading the cuttings, I am struck by the extent to which the productions of the Group during the season were positively received even when the plays performed were regarded with doubt and qualification.

With the success of *The Dog Beneath the Skin* in the New Year—it opened on 10 January and it became the thing to see it, so that by the end of its run it was playing to packed houses—the Group Theatre season was confirmed as a theatrical event of some importance. Historically it can still be seen as a small but recognizable landmark on the theatrical horizon of the thirties. The Westminster Theatre season established the Group Theatre in the public mind, but it also marked the moment in its history when a number of misconceptions about its style and philosophy, and the influences upon them, gained currency, and these have persistently coloured its subsequent reputation in ways that are not helpful to the writing of a true history. Although the more intelligent critics were able to distinguish between the ideas that might be presented in a play and the ideas that animate the company that presents it, there were others who confused them: because we had performed *The Dance of Death* and *The Dog Beneath the Skin*, and Auden was well known for his left-wing views, then the Group must be political. It is true that many of us involved with the Group were concerned about the issues of the day—unemployment, the struggle for democracy in Spain, the rise of Fascism in Germany and Italy. In this we were of our time. But the aims of the Group Theatre were essentially artistic—we were never interested in agit-prop or in straightforward politically activist theatre of the kind developed at Unity, although everything we stood for in drama was opposed to the comfortable voyeurism of the West End commercial theatre. Neither were we, as some have thought, an English offshoot of the continental expressionist theatre, in spite of Rupert's association with Reinhardt and his admiration for the work of Kurt Jooss. Bert Brecht we met a couple of times in the mid-thirties, but neither Rupert nor I saw any production of a Brecht play until long after. (Wystan always disclaimed any Brechtian influence on his dramatic writing, though it is clear that his experience of the cabaret in Berlin—and perhaps seeing *Die Dreigroschenoper* at that time—had some effect on him.) In a letter to *The Times Literary Supplement* in January 1935 Rupert had attempted to correct another misapprehension. The *TLS* had written in an article on the 'new poetic drama':

> Mr Auden is a practical dramatist, for he works in association with a band of players, the Group Theatre, disciples of the Compagnie des Quinze. This group announce their form as 'realistic fantasy', in which realistic incident and fantastic illusion are combined. . . .

We replied:

> . . . the article describes the Group Theatre as 'disciples of the Compagnie des Quinze' but as none of us have ever worked under

> their tuition, and as we began our work without any knowledge of their methods or results, this description can hardly be accepted as fair either to Monsieur Saint-Denis or ourselves. It is true that we share (in common with other theatres, such as the Moscow Arts Theatre and the Habima Players) certain basic ideas which have been expounded by theorists like Gordon Craig, Stanislavsky, Copeau and Granville-Barker. We believe, as they do, in the necessity of a permanent company trained together in a common style, and served by their own authors. But the tone and character of our work, so far as it has developed up to the present, is entirely unlike the lyrical mood of the Compagnie des Quinze.

This association was no doubt confirmed in some minds by the presence of Michel Saint-Denis in the Group's season, as the director of Jean Giono's *Les Lanceurs des Grains* (translated variously as *The Sowers of the Hills* or *The Scatterers of the Seed*) in late October 1935. The most widely read statement of the Group's ideas has undoubtedly been Wystan's famous 'Manifesto on the Theatre', *I Want the Theatre to Be. . .*, which we published in the programme of the Group Theatre season production of *Sweeney Agonistes* and *The Dance of Death*. This has led to the belief that Wystan was the progenitor of the Group's approach to drama. In fact, although Wystan wrote the final draft—as a brilliant controversialist he was obviously the best person for the job—the ideas were largely derived from an earlier and much lengthier version put to him by Rupert. This is what Wystan wrote:

> Drama began as the act of a whole community. Ideally there would be no spectators. In practice every member of the audience should feel like an understudy.
>
> Drama is essentially an art of the body. The basis of acting is acrobatics, dancing, and all forms of physical skill. The music-hall, the Christmas pantomime, and the country-house charade are the most living drama of to-day.
>
> The development of the film has deprived drama of any excuse for being documentary. It is not in its

nature to provide an ignorant and passive spectator with exciting news.

The subject of drama, on the other hand, is commonly known, the universally familiar stories of the society or generation in which it is written. The audience, like the child listening to a fairy tale, ought to know what is going to happen next.

Similarly the drama is not suited to the analysis of character which is the province of the novel. Dramatic characters are simplified, easily recognisable and over life-size.

Dramatic speech should have the same confessed, significant, and undocumentary character, as dramatic movement.

Drama in fact deals with the general and universal, not with the particular and local, but it is probable that drama can only deal, at any rate directly, with the relations of human beings with each other, not with the relation of man to the rest of nature.

September 1935

From the beginning the critically distinctive features of the Group Theatre's philosophy were its emphasis upon collaboration between writers, actors, artists and musicians, and its belief in the importance of keeping in constant touch with its audience not merely through a style of performance, and subscription membership, but through an active programme of lectures, exhibitions, classes and debates. Among those who gave lectures, demonstrations or readings, usually at the rooms in Great Newport Street, between 1932 and 1938, were Michel Saint-Denis, Kurt Jooss, A. S. Neill, T. S. Eliot, Herbert Read, John Betjeman and John Grierson. In June 1936 the *Group Theatre Paper* was started, with John Johnson as its editor, and set out to keep members informed of activities, to review plays and exhibitions, and to publish passages from work in progress by writers involved with the Group. The opening issue announced the formation of the Film Group, whose chief aim was 'to build up a creative movement in cinema which shall express the aim of the Group

Theatre'. As Basil Wright expounded it in the second issue of the *Paper*: 'The main objective is to give people an opportunity to acquire a thorough practical training in all branches of film work. . . .' I have no clear memory of how it was proposed to finance this venture, but I seem to recall that it was intended in the long run actually to *make* money. In the event the Film Group never really got off the ground, but its formation gives a good indication of the creative ambitions of the Group at this point in its fortunes.

In all this, we kept close to our declared aim in early 1934 to be 'a permanent GROUP of actors, painters, singers, dancers and members of the audience, who do everything, and do it together, and are thus creating a theatre representative of today'. At the centre of all this activity the driving force was Rupert Doone.

For me, personally, one of the most important experiences of the season was to work with Michel Saint-Denis on the design of the two sets required for *The Sowers of the Hills*. Hitherto I had worked only on the most rudimentary designs for Rupert's productions which generally required a minimum of scenery, if any at all, and on costumes and masks. I was ignorant of what was required for a three-dimensional stage setting, and I had never worked for an outside producer. It was from Michel that I learned the practical techniques of stage design. Before starting his own company he had been a stage director for his uncle, Copeau, at the Vieux Colombier, and he was a meticulous craftsman with great practical wisdom. No more exacting, or understanding, teacher could have been found.

One afternoon, not long before the opening of the season, I was working in the cubby-hole I had been assigned at the rear of the Westminster Theatre on the ground plans of the sets for *The Sowers of the Hills* when I was called to the auditorium. There was Wystan, highly animated, freely scattering ash from a succession of cigarettes, and talking with enthusiasm to Rupert about a young new composer, whom he had recently met at John Grierson's GPO Film Unit. He did not disguise the fact that he was disappointed that Herbert Murrill had already undertaken (with Wystan's approval I should add) to do the music for *The Dog Beneath the Skin*. It would have been at that stage impossible to change the arrangement, and in any case, after the success of the music for *The Dance of Death* it would have been churlishly unprofessional to do so. In the semi-darkness I discerned a slim young man, unobtrusively dressed in sports jacket and grey flannel bags, with irregular features and crinkly hair, and wearing a pair of slightly owlish spectacles, which emphasized his watchful reticence. In this way Benjamin Britten entered upon the scene and began his long association with the Group. I soon discovered that his diffident manner disguised a wiry personality.

Shortly after this meeting, Rupert and I were invited to a meal at his flat in West End Lane, Hampstead, before going on to a concert at some hall in Golders Green where an early string quartet was being performed. Over dinner and a bottle of inexpensive white wine Ben lost his characteristic reserve, and something of the complexity that lay behind the deceptively conventional persona was revealed. Later in the evening the music came as an exciting revelation, and we were immediately convinced that he should write for us at the first opportunity. Thus it happened that the first music Britten composed for the theatre was for Nugent Monck's production of *Timon of Athens*, given at the Westminster Theatre as part of our new season in December 1935. Thereafter Ben became composer extraordinary for the Group Theatre, creating music for the subsequent Auden–Isherwood plays as well as for Louis MacNeice's *The Agamemnon of Aeschylus* and *Out of the Picture*. Ben was always generous with his time and his talents. Like Wystan he could produce brilliant things at short notice, and he was always willing to give advice and help out; for *On the Frontier* he not only wrote the music and conducted the choir, but personally found the two first-rate horn-players that his music required, and played the piano: all this for no payment whatsoever. He carefully avoided any involvement with the executive, however, and declined our invitation to become Musical Director when Herbert Murrill retired in 1936. We were greatly indebted to Ben, and I think he got something in return for his commitment to the Group. Certainly he gained invaluable experience in working for a living theatre, improvising and making things in close collaboration with other artists within the limitations of a given script and production schedule. Much later John Piper wrote of the Group's ideal of a theatrical unity that was the outcome of creative collaboration: '. . . clearly the origin of the ideal was the Diaghilev ballet. I believe it remained a stage-ideal for Britten all his life, and is traceable in all his works involving collaborators.' This was an observation that would have given Rupert much pleasure, as it does me.

After the season the first opportunity for Ben to compose for us came with the production of Louis MacNeice's translation of *Agamemnon*. MacNeice's name had first been mentioned some time in 1935 when we were discussing the possible new authors and plays. He was at this time teaching classics at Birmingham University. He had written his first play and was uncertain about it, as indeed was Wystan, who privately suggested that he should be encouraged to proceed with the translation of *Agamemnon*. Some time before in a letter full of suggestions for texts and poems suitable for Group Theatre treatment, Wystan had mentioned *Agamemnon*, and added, 'There are no decent acting translations. Louis MacNeice is the person to do them.' Louis's own play did turn out to be unstageable, and he agreed to get on with the Aeschylus for a Sunday production at the Westminster. We were to look forward, also, to another play of his own, and his involvement with the Group would undoubtedly help him to an understanding of theatrical technique: of the quality of his genius we had no doubt from the first time we met.

Louis was a dandy and difficult to pin down. His slightly slanting, beautiful dark eyes, shaded by long black lashes, were always quizzically alert; watchful of the world, he kept much of himself secret. He was humorous, witty and convivial; but something in his manner suggested always an underlying sadness, a predisposition to melancholy. He was intensely Irish, proud of belonging to an ancient clan that could be traced back to a pagan world in which the sensory—whether visual or aural—was ascendant over the ethical: a world reduced now at Clanmacnois to

A huddle of tombs and ruins of anonymous men
Above the Shannon dreaming in the quiet rain.

This ancient background seemed to give Louis imaginative access of a rare kind to the Homeric world—the classics were living books to him.

Louis was temperamentally averse to making moral judgements or to pontification of any kind: he thought not to save a soul but to free it into the air like a bird, a curlew perhaps, to fly direct and swift above the moorland stone crops and peat bogs. The borzoi hound that he liked to keep was not so much a pet, I felt, as an aristocratic extension of himself. 'She's frightfully stupid', he would say, 'and very expensive to keep.' And when she was unleashed in Kensington

Gardens she was beautiful to see, bounding with incredible elegance, and leaping all fences effortlessly. This quality of imaginative grace endeared Louis to Rupert, and there were never to be the personal and artistic problems that beset relations with Wystan; fearing no judgements, Rupert felt less need to be defensive.

Louis had an Irish love of company and was a generous host. Shortly after our first meeting we went up to Birmingham one Saturday for a party to celebrate his move to London, where he was to take up a post in Greek at Bedford College. After dinner with Dr and Mrs Auden we went on, with Wystan, to Selly Oak where Louis had been living in a large studio room let by Mrs Sargeant-Florence—a retired Victorian bluestocking and artist. It was a splendidly memorable affair, which was reviving for further celebration at noon next day when Rupert and I left. Wystan, of course, had retired many hours earlier and gone home to his own bed. We were roused from the floor by Louis, a Jermyn Street bath-robe wrapped round him with negligent elegance, for a late breakfast of Guinness. Also at the party were Walter Allen, and R. D. Smith (later to be a close BBC colleague of Louis) who with his wife, Olivia Manning, I was to meet again in Cairo in 1942.

MacNeice's *Agamemnon*, a masterpiece of translation, was given two well-attended Sunday performances at the Westminster Theatre in 1936. (Greek drama in those days was not a great draw: even Sybil Thorndike's *Medea* could count on only a short run.) The play was given a brilliant treatment by Rupert, and with Britten's music and the fine acting of Veronica Turleigh, Vivienne Bennett, and Robert Speaight, it was certainly one of the Group Theatre's outstanding productions, and the one in which I was most pleased by the part I played in it. Entirely responsible for the visual effect, I was anxious to get it absolutely right. With Nigel Henderson to help me I dyed hundreds of yards of fabric for the costumes, which for the first time were made by professional costumiers. (Nigel was one of Rupert's talented protégés. After the war he went to the Slade, and went on to develop new techniques in photographic montage, which he has continued to exploit in his own individual way.) I also made all the costume jewellery, including Clytemnestra's torque and bracelets, and created the copper ornamentation of the fatal red carpet that was spread for Agamemnon to tread upon. I was understandably disappointed and angry when Rupert impressed me into playing one of Agamemnon's attendant soldiers 'to swell a progress, start a scene or two', and thereby deprived me of the opportunity to relax after my labours and enjoy from the front of the house the spectacular choreography of the drama's memorable ceremonies.

Louis's own play *Out of the Picture*, about the problems facing a dilettante artist in the social and political atmosphere of the thirties, and for which Britten again provided the music, unfortunately never got beyond two performances at the Westminster Theatre in the following year. It was written with characteristic freshness and originality, but it ran rather close to the Auden–Isherwood model and, for that reason perhaps, was not taken as seriously as it might have been. It deserved a better critical fate than the oblivion to which it has been consigned.

It was inevitable that Stephen Spender should become involved with the Group, and although his play for us was a long time coming (not surprisingly, given Stephen's extraordinary range of activities in the mid-thirties), he was an active member from 1933, even at times taking the chair at the rather chaotic meetings in Great Newport Street. (That was before we were brought to procedural order by Jack Beddington, who as Publicity Director of Shell-Mex was responsible for many important poster commissions, and created the imperishable catch phrase, 'You can be sure of Shell'.)

The Trial of a Judge was the most consistently poetic drama that we presented. Its theme of the crisis of the liberal conscience in the face of Fascism—a crisis in which we were all deeply implicated—unfolded with classical formality. Unlike the Auden–Isherwood plays its structure was symphonic rather than episodic, and its end was implicit in its beginning. Its deeply felt rhetoric expressed its author's scrupulous searching of his conscience, and if it ultimately failed as a play this was not so much the outcome of weaknesses in the dramatic construction (as was the case with *The Ascent of F6* and *On the Frontier*) as of a certain aural monotony, as if Stephen found it difficult to hear any voice other than his own.

By the time it was ready, in early 1938, much water had flowed under the bridge. The Westminster Theatre was no longer readily available to us, and to ensure a proper run we arranged with Unity Theatre that it should be presented at their converted chapel in Somerstown. This arrangement seems after the event to have confused a number of historians of the thirties, who have wrongly assumed that we were in opposing camps. This misreading of the situation is understandable. Unity was far more directly political than the Group—but in truth our territories lay side by side, and the rivalry between us was due to an overlap of interests, rather than an opposition of aims, different as they may have been. Certainly Unity could provide us with a politically committed audience, and we in turn could provide them with a prestigious production of a play with a declared political stance.

It was for this production that John Piper made his début as a stage designer. Being more of a non-figurative than representational artist at that time he was better suited than I was to provide the abstract architectural settings that Stephen's play required. The beginnings on *The Trial of a Judge*, however, were typically makeshift; once designed and built, the set itself had to be painted, and this we did together, for over a week, in the cramped and dungeon-like basement of the Phoenix Theatre. I think this aspect of our productions, of doing everything for ourselves, was extremely useful to him. Of his later work with Britten John wrote: '. . . the old principles (or, anyway, theories) of the pre-war Group Theatre—a united front by all participants from first note on paper to first night—still operated' and that he tried 'in each case to relate the designs to [his] own immediate practice as a painter as well as fulfil the composer's and producer's demands. . . .'

I had intended this chapter to be a personal history, but it has, perhaps inevitably, taken on something of a documentary character. There have been other accounts of the Group Theatre and there will no doubt be more, for the Group occupies an honourable place in the history of the British theatre. It was quintessentially a 'thirties' phenomenon, as well as being the prototype of a great many other minority theatres; a brave enterprise in lean times. It had high ideals perhaps most clearly expressed by Wystan Auden in the first number of the *Group Theatre Paper* in June 1936:

> Art is of secondary importance compared with the basic needs of Hunger and Love, but it is not therefore necessarily a dispensable luxury. Its power to deepen understanding, to enlarge sympathy, to strengthen the will to action and last but not least, to entertain, give it an honourable function in a community. . . . Experiments

> have to be made, and truth and error in their making. An experimental theatre ought to be regarded as as normal and useful a feature of modern life as an experimental laboratory. In both cases not every experiment will be a success; that should neither be expected nor desired, for much is learned from failure; but, in its successes important avenues of development may be opened out, which would not otherwise have been noticed.

It was above all an exciting time. Not only did we all feel that we were doing something revolutionary and important, but we had great fun. That Rupert managed to sustain, in spite of personal problems and disagreements, the integrity of the enterprise, was largely due to his intuitive ability to do the right thing at the right time. For me it was also a formative period, in spite of the fact that our joint creative activities meant that painting took second place for a while: a time when I came to recognize standards and principles in a life of art that I have lived by ever since.

10 Time out of Joint: the Group Theatre Post-War

At the time of the Munich crisis I was painting the Old Vic Safety Curtain with a decoration showing Emma Cons and Lilian Baylis (with dogs, of course) seated on one side, watching scene-changers at work, while various Shakespearian characters moved across the stage. The commission had been won in an open competition judged by, amongst others, Winston Churchill and Kenneth Clark, a success that had been as much to do with the aptness of the subject-matter to the commission as to any intrinsic artistic merit, about which there is no need for comment, as the curtain was soon to be destroyed by enemy action. These were strange days, during which we waited on what was universally felt to be an ineluctable fate, but what it was and when it would happen nobody could know. A few months later in June 1939 *The Ascent of F6* was successfully revived at the Old Vic (a production in which Alec Guinness was better cast as Ransom than the original creator of the part, William Devlin). Nothing could dispel the tension of waiting, however, and the departure of Wystan and Christopher for America now seemed a perfectly natural event of little consequence to our future.

When the war came it was to drive a wedge between everything that happened before and after. For Rupert and me it meant that our lives, hitherto conjoined, were drastically separated: for over four years I was to be far away in the Middle East, and when I returned things had irrevocably changed.

Rupert remained in London for the duration, having already begun a third new career, as a teacher. The Group Theatre funds, such as they were—a mere eight hundred pounds—after having been carried about in the back pocket of my trousers for some months, were finally invested, to be redeemed at such a time as the Group Theatre should be revived, and then only at the discretion of John Moody and Rupert. The funds, thus frozen, were to remain untouched for ten years, and the mixed fortunes of the Group Theatre ideal in that period and after are the subject of this short chapter.

In the autumn of 1939 during those last painful months before the outbreak of war threw everything into the melting pot, Rupert was asked by Mrs Eva Hubback to set up a theatre school at Morley College which was then as now a non-vocational college for adults pursuing part-time evening courses. At Morley a thriving music school, started by Gustav Holst and now run by Michael Tippett, was already in existence and the idea was to establish an equally vital theatre school. The project was well suited to Rupert's talents, and as he was not prepared to lower his artistic standards wherever and with whomever he worked, it came about that he created there an exceptional school for amateurs. He put a great deal of his heart into this work and among the professional artists who worked with him there over the years were Helen Gleadow, Nicholas Georgiadis, Anthony Milner, Stephen Dodgson and Louis MacNeice.

During the war the outstanding productions were of Purcell's *Dido and Aeneas* and a revival of Louis MacNeice's *Agamemnon*. Anticipating the revival of the Group Theatre, in 1949 he produced a remarkable *Dr Faustus*. But when the war was over he naturally looked to revive the Group Theatre in some form or other as circumstances might provide.

What looked like the first opportunity occurred in 1945 when it was suggested that Morley College Theatre School should amalgamate with a revivified Old Vic Theatre School and Studio Theatre to form a new unit under Rupert's direction. The war had put an end to the activities of the Old Vic School and the governors were uncertain of its future viability. There was a close historical link between the two institutions as they had been formed under the same charter; indeed, the first classes of Morley College had been held under the stage at the Old Vic. The proposals for a merger came to nothing in spite of the active interest of T. S. Eliot, Edith Evans and Nevill Coghill among others: but not before Rupert had drafted a characteristically ambitious discussion document, which stated that the 'policy shall be pursued to associate the organization with serious writers, composers and painters, and might be described as theatrical centre and workshop'. Such a centre would have provided for the first time a secure institutional base for Rupert to operate from, and one in keeping not only with the Group as it had been but also with the classical traditions of the ballet he had grown up in, in which the teacher, the *maître de ballet*, was also the creative producer and choreographer, and with the ideas of Gordon Craig and Stanislavsky, which after Diaghilev had been the principal influences upon him. Such a centre, coming immediately after the cessation of hostilities, could have had a positive influence on post-war theatre in Britain, which as a result of the folding, in 1940, of Michel Saint-Denis's seminal London Theatre had been left without a focal point for theatrical experiment.

The Group Theatre was finally reconstituted in 1950, largely through the energetic motivation of Véra Lindsay, one of the Group's earliest supporters, who had acted in its productions in the thirties before joining Michel Saint-Denis at the London Theatre Studio, in the formation of which she had played a vital—and largely unrecorded—part. Married now to Gerald Barry who was already deeply immersed in preparation for the Festival of Britain, Véra was well placed to organize a venture that would have to call upon the goodwill of people in disparate artistic spheres. Careful groundwork was done because it was felt necessary that if the Group Theatre was at last to rise again it must appear, fully armed, like Pallas Athene from the brow of Zeus, shining with the most influential and impeccable sponsorship. Its return was officially announced on 5 May 1950 at a party given by the artistic directors, Véra and Rupert, and the literary, musical and artistic advisers—an impressive list that included T. S. Eliot, Herbert Read (of whom it was observed that he was always present at the *beginning* of any new movement), Graham Greene, Lennox Berkeley, John Piper, and, from the New Theatre, Donald Albery, who, with Basil Burton, was Executive Director. In a manifesto calling for new membership published for this event, under the heading *Aims and Policy* was stated:

> The Aim of the Group Theatre, now as before, is the production of contemporary plays in a contemporary form. . . . Although run by

> artists, musicians, actors and producers as well as playwrights, its main preoccupation must always be to give the playwright and the actor the opportunity for experiment and the development of new forms.

To this was added a statement by T. S. Eliot quoted from a letter he had written to Rupert in reply to a draft manifesto sent for his comment:

> What I hope we shall eventually get is not one great dramatist, a solitary peak in a flat plain, but a cluster of dramatists. That would be a real dramatic renaissance. I regard our work today as that of the first generation only: my greatest hope is that we shall lay some foundation upon which others may come to build. The process is one of training and development of BOTH dramatists and audiences—and, I might add, of actors also—in which authors will teach audiences, and audiences will teach authors.

A statement which vividly demonstrated how closely sympathetic Eliot was to the original spirit of the Group. The members were to be given three Sunday productions a year of new plays and there was also to be some sort of association with the Institute of Contemporary Arts, recently established in Dover Street. There was, significantly, no mention of what plays the Group would actually perform. The only script left available from the old days was the Stephen Spender–Goronwy Rees translation of Büchner's *Dance of Death* which had been rejected as too problematic and unsuitable for an opening production.

In the event, the first production was to be a far cry from the intentions so proudly reaffirmed in the manifesto. The Group was invited by the Festival of Britain Committee to provide a programme for the opening of the bijou theatre in the Battersea Park Festival Pleasure Gardens, and a ballet based upon the popular stories of Orlando the marmalade cat, called *Orlando's Wedding*, was commissioned from Kathleen Hale, which was produced by André Howard to music by Arthur Benjamin. This was apt to the occasion and extremely charmingly done, but hardly likely to initiate 'a dramatic renaissance'. It provided publicity however, and presumably bolstered the exchequer, though I felt that it was an ominous sign of the difficulties that the new Group Theatre Productions Limited might have to face now that it was no longer part of a vital movement.

The next production, this time in line with our purpose and principles, and fulfilling our obligations to the members, was for a Sunday evening performance at the New Theatre (now the Albery), on 25 November 1951, of *The Flies* by Sartre, which had never been performed in this country, and which was the kind of play that would not be tackled by commercial managements. It also provided a suitable vehicle for Rupert's professional return. The settings were strongly and simply designed by S. John Woods, and featured two over-life-size statues of Zeus and Apollo provided by Bernard Meadows, and made by Bob Clatworthy and Elizabeth Frink at the Chelsea School of Art. The costumes were by Jocelyn Herbert, and the music supervised by Alan Rawsthorne. In spite of the logistical difficulties—there were two choruses (provided by the Morley College Theatre School) and a huge cast led by Yvonne Mitchell as Electra—the production reached a level quite unexpected of a Sunday evening performance and was enthusiastically received. Reviewing it in *Picture Post*, Denis Sidney wrote:

> Twelve curtain calls, we said. Maybe it was eleven? The Group Theatre, and everyone concerned, deserved it, in any event. No one was paid a penny, no one made a penny out of this Sunday night. And a thousand people who love the theatre got an evening of real theatrical excitement, and an equally splendid thing—something to argue about.

Sadly, though it did not mark the end of hopes, *The Flies* was to prove the last significant production of the Group Theatre. It was not so much a shortage of money that prevented an immediate exploitation of the interest that *The Flies* had created—although the costs of a Sunday production had mounted astronomically since pre-war days—but a shortage of new plays, and the only projects that met the quality sought for were translations of Brecht's *Mother Courage* and (by Wystan) of Cocteau's *Knights of the Round Table.* There were also adaptations, like that of Graham Greene's *The Power and the Glory*. All of these would have been extremely exciting to do, but they were beyond our powers without financial or commercial backing. Eliot's 'cluster of dramatists' never emerged. Perhaps we had proposed more than it was possible to fulfil. Perhaps the revival had been conceived on too grand a scale for a time not yet ripe. Or maybe, like other avant-garde movements, it had served its purpose in its time, and belonged to its moment. Anyway, the delays and indecisions served to point the differences between the ambitions and attitudes of the artistic directors. It might have been thought with some justification that Véra's artistic understanding and energetic management were exactly what was required if a revival of the Group Theatre, which no longer had the unique advantages it had enjoyed in the thirties, was to succeed in a competitive post-war climate. A new generation of producers were pushing against the door, and they would have to be admitted. Véra, who saw the situation clearly, was right to insist that as a matter of survival the Group Theatre would have to become a production company, albeit of a special kind. It would maintain its ideals of course, but it must nevertheless become part of the management system. But for Rupert the Group Theatre had been created and organized as a vehicle for his own expression as an artist working with artists. There was no longer a company or group of actors to train and work with and not surprisingly he felt displaced and threatened.

Inexorably, as some had foreseen from the beginning of the project, the conflict between Rupert and Véra brought Group Theatre Productions Limited to an end. The hampers were packed, to be left undisturbed in the attic of our house in Wimbledon until after Rupert's death in 1966. Unpacking them then I found the unfinished costumes designed by Isobel Lambert for the production that never was of Kathleen Raine's translation of Calderón's *Life's a Dream*, for which Elizabeth Frink, under my direction, had designed the settings, and for which the music was to have been by Alan Rawsthorne.

The impetus of the Group's influence, however, had not finally been expended: the ideas expressed in the 1950 Manifesto were taken over without acknowledgement by George Devine when he launched his 'Writers' Theatre' at the Royal Court in 1956.

This chapter would be incomplete if it did not mention the final reprise of the Group at the Globe Theatre on 24 January 1954. This was the memorial *Homage to Dylan Thomas*, who had died the previous November. The concert, which was sponsored by *The Sunday Times*, was devised by Rupert with Louis MacNeice and Véra Lindsay, and Louis wrote a special 'Requiem Canto' for the occasion. Edith Sitwell wrote a tribute which was read by Edith Evans. It was notable for the splendid drop-cloth designed by Ceri Richards, using the *memento-mori* motives of the heron, the owl and the flowering skull that were to recur again and again in his later work; and for Elizabeth Lutyens's settings of several poems which were sung by Hedli Anderson. Hugh Griffith and Richard Burton read, and Emlyn Williams superbly recited from memory Dylan's short story 'A Visit to Grandpa's'. The programme also included a live performance of extracts from *Under Milk Wood*, which was to be broadcast the following night for the first time. After the performance a supper party was given at the Hyde Park Hotel by Lionel and Isobel Berry to which everybody involved was invited, and at which the spirit of the dead poet in his most anarchic mood, ably abetted by Caitlin, predictably dispelled the formality of the celebration, somewhat to the embarrassment of our hosts.

11 A Cairo War: the Desert and the Sown

Speculation on what might have been had I awaited the call-up instead of volunteering is a waste of time; but had I remained in England instead of being sent to Cairo and the Middle East, I would have missed a turning-point. The fateful decision to write to the War Office offering my services as a camouflage officer was made after a meeting that Rupert and I had with Leigh Ashton, who was at the Ministry of Information. Looking out from the windows of his office, in the Senate House in Malet Street, on to the familiar backs of the houses in Gower Street, we discussed the available options. The British Army in France was being relentlessly pushed towards Dunkirk and the evacuation. Leigh suggested that Camouflage used artists and that I could apply for either the civil branch or the military. We learned to our surprise that the colonel in charge of Army Camouflage was the brother of our old friend Jack Beddington. To Colonel Frank Beddington we accordingly wrote and thus it was I eventually found myself, during the first week in January 1941, joining the largest convoy of reinforcements yet to sail for Egypt, in company with six other junior camouflage officers newly hatched from Farnham. We boarded the *Samaria* at the dead of night, with two thousand troops, and were confined in great secrecy below deck until the convoy was well under way. Hardly aware except by engine noise that we had started to move, we saw nothing until we discovered, to our astonishment, off the coast of Ireland, that we were part of a convoy of dozens of similar vessels, ringed as far as the eye could see by battleships (*Barham* and

Malaya), lesser cruisers and innumerable destroyers, and above us an umbrella of aircraft. There was no doubt about our importance.

It was as we approached Port Said, after a voyage that had lasted two months, that I found myself thinking of the personal implications of these events. How destructive to my relationship with Rupert might this war prove? The continuation of his career had been guaranteed by the Theatre School at Morley College. My career, however, had been more seriously disrupted. Chelsea School of Art had been closed, and by necessity I found myself earning three pounds a week with the Finsbury ARP during the quiet opening stages of the war. Several small pictures I had made of the First Aid Station off the Goswell Road were liked enough by Kenneth Clark for him to have bought them, and commission me as an official war artist for ARP. What seemed like a rescue from the boredom of the home front in the phoney war proved to be a mistake. The official pictures I painted lacked the freshness and originality of those that had led to the commission and I withdrew from the project. Now my sense of a personal debt to France combined with the necessity to make a living: I joined up, and the observer became a participant.

Behind all this lay deeper levels of feeling scarcely admitted into consciousness. Until the Group Theatre had claimed so much of my attention, Rupert Doone, the dancer, had not been habitually identified with Robert Medley, the painter, and in spite of the achievement of our combined energies in the making of the Group, I had come to have reservations about its effect upon my own personal ambition. The outbreak of war disrupted what might have become an irksome pattern, for I was beginning to feel that such a close association as ours had become might not ultimately be good for either of us; and that Rupert's growing dependence on me could act only to his professional and personal disadvantage.

At the time of the fall of France the war in Egypt had been forgotten, and when the letter arrived announcing my posting to GHQ Middle East Forces in Cairo we were both caught unprepared. My scarcely admitted wish that circumstances might intervene to make a break, albeit temporary, was fulfilled in a way I had hardly anticipated. Rupert, sensing as much, accused me of wanting to leave him. I could not absolutely deny the truth of this.

During the voyage it had been possible to avoid introspective enquiry, but as we lay off Port Said, motionless and awaiting disembarkation, the confusion of motives behind my actions rose to the surface, and after a while I was troubled by these reflections. Then, after a day of shimmering heat, a cooler evening breeze ruffled the mirror of the apparently tideless waters. A soldier standing next to me, leaning against the railings of the main deck and gazing at the dusty and barren hills opposite, gave vent to a common feeling—what on earth am I doing here?—by loudly announcing to nobody but himself, 'The white cliffs of Dover browned off!' and abruptly went below. At that moment, however, I was not feeling quite that way. The mountains, the colour of dusky moths' wings, changing to spectacular rose and violet, became an invitation. The sun set swiftly, and in the sky, now a deep and silent indigo, the stars came out. Conscious of being alone, and like a shipwrecked sailor responsible for my own fate, I experienced the elation of solitude, and looked forward to the adventure of the unknown.

On 1 March 1941 we docked in Port Tewfik, which is on the bank of the Suez Canal as it enters the Red Sea, and three days later we finally reached Cairo, exactly two months to the day after leaving Farnham. Temporary accommodation had been found at the Continental Hotel (second only to Shepherd's): from my own room I looked across the Ezebekiah Gardens towards the old city. There was a great deal of noise and bustle; strange smells, multitudes of people, clanging trams and camels crowded my first impressions of Cairo. Outside, taxis and dilapidated carriages (*gharries*) waited for custom. Spruced up, brass buttons shining on our tropical khaki drill (Alkits or Moss Bros), swagger sticks tucked under our arms, we presented ourselves at GHQ looking like a troupe of supers from an operetta. Spotted at once as new arrivals from London, we were treated as if we had just dropped in for the day. Somebody, however, took pity and directed us to Major Barkas's small office. Barkas who, for a week, had been anxiously awaiting our arrival, welcomed us warmly. Barkas himself had arrived, with Captains Ayrton and Hutton (the mural designer and decorator who later engraved glass for Coventry Cathedral), only in January and too late to take part in Wavell's advance into Libya—and there were, therefore, no camouflage officers with Western Desert Forces. Ayrton had gone off to round up Italians on the borders of Abyssinia, and Hutton, desperately in need of assistance, was coping with the docks and military installations in Alexandria. The general situation was not too good: the Germans were entering Greece which put the whole of the Levant at risk, and Wavell had been compelled to withdraw towards Tobruk. The troops as a whole had a poor appreciation of camouflage, and we would have a hard task. Barkas explained that his job at GHQ was to build up an organization in support of those in the field, and that our responsibility to GHQ was to keep him fully informed of our needs. With the theatre of war now spreading from Egypt to Greece, Crete, Cyprus and the Levant it is not surprising that he had been impatient for our arrival.

After a ten-day introductory course my Farnham companions were dispersed to various fields of action. There were to be no adventures, no risks for me; I was not to be tempered in the fire of battle; I was to be at GHQ. Thus it was that when Rupert was bombed out of our home in Islington I was perspiring at an office desk in a claustrophobic city that I had decided I hated. Struggling to overcome my initial incapability and to be of some use, I perceived that Barkas, a most lovable and admirable man, was in any case impatient of recognized staff procedures. We worked for long hours and without let up for three months before I had a full day off. At the end of each day, too tired to make the effort of conversation with fellow staff officers for whom I felt little sympathy, I simply fell into my bed.

One morning, as with ink-stained fingers I was endeavouring to draft yet another letter, and Barkas was banging out yet another memorandum, for he always thought very loudly at his typewriter, a young captain arrived from Wavell's office with a 'top-secret' and personal note from the Commander-in-Chief himself. It contained, together with rough pencil sketches, the suggestion that tanks might be made to look like lorries by adding some kind of lightweight superstructure. Could the superstructure be made to fall apart at the last moment before going into action? The lion disguised as a sheep! The General had provided the cue for which Barkas had been waiting and he kicked himself for not having thought of it himself. Under conditions of great secrecy, with the code name 'Sunshields', the General's proposals were worked out in detail in the engineering workshops.

Barkas seized on the possibilities that this opened up with characteristic energy and imagination. Reports from Tobruk and the Western Desert Forces had already suggested that a large part of the future for camouflage in the desert lay in misleading display rather than in concealment, which was practically impossible. From tanks as lorries why not *lorries* disguised as sunshields? The possibilities of deception seemed endless! It was clear that G(Cam) at GHQ could no longer function as an obscure sub-branch of another department. It must be given a position of its own and direct communication with Operations. It would need workshops for experiment as well as facture, and companies trained to maintain specialized decoys.

At this precise moment, in April 1941, an unfortunate brigadier charged with the reorganization of GHQ to deal with the problems of a rapidly growing army, and who knew nothing of 'Sunshields', transferred us to Military Training as MT3. Enraged by this disastrous setback Barkas exclaimed (and in the circumstances meant it), 'Well, Robert, you had better start learning Urdu—the Indian troops will need lectures!' The situation was saved by the unexpected appearance of Captain Ayrton who had managed to get a flight back from the borders of Abyssinia, where his job had come to an end. Tall, lean and sunburned, he gave the impression of an ascetic and humorous scholar. He was 31 years old and wore small metal-framed spectacles.

Tony Ayrton, who was a sensitive though modestly gifted artist, proved to be the perfect person to relieve the normally ebullient Barkas of some of the burdens of a crisis that might have put G(Cam) permanently up a blind alley. Unlike Barkas, who found the GHQ game hard to play, Tony was always cool and efficient, and thoroughly enjoyed the fun of it. Barkas provided the drive and Tony the wit. For me also he was a blessing, for I was able to relax with somebody who spoke the same language. At last I was able to look around and simply see where I was. Did I, after all, hate being in Cairo *that* much?

Certainly Cairo was not an easy city to come to terms with. Confined by the official British and military circuit to selected quarters and to the international tourist centre of the modern city with its banks, business houses, and shops strayed from Piccadilly, Bond Street, and the rue de Rivoli, it had not been immediately apparent that Cairo was the largest and greatest Muslim city in Africa. I had not yet discovered that it was possible to walk straight into the Eastern Desert from the walls of Saladin's twelfth-century Citadel and contemplate the Pyramids of Giza, eight miles distant on the escarpment that held back the sands of the Libyan Desert from the green and fertile strip of the Nile. The river itself was flecked always by the white wings of feluccas—surely the most beautiful boats ever to sail. The sharp division of the desert from the sown land—a contrast as dramatic as that of placing a narrow band of emerald upon a limitless field of pale ochre—was emblematic of the contrasts between poverty and riches in the city below, and of the traditional Arab way of life which countenanced great wealth amongst great poverty, for there were two classes only: masters and servants. There had been no stable professional and middle class until Muhammad Ali had begun the process of westernization, in the aftermath of the Napoleonic wars, little more than a hundred years ago; and this class still remained largely of European origin or of European education.

The British Army habit of referring to anybody in a jellaba and wearing a fez as a 'Wog' quickly struck me as an insulting discourtesy to a people who had not invited us to defend them, and who would much rather that we were not in the country at all.

By no means all British soldiers behaved insensitively to their surroundings. There was, for example, Sergeant Nolan. He was a 19-year-old corporal in the G(Cam) office when I arrived and though he rose to the rank of sergeant he never stirred from the Cairo office until I signed his demobilization papers in 1945. Young, healthy and fine looking—his features, taken alone, would have made him a likely casting for *L'après-midi d'un faune*—he was obviously intelligent and sympathetic and, as I discovered, exceedingly discreet. As he was about to leave finally for home I felt I must ask how he had managed to spend all that time in one office and never get out. (Though Liverpool-Irish he had never given a sign of wildness—though some mornings he had looked a bit red around the eyes.) He confessed that it had been his habit to break out of the barracks at night and, disguised in jellaba and fez, spend his time with Egyptian friends from whom he had learned to speak Egyptian Arabic as fluently as anyone can (the pronunciation is extremely difficult). This is how he had passed the duration. I was so struck with admiration that I refrained from asking the obvious question, 'What did you *do* with your Egyptian friends?' Years later I was patiently waiting in the queue for a taxi at King's Cross Station when there was a tap on my shoulder. Turning round I came face to face with a large and hirsute policeman. 'Major Medley, I presume? Corporal Nolan!' As he improperly hailed a taxi-cab in advance of other patient citizens, I asked myself the inevitable question: what mystery was now hidden beneath the parental corpulence of a married railway police sergeant?

Shortly after Tony Ayrton's, a further welcome arrival was that of Edward Bawden, also from Abyssinia, who was travelling as an official war artist. Edward's idea of the war was that of the single-minded artist, namely, to have as little to do with it as possible. He had found his subject-matter amongst the native tents and villages, and had arrived, unannounced, in the company of a young Sudanese servant and driver to whom he had become attached. Unfortunately Edward had not realized the elementary importance of the military document, and that this devoted young man would have no acknowledged existence at all without a piece of paper. Lacking an official movement order he hadn't even been able to get past the sergeant at the gates of the transit camp and had spent the night on the floor at Edward's hotel. When they were separated shortly afterwards, and the driver returned to Khartoum, Edward was saddened to lose a trusted companion. The independence of Edward's spirit in the conformist atmosphere of military life was very refreshing. Having known each other previously as acquaintances, we became, for two or three weeks, intimate friends. I found Edward's a complex character, rather like that of a cat which will approach closely but proudly maintain its separateness. I could never make out how far his shy reserve was natural, how far cultivated to protect his essential privacy. His apparent helplessness disguised a sharp mind and a strong will. While in Cairo, Edward made some finely characteristic drawings of the Citadel and the Muhammad Ali Mosque from the roof of the officer's mess. (Some of these are now in the Tate Gallery.) Before he departed we exchanged books and from Edward I received the *Oxford Scottish Ballads* (as romantic and rigorous as the donor) which kept me good company until in 1944 I gave it, in turn, to a Scots paratroop in Cyprus.

For many, Egypt was simply hot, dirty and disorientating, and the desert hostile. You either liked it or you did not. If you did, the desert could become an addiction. To be in the desert is to be lost in a landscape of the imagination. There are no destinations—only points of the compass and map references. The experience appealed to the adventurous and the navigator, and encouraged the romantic and the amateur. Some came out to play at being Lawrence of Arabia; others 'to keep up standards', spit and polish, and dinner at eight. The influence of such romanticism extended to the diverse liberties that were taken to adapt army uniforms to personal tastes, and which gave the Army in the Middle East its particular and unique style. Starched and strangling collars gave way to open necks, fly whisks dangled from wrists and soft suede replaced leather. The heights of eccentric dandyism were reached by the country-house corsairs of the 'Long-Range Desert Group', a law unto themselves, who marauded far behind enemy lines, and affected free-flowing scarves and a richly various headgear. This sartorial freedom flourished in the warmth of the Levantine air as the months passed towards August 1942, when, at El Alamein, the embattled armies faced each other across fixed lines, there was no possibility of encirclement, and the slogging began in earnest.

The fatal attraction of Egypt and the Nile is that it encourages extremes of behaviour: the first Antony was lost when he stepped on to Cleopatra's barge; the second Antony, the coenobite, endured his famous temptations in a hole in the desert not far from the walls of Alexandria and the pollutions of luxury from which he had fled. I was neither libertine nor saint when I went to Egypt. Although no ascetic, I had never been promiscuous; indeed I was surprisingly innocent for my age. It was ignorance as much as scruple that had inhibited me sexually until my enforced sojourn in the notoriously liberating airs of the Nile Valley. Thus it was that the war and the exigent requirements of desert camouflage brought the blessings of an increased knowledge of desire and the variety of its possible consummations. Before applying Occam's razor to confessions improper to a memoir I must say this: that it was from the commonplace promiscuity of wartime in a foreign place, in which affection, curiosity and lust all played their part, that I date the capacity for the freer and more sensuous handling of paint which characterizes my post-war paintings, and which is in marked contrast to the puritanical and English dryness of my earlier work.

That was an outcome to be appreciated in the future. In the meantime my nocturnal enjoyment of Cavafian delights had its dark and dangerous side—what night journey has not? A Faustian tug-of-war between the Good Angel and the Bad Angel set up a need within me for some creative activity 'wherewith to distract the mind'. In a poem I wrote called 'Egypt' (which John Lehmann published in *Penguin New Writing*) this deep-seated psychic conflict within found expression in a contrast between the 'false paradise' of Cairo and Alexandria and the reality of the desert 'where the flesh is fined down on the bone/by the love of sand for thin bodies'.

Before he went to the Eighth Army (the post-Wavell name for Western Desert Forces) Tony Ayrton had given me his immaculately kept box of paints and brushes. I could not use this for fear of dirtying it up and of spreading paint all over the *pension* bedroom floor, and more seriously because painting for me was a whole-time, messy, and totally absorbing business. The possibility of practising art as I understood it seemed far away, in another time and another country. Though I made a number of notes and water-colour drawings these have always remained outside the canon, uncharacteristic of my work. After the hours in the office I found it impossible to make the move into a purely visual world. I took to writing short stories and poems, and began the impossible task of putting into English favourite fragments of Baudelaire, a magnificently time-consuming project involving a pile of French dictionaries and great quantities of Egyptian brandy.

Until Churchill's dismissal of General Wavell, after the débâcle in Greece, the morale of the Western Desert Forces was high. In spite of the retreat from Benghazi, Tobruk was still in our hands and no Germans had yet crossed the border from Libya into Egypt. Wavell had had bad luck, but he had offered the troops their first taste of success and given the chance, under his command, they would do it again. They were therefore shocked by the sacking of Wavell and when 'Western Desert Forces' was renamed 'Eighth Army' they felt that they had lost an identity they were proud of. The fact that the 'Forces' were now to be an 'Army' scarcely satisfied the old hands.

The new Eighth Army got off to a confused start and was later to suffer a lack of decisive leadership. The rapid enlargement of the army in the field combined with the strategic importance of the Levant inevitably induced the fear that communication between those in the field and GHQ, in Cairo, might suffer. It was understandable that those men now fighting in the desert should blame those safely tucked away in the fleshpots of Cairo when things went badly for them. And indeed it was at the very worst moment in 1942, during the dark and anxious days when Auchinleck was holding back the German advance to within sixty miles of Alexandria at El Alamein, that Amy Smart (a painter who had studied in Paris where she had known Bérard and Tchelitchev), who was the wife of the Oriental Secretary at the Embassy, using her influence with the Abdin Palace, organized a midnight picnic to Shubra. This imaginative gesture of defiance was carried out in the grand manner, although it was a small party that packed into three open cars and set out accompanied by Amy's white-robed servants. The palace at Shubra, built by Muhammad Ali in 1811, stands in the centre of a royal *domaine*, a few miles north of Cairo, on the banks of the Nile. Turning off the main road at the broken-down old gateway we were directed to a rough track and bumped along, our throats choked with dust, between open fields, a scattering of mud-brick 'fellahin' cottages and palm trees whose fronds clattered in the light breeze of night. At length a dark silhouette loomed up in the distance and our flagging spirits revived. Shortly afterwards we came to a halt. Our darkened headlights scarcely illuminated an elegant portico set into the high retaining walls of the private enclosure. Here we were met by two armed guards, and an old man with a lantern, who had been expecting us. A large key was produced and the wooden doors unlocked. We skirted the banks of a lake, whose silent waters, now undisturbed by its old fountain, reflected the moon. Across its surface scurrying insects made silver threads. We arrived at the pavilion on the far side which was now provided with a few oil lamps. The old man showed us into a large and ornately gilded chamber, with an elaborately painted ceiling, which was still kept up for occasional receptions. Everywhere else was neglect. We finally reached the deserted private quarters of Muhammad Ali's harem and the cloister opened to the sky, surrounded by slender moonlit columns that supported the carved plaster vaults beneath which we were to dine. While the servants were preparing the feast on the marble dais of one of the four alcoves that closed the corners of this enchanting courtyard, and lighting the candles in the glass candelabra we had brought with us, we explored the adjoining chambers once used by concubines and eunuchs, and which now housed nothing but dusty wooden packing cases, old iron bedsteads and cast-out rubbish. The setting was strange and magical as a dream. The silence of the desert night outside was occasionally broken by the wild shriek, like that of a disembodied harlequin, of the Abyssinian curlew; within the court, beneath the visiting moon, in the light of flickering candles we danced to the music of Poulenc and Honegger, played on a portable gramophone. For a few hours the war did not exist; and yet such a ball could have happened only at such a moment, never to be repeated. My memories of that extraordinary interlude are touched by an added poignancy, for not longer after, Tony Ayrton, who was of the party that danced at Shubra, became sick and died. A few days later, Monty opened his famous battle with a barrage that could be heard in Cairo, and made Alexandria tremble. The war did exist, and we in Cairo were very much in the centre of it for those long months preceding El Alamein; the diurnal realities were of constant troop movements, as a continuous flow of reinforcements for the Eighth Army passed through the city.

At the end of 1941 my own ardent desire to join the Eighth Army was fulfilled and I left Cairo to join the Armoured Division of 30 Corps during the opening days of Cunningham's offensive in the Western Desert. Always slightly prone to claustrophobia, I was relieved to get out into the air and space of the desert. It seems impossible to convey the attraction of a limitless amount of sand and scrub and a landscape without identifiable landmarks on which to focus. At times, when under a sky of passing clouds or when the sun casts continuous waves of purple shadows across its surface, the desert can take on the appearance of the rolling hilltops of an endless grouse moor. All sense of altitude is lost, and there is no sense of place or home. For the few moments of dawn, when the eastern sky is lit with an astonishing spectrum of clear colours from lemon yellow to pale emerald, and the great sun rising swiftly flares into a flinty orange fire which melts the night, and rakes the earth with long shadows, there exists a brief consolation of time and place. This is repeated when the sun sinks below the western horizon in a blaze of copper and crimson, but between its rising and its setting the vertical sun, useless as a guide, becomes an enemy, and there seems no tangible reality beyond the sand at one's feet. This unaccustomed phenomenon upsets the normal Euclidean geometry of our perceptions. Space is no longer tangible, but an enveloping nothingness from an infinity, a deprivation of the sensual. And when the *khamsin* sandstorm, sweet and sickly-smelling and denser than any fog, comes, it blots out everything—eyes, mouth, nose and ears shut against its smothering sting.

Using only the narrow coastal strip of an immensity that spreads into and across the northern hemisphere of Africa, the opposing armies, even then, did not destroy the essential hostility of the desert to human life. They could not subdue it, but the thousands of men who invaded it with their vehicles and engines broke the fragile skin of the desert and created their own sandstorms. Railtracks appeared, and pipelines for water; petrol cans by the million littered the sand; encampments and wreckage and minefields pocked its surface. And in spite of all this it was still possible to get lost.

The winter offensive of 1941–2 meant a wide disposal of the Army over the Western Desert. My first real task in the field was to assist Captain Stephen Sykes in work on a decoy line that had been laid to distract enemy attention from the railway supply line to those in the South. This ran to what was to be enticingly baited as a tank delivery point. Here indeed my instinct for an effective *mise-en-scène* was deeply satisfied by the set created by Stephen Sykes. Inspired improvisation with two small camouflage units (also reminiscent of Group Theatre days) gave the appearance of a fully operational supply point; and when the performance began and the German bombers arrived to play their part I was highly delighted. The essential importance of the project lay in its use as a dress rehearsal for the infinitely larger role camouflage was to play, a year later, in the counter-plan at El Alamein. Shortly after this I joined a detachment of the Armoured Division of 30 Corps who were lying in one of the southern positions and waiting to be called forward. Here I found myself a bit of an odd fish in the company of the gay (in the old-fashioned sense) huzzars of a crack cavalry regiment, who when the war began had been in Palestine. The arrival of the 'artist' kept them amused; but what did I do if I was not a Munnings or a Seago? In the mess 'shop' was not allowed, and the conversation was confined to country-house huntin' and shootin' and fishin'. One young officer, who had been out on a recce, described it as 'hacking around on the old tin horse', and later confessed that on visits to London from the West Country, he had never gone further than the In and Out in Piccadilly, with the occasional foray to Piccadilly Circus. My daily job was to instruct the troopers in camouflage. When the evening came there was no slumming here, for dinner was served on a proper gold-and-blue-rimmed china service from the soup through to the dessert and the nuts. A few days later we moved forward and in their first skirmish with the enemy these truly gallant young men learned through bitter experience how far superior to ours were the Bofors guns of the German tanks, with their long range of fire. Later, I returned to Tobruk with Captain Edwin Galligan, an old Farnham hand (who after the war joined me at Chelsea School of Art, where he taught design). There we passed through the terrain—called Knightsbridge—where under the cover of dense clouds of dust our army had fought it out at close range with the German tanks, and won.

We were encamped in slit trenches which were part of the original defence lines. It began to rain, for it was February, the only month rain can be expected, and it was bitterly cold at night. Beneath the inadequate bivouac of the exiguous triangle of the issue one-man tent, I slept with every available covering piled on top of me. This did not last for long, for I had to own up to feeling distinctly unwell. My legs were raw and there were running sores. I went into Tobruk—which, understandably, I had strongly wished to see—to consult a doctor. Behind the blank and pitted façades there was no civil life, but there were plenty of army notices to this and that. The harbour was full of wrecks. Expecting the medico to provide a bit of ointment I was surprised that a serious view was taken of my condition and that I was ordered on to the next hospital ship to arrive. Thus ingloriously ended the active service that had been so eagerly anticipated on board ship at Port Tewfik a year before.

By the time we reached Alexandria I was feeling very ill. I was furious with myself, and with everybody, when with other officers who were walking cases we were greeted as we climbed aboard a waiting bus with the offensive remark 'more scum for Cairo'—a particularly nasty manifestation of class-ridden British aggressiveness. I was extremely glad to be put straight to bed at Kantara, and there I stayed for a long time as there were the complications of a thrombosis in my right thigh.

Before returning to Cairo in May I was given two weeks' sick leave in Alexandria. The first part was spent with Edwin Galligan at the Hotel Sosostris, which we had chosen because its name recalled T. S. Eliot's Madame Sosostris 'with her wicked pack of cards', and the second as the guest of Heathcote Smith and his wife at the British Consulate.

Now Edwin, a fiery Scot from Glasgow with ginger hair, and to whose original and inventive mind I owe the origins of the poem 'Egypt', was a lord of misrule. After the best part of six months in desert or hospital the time was ripe for a cathartic explosion, which was in no way hindered by the fact that his tastes were different from mine. The days were spent bathing from the beaches at Ramleh in the clear blue crystal Mediterranean that sparkled in the sunlight, and the nights in adventure. The city was filled with soldiers and sailors with leave or without, in search of the consolations of Dionysian abandon, for the distant rumblings of battle could be frequently heard. In this urgent climate, in the crowded bars and the blacked-out streets, sudden and intense relationships flared. One especially was so touching in its poetry that it lives in the memory still: two weeks later the boy was drowned. I remember his name but not that of his ship.

During the following days in the ordered calm created by the Smiths' warm hospitality, there was the relief of good talk of things other than military, and of music, for Mrs Smith was a fine pianist. This was the return to harmony after the frenetic dissonance of a Bacchic festival: for a brief moment I had known chaos, seen something of the darkness within. I knew that what had happened in Alexandria would have a profound effect upon me, not least upon my work as a painter, though I could not say what. It had been a necessary experience, in which the constraints of the individual ego had been loosened; in which the atmosphere of war, itself essentially orgiastic, and the general anonymity offered by that unique city at that extraordinary time, combined to allow a glimpse of one's own orgiastic anonymity. *Jadis, si je me souviens bien, ma vie était un festin où s'ouvraient tous les coeurs, où tous les vins coulaient. . . .*

The week at the Consulate was not without its moments of comic absurdity. Among Mrs Smith's tedious obligations was to play hostess to a regular sewing-bee for wealthy Alexandria ladies whose war effort was the hemming of slings and bandages. On one of these mornings I was pressed into service to join the ladies for coffee in the exchange and mart of gossip and chatter, and bring a fresh and unexpected masculine interest. Having never before been in a roomful of expensive Levantine ladies whose social position, as well the esteem of their husbands, was signified by the display of almost-discreet dress jewellery, it was quite an experience. I recall one of these diligent workers, engaged in the other-worldly activity—for the pile of finely stitched flannel grew but slowly—raising her shaped spectacles from the bridge of her nose with bejewelled fingers, and remarking as she gazed towards me, 'I kride so much when my husband dyte that I almost rruined my eis.'

On my return to Cairo in May I found things much changed. G(Cam), now standing on its own feet, had grown, and there was now a Camouflage School at Helwan. Barkas, now a lieutenant-colonel (GSO1), had been found a properly trained major (GSO2) so he no longer had to rely solely upon artists and designers who were novices at that kind of work. Brian Robb, who had joined us earlier, was able to join Ayrton at Eighth Army, and I resumed my old position as Captain (GSO3).

The six months from May to November 1942 were crammed with events that affected all levels of existence. The Germans might well soon encircle us by way of Persia and Iraq. And until Auchinleck won the battle of Heimeymat, south of Alamein, our ability to hold Egypt and the Delta was uncertain. There were plans for every contingency including that of carrying on the war from Port Sudan, Khartoum and Kenya. At GHQ there was a great burning of official and secret papers and a black soot, all that remained of grand and petty designs alike, filled the sky. G(Cam) was evacuated to a desert camp outside Maadi, a suburb south of the city. Then Churchill arrived, separated 'Paiforce' (Persia–Iraq) from MEF; and replaced Auchinleck with Alexander as Commander-in-Chief, and appointed Montgomery Commander-in-the-Field.

One day, Barkas handed me a 'top-secret' document scarcely a quarter-inch thick, saying, 'I don't think you are allowed to read this—it was GSO1 level only—but you will find it interesting.' It was Alexander's survey, for the War Office in London, of the situation in Egypt as he found it. It began with comments on the stability, or instability, of the Egyptian civil population under wartime stress, before proceeding to discuss the qualities of all the troops under command, not only of the British, Australian, Indian and New Zealand veterans, but of the whole army. What I found fascinating about this document was the accuracy with which he summed up the human factors which would determine the deployment of each component part of what had now become a complicated and multi-racial allied structure. It was written in plain English of the greatest brevity, the whole seasoned, for those who could read between the lines, with direct and amusing comment. The vast range of the Commander's responsibilities was unfolded in little more than an hour's reading. It was not only a model report, but a revelation of his powerful intellectual capacity. It ended with a clear-headed and honest estimate of the cost of the coming campaign in human lives (so many thousands), and the number of field hospitals that would be required for the wounded.

Alexander and Montgomery were, of course, perfectly cast for their respective roles. Monty with his flair for public performance immediately made his presence felt and everybody knew what kind of a man he was, while behind the scenes Alexander quietly held the reins.

I saw Monty only once and that was on the occasion of his sermon at the cathedral in Cairo, when he exhorted us all, several times over, to be full of 'binge'. Now we all knew what 'going out on the binge' meant but never before thought of being full of it, and this unexpected misuse of current slang suddenly revealed the innocence and other-worldly dedication in the speaker that helped to make of him a leader who knew that men as well as armaments win battles. Alexander I met twice: the first time a formality; the second when, having been shown round the school at Helwan, he found plenty of time for a discussion on painting before driving off in his staff car, the Commander-in-Chief's personal banner on the bonnet fluttering in the breeze.

Counter-operational planning (the misleading of the enemy before battle) made full use of camouflage for deception as well as concealment. The entire scope of the operation was known only to the Commander-in-Chief and Montgomery. Each department worked in ignorance of the others, for Intelligence, Signals, secret agents leaking false information and so on, were all involved. Even in our own organization only Barkas and Tony Ayrton at Eighth Army had known the full extent of the camouflage component. Under this huge cloak of secrecy my only visible contribution to the battle was the design of the disruptive pattern for the camouflage of tanks, with helpful notes on how they could be painted without paint brushes if there weren't any, for new tanks and armoured divisions poured in until the eleventh hour. This commission was urgent, but in the interests of art and doing my best I made the patterns as pleasing to the eye as possible. Shortly after the war there appeared on the bookstalls a souvenir magazine, entitled *The Eighth Army*. I bought a copy in the Charing Cross Road, and was delighted to discover therein a photograph of several unsigned Medleys careering across the desert like happy knights errant.

By the time that Rommel was being pursued towards Tunis and Algiers I had already been away from England for more than two years and the 'duration' was beginning to seem like forever. London would have seemed even further away had not Rupert written regular and complete letters. Through delays and losses at sea the post was erratic, and letters would arrive out of phase or all of a heap. The worst moment had been after a heavy London bombing. Not getting any answer to my cables I finally wrote and asked my mother to find out what had happened. Wharton Street had been hit and Rupert and Connie had been forced to move out and in the confusion a number of letters had gone astray. Louis MacNeice, who had been a frequent guest at Wharton Street, contrived a solution to the crisis by securing Byron Cottage in North Road, Highgate, a charming eighteenth-century house, which had recently been vacated by his sister. (Louis lodged there with Rupert and Connie until his marriage to Hedli Anderson in the summer of that year.) They had been firmly established by January 1942, but I did not hear of the move until early March, when I received in hospital a large backlog of correspondence including news of Rupert's production of *Dido and Aeneas*, with students from Morley College, at the Arts Theatre Club in Great Newport Street. The settings had been designed by the late Vera Cunningham (a much neglected artist who was also the subject of many of Matthew Smith's finest nudes) and the costumes by Elizabeth Briscoe who taught at Morley College and who had a unique gift for making silk purses out of pigs' ears. I learned that this was one of Rupert's finest and most characteristic productions, and hearing of it in hospital in Kantara, I felt a pang of nostalgia, for we had often planned together for a *Dido*, and I had in the event no part in it. I felt that it was about time that something similar should be seen in Cairo where there had been, as yet, no such entertainment for the troops. The first imaginative endeavour to fill this obvious lack was made by Christopher Scaife (Gillian's brother) who had mysteriously arrived in Cairo from Baghdad, where he had been Professor of English, in the autumn of 1942. Christopher, a close friend and collaborator of Tyrone Guthrie, and an excellent actor, gathered together an amateur company from some available troops, and calling itself 'The New Vic Players' presented James Bridie's *Tobias and the Angel.* When Christopher left Cairo soon after, the project fizzled out. I have always thought that in general the quality of the entertainment we provided for our troops could have been better in spite of the difficulties, and was less than worthy of the spirit—the tenacious bravery—that they displayed in the field.

In the cultural darkness left when the brief candle of the 'New Vic' was extinguished, Giles Isham and I shared fantasies about a production of *A Midsummer Night's Dream* in the elegant little Cairo Opera House that Ishmael Pasha had built for the entertainment of his royal and distinguished European guests on the occasion of the opening of the Suez Canal in 1869, and for which he had commissioned Verdi's *Aida*. Likewise remote from reality seemed a long evening I spent at this time with Douglas Cooper, who, like Giles, was involved in intelligence work and interrogation. Our conversation, mostly of painting and painters, took place in his furnished villa, the contents of which he heartily execrated. He had stripped the walls of their pictures, and removed the shades from the lamps. In this setting—reminiscent, I now feel, of an interrogation room—and seated on heavily upholstered thirties chairs (typical of the taste of Europeanized bourgeois Egyptians of that time) over an excellent meal prepared by the resident cook, Douglas reminisced of Picasso, Braque and Léger, bizarrely affecting, for reasons best known to himself, to be able to speak English only with a French accent.

In the hectic comings and goings that marked the preparations for the forthcoming offensive and in which the Meidan, the *rond-point* of Kasr-el-Nil, came to resemble Piccadilly Circus, I was suddenly surprised to come face to face with my younger brother Richard, now a lieutenant in the Royal Signals, who greeted me as casually as if we had just got up from the same breakfast table. Such encounters were not unusual in those crowded days when Cairo became for its brief moment an eye of the storm. A few days later, Edward Ardizzone, on his way as a war artist to join the Eighth Army, sought me out at GHQ. He had two pressing problems—where to replenish his stock of drawing materials, and how to get out of his unpleasant *pension*. I was pleased to be able to offer a solution to both: he should forthwith join the civilized mess at the Army Camouflage School at Helwan, where he could draw on the army stock of draughtsman's materials, and for the rest be within easy reach, by suburban train, of Schindler's, the excellent Swiss stationers in town. This arrangement had the added advantage that it facilitated the gastronomic experiment which was so characteristic an expression of Ted's enormous, not to say Pickwickian, zest for the variousness of things, and his infectiously generous conviviality.

I consider Ted Ardizzone, and Anthony Gross, who also passed through Cairo, but whom I missed, to be the best of the official war artists at rendering what life was actually like with an operational army. Both of them possessed the graphic artistry to describe in their own personal ways an immediacy of involvement with the event in its landscape—a sense of action set in a particular time and place. The best of their war drawings have a quality of the experience actually undergone, rather than observed from outside. By comparison Bawden's work of that period seems cool and remote; and that of Sutherland and Piper too predictably stylish and aesthetic: the art obscures the record. For all the fine work of the officially commanded artists of the Hitler war, very little was done that competes with the magisterial grandeur of Spencer's *Burghclere Chapel* or Paul Nash's *The Menin Road* and *We are Making a New World* (both now in the Imperial War Museum), from World War I. Something about our war made the grand statement impossible; the prevailing mood was honestly anti-heroic, humorously stoic: Ardizzone and Gross caught with perfect authenticity and sympathy this mood of brave irony.

After the enemy had been effectively cleared from North Africa, the role of Camouflage in the Middle East radically changed. An assignment to visit units engaged in various cover plans aimed at preventing the Germans from withdrawing troops from the Balkans gave me the chance to travel widely, from Algeria in the West to Lebanon and Syria on the Eastern Mediterranean seaboard. These expeditions provided me with a unique opportunity to explore Classical and Hellenistic sites from Cyrenaica to Damascus and beyond, and to see something of the Islamic antiquities. Interested in the Hellenistic and Islamic to the exclusion of the Ancient Egyptian,

I never explored further south of Cairo than Sakkara. What made the journeys to the Lebanon and Syria so rare an experience was that I was not a tourist in the ordinary sense, and each was accompanied by a sense of personal discovery. To be able to enter the Great Mosque in Damascus alone and unguided, and to sit unobtrusively watching the worshippers gossiping or telling their beads, grouped upon carpets that were spread on the marble floors, was to get a perspective of things that was restorative to the spirit after the disorientating unreality of life in wartime Cairo and Alexandria.

Once, entirely alone, I witnessed the sun rise over the ruins of Baalbec, and the next day enjoyed the hospitality of the Maronite Patriarch near the Cedars of Lebanon. After lunch I discussed English literature with the patriarchal secretary, a man who had translated Cardinal Newman's *Apologia* into Syriac, and was at that moment struggling with a long poem by Browning. After driving north from Beirut, I turned off the main road and visited the small and magical harbour of Byblos, with its Greek amphitheatre and fine Crusader church, and, looking into the transparent water of the harbour, I saw the broken marble columns of its Hellenistic past. In these places I experienced 'that spontaneous overflow of powerful emotion' that, 'recollected', became the basis for my painting after my return to London in 1945.

12 7 Cathcart Road, SW10

We finally sailed from Port Said in mid-June 1945 after several tiresome weeks of waiting for the embarkation order to come through. There had therefore been plenty of time to detach myself from the life I had created in Cairo, which in any case had become increasingly tedious ever since it had become certain that demobilization could not be more than six months ahead. Strangely I could hardly bother to wave a farewell as Alexandria and the north coast of Africa as far as Mersa Matrup melted away. What had passed was in the past, and in another place. Now suspended, as it were, between sea and sky, in time and space, it was better to become merely a parcel—one of several hundreds similarly posted home. To hide from myself the difficulty of thinking in any concrete terms about the future I read James Joyce's *Ulysses* (for the first time) and did not put it down until after Gibraltar and the Pillars of Hercules had closed the Mediterranean and we were in the grey Atlantic. The first view of Great Britain was of some darkly remote rocks and a spit of land in the ocean which unexpectedly I learned were the Scilly Isles. And then in the evening of the following day the cliffs of Pembrokeshire glowed in the incandescent rose of a Monet sunset. After these intimations of a sea-washed insular beauty it was somewhat of a shock to find on the following morning that we were moving, but hardly moving, through a grey and foggy drizzle up the Mersey towards Liverpool. Row upon row of blackened slate-roofed houses with closed front doors; meaningless trees; gas works and industrial junk yards under grey skies—if this was England then it appeared singularly uninviting. To arrive so grimly was a disquieting recall to reality, emphasized as it was by a distinct feeling of over-familiarity.

In the meantime there was an absurd amount of hand baggage to be gathered together. In addition to a bed-roll stuffed with clothes—it didn't matter what happened to them—were a number of cardboard boxes and biscuit tins filled with antiques, *objets d'art* and other fragile pieces for the decoration of the house I had not yet seen, and which I valued too much to pack in a trunk that might or might not safely arrive. Luckily there were no hitches in disembarking, though there was a great scramble and rush because there was not a sign of the Customs men in the shed by the early morning quay. Managing to grab a taxi I went directly to Lime Street Station, and from there sent a telegram to Rupert and Connie announcing my arrival in time for a late luncheon.

Rightly described in house agent's terms as 'a small freehold residence of exceptional character', 7 Cathcart Road was one of three detached Victorian villas, each separated by a small garden. It was not overlooked as across the road it faced the long back gardens of the houses in Tregunter Road, and next to us was an empty bomb-site. Rupert had chosen extremely well. The façade with the front door in the middle suggested a bigger house than actually it was, but the three principal rooms were large enough to allow for working and entertaining without feeling cramped.

After the flurry of arrival, the embraces, the food and the champagne, the smiles and silences because nobody could find the right words, and during which I felt, because it was Rupert and Connie who in London had borne the brunt of the war while I had been safely out of the way in Cairo, that the celebration was not so much for the return of the 'soldier' as the return of the 'prodigal', I was shown over the house and my approval sought. We went into what had been the drawing room on the first floor which was well lit by tall french windows that opened on to a narrow balcony—this was to be my studio, the best room in the house. Rupert reserved for himself the best bedroom. He had moved in only a month or so before my return and there had been no time to redecorate. Unlived in, it was almost equally strange to both of us but I was immediately sure that this was a good place in which to live and work.

For some weeks, however, the sensation of belonging and not belonging either to the house or to each other was overwhelming. Our relationship in the deepest sense had survived the war unchanged—there had never been any question that it would not—but in one important aspect, we soon discovered, it had changed. As Molière so precisely observed in *Amphitryon*, 'Virtue is a habit once broken can't be mended.' Rupert had been no Penelope, and I was no Odysseus returned to slaughter the suitors. Even without the protracted interruption—I had been away for four years—it might have been expected, as we entered our forties, that the intensity of our earlier life together should decrease.

Work was far more important. For Rupert my return was opportune, for our experience of working together would add to the strength of the amateur company of students he had formed over the previous years at Morley College. Though it was plainly understood that I should not be drawn into the theatre as much as I had been, we both felt that my involvement would re-establish an essential element in our lives. Starved for so long of intellectual and creative company I also wanted to integrate myself into the new circle of Rupert's friends, many of whom had been drawn together at Morley. And I turned once more to my own work. Rupert had kept all my materials, pictures and portfolios together, and to unpack them from their wrappings, left just as they had been when I went away, was a strange and disillusioning experience. Seen with a fresh eye, so many of them I had once thought worth keeping now disappointed me. So many drawings—so many ideas not carried through! I flipped through sketchbooks, and rereading random notes—'What is reality?' and 'Remember to buy five yards of hessian'—I experienced moments of total recall: there was my younger self sitting in the Express Dairy at the corner of Coptic Street and New Oxford Street having walked the streets for hours in search of an idea. I looked through sheets of sentimental drawings of the unemployed in Trafalgar Square. Among much that I now considered worthless there were things that didn't seem too bad. There were the gouaches that Rupert Wellington had shown at Agnew's in 1936 in a show that featured Francis Bacon, Graham Sutherland, Ivon Hitchens, Roy de Maistre and John Piper. These were better because they tackled their subject—which was essentially the frustrations of poverty—obliquely, and were free of the artificial symbolism that I had labelled 'realistic fantasy'. The best of these were *Tenement Buildings* and *The Jokers* (which featured Guy Fawkes grotesques with masked faces)—the latter I had also shown at the Surrealist Exhibition in

1936. In a review of that exhibition for the *Group Theatre Paper* I had written:

> The official surrealists see life today as two conflicting realities, the interior reality and the exterior reality in process of unification. But the truth is surely that these realities are part of a single Actuality, because everything we do is a mixture of conscious and unconscious.
>
> The surrealists in their pictures claim to act only on the unconscious. . . . This seems to be the result of exaggerating the interior reality at the expense of the outer reality. It gives the movement a clinical flavour that suggests experimental research. For it to become more than that it is necessary for the artist to see himself in relation to society and acting as part of it.

Thinking back to that time as I looked through the portfolios I recognized how much the intervening years and the travel and the events of the war had distanced one from that period. I knew that the time for major commitment to co-operative ventures was gone and that I must concentrate now on my own work. Not that I blamed my involvement with the Group for the small output of things I now thought worth preserving. Though the theatre is by nature ephemeral, and not much remained to show for the effort, through it I had nevertheless been part of the movement of the thirties—immersed in the spirit of the time—and I had had a recognized place in it. And I had done some work of my own that still stood up, paintings which were also, in their own way, characteristic of that time. These I preserved. The dustbin was filled with the rejects.

A new studio and a new house needing new pictures better than these was exactly the stimulus I needed to make a new start. Many of Rupert's new, and to me unfamiliar, circle of intimate friends lived nearby. (This had been one of the reasons for choosing to live in Cathcart Road.) They were centred on Kathleen Raine, who lived in Paulton's Square, and Rupert and Helen Gleadow (from Morley College) whose flat was on the Chelsea Embankment. I had space to work, the need to paint, and the stimulus of sensitive and intelligent friends: all was prepared for a new beginning.

Before the war Kathleen had lived up in Blackheath, and although she had never been a particularly close friend, our paths had crossed through our association with Tom Harrisson's Mass-Observation, which her second husband, Charles Madge, had co-founded. Now in Paulton's Square Kathleen had become the priestess to whom the Daughters of Albion were familiar spirits and *The Four Zoas* not yet quite an open book; she was also much absorbed by Coleridge; and in the Jungian wake of Simon Magus and the neo-agnostics of Syria and Egypt, came the visionary Yeats with his Gyres. The *ambiance* favoured the *anima* rather than the *animus*—the Visionary and the Fool rather than the Moralist. That element in Rupert which had been overwhelmed by Auden's and Isherwood's brittle demands, and had found no real outlet since *Peer Gynt* and MacNeice's *Agamemnon*, had been revived. Unfortunately Kathleen's translation of Calderón's *Life's a Dream*, made specially for Rupert, was never performed. This little group moved freely in and out of each other's houses—a neighbourly wartime habit that persisted. Helen and Rupert Gleadow for their part contributed a sophisticated and informed interest in magic and astrology. Neither Rupert nor I ever floated on the Astral Plane, but when Helen (a talented artist) designed the settings for the Morley College production of Marlowe's *Dr Faustus* in 1950, we made use of a rare seventeenth-century book of spells from which we copied various diagrams invoking fearsome demons, with horrible names, to make their appearance in the Doctor's study. Needless to say they did not materialize—but the settings were highly effective visually. Why should the devil have all the best designs?

The introduction of the newly returned prodigal into circles where a uniform was no passport—I was not to be demobbed until November—had been taken care of before I left Cairo, when via Rupert I had sent some poems and an esoteric fantasy called 'Tales that Alex told me' to John Lehmann. Rupert was writing a critical article, 'Three Shakespeare Productions', for *New Writing* and the idea was that John might also be interested in my pieces. This led to the publication of my long poem, 'Egypt', together with reproductions of several drawings brought back from the Middle East in *Penguin New Writing No. 19* very shortly after my return. This proved a timely boost which led not only to a lasting friendship but also to helpful commissions, when John went into publishing on his own account, for book jackets, and notably for the illustrations to Roy Fuller's *Savage Gold*, which I much enjoyed doing.

John Lehmann was a formidable presence in those years

immediately post-war, and he provided, in spite of rationing, a meeting place—not to say a salon—in Egerton Crescent. Here gathered not only some remarkable visitors from abroad but, more usefully for me, the homegrown artists and writers who were his particular concern. It was through John that I first met Keith Vaughan, Johnny Minton and John Craxton, the young painters of that very British manifestation, the neo-Romantic school, that had sprung up while I was away. There was also Lucian Freud.

At gatherings in Paulton's Square and Egerton Crescent an enlivening Greek presence was provided by Athens's new ambassador to London, the great George Seferis; at Kathleen's too one could meet Nanos Valoritis, the young poet, and Michael Cacoyannis, who was then training in London to become his country's best film-maker: the world of Alexandria and the Near East was not left entirely behind.

With so many people to meet, or renew friendships with—so many of them still in uniform—London *post bellum* was a lively place to be, and these seemed auspicious days to be making a new start, especially when the daily-bread problem was solved by Harold Williamson's return to the Chelsea School of Art when it reopened in September after its wartime evacuation to Northampton. Most of the pre-war staff were reassembled, including Raymond Coxon and his wife Edna Ginesi, and Henry Moore, now famous, who came to restart the Sculpture School before handing over to Bernard Meadows. The only defector was Graham Sutherland. Williamson, characteristically, took this as disloyalty and accused Graham of a swollen head. Whilst not sharing this over-simple view of a complex personality—Graham's was a highly strung combination of egotism and self-doubt—I nevertheless came to feel that it was a pity that he estranged himself from his roots and cut himself off in the South of France. His place at Chelsea as a teacher of illustration was taken by Frances Richards, and her husband Ceri Richards also joined the staff at this time. The next few years at Chelsea were particularly interesting because of the more mature students who came there in the aftermath of war (something similar had happened after World War I). Among the more notable students during this time were John Berger, Elizabeth Frink and Robert Clatworthy.

Having been inactive as a painter during the most important years of an artist's development, the years between the ages of 35 and 40, it was absolutely necessary to prove to myself that they had not been wasted even though I had returned with only a handful of sketches and a collection of photographs taken because they might prove useful. I discovered that the experience of those years had changed my view of life. I had been exposed to the ancient nakedness of the human condition, and my vision of things was no longer social and political as it had been so largely in the thirties; rather my sense of the numinous had been awakened. I looked at things with an enlargement of perspective that my experiences in the Near East had brought about. I had to come to terms with the realization that I was not a visual painter in the usual Post-Impressionist sense but a conceptual and philosophical painter, to whom the representation of the human figure was important, being, as it is, central to the greatest traditions of western art. Shortly after my return, thinking to start where I had left off, I succeeded only in mucking up a large picture of *Figures in Regent's Park*, and it then first began to dawn upon me—it came rather as a feeling than a thought—that I was happier working from the imagination in a more direct way, and that the old realist formulae would no longer do for me.

It seemed natural in making a new beginning to turn to allegory and ancient myth, and to bring to these my sense of more recent actualities. I drew directly upon the memory of two ancient beggars in a derelict side street in Cairo, whose stark nakedness was emphasized by the filthy and ineffectual rags clutched around their loins, for a painting of the meeting between Theseus and Oedipus at Colonus prompted by André Gide's novella *Theseus*. In *The Labyrinth of the Minotaur* the setting was the locality, referred to in my poem 'Egypt', of

> *the blue lamps with the thousand moons,*
> *and the dangerous shadows in the arcades,*
> *where love is an alabaster statue. . . .*

—the dark street haunted by male prostitutes and soldiers near the red-light district in Cairo. (At the time I could not set down things plain, and in the picture I disguised myself as the 'Fool'; later I tried to get away from disguises.) In another series of small pictures, I drew on the First Book of Samuel to treat the theme of Saul, David and Jonathan. I visualized these pictures in line with the traditions of Delacroix, as deliberately askew from the current neo-Romantic trends that were then to the fore as were the pictorial formalizations, derived from Picasso through Jankel Adler, in the work of Robert Colquhoun and MacBryde, which I underrated at the time because I wished to distance myself as far as possible from such conventions.

By the end of 1947 I had enough pictures of this kind, together with some more straightforward paintings, to declare my hand. Duncan MacDonald from the Lefevre Gallery, who had taken on Colquhoun and MacBryde, came to see them. Luckily—though I am still uncertain how much he really liked them—he offered me an exhibition in March 1948, and set me on my way. Cecil Collins showed thirty-two watercolours and gouaches in the first room, and I had eighteen oil paintings in the rather larger second gallery. Cecil, much the same age as me, had come to notice during the war and was painting, as he still is, personifications illustrative of spiritual forces, at that time easily identifiable with the (in the best sense) eccentric Blakean and surrealist tradition in British art. He therefore escaped the fashionable criticism of being derivative. My own openly confessed debt to French painting, to Delacroix and Matisse, was picked up and made a point of in even the favourable reviews of my exhibition. Since I have never been able to be rid of this misplaced objection to enduring affinities between the work of different artists in different times and places I have simply had to learn to live with it. This first exhibition was followed by one at the Hanover Gallery in February 1950, by which time almost everything that was to come later in my work was there *in potentia*—there were even two pictures on the subject of *Samson Agonistes* that were related to the paintings of 1946–7, and which treat a theme that was developed thirty years later in an illustrated edition with twenty-seven screenprints. The most significant pictures from the point of view of stylistic development were two paintings (the first of four) of *Bicyclists* which were the largest and most ambitious paintings I had yet undertaken. The third painting in this series, *Bicyclists against a blue blackground*, was to share the first prize with Lucian Freud's *Interior near Paddington* at the Festival of Britain exhibition *60 Paintings for '51* at the Burlington Gardens the following year. I was certainly very surprised when this happened! But then my career has always been one in which flashes of success have punctuated long periods of a self-doubt which is the outcome of a crucial lack of self-confidence. Some artists believe that everything they make is a masterpiece:

unfortunately I have no such sustaining belief and have confused matters by a restless seeking for my own answers to old questions. I have thus suffered from an instability of style that Erica Brausen (then Director of the Hanover Gallery) took me to task over when she declared in her gorgeously husky voice that 'really, by the age of 40 an artist cannot *afford* not to have found his own style', and that the best thing for me would be for her to take my pictures away before they were finished. Unfortunately I have never learned when to stop work on a painting, and I continue to ruin masterpieces!

At the Hanover Gallery, however, I was able to get a clearer view of what kind of an artist I was. Unlike Francis Bacon, I could not treat tragic subjects however much I might be attracted by the actuality of violence and alienation. I was not concerned with isolation but with integration and with seeking harmony—as in the grouping of the bicyclists in movement—rather than depicting disruption. In comparison with Bacon's, my work was diffuse, decorative and lyrical. If it was the pungent genius of Francis which dominated the scene—we were seeing a lot of him—it was with the work of Ceri Richards that I felt most professional sympathy.

Rupert and I had met Ceri and Frances Richards before the war, but at that time I was mainly absorbed by the Group Theatre, and it was not until 1946 when Ceri came to teach at Chelsea that we got to know each other well. Hovering on the borders of the conceptual and the figurative, we were both, for want of a better word, *compositional* painters. The idea of the figurative, as we understood it, is not to be confused with the notions of objective representation that were uppermost in the minds of those in the Coldstream school, who were so distrustful of the subjective that it was considered safer to look at nature with one eye only instead of two, and who regarded colour as a sensual and moral snare equivalent to the Scarlet Woman or the Whore of Babylon.

It is tempting to attribute Ceri's robust use of poetry and music to feed an imagination more continental than English to his Welsh ancestry and French grandmother; and Celtic indeed was his gift for the linear, his ability to create unfolding organic forms in fluid spirals. There were no inhibitions, and he drew freely and boldly on many sources in his approach to painting, and the intuitive geometry of his compositions was based more on the oval and the arabesque than on the strict Euclidean Circle and Square. The possible significance of this fertile preference was made explicit in a curious way much later when, doubtless in emulation of Matisse's *Chapel in Vence*, a number of modern artists, regardless of their beliefs, were commissioned to decorate the new Roman Catholic Cathedral in Liverpool in 1968. The Cardinal Archbishop, visiting his studio, objected to Ceri's use of the curved line in the early designs for the reredos as he found it too sensuously, even sexually, suggestive: Ceri's alternative design, using only straight lines, was eventually accepted. I haven't enquired if Elizabeth Frink's contribution suffered emasculation, but for some reason sculpture usually escapes from such censure, having perhaps a certain traditional *gravitas.*

Like Richards, I very rarely, if ever, painted directly from nature, preferring to rely more on an accumulation of images in the memory. The idea for the *Bicyclists* in the Hanover Gallery show came, conveniently, after the earlier exhibition at the Lefevre, when as the immediacy of the experience faded the Middle Eastern vein of imagery began to run out. I had felt I needed a more contemporary subject-matter and a change of locale. I was at this time beginning to explore new possibilities in pictorial space: both Ceri and I were exploiting Matisse's decorative convention of a uniform colour field which made it possible to evoke space without describing it in terms of either atmospheric or linear perspective. This convention—Byzantine and Islamic in origin—suited me well, especially as it would accommodate the human figure without the necessity of deforming it.

It was Robert Wellington who had originally suggested that Gravesend, so near to London, might be a profitable place to explore. There was a comfortable Victorian Hotel, the Clarendon, once General Gordon's headquarters, to stay at, or alternatively one could easily run down for the day. Beyond Eltham and Dartford, Gravesend lies where the industry of Greater London abruptly comes to an end. Upstream from the old cast-iron pier, with its lighthouse attached like a small minaret, is the river-front industry, huge paper works and cement installations, from which every evening in those days poured workers on their bicycles. Downstream is the public park that was once the fort defending the gateway to London, in front of which is a humble river esplanade. Beyond, except for a few small shipyards, is an endless expanse of deserted marshes—the marshes of *Great Expectations*. The river widens and becomes the estuary and then there is nothing but beckoning water on which the ships ride, the cry of seagulls and the vast sky. The immediate contrast between the busy and crowded and the empty and open, reminiscent of a classical port of embarkation, inspired in me a certain nostalgia, and stirred vague desires of escape such as might be enjoyed in the contemplation of a picture by Claude Lorraine. In the evenings the pubs—there had once been eighty of them—were filled with locals and the merchant marine of every nation under the sun: Gravesend presented a microcosm of existence.

I had taken to escaping there from the intensities of life in London, and it was natural that it should provide the change of setting I was looking for. The *Bicyclist* pictures originated from lounging about on a hot Saturday afternoon and watching the local youth on their 'bikes' on the waterfront esplanade descending like a flock of birds that might be scattered at any moment. The boys combed their hair and the girls lay on the paper-strewn patch of grass waiting for attention. One of the reasons for painting the pictures was to tackle the problem of relating the human figure to an intimate piece of machinery, and having no camera, I used for a model Ramsay MacClure, a student at Central School who was a close friend of Keith Vaughan. Ramsay, who had been working with me and several other students on the scenery for *The Rivals* which Rupert had produced for an LCC tour of suburban theatres, had the advantage of possessing a brand new and very smart bicycle.

Ironically, it was not through Rupert's activities as a teacher and producer that I maintained a close connection with theatre design through the fifties. In spite of several marked successes with my painting and increasing signs of critical interest I never succeeded in avoiding a dependence on teaching to make a living. What I earned from selling pictures always seemed a matter of chance and good fortune. I was never able to depend upon it. So when Bill Coldstream, who had recently moved from Camberwell to become Professor of Fine Art at the Slade, asked me, in 1949, to take over the Theatre Design section from Vladimir Polunin, who had just retired, I welcomed the opportunity, principally because I felt that teaching stage design would be less exhausting than teaching painting. Being less personally involved I could look at things more objectively, and maintain a distance between my own central preoccupations as a painter and the work I had to do for a living.

Though I had no sentimental feelings about returning to the Slade—it must have been at least twenty years since I had last set foot in the place—there was a dangerously satisfying sense of continuity when at the lodge gates in Gower Street I was greeted by a top-hatted beadle in a maroon frock-coat who turned out to be the same Connell who had formerly occupied the glass box and been in charge of the signing-in book as we entered the Slade school as students. The Professor had not yet been forced to disrupt the interior to suit the whims of students demanding individual spaces of their own—private dens in which they could work on large canvases and keep everything out (at times it seemed particularly the staff)—and from his room the Professor could still look down upon the life class and the paint-daubed walls. The large Antique Room, from which as a student I had been so anxious to escape, now looked splendid to me, its monochromatic calm relieved by one or two palms and shrubs. It remained, however, largely unappreciated and unpopulated, and so it came about that when I felt in need of a respite I took to working in there. I was only just in time, because the Antique Room soon changed: the sculpture became overtaken by more and more greenery, and there were also introduced, to my horror, several bubbling glass tanks mournfully occupied by horrid little tropical fish. And then antiquity was disposed of: the *Venus de Milo*, the *Discobolus*, the Michelangelos and Donatellos thrown out. Now everybody is beginning to regret sadly the destruction of so many irreplaceable Victorian plaster casts of the finest quality.

The pictures of *The Antique Room* which followed the *Bicyclists* did not by any means entirely depend on the visual appeal of the room. The move from Chelsea to the Slade was to some degree like moving over to the enemy camp, because Chelsea had always been highly critical of the Coldstream method of drawing, which however teachable it might be as a discipline depends upon analysis and measurement rather than vision. Carried to the extreme, this approach, with its emphasis on perception, encouraged the sensitive at the expense of the creative. I have always regarded this aspect of the Euston Road School's teaching as particularly suited to English taste—sensitive without being vulgarly emotional, and virtuous because it demonstrated by being apparently unfinished what great pains had been taken to get everything right. For my part I was more like a dancer who, finding it difficult, didn't want the difficulties to show in the final performance. A prolonged exposure to the disciplines of the realist approach, however, proved useful to me. Continually confronting the distinction between the actually perceived reality and the imaginatively conceived composition, intuitively arrived at, set up in me a productive tension. The subject matter of the Antique Room, and its inevitable associations, also acted as a corrective to the free-wheeling subjectivity of the *Bicyclist* paintings.

The first *Antique Room* pictures thus marked an important moment in my development. I had felt that there was a danger of falling self-indulgently into an easy decorative rhetoric that avoided the crucial problem of how to reconcile in a painting the imaginative with the visually perceived—i.e., what I thought with what I saw. Although the figurative element was still present, the immobility and the familiarity of the forms of the plaster casts made them unlike live models who are always different and surprising, and who change every few seconds: they were static, and their interior setting limited experimentation in pictorial space. They seemed to demand a discipline of detached accuracy, free from expressionist overtones: in short they required a Classical approach. Time and place were right for a move in that direction, for under the influence of Ernst Gombrich there was then much talk at the Slade about Alberti and the recurrence of harmonic ratios and 'divine proportion'. Without the help of Sam Carter, who taught perspective and was at that time deeply involved with an analysis of Piero della Francesca's *Flagellation of Christ* and its use of the Golden Section, the mysteries of the Square and the Circle might well have remained simply an aspect of art history. It was Sam, so intellectually involved with the perfections of theory that the painting of pictures had become an almost insuperable problem, who introduced me to Hambridge's *Dynamic Symmetry* and to Matila Ghyka's far more exhaustive (and exhausting) *The Geometry of Art and Life*, which dealt with canons of proportion in architecture, painting and music. And so, instead of ruling lines at random as I had done many years before when copying Poussin, I discovered the *Rules*. I also became aware that geometry was a means by which the material identity of man with his physical environment was established, and that this unity was to be discovered in space and sound by the application of proportional values. Proportion was, then, related in the most profound way to man's psychic well-being, his sense of belonging in the material world. These Pythagorean ideas which, going beyond Euclid, related the intervals of abstract harmony to the mathematics of organic growth—and through which a piece of architecture or of music, or a non-figurative painting, could become a metaphor for the human body—naturally appealed to me, particularly as they did not rule out the intangible or the subjective. Indeed, the most powerful feelings could be expressed through the formal structuring of a picture. As Sam pointed out to me, the pathetic figure of Christ before Pilate in Piero's *Flagellation* stands in the centre of a circle, the disc, seen in perspective, in the pattern of the marble floor. This circle symbolized, Sam suggested, the universe, and placed at its heart is the suffering of Jesus.

I knew already that pictures are not made with a set square and rule, but the objective disciplines of proportional composition did enable me to pursue my figurative concerns within an abstract framework that had behind it essentially humanist ideas. This had the unforeseen advantage that I was able to absorb the impact of the American abstract expressionists towards the end of the fifties without it throwing me off course. I was completely committed to the idea that paintings had to have a *subject*—the concept that the picture was *itself* the subject did not strike me at the time as convincing. I was able therefore to take what I needed from the example of the New York painters: it gave me the courage to leave an intuitive stroke undisturbed and to proceed towards further abstraction of my own kind by ruthlessly eliminating unnecessary descriptions.

The first picture in which I consciously exploited this American freedom of handling was, surprisingly, *The Education of Pan* of 1958. The more abstract paintings with fashionably ambiguous titles like *Movement in Rock Landscape* and *Red and Green Figuration* did not come until 1961, and even these were based on observation, and were made with a degree of intention that related to the figure and its place in the felt world. Drawing and design, moreover, were still essential to their formal composition. My earliest preoccupations, formed during the months of copying in the Louvre; the studies of Poussin; and my later interests in colour and space and in the signifying possibilities of proportion and the Golden Rule: all these things were by now part and parcel of my approach to painting.

During the fifties I had also become aware of the work of Giacometti whom I regarded as working in the direct line from Cézanne. In both his drawing and his sculpture Giacometti seemed to work from the centre outwards, not being concerned with the formal delineation of the human subject against its background, but with its inner experience of balanced weight, its physical and existential being in the world. Those stick-like figures, for all their economy, contain all the information you need about their subject. This added strength to my rejection of the literal academicism of the Coldstream school who worked from the outside in, and whose emphatic concentration upon measurable appearance—that which was visually perceptible—meant that they stayed permanently *outside* their subjects.

In spite of the responsibilities of having to teach two (and later three) days a week at the Slade, the fifties were a successful period for me, and my reputation as a painter became established as far as it ever would be, given the limitations of a fitful output, and a habit of stylistic experiment. The success of the Festival of Britain exhibition was followed two years later by the first large *Antique Room*, which won the first prize at the Contemporary Arts Society exhibition at the Tate Gallery for a picture on the subject of 'Figures in their Setting'. With this picture, much talked about at the time, I thought that at last I had made it. I was surprised and disappointed that it was not accepted by the Tate Gallery; instead it was sent to Huddersfield where until a proper civic art gallery was built it hung on the main stairs to the public library. However, the prize made possible an enjoyable celebration. We did not repeat the 1951 *folie de grandeur* of celebrating with a cocktail party at the Café Royal, but instead gave two parties at Cathcart Road which turned out to be equally extravagant but far more fun. The rooms were lavishly decorated with azaleas which Sir Charles Wheeler PRA, who had a studio opposite, had brought up from his country house near Reigate, and the drinks were served, as a penance, by two French boys from the Lycée whom we had caught several days earlier pinching the branches of cherry blossom which hung over the garden wall. These cheerful and unexpected Ganymedes turned out to be of the highest of *haute noblesse*—a prince and a viscount no less—and they brought unaffected grace and style to their service. It was at the conclusion of one of these parties that occurred the unique and memorable encounter of Wystan Auden and Francis Bacon. These two, together with Stephen Spender, had been invited to stay on for dinner. As it was a rather special occasion, Connie, whom everyone loved, consented to leave the kitchen and join us. Conversation was lively and everything seemed to be going well when in the middle of the main course Francis turned in sudden fury on Wystan: 'Never before have I had to submit to such a disgusting display of hypocritical *Christian* morality!' Declaring that he could no longer sit at the same table with such a *monster* who considered himself an *artist* he leapt to his feet and before you could say 'knife', was out of the front door and into the street. I hurried out, pursuing Francis halfway down Redcliffe Road in a useless endeavour to pacify him. When, rather breathless, I returned, Wystan was talking away much as usual.

These celebrations were highlights, but during this period we entertained frequently and this was made possible only by the economy and skill of Connie. Part-time work at the Slade and the sale of pictures—in spite of some public success my income from painting was still occasional and unspectacular—provided hardly enough for a living, and I was lucky that odd commercial jobs sometimes turned up: book jackets, illustrations, and though S. John Woods, posters and publicity material for Ealing Studios. This latter could be very well paid but unless you brought it off the first time it could be difficult and time consuming. For one of these commissions—for a forgettable film called *Saraband for Dead Lovers*, starring Stewart Granger, Joan Greenwood and Flora Robson—I got something between three and four hundred pounds, a lot of money in those days. However, unlike John Minton, I had no real aptitude for this kind of by no means uninteresting commercial graphic work, and I was pleased to be rid of it by taking on extra days' teaching at the Slade. In this way, I might complain, I became caught in the 'teaching trap'.

Here, in Shandian manner, I must interrupt myself on a point of order, and admit that it was not the time spent in teaching that should be blamed for my limited output of pictures over the years. Rather, it is something in my psychic make-up, a quirk beyond conscious control which has always made it difficult for me to follow up or exploit a success such as that achieved with the *Bicyclist* paintings or the *Antique Rooms*. The reader will certainly be aware by now that I have not been that kind of artist who could work in a particular style and then exploit its potentialities in the production of innumerable unmistakable 'Medleys'. I am not the first artist in this world who has found it difficult to produce art; and neither am I one of those who has enjoyed the difficulties as part of the fun. In my case it has rarely been fun. Each step forward, each success, has seemed to lead to a period of comparative failure, and I was always landed with the painful prospect of seemingly having to start again. Of course this is only partly true—as I have described earlier, each new development has actually embodied in some way all that I had learned—but I do seem to have had an exaggerated sense of the difficulty of things, and that has always inhibited my production, and encouraged me to put up with distractions. In the highly competitive world of artists and dealers, this erratic flow made it impossible to produce the expected one-man show every two years that would keep one's name before the public. Even Oliver Brown, anxious to promote a 'possibility', had to be kept waiting for three years between exhibitions at the Leicester Galleries. But, even so, the fifties were a time of achievement and consolidation, and the work I produced during these years, especially towards the end of the decade, formed a substantial part of the retrospective exhibition which was mounted in 1963 at the Whitechapel Gallery.

The great thing about the Whitechapel during those years, when Bryan Robertson was its Director, was that there was nothing institutional about it. It did not represent an official or establishment view of things: it was a place for living art. And because it was a public gallery, with remarkably high and consistent standards, it was an important and prestigious place to show. An exhibition there was an opportunity to take stock and also to indicate new directions. It was an opportunity for which many artists of my generation and the next have felt a special debt of gratitude to Bryan, whose remarkable eye, and breadth of critical sympathy, have made him an outstanding figure in the world of modern art.

During this period, with Bill Coldstream's support, I was also pioneering a Theatre Design section at the Slade, which was based entirely on my own experience of working in a non-commercial context with writers and musicians. The stage design room was equipped with a model stage to the scale of 1:12, designed by Robert Stanbury, which could be lit under conditions which approached actuality to a fair degree of accuracy. The approach I encouraged was improvisatory in which the imagination was not inhibited prematurely by the technical considerations that so often dictated design in the commercial theatre. And it was never, so far as I recall, formulated into a precise syllabus. People came and went much as they wished, and there were sessions when visiting producers such as Tyrone Guthrie, Peter Brook and Rupert discussed the settings required for a particular production. Opera and dance were not neglected and we were visited by John Copley and Ninette de Valois respectively to talk about the particular problems of design for those forms of theatre. Designing for the stage entails the highly sophisticated use of historical styles and considerable knowledge of the art, architecture, costume and manners of different periods—Nevill Coghill visited on one occasion to give a discourse on Elizabethan colour symbolism—and being an ancillary to the main school, confined to one of the smaller studios, we worked within limitations that forced us to concentrate upon the essential: the creative process of design for a particular text and a particular production.

I was lucky to have a series of gifted students, some of whom went on to form Theatre Design departments elsewhere, and to set up properly recognized diploma courses, and others who went on to make names for themselves in the professional theatre. Niko Georgiadis, while still a student, was commissioned by Ninette de Valois to design a Stravinsky ballet choreographed by the young Kenneth MacMillan. Peter Snow made his debut with his designs for the Morley College production of *Love's Labour's Lost*. For a time there was a great craze in the department for designing settings for grand opera. This was enthusiastically promoted by Ann Gainsford, who was later, appropriately, an assistant to Franco Zeffirelli, and by Philip Prowse, who became the director-designer of the Citizens Theatre, Glasgow.

In this way the work of the Theatre Design section at the Slade had an influence out of proportion to the modesty of its operation, and I think it is fair to say that through it some of the central principles of the Group Theatre were handed on to a new generation of directors and designers. Although it had never been intended to provide more than a subsidiary course in stage design for painters, as time went on more students began to arrive who wanted only to be stage designers. I had no wish to be caught up in an expanding department, and for this and other reasons I grasped with some alacrity the opportunity to move to Camberwell School of Arts and Crafts in 1958, where I was appointed Head of the Department of Painting and Sculpture. The 'other reasons' were mostly to do with the need for financial security: it was clear that Rupert was becoming increasingly dependent on my success rather than on any hopes of his own, and seized by an unaccountable restlessness that had been painful to both of us, he had insisted upon a move from Cathcart Road. Neither of us as yet recognized the symptoms in Rupert's behaviour of what was to prove an illness that would slowly and steadily worsen. We sold Cathcart Road and found a large house with a garden in Wimbledon. Knowing that I would have to guarantee an uncertain future with growing responsibilities I left the Slade, where I had never felt entirely at home, and took up the post at Camberwell. A new chapter in my life had begun.

13 Camberwell

Art education as it has developed in this country is the product of a particular history, and its origins are to be found in those ideals of the Prince Consort which were given their fullest expression in the Great Exhibition of 1851. In that spectacular display the alliance of Fine Art and Industry was proclaimed and exemplified, and one of its practical outcomes was the purchase of land for a Museum of Decorative and Applied Arts, named after the Queen and her far-sighted consort, which was, significantly, to house the Royal College of Art, and whose first Director, from 1860 to 1875, was an energetic career civil servant, Sir Henry Cole. The Royal College was founded to supply the country with teachers and artists appropriately trained to further the ideal marriage of Art and Industry. This was well suited to our national tendency to distrust artists and fine art *per se*, and appealingly suggested that the arts might be *useful*, and even add to the profitability of commercial enterprise, as well as bring prestige by association. Not surprisingly this led to a rapid growth in provincial art education as innumerable schools of arts and crafts were established, especially in the great industrial areas, often endowed by idealistic but hard-headed local industrialists. Many of these were housed in an architectural splendour symbolic of late Victorian high thinking and philanthropy, reinforced with a democratic idealism derived from John Ruskin and William Morris.

The Camberwell School of Arts and Crafts was a typical and by no means especially prestigious example. Built in 1890, in an enlightened Norman Shaw style, there is no mistaking its purpose; for the arts and crafts are symbolized at the entrance by the two sculptures of semi-draped nude figures, male and female—reminiscent of the work of Alfred Stevens—who extend a welcome to the dedicated student.

Associated with the school was a large department of printing, whose emphasis was definitely commercial, and the South London Art Gallery, the benefaction of a Mr Passmore Edwards, in which there is a marquetry and parquet floor (sadly now covered over) designed by Walter Crane.

By the end of the century municipal institutions like this had become firmly consolidated into a national grant and examination system at the apex of which stood the Royal College of Art. To be incorporated later were the numerous art schools such as Chelsea that belonged more to the Edwardian period of Quintin Hogg's influential polytechnic movement.

Standing outside this national system were the Royal Academy Schools, and, since 1873, the Slade School of Fine Art at University College, London, both of which were concerned with fine art only. They ruled their own affairs. It is not without significance that while the first director of the V & A and the Royal College had been a civil servant, the first Slade Professor, Sir Edward Poynter, was a painter and Academician, who was quickly succeeded, in 1875, by Alphonse Legros, the French painter and draughtsman, who had come over to England along with Monet, Pissarro and Sisley, to escape the Franco-Prussian war in 1871. This difference of functional emphasis explains something of the absurd historical rivalry between the Slade and the Royal College with its attendant envies and jealousies and competing claims to pre-eminence, which was brought to a head by Sir William Rothenstein, Principal of the Royal College from 1920 to 1935. By sheer force of conviction and personality Rothenstein swung an ossified institution, in which the teaching priorities of designing, applied arts, and painting and sculpture had become thoroughly mixed, decisively in the direction of fine art. And this in spite of its charter. The Royal College thus moved swiftly and laterally across the board to threaten the Slade on its own ground, and when a Queen moves so decisively the entire game is affected: the lesser pieces move position behind her. The Royal College, moreover, had continued to maintain control over the national examining mechanisms of art education, so that Rothenstein's move had far-reaching consequences; some of them for me, since from 1932 onwards I had, on and off, been involved in the business of teaching art, and had found myself shifting between institutions whose character and status had been determined by the great game in which Tonks and Rothenstein had been prime movers. Moving from Chelsea to the Slade had seemed a move 'up'; and when I moved to Camberwell I little suspected that the piecemeal developments and changes of emphasis over the previous forty years or so were soon to come to a climax in a revolution in art education that rivalled the scale and scope of the Consort's own radical initiatives of a century before. Ironically it was a Slade professor who was to be the proponent of a Rothensteinian elevation of fine art in the colleges of arts and crafts, and the transformation of the status of those institutions.

Arriving at Camberwell I found a climate that derived from the influence of Bill Coldstream, who until his elevation to the Slade professorship had imparted to the school an aura of particular distinction. Since his departure ten years before, painting at the school had been under the direction of Gilbert Spencer. Unfortunately Gilbert had been out of tune not only with the staff but also with the current mood of the students. The liveliest elements in the school, in fact, were those most closely associated with Coldstream. I realized that new initiatives were needed if things were to be revived, and that I must do what was necessary on my own terms. It was a bit like being presented with a motor car that was not firing on all cylinders. Having the advantage of a staff most of whom I knew, and were my friends, it was to be expected that the first real challenge would be presented by the students who were looking out, characteristically, for some indication of my worth. The ship may be a small one but how did this captain come by his command? In particular, a small group of local lads, who had been at Camberwell's junior school since their early teens and were now well advanced, watched points avidly, and their leader, a lively Irish-Cockney youth, took an early opportunity to observe that I was doubtless a teacher because I couldn't paint!

Savouring to the full the wounding cogency of this remark, I reserved my revenge until the occasion a few weeks later when taking over his palette and brushes I first wiped out his unsatisfactory life study and successfully repainted it for him. That a teacher should take such a liberty with a student's work would usually be regarded as outrageous, but in this case the ends justified the means. The real irony of the situation was that it suggested a facility that I neither had nor wished to pretend that I possessed, for it was my belief, common to teachers of my generation, that it was not the teacher's role to impose a technique from outside but rather to encourage the self-realization of the student. I had been at home hitherto in that tradition of teaching which blurred the distinction between the professional and the amateur, and which took the object of the course to be not the transmission of a style but the formation of a personality, in which commitment, not skill, was what mattered. Art was a vocation rather than a profession; and where there were so many styles to choose from it was no longer possible to say 'Do it *my* way.' I had found this approach congenial because I had no 'method' to teach nor personal axe to grind, but I came to feel that it failed to pay enough attention to the development of the traditional skills of the painter. It was obvious to me that if I was to justify my existence I had to make positive decisions in briefing not only the staff but also the students. This led me to separate out in my mind what could actually be taught from what was simply conveying a matter of opinion: 'I like this but not that. . . .'

By the end of the first year I had come to the conclusion that the teaching of painting in the school needed the added dimension of a tougher perceptual and intellectual discipline. The painting of sensitive pictures in an acceptable Sickert–Euston Road style which had become the norm at the school was all very well, but it left too much out of account, too many possibilities unexplored. Sensibility, so highly valued by the English that they think that is what a picture is about, is not enough. Delacroix put it very neatly when he said of the principles underlying the creative act: 'The Imagination conceives, the Intellect orders, and the Sensibilities execute.' What was required, I thought, was a bit more of the 'intellectual ordering': there was no shortage of the 'imaginary' and rather too much of 'the sensibility that executes'.

Instead of encouraging a greater freedom of expression, as had been expected by those who knew something of my background, I decided to initiate a course of training based on the analysis of the spectrum. This involved making it quite clear what are the relations of colours to each other and their relation to light and shade, all of which is relevant to a painter's decision to make a picture dark or light, or one in which one colour rather than another is dominant in 'pitch'. I had for years made tone and colour charts of my own and found them invaluable in 'finding' a colour, and such a discipline would inhibit students from just adding a little white or a little black to a colour if they wanted to make it lighter or darker. By imposing these and other limitations on practice—in some cases these ideas went back to my conversations with Tchelitchev in Paris—it was my intention to prevent students from painting 'from nature' without thought of the profound difficulties this actually involved.

Although I felt confident enough in dealing with some formal questions in a rigorously schematic way—the geometry of composition and its relation to general principles of interval and proportion had become very much my province—I needed somebody from outside the department to whom I could entrust the colour theory. It was, therefore, a matter of great good fortune when Bryan Robertson telephoned to ask if I could find a place on the staff for his old friend Charles Howard who, like many distinguished artists before and since, was hard up. I had met Charles Howard, the Anglo-American abstract surrealist painter, once or twice at Roland Penrose's Surrealist meetings in 1936 but had not seen or heard of him since. Over a dinner given by Bryan I quickly recognized that Howard was the man I had been looking for. He immediately understood the direction in which I had been thinking, and brought to my outline ideas a penetrating visual intelligence, though with characteristic modesty he insisted that I should draw up the teaching scheme.

The course we devised was made compulsory for all students who came to the first classes, a series of systematic colour exercises concentrating on the range of greys between white and black, in a state of sullen rebelliousness, objecting that this was all elementary stuff, classroom routine as opposed to studio experiment and expression. Had we not, after all, borrowed the prism from the printing department, whose priorities were in *commercial* design and lay-out? Why not borrow the spectrometer—a tiresomely accurate instrument used for the matching of colours in printing—as well? Charles and I, however, knew perfectly well that our systematic approach was intended to train the *painter*'s eye—and no instrument could improve upon the sensibilities that created an artist's vision. The limitations we imposed would ultimately be liberating.

The second part of the course was more fun, though it took some time for the students to appreciate it. A series of small still lifes were set up (a jug and a cup, a couple of bottles—as simple as that) against backgrounds deliberately calculated to create problems of visual and spatial perception. These had to be painted on a small board in monochrome, using only the limited range of the greys that had been used in the colour exercises. The object of the task was to raise a number of basic questions about the relationship between seeing and painting. How can the outline of an object be registered against a background of exactly the same tone? How are the areas in a composition related to the lights and darknesses that play around the objects in reality? Do we paint what we *know* or what we *see*? The exercise was instructive because in the composing process positive acts of judgement were required which nevertheless did not interfere with the operation of the individual sensibility of the painter. The results weren't practice sketches but considered pictures, and often—to the students' surprise—good pictures at that. The value of the experience was demonstrated by the way in which many of the more gifted students came back for more, and sought out Charles for criticism of their later work. If I were asked what was the most useful thing I did at Camberwell I would say that it was the appointment of Charles Howard. I was not the only person who was saddened by his early retirement in 1963. Howard was a remarkably interesting painter and a fine teacher, and he has been much underrated.

The other thing that I felt was needed was to offer some real alternative to the Coldstream manner of drawing which had become something of a formula at the school. Frank Auerbach, visiting once a week, provided the strongest antidote possible. The studios soon became deep in charcoal, heavily worked paper, and paint scrapings. Frank's dynamic and obsessive approach, with its intense emphasis on mass rather than on contour, was invaluable because my own style of drawing, unlike Bill Coldstream's, was too loose and eclectic to act as a positive model. His influence was inevitably powerful, and continued to affect practice and the school long after he ceased to visit, and moved on to the Slade.

For my part, a successful exhibition at the Leicester Galleries in 1960 was helpful in establishing that I was actually painting. Teaching and running the department were the activities that were visible but not by any means the only things I was doing. Things had gone well at Camberwell, and there had been changes for the better. But bigger changes were on the way. The publication in 1960 of Coldstream's notable report was to lead to a revolution in the long-established system of art education which I have briefly described at the beginning of this chapter, and which had such an air of permanence that I had thought it would last forever.

The examinations for the National Diplomas in Design (NDD) for Sculpture and Painting had long been regarded with something approaching contempt. They made the status of the award equivocal at best, and the whole business had become scandalous, for the best students (i.e., the most original and gifted artists) were habitually failed if their work did not match the preconceptions of the examiners. The form of the examinations was, in fact, ridiculous, requiring as it did such things as a 'composition' with a given title, such as 'A Street Scene' or 'A Decoration for a Dentist's Waiting Room'. The papers in Art History were perfunctory. The general effect upon the more imaginative teachers, especially younger artists, was inhibiting and dispiriting. By 1959 protests had become so vocal that something had to be done. Sir William Coldstream was asked to write a report and made recommendations for the reform of the art schools.

Coldstream cut through the complications of a piecemeal system at a stroke by proposing the abolition of the old examination and its replacement by a system which at once gave the individual art schools more autonomy and responsibility—they would devise their own courses and administer their own examinations, properly monitored by external assessors—and which raised the fine arts to the status of any other university subject, the study of which would lead to a Diploma in Art and Design which would be equivalent to a BA degree. Students would also be required to study the history of art, and undertake liberal studies, which were intended to extend their general education to a level proper to the academic status of a degree. This latter was a development with which I had great personal sympathy; as an examiner I came to value a school by the success with which it integrated History of Art and Liberal Studies into its total approach.

To effect the revolution a committee chaired by John Summerson was set up: there were a number of very tricky problems to be overcome if the national network of hundreds of colleges, great and small, was to be brought into an ordered system. Distinctions would have to be drawn between those schools that could award the new Dip.A.D. and the others; regional diversity must be respected; and within schools areas of study must be carefully defined, as between Fine Art, Graphic Arts, Textiles and Fashion, and the three-dimensional arts of Ceramics, Metalwork, Furniture Design and so on. I was pleased to be invited to join 'Summerson' as one of a team of teachers and artists who were to go round the country deciding which schools to recommend for inspection as candidates to award the new diploma, as this would provide useful insights into what would be required at Camberwell. And in the event Camberwell it was that became the first school to be inspected. Leonard Daniels had presented our case with readable precision and a lack of window dressing, and the school was a large and typical institution with the sort of reputation that suggested its suitability for the proposed new status. I found myself, then, at once on the giving and the receiving ends, and up to my neck in the ferment of change.

At Camberwell we tidied up studios, store-rooms and desk-tops, and scrutinized every aspect of the school's activities from the slide collection to lavatory provision in preparation for the grand visitation. The large number of inspectors who descended and occupied the school for two days included old friends like Merlyn Evans and Claude Rogers looking strangely unfamiliar in collars and ties and carrying bundles of paper and copies of a report that I had somehow never managed to read right the way through. Among faces new to me was that of Hubert Dalwood whose mastery of the documents equalled that of a QC acting for the Public Prosecutor. He seemed to my defensive eyes obsessed with such matters as academic status, channels of communication and degrees of responsibility, and I took an immediate dislike to him. But without fear or favour the team was going to make a proper job of this first inspection, and quite rightly so; and we did not emerge unscathed. Working with Hubert in many subsequent inspections I grew very fond of him as we learned how to operate with greater sophistication and a lighter touch than was possible at the beginning, when inexperience and over-enthusiasm, in this as in other things, could lead to clumsiness. We took the job seriously, perhaps too much so, because we knew just how much our judgements could effect the future of the colleges we visited, and of the people who worked in them.

One of the effects of a successful validation could be an increase in student numbers, for grant-in-aid students, no longer tied to their regions, could come from anywhere to the school of their choice. The painting school at Camberwell rapidly increased from just over twenty students to fifty, and by 1965 there were ninety. These were good years to be in charge of Painting and Sculpture in an expanding college of arts and crafts changing in ways that were long overdue and greatly inspiriting. The new order was not born without trauma, but Coldstream's radical break with the confused traditions of the past resulted in an outburst of creative energy in the art schools that was a fuelling element in the resurgence of British art in the sixties. It freed the students from the strait confines of the old examination and, more importantly, it created an atmosphere in which the younger generation of teachers could operate imaginatively and rigorously. The vitality and creative drive of the time was simultaneously chronicled and celebrated by Bryan Robertson, John Russell and Lord Snowdon in their splendid book *Private View*, which featured a section on the art schools, and in which Camberwell was generously described and pictured.

Snowdon's visit to the College was memorable for its professionalism and informality. He already knew Tony Fry and Patrick Procktor (who had recently joined the staff) and felt at ease and among friends. It had long been our custom to lunch at the pub round the corner from the school, where we could discuss school matters in congenially uninstitutional surroundings. Snowdon wanted to photograph one of these informal staff meetings and so we went to the pub for lunch as usual and, engaging a long table, we gave the landlord no indication that we would be feeding so royally famous a person. It was not until we were leaving that the penny dropped. Such anonymity could not be preserved in the studios but the students continued with their work with predictable *insouciance*, though I could not help noticing that some had taken the unusual step of brushing their hair. Snowdon was given freedom to move about the school at will and he was delighted by the informality. It was fascinating to see him at work. Behind the camera he seemed to disappear completely. When I finally came to fetch him away I had difficulty in finding him, so invisibly had he melted into the activity of the students.

If British art in the sixties was in part invigorated by the new vitality in the art schools, it also owed a great deal to the brilliant series of exhibitions that Bryan Robertson put on in those years at the

Whitechapel Gallery. These included influential shows by the younger generation of American artists, such as Robert Rauschenberg and Jasper Johns, and by the middle and older generation of British painters such as Charles Howard, Robert Colquhoun and Ceri Richards. The 'New Generation' shows in 1964 and 1965 were crucial in establishing the general atmosphere of experiment and originality that made possible so much good work by younger British artists during that period. My own retrospective at the Whitechapel in 1963 was an important occasion for me: it seemed to establish me at last as a painter with a past as well as a future. For all my doubts and uncertainties, the new beginnings and shifts in preoccupation, there was, undeniably, a body of work, a Medley *oeuvre*. And any rise in my personal stock was good for painting and sculpture at Camberwell, at a time when its reputation was still to be made under the new dispensation.

I approved of the Coldstream reforms and was active in implementing them. The basic form for the school of art that he proposed would be difficult to improve upon. But the application of rigorous logic to a muddled human situation meant that certain valuable features of the old system could not be taken into account. Raising the academic status of the better art schools, and firmly placing them within the higher-education stratum, put them out of bounds to the talented (and often middle-aged) amateurs whose presence under the old system had been so valuable as a social and cultural leavening in the mix. (I use the term 'amateur' here with proper regard for its true meaning: the difference between these and the 'professionals'—mostly aged between 18 and 22—was of approach rather than of quality of work.) Now they were to be regarded as a threat to academic standards. We became a closed shop. As well as losing this part-time amateur element, we had also to turn away the lively American, French and German students who came not to gain another diploma but to enlarge their experience. Here a crucial cross-fertilizing process was curtailed. Many of these students I now had to recommend to the Byam Shaw, the only private art school of any standing remaining in London. Academic elevation also meant that a good college could attract grant-in-aid students from all over the country. About this, too, I had certain misgivings. It was good for the more successful schools, but it meant a loss of the local rootedness which had been a positive feature of the old national system, and of course it favoured London, the magnetic centre, at the expense of the provincial cities.

My doubts about the way things were going were compounded in the early 1970s with the reinstallation of the art schools in the polytechnic sector, from which we had so specifically engineered their removal in 1962. I have always thought it likely that this decision was the outcome of a careless afterthought by some committee of the Ministry of Education which knew nothing about art education. At any event a great deal of debate was engendered which in essence recalled that of a century before, and which rehearsed themes that had been recurrent from that time. Perhaps art schools were too isolated from modern society and technology? Where does art education properly belong? Was it time to question the validity of the concept of fine art altogether? *Plus ça change*. . . .

One of the most serious negative effects of the change was that the art schools, with their needs so very different from those of more conventional academic departments, found themselves vulnerable to the conflicting priorities and struggles for place within the vast structures of the new polytechnics. The London colleges wisely took advantage of an escape clause and decided to stand apart, and under the ILEA they have managed to maintain some degree of flexibility. The provincial art schools were hit at their tenderest spot by the financial dictates of educational bureaucracies which made it difficult to employ artists as visitors on part-time contracts. For an art school this is equivalent to an engineering department being deprived of new machinery and the expertise to use it. The increasing administrative load and the pressures of internal institutional politicking have made it difficult for the polytechnic art schools to find heads of department who are also committed working artists.

One way or another I feel that the great hopes of the early sixties have been disappointed: the system has developed in such a way that society hasn't come to use its artists in the best way. An appalling amount of talent goes to waste at a time when we probably need it most. Perhaps the art schools should now be thinking how their doors might be opened wider, to potential teachers and students alike. The sixties showed how a dynamic situation in the art schools could vitalize art in society as a whole but perhaps that can happen only when society wants it. The eighties in this, as in other aspects, begin to look depressingly like the thirties. There is an important difference, however. In the thirties we at least had optimism: there was always hope that things could be made better by human, political effort. The mood today seems bleak.

The making of art and the need for aesthetic satisfaction is common to all of us, and there are times, especially now, when I am tempted to think that it would be a step in the right direction if we were to cease describing a certain category of art as 'fine', since it encourages the philistine heresy that art is a luxury, and one which we can no longer afford. Now as never before we need to nurture human values—which have nothing to do with monetary ones: the old battle has still to be fought although the terrain may have changed. At bottom I remain an anarchist, one of those absurd individuals who persists, despite all evidence to the contrary, in believing in the perfectibility of human nature.

In 1960 I had joined the Faculty of Painting of the British School at Rome. The British School was founded by the 1851 Commissioners with a charter which, like that of the Royal College, stressed the application of science and art to productive industry, and is appropriately administered from headquarters adjoining Exhibition Road and close to the Royal Albert Hall. In the early seventies the spirit of the original charter was indeed invoked, as tightening purse strings at the Treasury led to the scrutiny of all its funded institutions, and for a while the future of the school, which had developed an altogether more independent fine art and pure scholarship tradition than was originally intended, was called into question. The school and its prizes have survived; fortunately, for surely cultural representation of the kind it stands for is crucial in a civilized world? When in 1967 I succeeded Tom Monnington as Honorary Chairman of the Faculty I was particularly gratified to find, in the stout and noble volume that contained the minutes that it was now my duty to sign, the familiar signature of my first master, F. E. Jackson. A surprising wheel within a wheel had come full circle.

If in this chapter I have dwelt upon the public Medley it should not be imagined that the private Medley was not part of all I did. I had not gone into teaching as a 'career': it was simply a way of earning money. At Chelsea in 1932 my first concern was to do exactly what H. S. Williamson wanted and not get the sack. I had to take the first year NDD students for life drawing and had nervously wondered whether I had anything at all to teach them. It may have been the case that my very lack of method was an advantage. At any rate I had been, and I remained, suspicious of charismatic teachers who incite students to fierce personal loyalties and can 'inspire' anybody with a little talent to draw in a particular style. Neither had I thought of myself as an 'educationalist'. The practice of teaching I found exhausting enough without burdening myself with the theory. But I needed the job at Camberwell, as I have intimated, for reasons to do with developments in that part of my life invisible to those who saw only the public face I presented to the academic boards and art education committees. In that private parallel life there were difficulties that seemed perversely to increase in a sort of inverse ratio to my successes in the professional world. Indeed to some extent my commitment to the practicalities and responsibilities of administration and art education reform provided a relief from emotional turbulence and distress in personal matters. At least it was a world of objective realities where decisions were made by reference to agreed criteria and where responsibilities could be defined with some precision. None of that was true of decisions and responsibilities in the private domain. And I enjoyed the satisfactions of self-regard that accompanied successful operations in the public life. In all this I was of course following the traditions of the class and family from which I came; I was in fact returning to a mode of behaviour that was characteristic of my social and moral background. (It should be added that social responsibility had been no small part of the ethos of the thirties.) And perhaps some part of the satisfaction I gained from the execution of public service was to be traced to a feeling that my father would have at last approved: I was regaining something forfeited so many years before when I had left the Slade unqualified and gone to Paris to throw in my lot with that of a peripatetic ballet dancer. Who knows what private chaos, what desires, unconscious and conscious, fulfilled and unfulfilled, lie behind the poise of those in public places? These are imponderables that resist our speculation whatever the laws and mores that prevail. Autobiography can be no more definitive than any other account. Revelation may be a means of hiding the truth; reticence may give away more than a writer intends.

Personal imperatives, however, determined the course of events for me. In 1965 I resigned from Camberwell in order to turn my full attention to private affairs.

14 Beginning Again

I did not recognize the first signs of trouble. I can see now that the extraordinary outbursts of unmanageable obstinacy with which Rupert insisted that we leave Cathcart Road for no apparent reason signified an inner disturbance, a deep anxiety, that he could not communicate or explain, even to himself.

In 1957 we moved to an Edwardian house and garden on Wimbledon Common, which seemed a most unlikely place to find ourselves in, but with its handsome rooms and large garden the house chose us rather than the other way round. In exchange for the bustle of the Fulham Road there was the green space and open air of the Common. For a brief period the inexplicable internal clouds disappeared. The fact that we were now out of the centre of London and a longish way from our friends, and from Morley College and the Slade, did not seem to matter as much as I thought it might, for it was a splendid house for entertaining and for making special occasions. We replanted the garden, in which there was a fine ilex tree that looked as if it had come out of a Poussin landscape, and Rupert unexpectedly became a gardener. But there was a development in our relationship that worried me: this was an increase in Rupert's dependence upon me, which I taxed him about, for though it brought out a sweetness in his character, he seemed to be resigning from his own creative work and investing his interests in mine.

In the summer of 1959 we spent what was to prove our last real holiday together. We borrowed Tony Fry's house and studio at Longridge Box, near Bath. The sun shone in what seemed an endlessly blue sky, our closest friends came to visit at weekends, and I was able to do a lot of painting. It was a period of great contentment, and only when it was over did the clouds once more begin, imperceptibly, to gather. At first it seemed more like a failure of spirit than a physical decline. The doctor, a close personal friend who knew Rupert's temperament well, could find nothing wrong: it was imagination; Rupert had always been inclined to worry about his health. At Morley College Rupert felt increasingly unable to cope, and although his students covered up for him as best they could when things went badly, in 1962 he had to retire.

Throughout this period we resorted to various remedies—diet, homeopathy, and, at Mickey Salaman's suggestion, acupuncture, at that time a new treatment in the West—but nothing worked for long. For a while things would seem to be all right, and then not. After some time of indecision I insisted on a second opinion, and Rupert consulted a specialist at the Hospital for Nervous Diseases in Queen Square, Bloomsbury, where he was enrolled as an out-patient for observation, and given remedial exercises for loss of motor control. That summer, 1962, we went, carrying a medicine ball, once again to Longridge Box; but this time it was a disaster, and the rain fell ceaselessly. My father died suddenly and we hastily returned to London. There followed a bad year for us, but then typically rallying against adversity, Rupert summoned strength. There was my retrospective at the Whitechapel to be got together, which was scheduled for November 1963.

The exhibition was designed by Bryan Robertson who overnight had decided to repaint the whole gallery in white, and my pictures looked their best. It happened by a stroke of good fortune that Wystan was passing through London and staying with the Spenders and so it was arranged that we meet at the gallery before the private view and celebrate at a luncheon that Bryan had arranged at the Great Eastern Hotel in Liverpool Street—at that time one of the best in the City (maybe it still is). We were all delighted by the impressive and lively look of the exhibition and Wystan bought a picture, a still life, and Stephen a drawing. But on our way to Liverpool Street Wystan drew me aside to ask what was happening to Rupert. In spite of our efforts to hide it—and for all the years of his physical discipline Rupert was yet unable to sustain the social mask we had hoped would disguise his loss of control—it was evident that something was wrong. I told Wystan that I did not know, which was indeed true, because nobody had yet told me that it was the result of the progress of multiple sclerosis. At luncheon, seated at the round table between Rupert and me, Wystan looked after Rupert with the greatest of care and affection, but once or twice I caught a look of concern and curiosity. I have always supposed that Wystan guessed more than I knew. That was the last time that we were all to meet together.

It happens that if you are everyday very close to an invalid who is sometimes better and sometimes worse, and for whom you tenaciously hold on to a hope of recovery, you don't immediately notice alterations obvious to others, and so it was with Connie and me. It seemed vital moreover that no one should lose heart. Encouragement and love would surely do their own healing. It came about that Rupert, who had hitherto always been able to make the journey to hospital himself, required that I go with him. He was in a state of great fear and said that the electrical treatment they had given him tortured him, that they had put a band round his forehead and that there had been a terrible pain. I asked to see the consultant privately and after being kept waiting was finally shown in. The consultant's manner was professionally cool. Cold and polite, he plainly saw no reason to discuss his patient's medical affairs with a person who had no legal rights to information and he gave only the vaguest answers to direct questions. He would not give me a professional opinion on Rupert's health, and said that the electrical treatment was normal practice designed to measure the function of the brain. This cruel legalism, that kept from me the knowledge of Rupert's true condition, has been all too frequently encountered by homosexuals in similar situations. Whatever the rights or wrongs I understood now more than ever Rupert's hatred of institutions. This was no place for him any more. We left and never returned. It was a tremendous relief to find in Wimbledon Dr Bevan Pritchard, an adviser who immediately understood our relationship and took it into account, for as Rupert declined he had increasingly to look after us both.

In the summer of 1965, unable to continue looking after Rupert and going to the school, I retired from Camberwell. Not long after, Rupert's sufferings intensified to the extent that his personality was finally eclipsed.

Travelling up with him on an autumn morning, accompanied by two male nurses in a large Daimler, to St Andrew's Hospital, Northampton, where John Clare had died almost exactly a hundred years before, I did not know how far I secretly realized that Rupert would never return. Dr Pritchard had told me that his condition was irreversible, and also that it could last for an indeterminate length of time, but the arrangement agreed upon was that Rupert should be looked after for just three weeks while Connie and I took a well-needed rest. The doctor, of course, knew better, but mercifully he did not spell it out to me.

Rupert died on 3 March 1966, aged 62, and his ashes were scattered in Northampton. An obituary by Tyrone Guthrie and John Moody appeared in *The Times* on 8 March and on 25 June a memorial concert called *Rupert Doone Remembered by his Friends* was given at Morley College. The Emma Cons Hall was full.

I have never been able to forgive myself that Rupert died amongst strangers. It is no good people telling me that I did everything possible for as long as possible. A feeling persists in me that the finality of the journey to Northampton was a betrayal of loyalty. At the beginning, forty years earlier in Paris in 1926, Rupert the dancer had seen Life as a choreographed pattern, the meaning of which was in the shape we gave to it. In his youthful conception our ambitions, separate lives and mutual responsibilities were counterpointed in a potential life together, not given but chosen, and without legal ties to enforce its mutual obligations. It was an image of the loyalty that sustained our long relationship. That I was not there when he died to receive that final spark of recognition that must have flared between us still seems to me unforgivable. It has made it necessary to write this book, and to the best of my abilities complete the dance.

If Rupert never succeeded in achieving all he set out to do, he has never received proper recognition for what he actually did. He was fated to succeed in his own way and outside the professional theatre, but his standards were always those of the complete professional. He gave of his talents to the utmost and, in the business of sustaining the Group Theatre during the thirties, often in directions they were not naturally suited to. Avant-garde movements have a special but limited mission to fulfil and the Group's revival in 1950 came too late. The will-power which had driven him became in these later years antithetical and drove him inwards upon himself. Difficult with others, he was no less difficult with himself. He had great gifts as a teacher, and whether working with professionals or students he had an extraordinary ability to touch upon and bring to life within them the springs of creative action. To all things, personal and professional, Rupert brought an irrepressible enthusiasm for life, and a sense of humour that was positively bucolic, and sometimes rumbustious; for those who knew and loved him best it is the sheer fun of his company that is most immediately remembered. He was a wind that stirred and ruffled the waters.

After the celebration and tributes of the memorial concert, I went for an extended holiday in Greece and stayed for a time with Philip Sherrard and his wife Anna, at Limni, Emboiea, where also I found Kathleen Raine. I decided to sell Wimbledon, which was now too large, and return to the London we had always lived in. It would also be easier for Connie, now over 80 and still living as she had done since 1939 in Little Russell Street. It was not through a desire to break with the continuity of the past that I disposed of everything except those pieces of furniture which could not be parted with. It was a necessary stripping down to essentials. But the move, first of all to Camden Town, and then back to South Kensington, inevitably had both psychological and professional consequences.

Since the Whitechapel exhibition I had continued to make pictures that featured a deliberately ambiguous biomorphic imagery, and which depended for their effect upon an evocative *tachiste* handling of paint, the vitality of the expressive 'mark'. This use of open-ended forms discovered by chance, and the sensuous physicality of involvement in paint as paint, now began to lose meaning for me. I felt the need in my work as in my life for a new beginning: I knew that my new situation demanded certainty. Order must be imposed upon emotional turmoil. I turned to the rigours of geometry, not this time to regulate a composition that had other, referential, features, but as an end in itself. In order to prevent myself from wavering I turned to straight-edge abstraction, and to techniques and media (acrylic mostly) which made alterations to predetermined structures difficult to effect. At first I hated the deprivations of habit that these entirely non-figurative paintings imposed. Critics found them difficult to relate to my previous work, but the reader of this book will know that there were connections and continuities of a crucial kind. The discipline involved, though painful, yielded results. In 1972 I exhibited these new paintings at the Lisson Gallery with some critical success. A further outcome of this process was more surprising. Since making the representational paintings of 1949 on the theme of *Samson Agonistes* I had nursed an ambition to illustrate the poem, and the new abstract style I had developed suggested a way in which that might be possible. In 1978 I exhibited a trial run of sixteen large-format screenprints illustrating the poem, and specimen pages of a projected book. The idea for the prints had come when I had been experimenting with *papier collé*, and their semi-abstract, semi-figurative style perhaps owed something to the cut-paper pictures and designs of Matisse. An austere abstraction had led to the solution of a problem that had haunted me for years. The trial run was successful and in 1980 I published the book in a limited edition with twenty-four screen-printed images corresponding to passages in the text. The book, which was bound at Camberwell, was printed at Norwich School of Art under the supervision of Mel Clark, whom I had met whilst examining there in 1977. I regard this *Samson Agonistes* as one of the best things I have done.

The making of the *Samson* illustrations seemed to direct me once again towards representation. Since their publication I have returned to painting the figure, and to the looser, more expressive handling that characterized my work in the early sixties. Looking at a series of directly frontal self-portraits I recognize that their formal composition is a recollection of Watteau's *Gilles*, that so impressed itself upon me over fifty years ago. The artist in these late pictures however is not disguised as a Clown or as a Fool: he is naked.

The first sixteen screen prints that were to develop into a complete *Samson Agonistes* were shown in 1978 at the Artists' Market in Earlham Street, Covent Garden. Initiated by Véra Russell with the object of assisting painters and sculptors who were, even at the beginning of the present economic and social crisis, finding it difficult to sell their work, the Artists' Market Association was undoubtedly one of the most exciting and important experiments of the seventies. Its aim, clearly established by Véra at the outset, was to present the work of established and unknown artists over a wide spectrum from figurative to abstract art in a situation outside the commercial galleries and with a closer link to the public. The essential criterion was the quality of the work. Many artists who showed there strongly supported these aims, but the main burden of the project was borne by Véra, who created in the empty and threatened Seven Dials Warehouse in Earlham Street a unique and beautiful gallery which, with its open doors, was an invitation to anybody to come in and look.

And come in they did: we presented the work of over a hundred and fifty artists to the public, and as daily attendance averaged two to three hundred (often more) the Artists' Market proved beyond argument that it fulfilled a need. I am proud to have been closely associated with the enterprise in Earlham Street, being from its earliest beginnings a member of the closely knit group—we hesitated to call ourselves a committee—that directed its course. I was both angry and sad when the Arts Council would not increase its grant to cover the costs of a proper administration—Véra could not be expected to continue indefinitely, and an appointed director would need a salary. After protracted negotiations and with great misgivings we were forced to close in 1978. Véra wrote to the Arts Council:

> It is maybe a great indictment of our times that as successful an operation as ours has to go under, but we prefer to do so before we lower our standards, and deny our very large public the quality we have been able to give them. We are proud to have done it and only hope that our demise may be a warning to your organization.

The decade of the seventies defined a marked period in my life, and one in which Véra Russell came to play an important part. It had taken over two years to get the Artists' Market Association off the ground in September 1973, and from that period on Véra became not only one of my closest friends, but something of a prompter to action and a comrade-in-arms. We had of course worked together before, in the days of the Group Theatre revival, and more recently in 1965 when I had designed the drop curtain for the memorial concert for T. S. Eliot which she produced at the Globe Theatre. We have shared many battles, and understand each other very well. Véra has breadth of sympathy and a sixth sense of perception that must owe something to her Russian background. Her energies are prodigious and sometimes difficult to contain, and she is a great disturber of complacency and a fearless speaker of the truth. It was side-by-side with Véra again that I fought in the late seventies to secure a place for the Turner Bequest in a setting fit for it—the Royal Academy Rooms in Somerset House. This followed a letter I wrote to *The Times* in which I supported John Betjeman's brilliant original suggestion. I wrote saying that if Amsterdam could afford a gallery devoted to Van Gogh, why couldn't London afford a gallery for Turner? In spite of the support of Henry Moore amongst others the campaign failed and the entrenched forces of the Museum establishment carried the day. In retrospect I feel that the time and energy thus wasted might have been better spent in painting. That is the story of my life, as friends have so often pointed out: I am too easily distracted.

I am sitting alone in a room, with pictures that Rupert never saw upon the walls, and looking out of the window on to the trees of a London square not far from the house in Cathcart Road. But it is a room that Rupert would have recognized at once as ours, even if Connie in her apron is no longer in the kitchen scolding the potatoes that won't boil or cursing a spoon that has dropped itself on the floor. Dear Connie, born the Lady Constance Foljambe, daughter of the Earl of Liverpool, was a fugitive from a family that had not surprisingly refused to encourage her ambitions to go on the stage. As a nurse in France during the First World War she had made her escape from the family background final, and thereafter led a life of fiercely guarded aristocratic independence. She was of that courageous and selfless stuff, uninterested in money, class or success, that are indispensable to any uncommercial artistic enterprise. Finding in the Group Theatre in 1933 just such a venture as she could believe in she had thrown herself completely into its activities. She spoke verse beautifully, with natural understanding, and made a great success as Lucy in *The Dog Beneath the Skin*, and as Petra's mother in *The Trial of a Judge*. In 1935 at the time of the Group Theatre season she had decided, though warned that life would not be easy, to take charge of our housekeeping. Strong-willed and devoted, Connie became an essential part of our lives from that time on. She died in 1976, aged 92, having looked after me until she was 90.

One of the last occasions over which Connie presided must have been when Wystan, about a year before he died, came to dinner. This was a fairly complicated operation because by this time, with Wystan, everything had to be exactly timed. Strictly bidden to be punctual, the other guests were Véra Russell, who was planning the Auden/Henry Moore *édition de luxe*, and Gregory Brown, a young friend of mine whom he had already met and who was, if required, to drive him back to the Spenders' house, where he was staying, so that he could be in bed by 9.30 p.m. Arrival was timed for 6.30 and dinner for precisely 7 o'clock. Unfortunately, the dry martinis, put into the refrigerator some hours before, were neither strong enough nor yet cold enough, a double deficiency partly made good by the addition of a quantity of vodka. The roast lamb, however, was excellent, and Connie, at Wystan's command, broke her inflexible habit of remaining in the kitchen and sat down with us. It was to prove the last time that Wystan and I were to meet together, and, as if to mark the occasion with special regard and affection, the clock stood still. Wystan finally left for St John's Wood with Véra, who lived nearby in Hamilton Terrace, at the unusual hour of 11 p.m.

I realize that there are others who have played a greater part in my personal life than this chronicle would suggest. Friends like Bob Wellington, the most enduring from the earliest days, who can always be relied upon to give me a prod when he thinks it is required. Friends like John and Myfanwy Piper who have enlivened our times from the thirties onwards with an untiring celebration of the landscapes and townscapes, the art and architecture of these islands—who launched with Bob, in 1937, the adventure of *Contemporary Lithographs*, and who stimulated so much talk and thought through their work with *Axis* and *Pavilion*, to which in a small way I contributed. And there are the widening circles of other friends, some, like the great actor Ernest Milton, more important in Rupert's life than mine, but with all of whom 'the bread has been broken' and whose conversation has restored confidence and set new ideas flowing.

There are also the circles I have entered since Rupert's death, of a younger generation whom I taught or met through teaching. And though some of them, as painters, designers, producers and film-makers, are now in the public eye, and I enjoy their success, I would not like to name them at the expense of those unknown who equally reward me and make life interesting. Curiosity, supposed to kill the cat, keeps us alive.

I like change, and need it, but when I consider the facts I must value continuity more. I had wished, like Rupert, to launch out and distance myself from the point of my beginning; but it turns out the distance I have travelled is very small. I live in the same Borough of Chelsea in which, at 11 Edith Grove, I was born. Facing that home on the opposite side is Number 12, in the house and studio of which have lived and worked an extraordinary succession of friends: Keith Baynes the painter, a Bloomsbury friend of early days; John Dodgson whom I valued with affection as the most discriminating critic of my paintings in the period following the war, when I most needed encouragement, and who was an essential part of the Cathcart Road circle; and finally Ceri and Frances Richards, in whose lives and friendship Rupert and I recognized a deep-felt correspondence. Rupert and Ceri have gone; Frances and I remain.

At the end of it all I am reminded of the double-spiral staircase in the Vatican, on which, as you approach the *Day of Judgement*, you may find yourself turning on the axis and going down when you thought you were going up. That is a just image of the life I have led: its ascents and descents perpetually intertwined, and no ending that is not also a beginning.

Index